# ADVANCE PRAISE FOR WAVES ON THE POTOMAC:

WAVES on the Potomac is a work of fiction in the historical and women's fiction subgenres. It is suitable for the general reading audience and was penned by author R. Ann Bush. This fascinating read combines espionage and women's issues during the Second World War, which begins when our protagonist Meg Burke signs up for WAVES (Women Accepted for Volunteer Emergency Service) training in the year 1942. Early on in her new field, Meg proves herself to be indispensable when decrypting radio transmissions from Japan and outshines her male colleagues frequently. But success comes with a price, and Meg soon realizes that she's far deeper into the world of global intelligence than she could ever have bargained for.

Author R. Ann Bush delivers a high-stakes read that never overplays itself, and keeps readers as grounded in the reality of military intelligence as protagonist Meg herself is. There's no glitz or Hollywood-style machismo to Meg's work and attitude, and that in itself highlights the success of determined women like her who worked hard for their country's war effort in 1942 with little promise of glory. I really enjoyed the intimate narration of Meg's emotional challenges and the exploration of the pressure that she put on herself, the pressures she felt societally as a woman and a patriot in a country at war, and the danger lurking at every turn the deeper we get into the thick of the plot. Overall, readers seeking a realistic Second World War novel from a totally unique and truly eye- opening perspective should read WAVES on the Potomac. A recommended read indeed.

~ 5 Star Review by K.C. Finn for Readers' Favorite

*WAVES on the Potomac* is a novel following the evolution and experience of serving in the WAVES (Women Accepted for Voluntary Emergency Service) during World War II. It opens with Meg Burke's venture into unknown territory to help serve her country during a time of crisis.

Through Meg's eyes, as she moves from civilian to naval officer candidate at a time when women rarely entered upper ranks of military service, readers gain a perspective on history that has received relatively little exploration in fiction. Meg's choices and moves reflect more than olden times. Her actions chart the move from civilian to military support personnel from a woman's viewpoint, considering the motivations, inter-actions between different classes of officers of both sexes, patri-otism versus changing women's roles, and specific job descriptions that delve into the daily actions of WAVES:

*"My analysis work is a little different from most of the group's. I concentrate on the water transport communications, which are largely weather reports and certainly have a more limited vocabu-lary than the Fleet Code. I start working on a transmission the same way the other analysts do. I look down a vertical column and use the current additive to subtract numbers. I then rewrite the numbers horizontally." She stopped and took a deep breath. "But the complexity of the additives is sometimes a little much for the radioman on a fishing boat or a convoy ship. Occasionally, they forget and just send the message, so when an additive doesn't seem to be working, I go back and check if the message is uncoded."*

Through Meg's eyes, the process of code training, indoctrination and training, and changing social and political influences of the times are revealed.

R. Ann Bush's novel embraces this world with such an attention to daily details that the complete impact of this changing world on women's lives is finely tuned. Meg's confrontations, growth, examinations, and revised duties and perspectives receive central examination, as do her friendships and relationships; whether with colleagues or fellow leaders. Along with this history comes a portrait of changing social conditions which lends added value to the history of Meg's experience of the WAVES.

The result is a thought-provoking story that brings readers into the milieu of World War II and the motivations of one young woman to contribute to her country's efforts, including a note of intrigue that challenges Meg to rise above and beyond her training to view the bigger picture around her.

Collections looking for fictional accounts of WAVES will find much food for thought and historical background in *WAVES on the Potomac*, bringing history and experience to life.

~Diane Donovan, Senior Reviewer, Midwest Book Review

With crisp and transportive detail, *WAVES on the Potomac* is a coming-of-age story that will have you cheering for lovable, diligent Meg Burke as she puts her methodical math mind to work for the U. S. Navy during World War II. From her training at Smith College in Massachusetts to her post in Washington D.C., Meg's lipstick color choice is deemed imperative while the menial tasks expected of women during the era disguise covert assignments that she can't even share with her family. Whom can she trust in her code- breaking mission? The three women Meg trains with are fast becoming friends while she navigates working beside a charming professor, a pining church choir member, and a misogynistic lieutenant. Each will test her ability to keep secrets or face the consequences in a game she didn't even know she was playing as Meg rises through the ranks amid the first women to serve in uniform. Witty, charming, and well-dressed as a black and white cinema classic from the 1940's, WAVES holds riveting plot twists and a misty-eyed ending reminiscent of the cherished soda bread recipe she keeps close to her heart: wholesome and satisfying to the last page.

~Christy Baker Knight, author of *On Display, a novel of natural history*

# WAVES ON THE POTOMAC

# WAVES ON THE POTOMAC

R. ANN BUSH

KONSTELLATION
PRESS

*To Sarah Crowley and so many women whose stories we are still waiting to hear.*

# 1

Meg's world changed dramatically the moment a letter addressed to Miss Margaret Burke dropped through her mailbox in Brooklyn. It announced she had been admitted to the inaugural cohort of Women Accepted for Voluntary Emergency Service, known as the WAVES. She was directed to report to Smith College in Northampton, Massachusetts, for officer training on August 28, 1942. Since everyone called her Meg rather than Margaret, she felt the letter, and the adventure, belonged to someone else.

Neither Meg nor the Navy were prepared for female officer candidates. The letter had directed her to pack simple civilian clothes to wear until their uniforms were ready. Ready or not, the lure of studying ships, naval history, physics, and military etiquette convinced her to hastily resign from her teaching position. Besides, Meg wanted to do her part to help her country.

The morning before leaving home, Meg ate a slice of toast and drank a cup of tea, which was as much as she trusted to put in her nervous stomach. Her father worked as the elevator man at the Iroquois Hotel in midtown Manhattan; his start this morning had been even earlier than her own, but he had left a ten-dollar bill he could not really spare under her cup as a good-bye. As Meg picked up the money, she saw her mother, Annie, not only acknowledging her father's gift but also trying to give her a smile of encouragement. The previous night they had decided to take the subway together, allowing her mother to see Meg to the train station before continuing on to her housekeeping job in Manhattan. Annie put a small, waxed paper parcel into Meg's hands.

"They may not have dining service on the train; I packed apples and soda bread," she explained.

Meg took a final quick look around the dining room, which opened into their small front room. She had so many happy memories of life in this house with her parents and three brothers, reading aloud to each other or listening to Brooklyn Dodgers games. She tried to imprint the pictures in her mind, ready for recall when needed.

"Time to go, dearie." Her mother was holding back tears. Meg ushered her out the front door before either woman started to cry. Both women were tall and thin; with their long legs, they matched steps as they walked the few blocks to the subway station, deposited their tokens, and brushed through the turnstile. The warm air from the platform engulfed Meg as they started down the stairs to the tracks.

"I wish there were someone to help with your bag," her mother said.

"Really, it's not that heavy, because I'm not bringing much," Meg reassured her. "They'll soon be giving us uniforms. I just need a few things until then."

As they entered the crowded subway car, two men got up to give Annie and Meg their seats. Meg kept trying to think of something to say to her mother, but she felt the words catch in her throat. Any other day, mother and daughter would have been commenting on the news or the results from yesterday's

Dodgers game, but today they could only reassure each other with forced smiles.

Mentally, Meg ticked off the more than a dozen stops, her stomach jumping as Grand Central Station neared. Her legs felt spongy as she climbed the stairs to the frenetic main station floor. To Meg, Grand Central always managed to be more chaotic than even the city it served. Today was no exception. Gas rationing had started, so many people who used to commute by car were now taking the train. The young men in Army and Navy uniforms almost marched as they moved to their assembly points while businessmen streamed in from the suburban tracks to their banking and insurance jobs, lost in their own worlds. Meg marveled at how these commuters never appeared to make eye contact with anybody yet never collided. To her it resembled swimming. When she swam, she knew exactly where the wall of the pool was by how many strokes she had taken. Those around her must consciously or subconsciously count steps.

"Do you have your ticket?" Annie asked.

"Yes, Mother."

The large board above them clacked as it updated with train numbers, destinations, track assignments, and departure times.

"There it is. The ten a.m. to Boston's South Station via Providence. Track eleven," Annie announced. This was it. Meg's mother walked with her to the tunnel entry and squeezed her arm.

"I know you'll do your best, dearie. I'm proud of you, Meg." Annie gave her daughter a hug, then squared her shoulders, adjusted her purse, and was soon lost in the station crowd. Meg took a deep breath and walked to the tunnel entrance where the guard called, "Tickets. Get your tickets out." Meg felt another wave of panic. She'd thought she had until she was seated, but luckily found her documents at the top of her purse.

Her bag now felt heavy and hit her leg with every step. She was sure there would be a bruise later to mark her passage.

There were no conductors to help her with her bag. Meg realized many of the able-bodied men had left to join the military. This was the first of many times when she would have to make things work on her own. Swinging her bag up before her, Meg tripped on the platform but caught her balance at the last minute and got both feet onto the carriage steps. She hoped no one had seen how clumsy she had been.

The conductor blew his whistle and Meg steeled herself for the train's start. She laughed inwardly, acknowledging the irony that for her, joining the Navy began with a long train ride. It was just ten in the morning, but the tunnels in Grand Central held the summer's heat. On this late August day, the air in the train carriage was oppressive, and the feel of sweat dripping down her spine as well as her thick, curly black hair escaping from the knot at her neck did nothing to help Meg's confidence. She was glad those around her did not know that she felt slightly nauseous from the heat and her own nerves.

Meg needed the air to circulate, especially as she was standing at the end of the carriage in the small gap between the door and the rows of seats. She propped her suitcase against the back of the nearest seat and put her weight into loosening the latches on the window at her side. The latch on the right side finally budged and the window slid down with a loud thunk. *Success*, she thought. Once the train started, the air would move about. "Let's go," she encouraged the train under her breath.

As if the engineer heard her plea, there was a small lurch and the platform column next to Meg's window shifted slightly. The train passed the second column, the third, and Meg began to relax a little. There was a thud and a hiss, then quiet as she bounced against the carriage wall with a slight crash from the aborted start. To her relief, in a few seconds the train was underway and Meg realigned herself, standing in front of the window to try to catch the breeze. The train's progress mirrored her emotions. She was more than a little unsure of what she was about to do.

The air streaming through the open window helped relieve some of the nausea, but Meg's mind was racing faster than the train. As a high school math teacher, she had planned her professional life to the minute. In contrast, the past three weeks had been the most uncertain of her life.

The train slowing for the first stop at New Rochelle brought Meg out of her reflections and into the present. If she did not focus on getting a seat at this stop, she might have to stand until Boston. As Meg looked around to see who was getting off, she spied three well-dressed, attractive young women seated together at the opposite end of the carriage. A bag on the open seat was likely saving the spot for someone else, but Meg knew she had nothing to lose. Making her way down the aisle, she murmured, "Pardon. Excuse me. So sorry," as her bag brushed against those seated. One of the three women called to her.

"Aren't you going to Smith?" asked a woman with a blond braid and a broad smile.

"Yes, I am," Meg said. The woman grabbed the bag, tucked it into the space under her seat, and motioned to the now empty seat.

One of the men standing nearby said, "You told me you were saving that seat for a friend."

"And she's here now," the young woman confirmed brightly.

He muttered and gave both women a scathing look. Once he looked away, Meg mouthed, "Thank you," to the gracious woman.

"I wondered where you had disappeared to," the young woman said in the direction of the scowling man as she stood up to help Meg with her bag. Even on her toes, with braid bouncing, she could not quite reach the luggage rack. When she looked sideways at Meg to check on her progress, she said, "My, but you are tall. Does everyone say that to you?" Words bubbled out of this petite and energetic young woman. "Tell you what," she directed Meg. "Move your bag toward my seat. I'll hold the bottom while you hoist it up." Meg smiled gratefully. Together they were able to get the suitcase into the rack above the seats. Meg was not sure how they would get it back down, but they had hours before arriving in Boston to figure that out.

As Meg sat down, she said under her breath to the woman, "Thank you. I don't know what I would have done if I had to stand all the way to Boston."

"I saw you get on in Grand Central, but I couldn't catch your eye. I knew you had to be WAVE. You're tall and slender, the way a WAVE is supposed to look!" Meg's new companion said with enthusiasm. "Where are my manners? I feel as though we already know each other, but you have no idea who we are. I'm Julia Bowen, but everyone calls me Julie. My friends are Cynthia and Vivian Collingsworth." She gestured to the two riders who made up the seat quartet. "You would never know they were sisters, would you? They don't look a bit alike. Cynthia is the tall one, who is constantly frowning, and Viv has the gorgeous auburn hair."

"I'm Margaret Burke. Everyone calls me Meg." She tried to smile but felt like her face was not responding. As Meg sat down, she felt the eyes of the tall woman, Cynthia, appraising her. Meg had a sixth sense Cynthia had already decided she was not worth getting to know.

Julie continued, "Cynthia, Viv, and I went to Wellesley together. We knew Dr. McAfee before she took charge of the WAVES. Dr. McAfee is why the three of us are on this train."

"She's not the Wellesley president any longer, Jules," Cynthia corrected. "Hopefully, *Lieutenant Commander* McAfee is working on making sure we get our uniforms. Can you imagine if we were commissioned without our uniforms? It's bad enough they aren't ready for us today."

"How well did you know Lieutenant Commander McAfee at Wellesley?" Meg asked, trying to change the subject.

"Well, I'm sure she specifically selected the three of us for appointment." Cynthia smiled at Julie and Vivian.

Meg looked more closely at the woman with whom she would be spending the next few months of training. Like her, Cynthia was almost six feet tall, with brown hair that looked as though highlighted by the sun, but Meg thought more likely at the beauty salon. She had a rangy build, and Meg was sure she had played several sports. Meg thought Cynthia radiated "born leader" and had probably been the president or captain of most of her college organizations.

Cynthia continued, "It made sense for the Navy to recruit Seven Sisters graduates. We already all knew each other and had been watched over by our house mothers and chaperones, so the Navy knew we would almost certainly pass the background check."

Meg was sure her own mother was stricter than any house mother but nodded appreciatively. The conductor made his way down the aisle, and the conversation stopped as he punched their tickets and put pink tags on the back of their seats indicating they were going all the way to Boston. The train began to slow for its next stop, at Stamford, Connecticut. A few more seats opened, and the man who had been glaring at Meg sat down. Julie smiled and whispered, "Do you think you can relax now?"

"Maybe," Meg said doubtfully.

As the train pulled out of the station, Cynthia resumed speaking and Meg wondered idly if she was a swimmer. She did not seem to have to come up for air. Cynthia had begun to describe her family to Meg. One brother had graduated from Annapolis and the other Princeton but had become a naval officer. Meg was not particularly surprised to hear Cynthia's father had attended the Naval Academy, as had her maternal grandfather, but thought it interesting only one of the two Collingsworth sons had an academy appointment. She was sure Cynthia's Princeton brother had to have overlapped with at least one of the sons of the family her mother worked for. Meg had probably met members of Cynthia's family while helping her mother by passing trays of hors d'oeuvres during one of the Taylors' glamorous parties.

"Of course, when it was time for me to go to college, I wanted to go to the same school as Cynthia," Vivian said. Meg was happy to note the sister could speak, even if briefly. Cynthia unlaced her fingers and replaced them in the opposite position. She paused for a moment and then turned to Meg.

"My understanding is WAVES officers must be a college graduate. Where did you go to school?" she asked.

"Brooklyn College," Meg responded in her best teacher voice whose tone reminded the class that she, rather than the students, was in control. She continued, "I majored in mathematics and have been teaching for two years." She thought it seemed petty to add she had graduated with honors. Julie had a look on her face that Meg thought she would have had if she had met Katharine Hepburn, or another sophisticated movie star.

"The three of us were English majors," Julie shared. "I doubt I could have passed a college math course. I barely got a 'C' in high school trig, which I took only so I could apply to college. We all speak German, though. How about you, Meg? Do you speak German?"

"I took German in high school, so I'm a bit rusty. I started brushing up once I got the letter."

"The dining car is now open! If you wish to dine, please proceed to the car now. The dining car is two cars ahead!" the conductor bellowed as he walked down the aisle.

"This morning has flown!" Julie exclaimed. "If it's time for lunch, we're nearly halfway there."

Cynthia and Vivian rose from their seats with the grace of ballerinas. "We didn't have a chance to eat breakfast, so we'll go first, Julie. You'd better stay and save the seats. We can bring something back, or the two of you can go to the next seating." Cynthia had quickly assumed command. "Do you want anything?" She was looking at Julie rather than Meg.

"Oh, bring two sandwiches back, would you?" Julie responded.

"Make it one," Meg said. "I have some sandwiches with me."

"Of course you do," Cynthia said.

## 2

-------

Meg's stomach stopped churning and switched to loud growling. Her breakfast was at least four hours ago. She sent what she hoped was an apologetic smile to Julie to excuse her stomach as she twisted around to retrieve her smaller bag from under the seat. She opened the waxed paper covering the loaf and the sweet smell of the bread engulfed their seating area. Her mother's soda bread was legendary. Somehow buttermilk, raisins, butter, flour, and baking soda formed a hard-crusted but moist bread that traveled well and was as tasty as it was filling. Meg saw her mother had added extra raisins and generously buttered each slice as a special treat. She extended the opened package to Julie and explained, "Irish soda bread. It's sort of like a giant scone. Filling and travels well. Please. Have a piece."

"You don't have to ask twice," Julie said as she grabbed a piece. "Thank you." She had barely swallowed her first bite when she exclaimed, "This is so good! I hope your mother will send care packages during training."

Care packages. From home. Meg knew what they were, but she had never thought of her family sending them, especially as this was the first time Meg had really left home, since she did not count her summer as a camp counselor. Her eyes welled as she thought of her parents. Julie saw her tears and patted Meg's arm gently.

"It's going to be fun. I can't wait until we get our uniforms, and everyone will want to look like us. But I'm sure you volunteered for more than the uniform, Meg. What made you apply?"

"Do you want the short answer or the long one?"

"Today I think we have time for the long answer, don't you?" Julie smiled at her.

"I'm not sure how interesting my story is," Meg confessed.

"I'm pretty sure it is more interesting than our three stories combined. Tell me."

Meg smiled. She was not used to being the center of attention. When she taught, she communicated information, which was not the same as sharing about herself. In fact, her usual approach to any social situation was to watch others, engaging as little as possible, while she stood discreetly at the edge of the group and gave herself a chance to get her bearings.

She took a breath. "My story begins on a Sunday in December at home in Brooklyn. We had just sat down to Sunday dinner of lamb, which is my favorite."

"With mint jelly?" Julie interrupted.

"It's not lamb without mint jelly," Meg agreed.

"The telephone rang and my father looked cross. Sunday dinner is sacrosanct. The telephone should not ring and there should be no knock at the front door. He looked at my brother Tom because the telephone was almost certainly for him."

"You have a brother?"

"I have three. Tom is four years older than I. He's closest in age. My middle brother, William, is a year older than Tom and was at his fiancée's house. My oldest brother, James, lives in New Jersey with his wife and two children. He's a salesman with Burroughs. They're all wonderful brothers, but Tom is probably the most interesting."

"And single," Julie interjected.

Meg chuckled as she thought about how best to convey the essence of her brother to someone she had just met. "The thing about Tom is he's never met someone he couldn't talk to. He has the most amazing ability to cut through formality to talk to men *and* women. He immediately puts them at ease so they feel comfortable and want to be his friend. None of the rest of my family is like that. I'm not quite sure where he got the talent. It must have skipped a generation or something." Meg looked at Julie to see if her explanation made sense.

"I have a feeling you have the same skills," Julie remarked. "You've never had the same opportunities to practice it. But go on. I want to know who was on the phone."

Meg continued, "After the third or fourth time it rang, my father gestured to Tom to answer it. As Tom listened, we could hear the caller's emotion even if we could not make out the words. After a few moments, Tom dropped the receiver to turn on the radio. The tube took forever to warm up, but eventually we heard the Japanese had attacked Pearl Harbor. Even though Tom and William were working at the Brooklyn Shipyards as electricians, they both volunteered the next day. My mother, of course, has been worried about them ever since."

"What about your oldest brother?"

"James and my father both have terrible eyesight. Cataracts. What about your family?" Meg asked as she leaned back in her seat and grabbed another slice of bread. That was the most she had talked about her personal life with anyone outside of her grammar school friends. She was happy for Julie to be the main attraction for a few minutes.

"I'm an only child. My father is in the diplomatic service, so we move frequently. My four years at Wellesley were the first time I had ever been in one place for more than a three-year rotation."

"Where have you lived?"

"London, Paris, Munich, Argentina—twice." Meg marveled

at Julie not only having visited but actually lived in such interesting places.

Julie took a moment to point out the window. "I'm still amazed by how quickly the Northeast can become rural once you get away from New York or Boston. And how beautiful the coast is. Meg, you should be sitting in the other window seat. We've already gone through New Haven and the train is going to turn inland after New London. After that we won't see any more lighthouses or fishing villages."

"You don't think we'll be seeing the seashore while on assignment?" Meg asked.

Julie laughed. "We're going to be seeing the inside of an office. No seafaring for us."

Once Meg had moved across from Julie, she inquired, "Why did you apply to be a WAVE?"

"Part of it was I was asked to."

"Asked to?"

"Dr. McAfee knew I was fluent in multiple languages because of where we had lived. Also, I'm familiar with the politics of a bureaucratic system, which probably won't hurt." Julie smiled knowingly at the rules and regulations they would be running up against. "Dr. McAfee visited my parents and flattered them by saying I was exactly the type of lady they needed, while assuring them I would be perfectly and completely safe. I was all for it. Especially after my debutante year, which I hated," Julie said with a sigh as Meg looked at her blankly.

"I'm not familiar with the debutante year," Meg confessed.

"On the surface, it's a merry-go-round of dances in which all the young women wear a different gown for each event. Only certain men qualify to be a dance partner or more formally, escort, to limit your chances of meeting the wrong man. In reality, it's a barely disguised advertisement to society that 'My daughter is looking for a rich husband.'"

"You didn't meet the right man?" Meg asked.

"I didn't meet the right man because I wasn't looking." Julie grinned at her. "For this single college graduate who was unwilling to go with my parents to my father's next assignment, becoming a WAVE was exactly what the doctor ordered. Besides, it sounds like college without exams!" She laughed heartily. "I can't wait to start. Speaking of starting, do you think Cynthia and Vivian are ever coming back? This has to be the longest lunch ever!"

Meg laughed politely. She had no idea if this was the normal amount of time for lunch on a train and took a moment to look through the window at the landscape. The hayfields had just a tinge of yellow, indicating summer was near its end, but the tree limbs were still bent toward the ground with heavy green leaves. As she gazed at the scenery, she thought about Julie's life. Multiple languages, international assignments, and a debutante year. Meg was familiar with people who lived like this, albeit secondhand. Her mother had risen from house cleaner with the Taylor family on the Upper East Side to eventually becoming their trusted housekeeper. It was different to work for such people rather than live and go to school with them. During the few hectic weeks between getting her letter and leaving for training, Meg had focused on the mission and the idea of becoming an officer. She had not really thought about the day-to-day and how nervous she could be mingling with so many different classes of young women. Meg took a deep breath before continuing the conversation.

"My brother Tom sort of encouraged me to join."

"Really? What did he say? 'Meg, I suggest you join the Navy'?"

Smiling, Meg said, "One afternoon Tom was reading the newspaper and he asked me what I thought about Mrs. Roosevelt suggesting women be drafted for a year of compulsory service. He joked, 'I could introduce you as my sister the mechanic. That would *really* make Ma proud.' Later, he slid the application information under my door with a note teasing that they might not take Brooklyn College graduates. Proving myself was a powerful motivator." *And the salary of fifty dollars a month,* Meg thought to herself.

"Providence in five minutes. Providence station in five minutes," the conductor announced as he walked down the corridor.

"Thank goodness you had the bread, Meg. We're never going to get to lunch," Julie exclaimed. "Where and how are your brothers serving?"

Not for the first time that day, Meg thought Julie had one of the friendliest smiles she had ever seen. She made it so easy to talk to her. If all the WAVES were like Julie, Meg was going to enjoy the experience.

"In January, both were sent to training in the South— William in Norfolk, Virginia, and Tom in Texas along the Gulf. Even with censored letters, they couldn't hide how excited they were about their training and meeting interesting people from all over the country and all walks of life. They were both having a great adventure."

"Just like we're going to have," Julie confirmed.

"Tom's letters were especially colorful because he captured the dialect and colloquialisms of his fellow recruits. Also, Tom's not above making the joke about himself when he misunderstood what others were saying. He made it sound as though he were constantly in scrapes. Tom almost didn't eat dinner one night because the men said the chicken wasn't barbequed. He didn't realize that meant it didn't have sauce on it. He thought the men meant it wasn't cooked."

Julie laughed. "My entire childhood was spent not entirely understanding what was going on. It gives you a thick skin. Something catastrophic has to happen for me to be embarrassed because it happened so frequently growing up." She smiled warmly at Meg and her eyes danced. "Tell me more about Tom."

Talking about her brother was easy. "Tom couldn't believe Corpus Christi's warm winter. He and some friends used a few hours of leave in February to swim in the ocean. My mother was concerned because Tom had not taken his swimsuit when he left and thought it was unlikely the Navy had issued swim trunks. My father and I could hardly keep from laughing. I'm not sure if my mother caught on to what they were or were not wearing." Meg and Julie giggled at the thought before Meg continued, more somberly, "Unfortunately, during an appointment for a twisted ankle, of all things, the doctor diagnosed Tom with a heart murmur and he was medically discharged."

"What a shame," Julie commiserated.

Meg skipped sharing her parents' shock and disappointment. She pictured them at the dining table as Tom explained, "The doc asked if I had ever had scarlet fever." He'd turned to his mother and said, "Ma, I remembered you telling the story about how everyone was so worried baby Meg would get scarlet fever from me."

"You had a physical before you were on the swim team and again when you first volunteered," his mother said, frowning. "It's strange the heart murmur was only discovered now." Meg and her father knew the look. Meg's mother was blaming herself that the Navy rejected Tom.

"The Navy has great doctors who discovered what those others couldn't diagnose," Tom quickly responded. The next surprise was that rather than going back to his job at the shipyard, Tom began to drive a taxi. Meg's parents loved their son, but it was difficult to ignore the jabs of neighbors who suggested Tom was a healthy young man who was avoiding service.

"Meg? Meg? Are you okay?" Julie asked her as she touched her arm gently.

"Sorry. I was thinking about home," Meg replied. "I got distracted thinking about my family."

Before Julie could say anything further, Cynthia said, "I'd really like my seat back."

Meg was not sure why she felt as though she should apologize as she moved into her original seat next to Julie.

Cynthia was barely paying attention to her and said, "They were short servers and food. It took forever to get lunch. You must be starving, Julie. But you didn't miss anything by not getting lunch in the dining car. The only choice was stew. It was just like the Wellesley cafeteria. We had to eat mystery meat. All I could get for you was a couple of rolls." Meg tried to ignore Cynthia's rudeness as Julie quickly responded, "Meg had the best picnic lunch, which she shared with me. Maybe if you're nice, she'll share some of her delicious soda bread." Friend or not, Meg noted that Julie seemed willing and able to put Cynthia in her place. "Cynthia, I put you in charge of getting food because normally you are the world's best hostess. Plenty to eat and wonderful conversation. I guess today is not your day."

After raising an eyebrow at Julie in quiet acknowledgment, Cynthia announced, "We're only about an hour away from Boston. I'm going to take a quick nap." Within a few minutes, the rhythmic clacking of the train put the two Collingsworth sisters and Julie to sleep, while Meg enjoyed looking at the farms and the small villages that appeared every few miles. Meg was glad Julie was dozing so she was not tempted to comment on the fact that the beautifully put-together Cynthia was drooling in her sleep.

# 3

As they neared Boston, the scattered villages turned into rows of houses. Meg felt the train starting to slow and Julie sat up with a jerk. Julie caught Meg's eyes as she glanced at Cynthia and Viv sleeping.

"Better you than me," whispered Meg, and as Julie reached tentatively over to tap Viv, the conductor entered the car bellowing, "South Street Station, South Street Station. Last stop, South Street Station."

Cynthia woke with a start and looked confused. Her once perfect hairdo was now plastered to her head where she had lain against the headrest, and she looked dazed. Julie leaned over and quietly reminded her they were on the train to Boston. Viv did not stir. Julie started to tap her.

"Oh, that will never wake her." Cynthia grabbed Viv's shoulders and looked like she might be shaking food loose from her sister's windpipe rather than waking her.

As the train slowed for its final creep into the station, Meg sucked in her breath and prepared to wrestle with her bag. As she stood, she noted that at some point during the journey a pair of Army soldiers had slipped into seats a few rows behind her. Meg had barely started to reach toward the rack when one of the men said, "Allow me, ma'am." He hoisted her suitcase from the rack and onto the floor in one motion while grinning at her.

"Thank you," Meg said as she felt her face flushing. She could not help but notice how the tailored olive jacket accentuated his broad shoulders.

"Where are you going?" he asked, as Cynthia frowned in Meg's direction.

"We need to find a bus to Northampton. I'm not familiar with the station," Meg replied.

"That's okay. There will be a sign or two," he said helpfully as the train came to its final stop. "We'll go with you until you find the assembly point."

"You certainly have his attention," Julie whispered to Meg. "He's cute. But the wrong service."

"I'm not going to tell him," Meg confessed quietly as Julie looked at Meg admiringly.

"At least wait until our bags are off the train," Julie said with a quiet giggle.

When the train stopped, the friendly soldier announced, "I see a cart against the station wall." As he jumped off from the end of the car to the ground, he called, "I'm going to grab it. My buddy here will help you get your bags off the train."

Wordlessly, the other soldier grabbed Meg and Julie's bags, and Meg followed him off the train to the luggage cart.

"I'll stay here and watch the bags if you can go back and help the others," Meg offered. He smiled at her and a few minutes later, all the bags were on the cart.

"Just as I thought. I bet all your male students were in love with you," Julie said under her breath as she joined Meg on the platform.

"I can't believe Army guys are helping 'about to be Navy' gals. I'm pretty sure we would be getting stink-eye if we were in uniform," Meg said.

"Or they'd tease us for not being able to carry our bags," Julie added.

Walking through the station, Meg noticed that people moved out of the way and smiled at the two men in uniform. Would the same happen when she was in a uniform? When she saw the sign for the buses, she called out in her classroom-trained voice, "This way!"

As they entered the outdoor bay, Meg saw several other young women waiting next to two buses marked "Northampton." A woman in a poorly fitting naval uniform carried a clipboard and scanned her list several times before finding their names. She was too distracted to see the approving eyes watching the two handsome soldiers push the cart up to the bus. Once the bags were stowed, the soldiers smiled, saluted, and left to a round of applause.

"I feel as though we are going on a school trip," Vivian reminisced. "I loved going to the Natural History Museum, eating lunch, and then playing Red Rover on the front lawn."

Maybe Vivian had the right idea. Meg could try to think of training as a very long school field trip, but as soon as she stepped on the bus, she felt her nerves return. She was training to be a naval officer rather than going on a field trip or to summer camp. Meg was filled with relief when she saw Julie had grabbed seats to keep the pair together. As Meg sat down, she heard Julie's stomach growl.

"It's still hours until dinner and the rolls weren't filling," Julie said under her breath to Meg. "Is there any chance you have any food left?"

Meg carefully and quietly opened her purse to slip a slice of bread to Julie.

As the bus got underway, the exuberance of the train ride evaporated into weariness, but Meg found herself keyed up with thoughts of the unknown. She tried to calm herself with glimpses of Boston, spotting a sliver of the Boston Gardens a few blocks from the station, as well as enjoying the riverscape as the bus followed the Charles.

Meg recalled how as school ended, she had settled into a summer of revising her lesson plans and listening to Red Barber call Dodgers games on the radio. She frequently stopped ironing or mending when he used expressions such as "tearing up the pea patch" to denote a batter or team going on an offensive charge, or to describe a batter facing the pitcher with three balls and no strikes as "sitting in the catbird seat." With Red announcing, she was at the game rather than merely listening to it. She hoped the Dodgers could win the National League pennant, as they had done the previous year. Her one extravagance was doing two crossword puzzles on Sundays, when she quietly purchased the *New York Post* or *New York Daily News* in addition to her usual *New York Times*. The Taylor family had increased their war-related entertaining and Meg went into the city with her mother to help in the kitchen and, occasionally, to pass trays during cocktail parties or serve at dinner. She felt her working-class background was so different from the illustrations in the WAVES recruiting materials that she had told no one, not even Tom, before she took the bus to the Brooklyn Naval Recruiting office. She did not want to have to tell her family she had been rejected on sight.

At some point, her exhaustion overcame her nerves, because she was jolted awake as the bus stopped. It took a moment for Meg to register she was on a bus in a hotel parking lot. A voice from the front of the bus was telling the passengers to exit and retrieve their luggage. As she stepped off the bus, she could see a sign reading "Hotel Northampton."

Meg and Julie watched with some trepidation from the edge of the lot as one bus driver unfastened the net holding their suitcases to the roof and tossed the bags down to another driver on the ground. There were cries of dismay as the receiving driver missed several tosses and dropped the bags. They moved forward to grab their luggage. Julie rubbed a new scratch on her bag, which was not going to go away. Meg was thankful that she had brought Tom's previously dinged bag.

"We might as well go inside. Our watching isn't going to make us feel better," Meg suggested, so she and Julie moved into the hotel lobby. Meg noticed the lobby's grandeur. Tasteful, with an elegant chandelier, egg-and-dart molding, beautiful yellow-and-white-striped silk drapes covering the federalist-style windows, as well as stern portraits of men whom she assumed had started the hotel as an inn and tavern. As Meg looked around at the tired group, several women approached her and asked if she knew what they were doing next. Although exhausted, she was holding herself in what her brothers teasingly referred to as teacher posture.

"Line up next to your seatmate with your luggage," Meg instructed. "It will make it easier for check-in and room assignment." Meg had no idea if it would help, but it would give them something to do; busy students were less likely to get in trouble. The women started moving into a line and Meg caught Cynthia giving her an astonished look. Meg smiled at her and Cynthia quickly turned away as an officer with a clipboard started speaking,

"Welcome to the USS Hotel Northampton. Because of travel, tonight's dinner will start in the Mess at nineteen-thirty hours. Normally, you will report for dinner at eighteen hundred hours."

A young woman near the officer raised her hand. The officer nodded at her. "How do we know who our roommate is?" Even at a distance, Meg could see from the officer's facial expression that no one had thought that far ahead. She was impressed when the officer quickly and evenly replied, "For tonight your roommate will be your seatmate."

Meg felt a rush of relief to be paired with the apparently easygoing Julie. As Meg and Julie stood in line to get their keys, she could hear Cynthia telling Vivian it was a good thing they had sat next to each other on the bus. Their next surprise was an officer standing to block the elevator, announcing, "You must use the stairs." The women started to grumble as they turned into the stairwell door, but the officer whistled and demanded, "Enough. No complaining. You're in the Navy now!"

At the second-floor landing, Julie and Meg said good-bye to Cynthia and Vivian, who were assigned to the third floor. When Meg unlocked their door, they found the room no longer had double beds; it had been fitted with a bunk bed, but it still had soothing dove-gray walls and a full bath with a tub only they would have to share.

"Thank goodness! I almost said 'no' to joining the WAVES because I so disliked walking to the bathroom in my robe at Wellesley," Julie confessed.

Meg just smiled. Julie did not need to know that Meg's entire family shared a bathroom or that this was the first time she had stayed at a hotel, even if the Navy had requisitioned it. As they went back down the stairs, she listened to the women's chatter, wondering about dinner, their training, and their uniforms.

Meg's stomach gurgled when they reached the restaurant doors and she smelled food. While waiting, as the women took open seats in the order in which they arrived, Meg counted sixty women including herself. Soon the room sounded like a high school cafeteria. Instead of talking, she tried to look around as inconspicuously as possible and noted the buffet line was new. In its civilian incarnation, the elegant dining room would have had waiter service. The chicken and potatoes were surprisingly good, although she was so hungry, she might have eaten anything. Meg especially enjoyed the scoop of vanilla ice cream. She was in a daze as she and Julie took the stairs back to their room.

"Julie, why don't you take the bath first," she suggested. "I think you're even more tired than I am."

It wasn't true, but Meg wanted to unpack her things without Julie seeing how inexpensive her underclothes were. She could maintain some privacy for a little longer. Julie returned the favor by bathing quickly and within the hour, both women had bathed, brushed their teeth, and turned the lights out. Meg barely registered Julie asking her something as she was falling asleep.

# 4

Meg awoke to a chorus of birds chirping and, for a moment, had no idea where she was. Luckily, she remembered she was in the upper bunk before she started to get out of bed. It was barely light, and she was sure she had a few minutes before she had to start the day. With the combination of exhaustion and the fact that it was easily 15 degrees cooler than in Brooklyn, she had slept surprisingly well. She heard Julie's even breathing below her and readjusted herself quietly to look around the room. The egg-and-dart molding she had admired downstairs ran along all sides of the room where the walls met the ceiling. There was an elegantly brushed hanging lamp with light bulbs designed to look like candle flames to illuminate the room. Its ceiling fastening was surrounded by a delicate circular relief of plaster leaves. While the drapes were not the silk of the lobby's, they were a heavy blue-and-white damask, which would block draughts as the weather cooled.

A loud buzzer, like the air horn indicating the end of time at a basketball game, interrupted her thoughts and nearly jolted her out of bed.

"What is that noise?" moaned Julie from underneath a pillow on the lower bunk.

"Reveille. It's six twenty. Up and at 'em."

That was what Julie had been asking her as she fell asleep. How would they know when to wake up? Fortunately, Tom had warned Meg. The two scurried to put on their clothes. Meg also quickly made her bunk while balancing on the edge of Julie's bedsprings. Last night, Meg was drained and had not listened carefully to the brief announcements but was sure the hotel's housekeeping service would not be cleaning their rooms. She smiled inwardly as she thought about how this might be a shock for many of the other prospective WAVES.

Julie smiled weakly at Meg and asked, "Shall we go?"

After a plain breakfast of toast, cereal, orange juice, tea, and coffee, the young women filed into the hotel's ballroom. While ideal for a reception, the chandelier light was too dim if they were going to be reading training documents. Someone had pulled open the curtains from the few windows on one side of the room, but the windows were small and admitted little natural light. The room was designed for night and not day. Gone were any cushioned chairs, flowers, or decorations. The orchestra's music stands, crowded in one corner, stood as a reminder of the room's former purpose. Breakfast had not quieted Meg's nerves and she was glad for the opportunity to sit next to Julie. Initially surprised when Cynthia and Viv sat next to them, she remembered Julie knew the two women well; it was natural for them to stick together. Throughout breakfast, Cynthia told stories about her brothers frequently destroying the banisters in various houses in which they lived as they raced to see who was the fastest. The stories weren't very funny, but Meg appreciated Cynthia's attempt to keep their minds off the unknown they faced this morning. Meg also had her eye on Vivian, who she was worried might pass out from anxiety.

This morning's lead officer stood at the front of the room.

Her black hair was more successfully pulled into a bun than that of last night's officer in charge, but she lacked her colleague's powerful whistle to get the young women's attention. Meg wished she could give her a ruler. There was nothing like rapping a ruler on the desk to get the students' attention in her class. With some help from the audience nudging each other, the room quieted.

"Good morning, Seamen. I am Lieutenant Fowler." There were several giggles as she said "men" and the officer scowled. "Seamen," she repeated and continued, "let's begin with your first naval terms. For the next few weeks you will be known as seamen in training, which is called Indoctrination." Ignoring the buzz of response, she forged ahead. "Before you ask, let me assure you your uniforms are on their way. I'm sure you have all seen pictures of the Mainbocher-designed uniform in newspapers and magazines. We are just as excited as you for their arrival and the manufacturing company is running double shifts sewing your uniforms." There was a hum when she mentioned the designer. Meg knew he designed for film stars as well as duchesses and countesses. She was not the only WAVE to be excited by the idea of wearing designer clothing. Fowler tapped a nearby table to get the women's attention. "For the next few weeks, the Department of the Navy will issue you two white blouses and two white skirts, which are your responsibility to launder. When you are not in uniform, you will wear the simple tailored skirts, blouses, and sweaters you brought with you. WAVES will maintain a neat, clean, well-pressed appearance at all times." She looked specifically at one woman and said, "A patterned scarf is not appropriate dress."

The woman wearing the scarf flushed, but Meg noted she did not immediately take it off. This was not a group used to taking orders. Idly, Meg wondered whether the Navy considered cashmere appropriate. Last night several women had worn cashmere sweaters to dinner, which were lovely even if Meg thought them unnecessary in August.

The officer decided it was time for the WAVES to learn to follow orders.

"Stand!" Fowler commanded.

Meg, Julie, Cynthia, and Vivian stood rapidly. Meg guessed the Collingsworths were used to orders given their family's naval history, but several of the women stood slowly, scraping chairs and giggling as they did so.

"Sit. We're going to repeat my command until you stand together in fewer than five seconds," Fowler directed. There was a laugh from the back of the room.

"We have a dozen people waiting on you. You are wasting their time. YOU are wasting resources," Fowler instructed. There was silence.

"Stand," she commanded again.

Although they did not rise uniformly, the process was much quicker and quieter than the previous attempts.

Lieutenant Fowler kept them standing as she announced, "The Plan of the Day is uniform and shoe fittings as well as immunizations before lunch. Lunch will commence at twelve hundred hours. At thirteen hundred hours we will begin training in basic duties. As mentioned last night, dinner will take place at eighteen hundred in the Mess. You will have a few hours of recreation and lights out at twenty-two hundred." A few hands shot up. Lieutenant Fowler smiled grimly and motioned to a young woman in front of her.

"Will we keep our roommates from last night?"

"That policy is under review," Fowler replied.

"Can we walk around campus after dinner?"

"That policy is under review," Fowler responded.

"When will we get our real uniforms?"

"As soon as they arrive," the officer answered curtly.

"When will we start our physical training?"

"As soon as the training clothes arrive." Lieutenant Fowler paused. "Seamen, dismissed to the back of the room."

Quickly, the morning started to feel less like a military

activity and more like a giant back-to-school morning. The newly designated seamen formed half a dozen lines to go behind screens and disrobe to their underwear as women from a local department store measured them for blouse, skirt, glove, and hat size.

The whispered commentary made Meg smile.

"There are nurses who are missing their uniforms," complained a seaman.

"Be thankful we are in blouse and skirt in the heat!" said another.

"Maybe they needed our actual measurement to make the uniforms," suggested another.

"What do you mean?"

"Do you think the Navy knows anything about women's sizes?"

"Navy men do," came the saucy reply.

Once they had two sets of blouses and skirts, they moved to the far corner to the pile of hundreds of shoe boxes and half a dozen civilian men, who took considerable time fitting each of the WAVES in black shoes with a heel of slightly over an inch. Because of the combination of her height, hours standing in the classroom, and her considerable daily walking, Meg generally wore nearly flat shoes, but when it was her turn to try on the shoes, she found them surprisingly comfortable. Even so, Meg envied Navy men who wore boots or flat-soled shoes, since for her, heels were treacherous in wet environments. The next rainy day was going to be a challenge!

From the ballroom, groups of a dozen were ushered down the hall into a smaller banquet room with closed and curtained windows for privacy. The room was warm and the air stale with so many individuals standing in a too small, closed space. Meg began to feel queasy.

Although Meg had spent several hours at the Brooklyn Naval Recruitment Center filling out induction paperwork and undergoing a brief physical, she found herself filling out the same medical history but without the help of a small notebook in which her mother had recorded every illness, with date and duration, Meg had ever experienced. She tried to remember if she had measles in first or second grade. She finally decided to report the date of fall of second grade. If the recordkeeping she had seen so far was any indication, it was unlikely anyone would ever compare her two information sheets. Once finished with the forms, she was instructed to undress to her undergarments again so the medics could check for scoliosis and so her arms were free for immunization. Even though she was used to the communal changing room at the pool, Meg felt her perfectly clean, but clearly cheaply made undergarments did not compare to the more luxurious styles other WAVES wore. She focused on a spot on the wall across from her, thankful Cynthia was not in her group, and thought how amused Tom would be to address her as Seaman Burke. In no time, the efficient medics started at either end of the two lines of women and administered diphtheria, smallpox, typhoid, and tetanus immunizations.

"Oh, my arm is going to be sore," Meg commiserated with the woman next to her. Several of the WAVES looked a little woozy from the closeness of the room and their own nerves. Meg realized as she walked back to the ballroom that everyone in the medic call was too concerned with their own issues and fears to focus on her.

"There you are," Julie exclaimed as she rushed over to her.

"How are your arms?" Meg asked.

"They already ache. Come with me to see if I can change out my shoes. They're pinching my toes. Although maybe I should keep them. If I'm thinking about my toes, I'm not thinking about my arms," Julie quipped.

Meg watched Julie smile at one of the shoe men as she took off her shoes and delicately wiggled her red toes. The man grabbed the sizing slide and took her measurement.

"I apologize. You were given shoes a size too small, madam. Let me get you a new pair."

Meg raised her eyebrow at Julie, who was barely containing her giggles. Lieutenant Fowler used a chair to climb onto the small ballroom stage. She now wore a whistle around her neck, which she blew to quiet the room.

"Please return to your rooms, change into your 'uniforms,' and report for lunch at twelve hundred hours."

Back in their room, Meg quickly hung one of the sets of "uniforms" in the closet as Julie erupted into giggles.

"I know they took my measurements, Meg," Julie choked the words out as she laughed, "but I'm dressed for the last war rather than this war. My skirt is almost down to my ankles!"

Meg looked more closely at Julie and burst out laughing. "You can't wear that," she agreed. "But I don't think we want to miss lunch, either. I brought some safety pins, which you can use for now. Tonight, I'll hem your skirts for you."

"You know how to do that?"

"Of course," Meg said naturally, thinking Julie would be in shock if she ever brought her home to Brooklyn.

"I wish I were tall like you, Meg," Julie observed as Meg knelt down and tried to pin Julie's skirt evenly. "You can wear anything and you look great. Do you think I could grow tall like you if I started swimming now?"

"You can try." Meg had to smile at Julie. "It would be a good experiment."

In the dining room there was a great deal of pulling down on waistbands and hunching up of skirts, depending on the height of the WAVE, as they ate their lunch of homemade tomato soup and grilled cheese sandwiches. They returned to the ballroom to find someone had wheeled a bed into the center, where Lieutenant Fowler was ready to demonstrate how a seaman made a bed. Standing in a circle, the women craned over each other's shoulders to watch the lieutenant strip the bed of all linens and put the sheets on using square corners.

*That's easy*, Meg thought to herself. She already did that. She was not, however, familiar with blanket folding. She watched the lieutenant fold the blanket in half, then thirds, and then half again, after which she put it at the bottom of the bed. There had to be a reason for that, but the instructor did not explain and Meg did not want to ask such a question on the first day. Lieutenant Fowler then dismissed the women. "Go back to your rooms. You have thirty minutes to make your beds according to regulations." The worried looks confirmed Meg's hypothesis that many of the women had never made a bed. She quickly made up her bed and then helped Julie with her square corners. Julie marveled at how quickly she was able to do it.

"I used to make five beds a day, sometimes more," Meg explained.

Lieutenant Fowler came in for inspection. She flipped a quarter in the air over Julie's bed and it sank.

"Strip it and start again," she ordered. The officer looked irritated and stepped carefully around the mattress and onto the lower bunk's bedsprings to try Meg's bed. She looked surprised when the quarter bounced and turned to Meg.

"Lucky you. Come with me, Seaman. You will show the others on your floor how to do this."

Lucky her, indeed. Meg had not expected to keep her background a secret, but here it was, out in the open. It was obvious, she thought, that only someone who had worked as a household servant could make a bed so well. *Damn*, she swore to herself.

"Also, rearrange those shoes. Toes face out, not in," Fowler commanded as they walked out the door. As Meg turned back to move the shoes, she saw Julie smiling at her reassuringly. Meg needed the encouragement as she accompanied the lieutenant to the remaining nineteen rooms on the floor and demonstrated the tricks to getting square corners. In her best math teacher persona, Meg tried to stress the geometry rather than the domestic nature of bed-making. She also tried to learn some of the names of the other women, but unlike her brother Tom, she saw only a sea of faces. Meg also wondered if she had a counterpart on the third floor and what her story might be. When she returned, exhausted, to her room to prepare for dinner, Julie was waiting for her.

"I ran a bath for you. I think you have just enough time before we go to dinner."

As Meg got in the bath and closed her eyes for just a moment, she realized she was very lucky to have Julie as her roommate.

## 5

_____

"I was stirring before dawn because I thought it would be less upsetting to wake up before the buzzer than because of it," Julie confessed over breakfast.

"Julie, that doesn't make sense," Meg replied in a befuddled tone.

"What do you think would happen if we were late to a meal?" Vivian asked, as she and Cynthia slipped in to join Meg and Julie at their table.

"You'd have to stand in front of the flagpole and repeat a dozen times to the group you will not be late again," Meg replied. She was still irritated from demonstrating bed-making the previous afternoon and, as her fellow seamen were about to learn, was not a morning person. Her family knew of her affliction and stayed away until after she'd had her first cup of strong tea. Having to socialize with others at breakfast was going to be a trial. Mainly for them.

"She's making that up," Cynthia reassured Vivian and looked remonstratively at Meg, as though she had just kicked a puppy. Meg was glad to see Cynthia could be compassionate, at least toward her sister.

From the front of the Mess a whistle blew.

"Good morning, Seamen."

"Good morning, Lieutenant Fowler."

"My first announcement is that we will not be changing the room assignments. You will continue to bunk with your current partner." Meg said a quiet prayer of thanksgiving and promised not to tease Vivian again.

"Second," the lieutenant continued, "this morning we're going to go to campus, but first you need to learn to march. We will assemble in the parking lot at oh-eight-hundred."

Ten minutes later the women were milling around the parking lot in their all-white uniforms, looking as though a bag of cotton balls had been opened and was now floating in the breeze until a male instructor, with a much deeper voice than Lieutenant Fowler's, easily got their attention and without a whistle.

"Seamen, line up by size." There were still a few giggles when they heard themselves called seamen, but fewer than the day before. Meg immediately moved to the back of the line. She was usually one of the tallest and always in the back row of any photo, even when it was a co-ed group. Cynthia was also waiting at the back. The two women farthest front were most responsible for the speed, but it would be up to Cynthia and Meg, as the tallest and the anchors, to watch for individuals who were falling out of cadence. Once organized in two lines, the women began to march. The initial march looked like two independent snakes, but after the instructor taught them two songs to sing while marching, the beat helped the women to step more uniformly. Since arriving in Northampton, the seamen had not been outside beyond the hotel courtyard and welcomed the ten-minute walk—or march—onto the Smith campus.

Their first stop was the newly built Alumnae House. Dedicated in the spring of 1938, the Georgian and Neoclassical–style building's bricks were painted a crisp white, offset by dark shutters. Meg marveled at the balcony along the back, which could also double as a stage, accessed by an elegant double-curved staircase. She imagined women walking gracefully across when called by name as part of ceremonies marking their achievements. Now there was a freshly installed sign designating the building as the United States Naval Reserve Midshipmen's School. Perhaps they would use it for graduation. Or would it be too cold in December? There were too many seamen to fit inside, but an administrator came outside and introduced herself as Dr. Mary Philpott, Smith's dean for juniors and seniors.

"I welcome you all to Smith and thank you for your commitment to your country," she said. "During the Great War, the Smith College Relief Unit went to France to rebuild the lives of villagers in the Somme. Those brave alumnae went from village to village providing medical care as well as bringing milk for the children, building materials, and warm clothes, which prevented starvation and death. Your service will help to continue this proud tradition."

As Meg and the others walked farther onto campus, Meg overheard one of the WAVES telling another her aunt had been part of the group detached to France. They entered the classroom building and as she climbed to the second floor, Meg felt the worn dips in the stairs, eroded by several decades of female students' footsteps. She got chills as she reminded herself she was now one of them, even if they were from different classes. Meg always thought Brooklyn College smelled a bit like a hospital; she noted the aroma of Smith hallways was a combination of chalk dust, musty books, and leather, which she decided was the scent of learning.

The seamen entered one of five classrooms according to a list of last names; Bowen, Burke, and Collingsworth remained together. Inside the classroom, they found identical notebooks waiting on the desks as well as pens stamped "US Government property." Julie raised an eyebrow and Meg struggled to keep from laughing. Knowing the pens were not theirs made it seem both more real that she was in the Navy and a bit absurd.

A woman in her late twenties entered the classroom briskly and rapped on the lectern. Dressed in her unofficial white blouse with white skirt and only a few years older than most of the recruits, she easily could have been mistaken for one of the new seamen. Unlike them, she had managed to tie her black silk scarf in a perfect sailor's knot under her collar and her blouse and skirt were tailored to fit.

"Good morning. I'm Lieutenant Roland. Before I became a WAVE, I was a physics instructor at Radcliffe. Over the next twelve weeks I will teach you about ships, naval history, teletype, and physics." As soon as she mentioned physics, several eyes rolled and someone behind Meg groaned. Roland rapped on the lectern again.

"When you were a civilian, you could be emotive. As an officer, you must learn to maintain your composure. You're the first selected for an officer commission from more than twenty-five thousand applications. The Department of the Navy chose you for your education, your commitment, and your comportment. Everyone is watching you; some want you to fail. We must not let this happen!"

Lieutenant Roland walked to the chalkboard and wrote a list of times and activities. *Structure! Finally!* Meg inwardly breathed a sigh of relief. She did much better when she had an agenda or a list. As a fellow teacher, she was envious of the instructor's white uniform. Meg's dark clothes frequently looked like she had walked through a chalk storm by the end of a day of teaching.

The lieutenant continued her review. "Seamen will wake at oh-six-twenty Monday through Saturday. You will have forty minutes to dress, make your bed, and help your roommates with their beds or any other necessary housekeeping, such as shining your shoes. At oh-seven-hundred you will arrive for breakfast. You will all assemble after breakfast and march to campus from the USS Northampton down Main Street in formation for instruction beginning at oh-eight-hundred." Meg was sure a few of the women wanted to say, "That's not fair" or "That's too early," but they were a bright group and there was no further verbal "emoting." Roland continued, "In addition to your courses, you will have group lectures, and two hours of exercise drills on the playing field or in the gymnasium. You'll end the day with two hours and forty-five minutes of study hall. The good news is you will have two hours of liberty each day, with a bit more on Sunday. In the beginning, you will need the time to make sure your uniforms and gear are ready for inspection. Now, I want you to stand up. We're going to learn to salute."

Roland never broke into a smile as the women began awkwardly saluting based on what they had seen in movies, but Meg was sure she saw a twinkle in the lieutenant's eye. She thought Roland had probably learned to salute just days ago.

"The salute is one motion, with an exact placement on your forehead, and eye contact with the recipient. If you have all three of those ingredients, you can't go wrong," Roland counseled as her session with the WAVES ended.

Meg was surprised that their next course was taught by a man. She had thought all of the instructors might be female. As Lieutenant Webb passed out copies of *The Bluejacket's Manual*, which every naval recruit received, he stared fixedly at something at the back of the classroom. He acted as if he were unable to see the women around him. His awkwardness only seemed to emphasize his red hair, clear blue eyes, and athletic build.

"Open your manual to page one," he said in a monotone. Meg's mind drifted as he read the manual, word for word, to them.

"Sir?" A voice from the back of the room jolted Meg awake. Webb looked up as if he had forgotten the WAVES were there.

"I don't see the term for a converted hotel among the types of domiciles." Someone giggled at the back of the room.

"Could you diagram how we are supposed to walk if we are the senior or junior officer?"

Speaking before she had really thought it out, Meg blurted, "Maybe we could take turns being senior or junior officers so we learn to walk on a senior officer's left?"

Webb did not have time to answer before another voice asked, "Could you clarify the section on fraternization? Are there any ranks we are allowed to date?"

"Down on the floor. You will all do fifty pushups for interrupting class," he ordered.

"In skirts?" Julie asked with concern.

"Fifty jumping jacks," he demanded, and Meg noted he had gone beat red.

Meg started counting for the group: "One, two, three . . ."

There was a knock on the door and Lieutenant Roland demanded from the doorway, "What's going on?"

"A demonstration of naval discipline," Webb explained.

"I see," Roland replied, and waited for further explanation. When she saw no more was forthcoming, she walked away but left the classroom door open.

"Bet this is discussed among the instructors tonight," Julie whispered to Meg.

After the jumping jacks were completed, the WAVES quietly took their seats, and there were no more interruptions until the session ended and Webb thundered, "Seamen dismissed."

That evening after study hall, which they learned meant time in their rooms to study, Meg and Julie sat on the lower bunk as Julie practiced her sailor's knot and Meg hemmed Julie's skirt. They had opened the drapes to let the early evening breeze in their room after checking their screen was in place.

"I heard that squirrel bustling in the tree, but both screens look secure," Meg said. "We shouldn't have any unwanted visitors joining us in the middle of the night."

"What about wanted visitors?" Julie countered.

"You don't have a crush on Lieutenant Webb," Meg said incredulously.

"Oh! Not him. But we do have quite a few other men to choose from. In fact, I'm surprised there are so few female instructors," Julie said. "Other than Lieutenant Roland teaching physics and Lieutenant Fowler teaching the radio/signals class, all our teachers are male. Look at me. Is the bow straight?"

"Still longer on the left side," Meg observed. "You have to make sure you start with an equal amount of tie on both sides."

"You're a math person. You get the geometry."

"You were a debutante. You should know how to dress," Meg teased, as Julie got up from the bed to look at the mirror in the bathroom. Meg could hear her sigh loudly.

Meg called to Julie, "I'm used to only having male professors, so I was surprised we had two female instructors. Including one with a PhD in physics!" She clapped as Julie emerged from the bathroom and paused for inspection. "Julie, you finally got the tie even," Meg exclaimed, and Julie took a slight bow.

"And those male instructors do not want to be here, do they! Especially Lieutenant Webb. It looks like it's torture for him," Julie observed.

"I think it must be tough to be Fowler or Roland," Meg remarked. "Although experienced teachers, they've had no time to become naval experts. That would make me nervous."

"Too bad Cynthia can't teach protocol," Julie observed as she tried to work on her tie without the mirror.

"Not sure about Cynthia, but maybe her mother. Speaking of being an expert, I wrote home that I'm looking forward to taking my first watch and I have a bunk on the second deck," Meg said.

"Did you tell them about bathrooms being heads?"

"My brother already knows and my mother would rather she didn't."

They both laughed.

"You have me thinking about Fowler and Roland. Most of my college professors were women and I'm used to working with women," Julie said. "I'm sure Dr. McAfee would like to have more female leadership."

"Julie, don't you see, we will become that leadership!" Meg exclaimed. "Once we finish our Indoctrination, we may be trainers at the next session! That is, only if you can get your tie straight. Have you gotten it straight two times in a row?"

Julie made a face at her. "You, maybe. I can't imagine doing that. Did you learn how to stand up in front of a crowd in college?"

"Because I majored in math rather than education, I didn't learn to teach until months after I had the job."

"Yikes! We've got ten minutes to lights out and I only tied this once," Julie moaned.

"You're fine if you use the mirror. You don't have to do it by feel yet," Meg said to comfort her.

After brushing their teeth and turning out the light, Julie asked, "If you weren't in the education program, why did you become a teacher, Meg? Did you think you would do something else?"

Meg took a deep breath and felt like she was on the edge of the diving board. She still had a moment to quickly change the subject. She could ask Julie to tell her more stories about her beloved Wellesley and Dr. McAfee. Instead, she dove in.

"I sold my going to college with the proposition that I could be a high school teacher." She rushed on with her story before she could chicken out. "I calculated how much I was likely to earn in the four years immediately after high school plus the cost of subway fare and books. Then I calculated how much I would make as a first-year teacher. Even without a pay raise, by my third year of teaching I would have earned more than seven years of a non-degree job and have a degree."

"Your parents must have said yes immediately," Julie said.

"Not exactly. My mother was afraid I might become a radical. I reminded her that in the first two years at Brooklyn College, women only take classes with other women and I would be too busy studying and working."

"And she gave her permission?" Julie asked.

"My father almost derailed the idea when he suggested I would be twenty-four at the three-year mark and married, so they would have lost money." Meg stopped to remember the twinkle in his eye as he mentioned marriage. She knew at that moment, if she were accepted, she would be going to college with her parents' blessing.

"Since you only taught for two years, you'll never know if you would have gotten married in year three," Julie joked. "I think I want to meet your family. They sound nice. Maybe at Christmas you'll introduce me to them and I can meet your single brother."

Meg knew she could not bring Julie home and said instead, "By Christmas you'll be engaged to Lieutenant Webb."

Julie began to laugh so hard she planted her face in her pillow to deafen the noise. They did not want to be written up for not observing lights out.

When she regained her composure, Julie probed, "Was it hard to get a teaching job?"

"Much harder than getting a job at a grammar school where there are many women. High school pay is better and attracts more men. Even with my degree, several interviews ended when they said they were going to hire a man because he needed a job. I was lucky to find a high school principal who was willing to give me a chance. Even so, he had to reassure the hiring committee that he could hire two people if he hired me."

"How did he do that?" Julie asked.

"How do you think?" Meg responded.

"Oh."

Meg let the silence lie for a moment or two until she said softly, "My commission is the most money I have ever had."

In the dark, Julie's breathing was regular and she was quiet. Meg was not sure if she had heard her.

## 6

I t did not take long for Meg to adopt the breakfast strategy of drinking a strong cup of coffee in relative isolation at one of the tables toward the back of the dining room, preferably with a crossword puzzle, and wake up during the march to campus.

Meg was surprised to see Julie approaching her table balancing a brown paper parcel and a mug of coffee. As Julie sat down next to her, she took Meg's knife and started to saw the string wrapped around her package. Cynthia must have spied the package; she and Vivian stood up from another table and carried their trays over to join them.

"Mother sent a care package," Julie shared. Just then, she broke through the twine and pulled at the paper. A huge smile broke on her face. "I have cocoa!"

"Ohhh," Vivian and Cynthia exclaimed together as the paper came off.

"Do you think we can fix it during study hall?" Vivian asked.

"Of course we will," Cynthia answered.

"I'm not sure where we're going to get the milk or heat it if we do," Julie said.

Meg raised a quizzical eyebrow at her.

"We spent most of junior and senior years sitting in the common room in our flannel nightgowns and robes chatting over cups of cocoa," Julie explained.

"It's still summer and a little warm for flannel, isn't it?" Meg asked.

Vivian giggled and smiled at Meg's remark. "I think I learned more over cocoa than in classes," she said.

Cynthia stood up. "I'm going to ask the kitchen to provide warm milk tonight."

And it was decided, Meg realized. Cynthia would make it happen.

"Meg, where are you?" Julie was nudging her. "It's time to go. You were a million miles away." Cynthia was back from the kitchen and standing hands on hips with a pleased expression on her face.

"I told you milk wouldn't be a problem," she reassured Julie before turning her glance toward Meg. "You're going to get us all in trouble if you are late to march."

"Right. Let me put my mug on the dish rack. I'm right behind you," Meg assured the group.

After depositing her dishes, Meg went out to the parking lot and joined the other young women assembling themselves by height. As she and Cynthia walked purposefully to the back of the line to anchor the march, Meg began to sing, "I want to be a Navy WAVE, MMM, and a little bit more," to start the march. The line joined in:

"I want to be an Ensign, too, MMM,
And a little bit more.
I want to wear a suit of blue, MMM,
And a little bit more.
One blue stripe would be all right.
But oh, for a little bit more."

In addition to marching everywhere in their heels, they had daily calisthenics on the field and once a week went to the gym to climb ropes. As a swimmer, Meg had no trouble shimmying up a rope, but several of her fellow WAVES did not have the upper-body strength. Luckily, the WAVE regulations permitted a team approach so those who were stronger could help boost others up the rope as they gained strength. It reminded Meg of combining forces with Julie to get her luggage on the train rack. This morning several WAVES were struggling.

"I can't do it," Vivian cried with tears running down her face. She crumpled to the floor.

"Sure you can," Meg said. "I'm going to get your left side and Cynthia is going to get your right. We're going to boost you up and push so you get a feel for going up the rope. Cynthia, you ready?" Cynthia glared at Meg as she moved the rope over to Vivian.

"One. Two. Three!" Meg called and Vivian squealed, but made it a few feet up before sliding down, rope burns on her legs and arms.

"Let's tape your hands and try again," Meg coached. "You started to get the feel for it and you don't want to stop now. It will take a few weeks, but you'll get it."

That night at their hearty dinner of stew with peas, carrots, and cubed potatoes, Cynthia looked inquisitively at Meg and said, "Meg. Tell us more about teaching. What was it like to be so young and teaching at a large public school?"

"Busy. Interesting. Challenging." Meg hoped to avoid whatever game Cynthia was playing.

"Don't all new teachers have to work their way up?" Cynthia pressed. "I thought high school jobs only went to men who had families to support since those jobs pay better."

"They also go to women with a math degree rather than a normal school credential." Meg took a deep sip of her milk. Their milk was from a local farm and contained more cream than the milk she drank in the city. Meg carefully wiped her mouth. She did not need to sport a milk mustache as Cynthia volleyed her next insult.

"Do you really think you had the students' respect?" Cynthia continued. "You're young and from their neighborhood. How did you discipline your students?"

Cynthia was certainly perceptive. During her first week of teaching, the librarian refused to give Meg textbooks because she thought Meg was a student pulling a prank rather than the new math teacher. After that experience, Meg tried to dress as "old" as she could, wearing plain dresses and pulling her hair back in a tight bun.

"A few people did think I was a student," she admitted, "but I grew up with brothers."

"How does that help?" Cynthia asked.

"I can almost always solve a problem based on something my brothers did, even if it was getting in trouble. I reminded myself that if my popular brother liked a teacher, everyone else did too. I quickly learned the secret to teaching high school is to figure out who is the ringleader of the biggest clique. Get him on your side and he does all the hard work."

"You sound like our father," Vivian interjected. "He does that sort of thing when he's planning operations with his men."

"It's all the same sort of strategy," Meg agreed. "You'll have to excuse me. I need to work on my sailor knot."

Meg sighed deeply before deciding to go to the library to send a brief note to her family, for whom she was more homesick than she wanted to admit. After mailing the letter in the box outside the hotel, she went upstairs to her room and walked over to the window. She was staring at a squirrel frolicking in the tree and decided she did not have the emotional energy to have cocoa with Cynthia as Julie walked in.

"Julie, I'm going to have to pass on cocoa tonight."

"Not an option, Meg. They're coming here. I knew you wouldn't join us if I didn't have it in our room."

"I'm not going to say anything," Meg replied.

"Fine. I dare you to be quiet!" Julie said with a smile. "You've never really seen Cynthia in a social gathering. She can coax even the most reluctant wallflower into the conversation. After tonight I think you'll agree she can be a lot of fun."

"She has to like the wallflower," Meg muttered.

At 19:30, there was a tap on the door. Cynthia was holding a carafe of warm milk and Vivian was grasping four mugs, focused on every step she took. Holding the mugs had upset her precarious sense of balance.

"Julie, I'm putting the mugs on the bathroom counter before I drop them," Vivian explained.

"Here, let me help!" Julie said. Meg saw Vivian sigh with relief. Julie carefully tapped the powered cocoa from the tin into the mugs, without any spills. She was practiced in the transfer. When Cynthia doled out the milk, Meg was surprised that she poured four equal portions. Meg was prepared for whatever remained.

"We don't have spoons!" Julie exclaimed.

"Wait," Meg commanded, heading to the sink. She took her toothbrush, washed the handle with a little soap, and grasping from the brush end, used the handle to stir the hot liquid.

"You never cease to amaze me, Margaret Burke," Julie complimented her before turning to Cynthia and Vivian saying, "You're our guests. You take the lower bunk. Meg and I will sit on the floor."

Meg carefully lowered herself to the floor and took a small sip of cocoa. The milk was creamy and the chocolate sweet. She could see how the treat could easily have become a ritual.

Not surprisingly, Cynthia was the first to speak.

"Meg, I'm sure you haven't heard my story about the time I went to the Yale homecoming game?" she began.

Meg had expected Cynthia would talk about her college exploits and name-drop so everyone, especially she, knew how well connected her family was. She wondered if the Taylor family would be mentioned; its omission so far intrigued her.

Cynthia continued, "I went to that dance with Peter Miller. Or was it James Guittard? At one point I had to put my suitors' names on index cards to remind myself who they were and how I knew them." Meg wondered if the cards had a line for estimated family worth.

"Cynthia's rejects were every other girl's dream, so it paid to stick around," Julie noted.

"Can you imagine if I got their backgrounds confused?" Cynthia turned to Meg. "I suppose it was easier for you. Not so many suitors to remember and all named Michael and Patrick." Meg was exhausted from Cynthia's attempts to provoke her. She tried to let it wash over her, wondering how Tom would handle Cynthia. He could win her over and say the right thing. Instead, Meg took a careful sip of her drink, focusing on the chocolate rather than the fact that she was a fish out of water, helplessly gulping on a table.

"Do you remember the rhetoric instructor my senior year?" Cynthia asked. "He was so handsome. He looked a bit like Cary Grant and had the loveliest diction. He followed me around like a lost puppy. I might have broken his heart when I graduated."

"I remember the instructor," Julie said. "His crush was on Vivian, who was Katharine Hepburn to his Cary Grant. What I remember is your father arriving on campus to make it clear to him that someone with so small a salary had better leave his desirable daughters alone."

"He liked Cynthia," Vivian said firmly.

"He liked you," Julie said, reaching over to pat Vivian gently on the shoulder. "And he was a nice person. I had no trouble picturing the two of you living on campus. Your children thankfully breaking the monotony of chapel when they said something funny." Meg saw a few tears escaping from Vivian's eyes.

"Cynthia, you can't pretend to have all the fun. You need to be a better older sister," Julie said firmly. "Meg, Cynthia is doing her very best to hide it, but she can be selfless. Our sophomore year she was determined our class would break a decades-long streak of losing to the juniors in field hockey. She recruited new team members based on height and single-handedly taught them to play the game. Once we had a new backfield, Cynthia had the entire team up before dawn so we were ready to practice the moment there was enough light, even when the field had frost on it!"

Meg took another sip of her drink and tried to picture Cynthia in Julie's light. She was savoring the warmth and sweetness of the cocoa when Julie's voice startled her. "Meg, what do you want to talk about tonight?"

"Why are we called 'seamen' but the subject on which we seem to spend the most time is reviewing the proper posture for sitting at a desk?" Meg replied. "I am tired of hearing 'Self-respecting WAVES will not slouch over desks and counters.' The three of you are experts on posture from your debutante days. Is learning comportment and how to look graceful always so time-consuming?"

"It is, actually. I spent a lot of time on that," Cynthia said. Meg noted this was the first time she remembered Cynthia admitting to being slightly less than totally competent.

"I don't think anyone in our family is graceful," Vivian chimed in. "But I am far worse than Cynthia. My mother was so worried I was going to trip when I was presented at the debutante ball. The more she worried, the more I worried. The only good thing was I agonized so much I lost weight, so my dress fit correctly. When I get married, it will have to be at a justice of the peace so I don't have to fret about walking into a church." Julie reached over to pat Vivian's arm comfortingly.

"I've learned something from our lessons on lipstick color. The right color does make a difference in the way we look," Julie admitted. "Lieutenant Fowler told us that one of the first things Commander McAfee brought up during their training is that the correct lipstick is the difference between appearing tired and looking prepared for duty."

"It is also a symbol of why we're fighting. Since Hitler won't let women wear lipstick, it's important we do wear it," Cynthia confirmed.

"Lieutenant Fowler always looks rested, so she must have found the right color." Meg had finally found a topic on which she could comment. "The Montezuma Red the Navy is supplying works for most people, but it's too orange for me. So is Elizabeth Arden's Victory Red. I look like a ghoul. I need a bluer red. Until then, I will look tired! Maybe even ghostlike." Julie and Vivian laughed with Meg as the three clinked their cocoa mugs together.

"But back to walking during your debut," Cynthia began.

"Cynthia, you are just being mean!" Julie exclaimed. Meg looked quizzically at the other women, surprised that Cynthia could be almost as trying with her sister and her friend as she was with her.

"Julie did what I was so scared I would do," Vivian said quietly. "She tripped on her dress and fell down a small flight of stairs as she was announced."

"It's become a bit of a joke," Julie said lightly.

Meg decided it was time to change the subject. "Julie, I'll give you my dessert tomorrow night if you trim my hair," she coaxed. "Meeting the Navy regulation of keeping our hair above our collar is tougher than I expected."

"You'll need to stand up for me to get the right angle," Julie replied

"Let me get a towel to capture the trimmings." Meg stood up, went to the bathroom, and returned to take her place in the middle of the towel.

"I'll need several more weeks to get better at cutting your hair, but it feels like December is around the corner. I want you to look beautiful in our graduation picture," Julie continued as she gingerly trimmed Meg's ends. "Speaking of pictures, I was helping to sort boxes in the Alumnae Center . . ."

"You mean Naval Reserve Midshipmen's School," interrupted Cynthia.

"Yes. Alright. Naval Reserve Midshipmen's School. Do you want to know what I overheard or not?" Julie waved the scissors at Cynthia.

"Stop interrupting her. Drink your cocoa," pleaded Meg. "I don't want my hair to be lopsided." Vivian started to giggle as she took a sip and it turned into a slurp, which made them laugh harder.

"While I was quietly sorting boxes, I overheard that Eleanor Roosevelt will be coming to inspect us at our Midshipman ceremony!" A small ceremony was planned for next week to mark a month of the training and their promotion to midshipmen.

"A perfect chance for good public relations. Maybe you and I will be featured as multigenerational Navy officers," Cynthia said to Vivian. Meg furtively rolled her eyes at Julie.

"It would make sense to have the First Lady there. She was instrumental in making sure women could be in the military," Julie continued as if she hadn't heard Cynthia.

"And it explains why Lieutenant Fowler is even more jumpy than usual," Meg noted. "She is probably in charge of the logistics," Cynthia suggested.

"And lipstick color!" Vivian said. They giggled.

"We'd better pray it isn't wet or damp. Can you imagine a group of us marching and slipping?" Julie asked.

"We still don't have our uniforms. It won't look good for the pictures if we go to Washington in our 'nurse uniform,'" Vivian worried.

"Maybe. It should cut down on any male attention!" Cynthia responded.

"They'll have to have us in uniforms before they let us out," Meg observed. "We've spent so much training time on making sure we look immaculate, they aren't going to send us out with cheap blouses that don't match our military-issued gloves."

"You've spent time thinking about this, haven't you," Cynthia noted.

"I have. In between lipstick color," Meg said with a smile.

"But what I am thinking about now is that you need to take your carafe and mugs and head to bed. It's almost lights out."

"Always the teacher, aren't you," Cynthia complained.

"This was fun," her sister said. "We need to do it again soon. See you tomorrow." Her smile to Meg conveyed such warmth, Meg was not only surprised but touched.

As the door closed and Cynthia and Vivian hurried to get back to their room, Julie remarked, "That wasn't so bad, was it? Vivian really admires you, Meg."

"Yet another reason for her sister to dislike me," Meg grumbled quietly.

Rinsing the mugs took longer than expected and the whistle blew for lights out while Meg and Julie were brushing their teeth; they crept to bed in the dark. Pulling the sheet up, Meg wondered why Cynthia was so brusque with everyone but could not come up with a good reason. She switched to thinking about what lipstick color would make her look less tired and quickly fell asleep.

# 7

---

**M**eg was having trouble memorizing the plethora of acronyms, or alphabet soup as they called it. They'd had an acronym test today; Meg had made lists and propped them against a folded towel on the bathroom counter, studying them while brushing her teeth. Julie made index cards. Meg realized acronyms might be the one thing that would prevent her from graduating. At least, she had made it as far as the Midshipmen ceremony. Unfortunately, it had been only a rumor that Mrs. Roosevelt would be there.

"What does BCD stand for, Julie?" Meg quizzed as they walked to the Mess Hall.

"Bad Conduct Discharge. And for fifty cents, what if I add an additional 'D'?" Julie responded.

"Bad Conduct Discharge and Demotion?" she guessed.

"Base Construction Depot Detachment."

"Of course it is. My favorites are the two MRSes. Officially, Military Railway Service or Movement Report Sheet. Unofficially, Officer's Wife designation."

They both giggled. As they walked into breakfast at the USS Northampton Hotel, Meg could not shake the feeling that she was on an extended vacation; she had never had this much free time. All her meals were prepared and someone else washed the dishes! When she wanted to go into town when she had liberty, she could take a bike from a Smith student who tied red, white, and blue ribbons to the handlebars to indicate it was available for loan to a WAVE. Even the classes were different. Everyone started the day well rested and ready to ask questions. The contrast to her college days was stark. Meg did not tell her fellow WAVES about the semester she gently prodded awake the young man who sat next to her in calculus who had already delivered milk for several early morning hours before coming to campus.

Meg loved her class on radio communication; she tutored other WAVES and explained the physics in a way her confused classmates could understand. One of her favorite afternoons was a quick course on how to talk her way out of a classroom-rigged emergency. Lieutenant Webb had asked the seamen what they would do if they were followed. Some of the suggestions had been "always walk with a buddy" and "find a policeman" and "try to find a crowd."

"I would look in store or office windows to see who was following me. If I felt really unsafe, I would start walking in the middle of the street to attract rather than detract attention," Meg said.

"Good examples," Webb said. "You have to be aware of your surroundings and be able to use whatever you have, such as a store window or an approaching car if the area is mainly deserted, to help you out."

There were several discreet looks among the class. This was the most positive statement Webb had ever made.

"Class dismissed," Lieutenant Webb commanded. "Seaman Burke, please stay back."

When the rest of the class had filed out, he asked, "Do you have a background in police work?"

"No. I'm a math teacher," Meg answered.

"Have you been followed?"

"Yes."

Webb raised an eyebrow but said nothing.

"Another teacher I did not like as much as he liked me." She flushed. "May I be excused, sir? I need to get downstairs to march with the group."

"Of course."

Meg thought he looked very puzzled and surprised. *He must not have sisters*, she thought as she raced to join the line to march. When she entered the meeting point, Cynthia frowned at Meg as she took her position at the end of the line.

"You're late! Are you running on Irish time?"

Meg mentally kicked herself when she could not think of a comeback and focused on starting the cadence for her side of the line with more force than necessary. Once underway, a WAVE in the middle of Cynthia's line broke a heel.

"We've got one down!" her partner shouted.

"Oh no!"

"Are you hurt?

"Can we stop?"

"We need to stop."

"Keep up! Keep up!" Cynthia urged as her line started to snake. In the confusion, she hissed at Meg, "You know you're never going to be one of us."

Meg called out, "Halt." As the line stopped, she went up to check on the woman with the broken heel, who was laughing rather than crying.

"Are you okay?" Meg asked. "Do you need any first aid?"

"Only for my shoe," she said, grinning.

"I'm not certified in shoe first aid," Meg joked. "Can you hobble back?"

"I'll try to march on my toes. It isn't far!"

Meg went back to her position and called, "Forward, march!"

When they had reached the hotel parking lot, the women

started heading indoors, but Meg was not going to let the insult go. She walked over to Cynthia and blocked her path to the building.

"Cynthia, I'm one of the few women you will ever meet who has a math degree and professional experience as a department chair." Meg continued, "The US Navy had to over-look the fact I was Irish American and Catholic when they accepted me. You don't have to like me. We certainly don't have to be friends, but you have to accept the fact that I do belong here."

Only as she finished did Meg look up and realize some of the group, including Julie and Vivian, remained outside and had been listening to her. She felt her chest constrict. Cynthia had two bright red circles on her cheeks; Meg realized she probably had twin flushes on her own face. Without a word, Cynthia turned on her heel and walked inside. After the incident, she and Vivian avoided her; Meg did nothing to seek them out.

That night after lights out, Julie said, "There's something you should know about Cynthia."

"Even you, the eternal optimist, don't think she and I are going to be friends, do you?"

"I hope you can be, but I know it's not going to be this week or next." Meg could feel Julie smiling in the dark.

"When I met Cynthia at eighteen, she had the self-confidence of a thirty-year-old," Julie continued. "She was witty. Because of her parents, she was invited to all the right parties and her brothers ensured an ever-present pool of eligible males. She always had fresh flowers in her room and candy to share with the rest of us. Unfortunately, after her debut junior year, spirited became self-centered," Julie sighed. "But when I was so homesick at Wellesley and wanted to leave, she was the person who was always convincing me to stay. I love that Cynthia and I know she is still in there."

Meg said thoughtfully, "There's more to it than that."

It was several moments before Julie replied, "I don't want to be a gossip."

"Of course."

Meg thought Julie had fallen asleep, but as she rolled over, Julie said quietly, "The summer before senior year Cynthia developed a horrible crush on an officer reporting to her father."

"Never a good idea to date the boss's daughter. I'm going to guess even worse in the Navy."

"Spot on as always, Meg. Although it wasn't a problem until Cynthia was sending three or four letters to his one. He tried to extract himself gracefully. First he became much busier after war was declared in Europe, then he found excuses not to visit, and finally he asked for a transfer."

"Disappointing, but that doesn't account for the chip on her shoulder."

"She had hinted widely that they were about to be engaged."

"Oh. That does hurt. I'd be upset too."

As she worked on her crossword puzzle the next morning, Meg thought about a conversation with her mother before joining the WAVES, which kept spinning in her head.

"Should you go?" her mother asked. "You're already head of a department. Of a *high school*. In a few years you will be a principal." As much as she enjoyed the comradery, especially with Julie, and the experience of being a student at Smith, Meg was not sure she was going to be making a more significant contribution to the war effort than if she were teaching. She drank her coffee and reassured herself that right now she was earning more money than she had teaching; once she finished Indoctrination, she would be more involved and her role clearer.

A few days later, during Physics, Meg's favorite class, an unfamiliar officer joined the class to make an announcement. Although properly attired, he was not yet comfortable in his uniform and unlike many of the male officers, he seemed amused to be in a classroom of women. He was in his late twenties, well over six feet tall, with dark brown, almost black hair and gray-green eyes. He looked and carried himself like an athlete. Maybe a swimmer, she thought. Picturing him in a tweed jacket, she concluded he could be an academic.

"Good afternoon, Midshipmen. I'm Lieutenant Robert Prescott. I'm representing the Naval Communications Command."

Meg felt the buzz in the room as he spoke.

He continued in his upper-class Boston accent, "This evening, at nineteen-hundred hours, I invite those of you who like puzzles to participate in a friendly competition in the USS Northampton Ballroom."

It was a good idea, Meg thought to use the ballroom rather than the lounge; there should be a good turnout for the handsome lieutenant. Cynthia shot a triumphant smile at Meg to indicate she had already won the challenge. Meg told herself she was going because she was bored and working on the puzzles was the challenge she needed; it had nothing to do with Cynthia or the lieutenant.

Later that evening, as she wandered into the ballroom, Meg noted that most of the hotel had easily adapted to the influx of young women and its transformation into a training center, but it was as if the ballroom were the staunch holdout. The chandelier light was uneven—too glaring directly underneath the fixture and too dim in the corners. As people walked through the room, Meg thought they became different characters. In the dimmer periphery, Cynthia looked young, even vulnerable; but as she came into the brighter light, the dominant feature of her strong chin returned and she looked as though she was ready to battle with an unsuspecting waiter, finding fault with her order or sending back soup for being too cool.

Four tables meant to seat eight were set up with four chairs each. Only a dozen WAVES were there (the handsome officer was not as much of a draw as Meg had expected), leaving plenty of space around each of the attendees. There were a few pages of blank paper and two pencils at each spot. All the WAVES stood and clustered nervously around the tables, waiting for further direction. Cynthia squared her shoulders, walked up to the young officer, and gave him her hundred-watt smile as she said, "Good evening. I'm Cynthia Collingsworth."

"Ah, John's sister. That's why you looked so familiar," the officer said tersely. Meg could see him frowning. "I've got to administer this test, so I can't chat now," he added.

"That's okay. We can catch up after the exam," Cynthia replied.

Lieutenant Prescott said, "Hurry, ladies . . . ah, Midshipmen. Sit down. Please leave the papers I am passing out facedown until I tell you to flip them over. During the thirty minutes, you must keep your eyes on your paper and not disturb the others. If you finish early, please turn your papers over and wait quietly. At the end of the session, I'll collect your sheets."

Every pair of eyes was on him as he passed out the work-sheets. *Only recently finished graduate school*, Meg concluded. A seasoned teacher would have selected someone not taking the test to help pass out the papers. She also wondered if he would use all thirty minutes to figure out a way to escape from talking to Cynthia.

"You may begin now!" Meg flipped the page. She wasn't sure what she had been expecting, maybe a crossword puzzle or a word search grid. It was neither. She was sure they were famous passages of text, but not written in English or another language she recognized. The first was easy. It was the Pledge of Allegiance, with each letter off by seven letters. The second was Psalm 23, but in numbers. She recognized the length visually and checked a few of the numbers; she saw A = 13 and confirmed B = 14. The third took a little more time, but once she realized it was FDR's speech, in German, from the day after Pearl Harbor and used the German alphabet flipped from beginning to end, she quickly completed it. She quietly turned her paper over and put the pencil down on it.

The officer gave her a disappointed look. *He must assume I've given up,* Meg thought. A few minutes later, Cynthia's hand shot up and she cried, "Done!"

Lieutenant Prescott shot her a scathing look and mouthed, "Quiet." Meg would have blushed after the correction, but Cynthia continued smiling. She seemed even more pleased with herself when Prescott walked over to her seat, crouched next to her, and whispered in her ear. Cynthia got up and tiptoed out of the room but failed to catch the heavy door as it closed with a bang and the remaining WAVES jumped in their seats. Meg watched Prescott scowling at the door. Meg was the last WAVE to leave the room after time was called and the papers gathered; she thought the officer looked as if he wanted to say something to her, but she left before he had the chance.

Cynthia was leading a testing postmortem in the corridor:

"Did you get the last one?" she demanded of another midshipman.

"What was the last one?" the midshipman responded.

"I have no idea what the middle one was about," replied another.

"How about you, Meg? You're always doing the crossword; did you get any?" Cynthia asked with an arched eyebrow and her funny way of looking down at Meg, even though Meg was slightly taller. It was the first time they had spoken since their encounter in the parking lot.

"I got the first one. There wasn't a lot of time to work on them, was there?" Meg shrugged her shoulders to suggest resignation to not having done well. Why didn't she say that she had solved all three? And quickly, too. For some reason, she kept it to herself.

Julie was waiting in their room to hear about the test and the lieutenant as she washed out the day's uniforms, which Meg would press for tomorrow. Meg did her best to imitate

Lieutenant Prescott's Boston Brahmin accent explaining the directions and Cynthia's outburst when she solved the puzzles, sending Julie into a fit of giggles.

"I think Cynthia already knows the officer. Or at least her brother does," Meg noted.

"That makes sense. They probably went to school together," Julie confirmed. "But who cares about that. Do you think you'll get to work with Lieutenant Prescott on whatever project it is?"

"That wouldn't be so bad, would it? He's handsome; he looks like he swims. With that accent, though, I'm pretty sure he is only working with elite officers."

"Margaret Burke, I was beginning to give up on you! He stared at you the entire time he gave the announcement today. I couldn't believe you didn't notice. He isn't a swimmer. He's a rower."

"A rower?"

"Crew. Men in boats on the river. You can tell by the shoulders."

"Oh."

"And, why has it taken me this long to find out you are such a mimic?"

This was a much better subject as far as Meg was concerned. "I always liked reading out loud and giving my characters voices, but I'm not always sure if anyone will appreciate it. I guess I know you well enough now to know you would. I would have liked to be in the high school play, but . . ." Her voice trailed off. "I was always too busy."

"I think you would have been terrific," Julie confirmed. "You could have played Desdemona or Olivia. Yes. A fabulous Olivia. A wealthy countess but a little naïve. You might fall in love with a woman dressed as a man, but only because you wouldn't get close enough to see she wasn't a man."

"That's ridiculous. I grew up with three brothers. I can, literally, smell a man at twenty-five yards, especially if he has socks on." They fell into another fit of giggles, put their uniforms out for the next day, and turned out the lights. They were so busy and often so tired that they did not wait for the lights-out bell to get into bed.

But once the lights were out, Meg couldn't fall asleep. She had solved all three puzzles rapidly. They were not puzzles, of course. They were simple codes. Far simpler than anything the military would be using, she thought. She remembered one of her college professors talking about machines that generated codes. He had lectured about the mathematical complexity of cryptology and demonstrated a few examples. Meg had been interested in the idea and learning more about cryptology; this was one of the reasons she would have liked to go to graduate school. But this wasn't graduate school. Why were they testing WAVES on their ability to recognize codes? Wouldn't the Navy reach out to university professors to work on codes? Meg turned over in bed and tried to think about the mechanics of the code pattern she would suggest to the Navy if asked. As hard as she tried, she also could not stop thinking about the lieutenant. She knew she had met him before.

## 8

Fall weather had arrived in New England, with crisp nights and a sky the deepest blue Meg had ever seen. Here, without the city pollution, Meg saw a slow turn of color including leaves in vibrant orange-reds she was sure were unknown in Brooklyn. She had grown to like marching in the fall air.

As they returned from classes to the USS Northampton the day after the puzzle test, Cynthia called to Julie, "Take a quick walk with me." She smirked at Meg and said, "You should probably come too." Cynthia waited until they were a few blocks from the facility and said, "I've done some homework."

"Really? What type of homework?" Julie asked.

"I remembered a Prescott rowing with my brother and my dancing with him at some point, but I did not get a chance to follow up with the officer who gave the test last night." Meg tried not to roll her eyes as Cynthia recounted another man she pretended to have barely met. "I called my brother at lunch," Cynthia continued, "who confirmed he went to school with Robbie Prescott."

Meg wondered what a midday long-distance telephone call

cost. Before she could stop herself, she asked, "He went to the Naval Academy? I'd have guessed he was pulled from academia."

"Not that brother. The one who went to Princeton," Cynthia replied. Meg felt a boost of self-confidence. She had recognized the lieutenant was recently a civilian. If he went to Princeton, it might also explain why she thought he looked familiar. The Taylor sons attended Princeton; Meg might have seen Lieutenant Prescott while working at their house.

Cynthia was off and running with her commentary, and Meg noted Julie had to do her half-hop to keep up.

"Cynthia, slow down," Meg commanded. "We aren't marching."

Cynthia looked around before whispering, "His name is Robert Tait Prescott."

"Why are we whispering, Cynthia?" Julie asked.

Cynthia flushed and in a normal tone continued, "Everyone calls him Robbie. Still. I guess because his father is Robert. He rowed with my brother. Normally, Princeton's crew is a perennial third, but his boat won Head of the Charles his senior year."

"With your brother?" Meg asked.

Cynthia glowered at her before responding, "Different boat." She turned back to Julie. "Apparently, everyone loves him. His classmates, his professors, his nanny."

"And girls." Julie had almost caught her breath from jogging to keep up.

"And girls," Cynthia confirmed. "From what I can tell, attending Princeton is the only thing he has ever done to upset his family. Generations have gone to Harvard. Also, he majored in math rather than economics. He recently finished his PhD at Columbia and started to teach there. His family is connected to a Boston bank, but now his father is in Washington, DC, doing something at State or maybe something with Treasury. Apparently, his parents are friends with my Aunt Isobel. Also, he has a sister at Smith. That's probably one of the reasons he was sent to give us the test during Indoctrination. The Navy felt he would know how to behave. I'm sure his position is probably all hush-hush. Just think, Meg, if you had gone to Barnard, he might have been one of your math professors." Meg ignored her comment.

"I bet he can dance. He looks like he can dance." Julie said. "What do you think, Meg?"

"Ask Cynthia. I thought she had already danced with him," Meg replied. Cynthia's hurt expression surprised Meg. She had struck a nerve. If Cynthia previously met this man as she claimed and he knew her family, why hadn't he wanted to chat after class or said hello when they arrived at testing? Surely that was allowed. Had Cynthia's reputation preceded her, and he knew to avoid her?

A few days later, at lunch, Lieutenant Roland directed Meg to attend a meeting after lunch at the USS Northampton instead of returning to campus for class. Meg's first thought was what her absence would do to the marching formation. The second was whether the meeting was related to the other night's so-called puzzle competition. Lieutenant Roland told her to report to the lounge at 1300. Meg quickly went back to her room to check her uniform and combed her hair.

As Meg entered the room, Lieutenant Prescott sprang to his feet but did not immediately salute. Surprised to see him, she noted he was still following deeply ingrained civilian manners rather than naval protocol. Meg did not enjoy interviews in the best of circumstances; the idea of sitting one-on-one with this handsome officer threw her off balance until her inner voice started scolding her. Given all the situations she had success-fully navigated over the past few weeks, she told herself she most certainly could speak coherently to this man.

The lieutenant had several folders on the table, which he kept rearranging. He settled on one and took a moment to skim the contents. Meg was sure he had already studied her file and likely memorized its contents. Was he stalling? No, she realized; he was nervous too!

"Thank you for joining me today," he said. "I want to ask you a few questions about your background. Let's start with you describing the math and science courses you took in college."

Meg knew the Navy already had that information several times over. She quickly realized this interview was not about content but about measuring her composure. He was determining if she could look him in the eye and speak articulately. As he continued to smile encouragingly at her, she decided she was doing okay. His next question surprised her.

"Do you know anything about radios?"

"Actually, I do." She chuckled slightly. "My brother Tom received a radio kit as a present when he was in high school, and I helped hold the different pieces as he soldered the wires." She smiled. "He let me solder a few of the easier joints."

"Does your brother still build radios?"

She laughed. "Not for years. Once we discovered baseball on the radio, we bought a commercial model."

"Who do you root for?"

"The Dodgers."

"Of course. Brooklyn," he replied. He had read her file, Meg thought. Closely. He was well aware of her working-class roots, reinforced by her devotion to a blue-collar team.

"They had a good season last year," he continued evenly. "Not quite as good this year."

"This fall I wasn't there to help them pull through to make the World Series."

He grinned at her.

"There's another reason I know something about radios."

"What's that?" He leaned forward in his seat, looking a little surprised.

"This past year, after Pearl Harbor, I did everything I could to make my math classes relevant to the war effort. I taught my students about the amplitude of radio waves." Meg could see him making notes.

"Tell me more about what you did as a camp counselor," he requested.

"Mainly I focused on keeping the girls busy. I taught them to swim and spent the rest of the time lifeguarding. I helped them discover homesickness is not fatal."

He chuckled. Should she tell him that camp had been her first experience with the dynamics of an all-female community? She decided it was better to continue to answer his questions simply. Even baseball might have been too much of a tangent.

"Did you swim in school?"

"No. Only during the summer."

"What hobbies do you have?"

"I read and do crossword puzzles. While I commuted to college, I could do both while on the train or the bus."

"Do you play bridge?"

"No, I don't," Meg replied as she shook her head. She started to explain her limited knowledge about the card game came from it being used as a distraction in numerous Agatha Christie novels, but caught herself just in time. The lieutenant seemed so friendly she found herself opening up to him, which was contrary to their daily reminders to disclose as little as possible about their current training and themselves.

"It's a fun game. Since you like puzzles and numbers, you should give it a try." He cleared his throat. "Thank you for taking the time to talk to me this afternoon."

She saluted, disappointed that was all there was to the interview. After her case of nerves, she wished it had been more of a challenge. He could have asked her about the politics of Brooklyn College students or specifically what she knew about cryptology, but instead, seemed to have decided about her when she declared herself a Dodgers fan.

On Sunday evening, Meg found a plain envelope in her

mailbox addressed to Margaret Burke. The brief letter informed her the US Navy had selected her to receive additional communications training. She should report tomorrow morning to Dewey House, Room 10. Now she would have something to think about other than the dreaded acronyms.

## 9

At breakfast on Monday, as she got in line for food, Lieutenant Fowler pulled Meg aside.

"Grab a cup of coffee or a piece of toast and report to your new assignment," Fowler instructed.

"What about the marching line?" Meg asked, worried. Fowler smiled at her.

"We've got it under control," she assured her. Meg used the time to drink not one but two cups of coffee before taking a few pieces of toast to eat as she scurried to campus.

Meg was the first to arrive. After a brief salute, her instructor offered her hand and said,

"I'm Lieutenant Josephine Carrington. Tell me about WAVE indoctrination. What has the experience been like?"

"It's nothing like anything I have ever done, ma'am," Meg said truthfully. "I commuted to college, so living in the dorms, I mean barracks, as well as the esprit de corps, is all new to me. I really feel as though I'm part of something."

She heard footsteps. Cynthia and four other midshipmen entered the classroom. *Of course, Cynthia was selected*, Meg thought.

"Everyone, take a seat," Lieutenant Carrington directed. Once they were seated, she continued, "A little bit about myself. I earned my PhD in zoology at Columbia and I've been teaching zoology at Smith for three years." As Meg watched this lean, handsome woman with brown hair and hazel eyes, which sparkled behind her glasses as she spoke, she wondered whether she could attend graduate school and then teach at a college or university. Meg also wondered if Lieutenant Carrington knew Lieutenant Prescott from Columbia.

"We're going to dig into our training material in just a few moments, but before we do, I need to talk to you about something even more important." Carrington had captured the WAVES' attention with not only the earnestness in her voice but also her serious tone.

"It is *vital* you do not talk about what you are about to learn in this training or even tell others you are part of this training. It is TOP SECRET. Not a word to your roommate, your parents, or a boyfriend, even if he is in the military. You cannot discuss what we are doing with the other WAVES at dinner. Or anywhere else," she clarified.

She paused to gaze at the six women. With that statement, Meg realized her future war experience had just dramatically shifted from the expected menial tasks of filing paperwork to something far more exciting and serious. As she looked at the solemn expressions on the other young women's faces, she recognized that they, too, were processing what they had just been told.

Carrington continued, "You can't talk to the other women in this course about what we are doing, except in this classroom. Is that clear?" She paused to make eye contact with every WAVE before continuing. "When the other midshipmen ask you what you are doing, you must simply say you are taking a communications course."

Lieutenant Carrington had been pacing at the front of the classroom and suddenly pivoted. "Who can you tell?"

"No one!" the six midshipmen responded in unison.

Carrington was apparently convinced she had communicated successfully the secret nature of their work and passed out mimeographed sheets, notebooks, and the ubiquitous US Government property pens before continuing, "You will need to leave the materials in the classroom each day. Not only is it important to keep things secure now, but it will also get you in the habit of being careful to confine your work to an approved location." She paced for a few moments before turning to face the group again, saying, "You are here for several reasons. You had high scores on a test indicating your ability to decipher codes. You are highly educated. Finally, you have shown aptitude for military operations during Indoctrination. Now the US Navy is challenging you to take on a special responsibility. Over the next few weeks, I will be preparing you to join and to support the US Navy's Combat Intelligence Unit, called OP-20-G, which is dedicated to breaking Japanese ciphers."

As Lieutenant Carrington stopped to take a breath, there was a silence in the classroom. Meg felt her chest constrict slightly and her stomach do its familiar anxious flip-flops. She had recognized that her rapid acceptance into the WAVES was because of her math degree, but she had allowed the novelty of Indoctrination to distract her from considering what she might really be doing as a naval officer. Given the hush in the room, it felt as though the other midshipmen were also just realizing what their true assignment would be.

The six students waited with pens poised over their paper.

"This morning I'm going to provide a historical overview of codes and ciphers. The terms *code* and *cipher* are often used interchangeably. But to be precise," she stopped to smile at them, "and you were selected because you are individuals who are precise, I will review the differences. A code is a system for disguising a message by replacing one character or string of characters for another. A cipher requires the decoder to apply a mathematical operation, such as subtracting a designated value called the key, from a string of numbers and before decrypting those values."

Cynthia raised her hand but did not wait for the lieutenant to call on her. "We did both as part of the exam we took."

"Yes. You did," the officer responded. "But the examples you worked with were much simpler than any cipher used for military communications." That confirmed Meg's earlier conclusion that the exercises were unsophisticated. Meg was still surprised only a select group had seen the patterns that night in the ballroom.

"You will learn how to analyze and to break sophisticated ciphers, ciphers used by the Japanese to mask communications about troop movement, supply routes, and other critical war-related information."

Meg felt as if the room had gone dark when Carrington mentioned the Japanese, but as she looked out the window, she saw it was clouds blocking the sun rather than tension darkening the room. A storm was quickly moving into Northampton. By this afternoon there would be cold rain, possibly freezing, if it continued into the night.

Carrington saw Meg looking out the window and remarked, "Winter is knocking on the door, isn't it?" Meg was embarrassed the teacher had seen *and* commented on her looking out the window, but Carrington did not seem upset as she continued, "Even before the Great War, the United States had an agency scrutinizing other nations' ciphers. Then, in the 1920s, as navies around the world adopted radio communication, they quickly learned they could eavesdrop on each other. So they developed methods of both encrypting and deciphering messages. We noticed the Japanese had an advantage because they used a different type of Morse code than the rest of the world, which added a layer of security to their communications."

"Will we need to learn Morse code?" Cynthia asked, and Meg noted the apprehension in her voice.

"Probably not," Carrington said. "Most of that work is done

in another department, before you could even begin to work with the transmissions." She leaned against the chalkboard and sighed. "It did take us a while to train people to work with Japanese Morse code. The Japanese use syllabic Morse code, which corresponds better to their characters-based language. The more common Morse code is based on individual letters." Carrington looked around the room and said, "Stop frowning!" She laughed, although none of the others joined her. "I've gotten most of the bad news out of the way. Now I am about to tell you about Yankee ingenuity!"

Meg looked around the classroom and noted smiles returning as Carrington continued her narrative. "In 1933, when the Japanese brought their entire fleet together for maneuvers in the Pacific, they did not realize our radio stations were picking up their transmissions. We spent months putting the information together." Meg looked around and saw she was not the only WAVE sitting on the edge of her seat.

Carrington paused and looked thoughtful. "When the Army Signal Intelligence Service broke the encryption system the Japanese use to send diplomatic messages, this was a huge breakthrough. We now refer to this cipher system as Purple."

Carrington was a good storyteller and Meg realized she had stopped taking notes. She quickly jotted *Purple, Army, diplomatic code.*

"The system you will be working on is called JN-25." Carrington smiled again. "You will probably start to dream about JN-25. The Japanese adopted this cipher methodology in June 1939 and are still using a version to send naval communication."

Meg raised her hand and waited for Carrington to nod. "What does JN-25 mean?"

Carrington laughed. "It's probably one of the most straightforward naval designations. *JN* merely stands for Japanese Navy and the *25* indicates a version. *Twenty-five* has remained part of the name even with subsequent versions. The code name for JN-25 is 'Magic.'"

"We're working with Magic and Purple," the midshipman behind Meg blurted out.

"No one would believe us if we talked about this," Cynthia remarked. "Not that I am going to," she added quickly.

Lieutenant Carrington continued, "Because the Japanese language is character based, the Japanese assigned a numerical value to every word or syllable likely to be used in a radio message. This is the code part."

Another hand went up. "How many codes are there?"

Carrington thought before she answered. "Truthfully, thousands."

A few quiet groans drowned out Meg's quiet sigh.

"The system involves more than codes," Carrington continued. "Before the Japanese Navy sends any coded message, they also use an additive."

Meg glanced around the room and saw that the others looked as confused as she was by the word *additive*. Carrington read her students' uncertainty.

"After the message is coded, the clerk opens a second book. This book contains one hundred pages of random numbers sets." Meg heard a muffled groan behind her. Carrington ignored it and continued, "He may be directed to use a certain page or he may decide on a page; once the page is identified, he adds the first of these random additives to the first code group of his message. He adds the second group of random numbers to the second part of the message, and so on. It only works if the clerk also buries what is called an indicator in the message to tell the recipient the random number page he used. The clerk at the other end turns to the same page and strips off the additive before looking up the actual code."

Meg quickly looked around. The expression on the faces of the other five WAVES confirmed they were as baffled as she was.

"Let me give you a specific example," Carrington said, seeking to assure them. "I'm a Japanese sailor." She grinned as there were a few nervous giggles. "Let's say I need to send a message communicating 'the transport ship will arrive on Tuesday.' I would look up the code for all seven words of that message. *The* might be represented as 5731, *transport* as 7234, and so on. Next, I pull out my additive book. I've been told by my superior officer that today we are using page forty-nine. Let's say the first number on the page is 3459. I would add 3459 to 5731. The word *the* will be sent as the number 9190. The next additive is 2397. Transport would become 9631, and so on. Does that make sense so far? Why don't you do the arithmetic to help the concept stick."

Meg raised her hand. "So at the other end, the clerk would know to open to page forty-nine and subtract 3459 from 9190. When he got 5731, he would look that up and see it is the word *the*."

"Exactly," Carrington confirmed.

"It sounds exhausting," Cynthia said.

"It certainly is time-consuming," Carrington agreed. "With practice, a good clerk can code or decode about fifteen words a minute. Even when we know the additives, the sheer volume of messages means we are always behind. In a military conflict you want to be ahead."

Another midshipman named Sarah, who Meg recognized from helping to bring up the back of the marching line, asked, "Did I follow correctly? We have broken the code before, but the Japanese change it frequently?"

"Exactly!" Carrington confirmed. "Just before the war started, Commander John Rochefort gathered a team in Pearl Harbor and they were able to crack JN-25."

"How did they crack it?" Cynthia asked.

"It took several steps," Carrington said as she moved to the chalkboard and wrote a *1* followed by *codebook* and explained, "The first step had nothing to do with the team in Pearl Harbor.

It had to do with an event several years earlier. In the 1920s, a copy of the Japanese Navy's Red codebook was secretly photographed in New York City and laboriously translated by linguists. Obtaining the book was more American industrial espionage than military strategy. Fortunately, we started the war with some knowledge of their codes."

She turned and wrote the number 2 and *no additive book*. Meg was not sure what that meant.

Carrington explained, "We had the code manual but not the additives—again, that is the long list of random numbers being added to the codes to further disguise the information. Luckily, Rochefort knew something about large-scale computation." She added *3 – computation*.

"Using the raw Japanese Navy transmissions, Rochefort had his team use IBM punch cards to identify patterns. His team would laboriously transfer the numbers onto cards run through what are essentially large adding machines, which calculated the frequency of each number used. Using this data, the Navy cryptanalysts began to note the indicator numbers in each message were not as random as they should have been. Japanese code clerks get busy and tired, too. They were reusing the same pages of numbers, which allowed Rochefort's team, eventually, to crack some of the additives." Carrington stopped to take a much-needed breath.

"Wow!" exclaimed one of the midshipmen.

Carrington laughed gently. "Wow indeed. It was an intense project. After a year of leading the command, Rochefort went back to serving on a ship to recuperate. Also, given the importance of the project, the primary code-breaking efforts are now in Washington, DC, rather than Hawaii."

Cynthia and Meg caught each other's eye from across the room. They would be going to Washington, DC, when Indoctrination was over.

"If the additives have been identified, why do they need us?" Cynthia asked. Meg had been wondering the same thing.

"Because the Japanese introduced fifty thousand new additives last summer and we are working with only a partial list of the random numbers."

"How much do they change the additive list, ma'am?" Meg asked.

"What do you mean?" Lieutenant Carrington's eyebrows formed a *V* when she was asked a question.

"I would imagine the Japanese are short of time, and people are less likely to make mistakes if it is not completely different. Isn't the list updated rather than brand new?" Meg suggested.

Lieutenant Carrington looked slightly stunned. "That's excellent insight, Midshipman. Usually, we can find a pattern as to how it has been modified." She smiled ruefully. "It still takes time for us to do so."

"Ma'am," Cynthia interrupted. "How can we be expected to do this when we don't know Japanese?" Meg had wanted to ask the same question herself but hadn't wanted to throw the lieutenant off her speech.

"Almost no one working on the project started with any knowledge of Japanese. In fact, when he started working on the transmissions, Commander Rochefort knew as much about cryptology and as little Japanese as you do now. But, like many of you, he was selected because he worked on crossword puzzles during his free time. To be successful in this work, you need to have a mind built to solve puzzles. You don't need to know Japanese."

"But we do know German," Cynthia persisted. "Shouldn't we be working on German codes?"

The lieutenant sighed and pressed her lips together. Meg had noticed her doing this several times this morning. It was as if she was about to say something and then thought better of it. The lieutenant took a moment before speaking again. Meg watched as she straightened her back and squared her shoulders as if she expected a negative response to her news.

"As you have no doubt learned or are hopefully learning,

many decisions are political rather than logical. Several months ago it was decided the Army would focus on transmissions from the European theater and the Navy would work with Pacific theater transmissions. As the Navy sails in the Pacific, they intercept a huge volume of communications, so the assignment was for both political and practical reasons."

Cynthia looked disdainful as she heard this explanation, and Meg thought she was going to say something more but decided against it. Meg looked at her watch and was surprised it was lunchtime. She was so engrossed in the class, she had not noticed her stomach rumbling to complain about getting only toast and coffee.

## 10

That fall, Meg and the other five coders arrived early for their daily training sessions. Their faces were red not only from the increasingly chilly mornings but also from excitement as they hurried to the classroom through the falling leaves and negotiated icy patches while nibbling on toast.

Lieutenant Carrington taught them clues to help them uncover the hidden messages. The first insight was that some letters, or in the case of Japanese, characters, are used more frequently than others. Looking for uneven character frequency was a good first approach to analyzing a message. She told them that even though code clerks were reminded not to use stock phrases like "good morning" or even "dear sir," often titles were not omitted in communications because the message sender did not want to upset protocol to preserve the randomness of the message. The class discovered longer messages rather than shorter ones were more likely to be decoded, since they had more characters and provided more opportunity to see frequently used or repeated symbols in context. In comparison, a code-breaking team might have to review thousands of short messages to find the additive overlaps.

Carrington advised, "When you first look at a message, start by counting how many times each symbol occurs. This is a way to 'get to know your code.' Another approach is to combine messages and identify high-frequency character combinations. If you notice the same number used in concurrent messages, it makes sense to think it might be a common word like *ship, rain,* or *delay.*"

As they reviewed centuries-old practices of communication disguise, Meg realized the acronyms she had trouble memorizing were a type of code. She wondered why she had so much trouble with the acronyms when she could clearly break through codes. Maybe the acronyms were an example of inefficient coding: something meant to save time, yet which took more time and certainly caused more confusion among its intended audience than it helped.

They progressed from history and theory to working with codes and ciphers. The midshipmen started with simple cryptograms and moved on to ones that were more and more complex. As a teacher, Meg knew she might talk about how to do a math problem for hours, but the students had to solve the problem by themselves to learn the concept. In the same way, Carrington let them decipher an example for at least an hour before she pointed out mistakes so that the midshipmen had the experience of working on the problem, getting frustrated, and even restarting using another approach.

One of Meg's favorite techniques was cribbing because it reminded her of the game Hangman, in which she would start with several blank spaces representing the missing letters to make up the word. When cribbing, she did something similar. Meg would make an educated guess of a few key words in a transmission and then see if the resulting letter assignments produced text elsewhere in the message.

Far more challenging than cribbing was the Vigenère

square, a method of using a table to disguise letters. In this approach, they used a grid of twenty-six by twenty-six characters in which each letter of the alphabet is written but shifted left by one character in each subsequent row. Carrington gave them graph paper to make their own square, and they wrote *A* through *Z* in each box of the top row of the paper. In the next row, they wrote *B* first and ended with *A*. They continued until the last row started with *Z* and ended with *Y*. Next, Carrington gave them the message *Go Navy Codebreakers* and the secret key of *quizlost*, which needed to be repeated for as many characters as there were letters in the message. They wrote:

GO NAVY CODE BREAKER

QU IZLO STQU IZLOSTQU

Looking at the square, they found the character that is the intersection of the column (top character) and the row (bottom character). *G* and *Q* intercepted with a *W*, and *O* and *U* with an *I*, and so on.

Already, Meg liked Lieutenant Carrington and admired her instructor's ability to break down difficult concepts, such as the Vigenère square, into smaller understandable steps. While the work was challenging, not talking about it was even harder. Meg tried not to see Julie's hurt expression as Meg sailed through the Mess and grabbed a piece of toast to eat on her walk to campus rather than sitting down to breakfast.

"I volunteered to take on an extra communication course," Meg said by way of an explanation. Julie gave her a funny look, but her roommate was astute and did not press her for details. Meg longed to show Julie how to crib and suspected her brother Tom would be even quicker at using a Vigenère square than she was.

Julie and Meg could talk about their newly arrived fill-in cool weather uniforms, which augmented the summer-weight "nurse's uniforms." Keeping the white blouse, they now had a drab, drooping gray cardigan and scratchy gray wool skirts.

"How could they possibly have made the skirts worse?"

Julie moaned. The skirt was so long on her, it almost formed a train in back.

"I don't know what you are talking about," Meg teased. "The skirt shows off my ankles. I do like the gloves, though." The gloves from their official uniform had arrived, and they had been encouraged to wear them to become familiar with them. As Meg helped Julie hem her skirt, Julie asked, "Can you believe we are only weeks away from leave? What movies do you want to see at Christmas?"

"Anything with Bing Crosby," Meg replied. "By the way, how is poor Lieutenant Webb doing?" she asked, thinking that was probably a safe topic. She was surprised to see Julie blush and blink her eyes quickly.

"He's fine. He's teaching Morse code."

"So how do you say Bing Crosby in dots and dashes?" Meg said quickly, and then watched as Julie swallowed quickly. She hoped Julie did not often play poker.

"It's hard for me to say it. I'm getting so used to tapping it. I'd have to do it that way."

"That makes sense." Meg decided to let her off the hook. "Since you are learning the code, do you think you'll be assigned to a radio unit?"

"Probably. Damn!" Julie had just stuck her finger with her needle and quickly moved to grab a towel before getting blood all over her uniform.

Meg said, "I wonder where we will be sent." A pang of sadness hit her as she realized that in a matter of weeks, she and Julie would no longer be rooming together. In fact, they probably would not see each other once their training was finished. She continued, "Do you think any of us will be together?"

"I hope so. But I've heard that some of the radio group is going to Dayton, Ohio. I figured if you and Cynthia go to DC, I'll be in the Ohio group. Or, vice versa. Maybe Vivian will be with me to keep me company," Julie answered with none of her usual optimism.

"I'm sure the food will be better in Ohio. Closer to the farms."

"And the ice. And the middle of nowhere. DC will have all of the good-looking officers," Julie said ruefully.

Meg had roomed with Julie long enough to know the radio communication class was a cover. She was so preoccupied with trying to keep her own secret, this was the first time she had realized Julie was also keeping secrets. What was Julie up to? Meg wondered. For one thing, she was sure it was not transmitting messages using Morse code!

## 11

The next afternoon, Lieutenant Carrington started the session with her small group of cryptology students by saying, "I want to talk about how to keep your work secret. If you think it has been hard while you've been on campus, it's about to become much harder when you go home for Christmas and then on to your assignment."

After her awkward conversation with Julie, Meg had started thinking about what she was going to say at home, especially as she knew Tom was not going to believe her if she said she was going to be filing and answering the telephone. Lieutenant Carrington continued, "If you are asked what you do when you are out in public, and I can guarantee you will be, you need to be ready to say something like, 'We empty trash cans and sharpen pencils' in a believable tone."

Cynthia asked, "What are you going to say, Meg?"

Meg looked out the window, took a breath, and tried to keep her tone even. Outside the classroom, it was almost dark at four o'clock and Meg realized the fall had flown by while their eyes were focused on small pieces of paper inside the classroom.

"Oh, I'll say I make coffee and wash mugs."

"It isn't that far from the truth, is it," Cynthia replied and smirked.

At the end of four weeks, they had covered twelve lessons. Lieutenant Carrington did not have any more materials for them to work on, but she asked them to come in on the Saturday of the last week for a brief of their assignment. At this point in the training, Saturday had become a day to do laundry and to finish any assignments not completed during the week. The others might have noticed the group's absence were it not for the fact that several of the WAVES, including Julie, had decided to go into town and begin their Christmas shopping. Meg was prepared to say she was joining another group of shoppers if the question came up, but that morning she walked out of a largely deserted USS Northampton through a similarly quiet campus to her classroom.

Once the WAVES were in their seats, Lieutenant Carrington began, "Last year at Smith and Wellesley, the administration selected a group of seniors to take a special course. Over several months, in secret, they met and finished the lessons you have just completed in a very accelerated four weeks." She peeked over her glasses to emphasize *accelerated*. The class giggled quietly as she did so. "During the spring of 1942, as they were about to graduate from college, these women received personal invitations from the head of the Navy's code-breaking program to join the effort." When Meg heard *code-breaking*, chills went up and down her spine. For the first time, her upcoming assignment felt real. She even allowed herself to admit that being part of a team in Washington, DC, working on codes was a far more exciting job than being a math teacher. She pictured herself, in her dark blue, tailored uniform, walking briskly down the Mall with other similarly focused military personnel.

"Although not every student finished the lessons or wanted to work for the Navy, many did," Carrington continued. Meg forced herself to focus on the lieutenant's presentation and stop daydreaming about Washington. "These women became assistant cryptanalytic aides. Housing in the Capitol was at a premium, but, thankfully, Smith and Wellesley alumnae were instrumental in finding 'appropriate' housing for the graduates." Meg started to roll her eyes at Cynthia at the use of the word *appropriate* but remembered she still could not share a joke with Cynthia the way she could with Julie.

"Today you will get a chance to meet two of the women who have just arrived at the USS Northampton for their abbreviated thirty-day Indoctrination. I've invited them to talk about what they have been doing so you'll be less surprised when you get to Washington, DC," Carrington explained.

There was a knock on the door, and two young women entered wearing their temporary, baggy wool skirts and gray sweaters. Meg could see the glint of the safety pins holding up one woman's skirt as the woman started to hug Lieutenant Carrington before abruptly stepping back and exclaiming, "I don't think I am allowed to do that in uniform."

"Seaman Franklin was a student in my dormitory at Smith," Lieutenant Carrington explained. "Let me also introduce Seaman Proctor. Or are you midshipmen? How is this working?" Lieutenant Carrington gave a small laugh at the end of her question. Meg again started to catch Cynthia's eye and was surprised to see she was struggling to fight back tears. Cynthia turned her head toward the wall so the others could not see her.

"I think we're now midshipmen. We were seamen when we arrived five days ago," Midshipman Proctor said. She had a beautiful laugh and turned to the class with her eyes twinkling. "We're here to learn naval protocol. I think that means we have twenty-five more days to learn to salute. What do you think are our chances?" The group laughed. Proctor walked into the room expecting everyone would want to listen to her—and they did.

"My fellow midshipman and I have two related presentations to share with you," Midshipman Proctor explained. "I'm going to tell you about cracking codes and Missy, ah, Midshipman Franklin, is going to tell you about her library work."

Meg wished she had some paper so she could scribble or doodle. Although she loved books, she didn't want to spend a Saturday morning learning about libraries. As she panned the faces in the room, she noted the lack of enthusiasm. Hopefully, the presentation might finish early, and they could join the shoppers in town. Meg looked out the window and saw fat, lazy snowflakes starting to fall. By lunchtime there might be enough snow for a snowman. Later in the afternoon they could likely have a snowball fight.

"I'm actually going to go first," Franklin spoke. "Hopefully, some of what I am going to say will give you better context for the code work. I'm going to begin by telling you I was an English major and I thought my next step after graduation was to get a degree in library science. At least that was my plan before the war." She smiled. "But everyone in this room is probably doing something different than they thought they would be doing." Several heads nodded in agreement.

"Although the classroom is beautifully neat right now, I imagine when you were practicing, there were papers all over. Cracking codes requires volumes of regular-sized paper, and small scraps with different letter patterns written, as well as graph paper to try to move symbols into some sort of readable order." Again, heads nodded in agreement. She continued, "Imagine you have thirty people working on code-breaking and trying to keep the messages organized by the area from which they were sent, or maybe by time sent or if it is an urgent communication rather than a routine message. Our command was a mess of scraps until, because of a mistake in paperwork, an officer who was a librarian in his civilian life was assigned to our group. While waiting for his next assignment, he organized the thousands of coded messages by time sent, which apparently helped with more decoding."

"The librarian was a fortunate mistake," Lieutenant Carrington commented.

"Exactly," Franklin agreed. "And life-changing for me. Last spring, as I was finishing my degree, I was also working one-on-one with a Smith librarian to learn in just a few weeks what is normally covered in a master's degree. I've been able to continue to implement library cataloging processes and systems, but there is still an enormous backlog of decoded transmissions." She paused for a moment to look at the group and smiled. "And naval communications don't require overdue notices and none of the cryptographers have made-up excuses about how they lost a library book. But give it time." She laughed. "Any questions so far?"

Cynthia's hand shot up. "What do you tell people you do?"

"I file papers, which is exactly what I do. Simple. Boring."

"But that's not all you do?"

"No," Franklin replied. "I haven't told you about the really exciting part. I also do intelligence work."

"As a librarian?" Cynthia blurted. Meg noted she was apparently over her earlier tears.

"I didn't believe it at first either. It turns out you can obtain a huge amount of information about the enemy from publicly available books, newspaper articles, and magazines."

"I didn't think Japanese newspapers were easily available in Washington," Meg said.

"They aren't," Franklin agreed. "But, it turns out you can get some Japanese news in Lisbon. A year ago, I knew nothing about Portugal and the country's role in the war. Remember, I was an English major who planned on organizing story time at the library. Briefly, Portugal has a long-standing treaty with Great Britain preventing the country from entering the war even though its dictator, António de Oliveira Salazar, is sympathetic to the fascist movement. As a result, Portugal is neutral and Lisbon, its capital, is a magnet for exiles, diplomats, and foreign correspondents as well as refugees from occupied countries who are waiting for exit visas. Sometimes the refugees are waiting for months. One of the things they do while waiting is read. Newsstands carry European newspapers and magazines from every major country on the continent. Luckily for us, the Germans report on the Japanese."

Meg raised her hand. "Did you go to Portugal?"

"No, and now that we are becoming WAVES, we won't travel abroad," Franklin answered. "But the US Government does send librarians, whose cover is as officials collecting books for the Library of Congress and other libraries. Sometimes they send the actual books or periodicals, but what works better is for them to take microfilm pictures of the books as well as Axis scientific periodicals and technical manuals. They've sent back thousands of microfilm images through diplomatic courier bags. Once it comes to us, we study the pictures."

"How do you find useful information? How many languages can you read?" Lieutenant Carrington interjected. "Aren't you looking at massive amounts of information?"

Franklin nodded. "I can read some French and German. My Italian is improving, but even with those skills it is hard to weed out the useful from the fluff. Our group passes the really technical information to a different department with scientists and engineers when we come across it. Our mission is to be a sort of clipping service. Interestingly, some of the best information is from materials we don't need to translate. I look at the society pages and see who is attending parties with each other. Or there will be pictures of a new ship being christened, which might match a transmission a cryptologist is working on. It took me a few weeks to get used to skimming through the film, but it is an ideal process. The microfilm is compact, cost effective, and takes a fraction of paper document storage space. We just need to get more eyes to mine it."

"I should do that!" Cynthia exclaimed. "I can figure out

whose parties are or aren't being featured on the social page or whose picture is or isn't being included. You can always find out a lot of information by paying attention to who isn't speaking to whom."

Meg silently agreed Cynthia's personality made her an ideal person to look at newspapers for clues; she could thrive at working on a clipping service. Meg's stomach grumbled as Midshipman Franklin finished her explanation. She made an apologetic smile as the others heard the noise.

"Thank goodness someone else is hungry. I'm going to topple over if I don't eat something!" Franklin exclaimed.

Lieutenant Carrington stood up and addressed the group. "There should be sandwiches in the next building. I did not want the catering delivery to overhear our discussion today. Let's grab some food, and then we will come back to hear more about code-breaking."

The women walked carefully to the adjoining building. There was enough snow that their heels sank into the accumulation, and they walked gingerly to avoid slipping. Meg quickly scraped the snow off her shoes as they entered the building so it could not melt. She did not want to sit through the afternoon with wet feet.

As promised, there was a large platter of roast beef sandwiches on thick hotel-baked bread waiting in the adjoining building, as well as several thermoses of coffee. The cook used mayonnaise on one side of the bread and a very thin spread of horseradish on the other, giving the sandwiches a hearty, slightly spicy flavor.

"Enjoy this while you can," Midshipman Proctor advised. "We've plenty to eat in Washington, but we don't have this wonderful bread or thick-cut roast beef. We eat a lot of fish since we're close to the Chesapeake, and it's cheap."

Both Proctor and Franklin helped themselves to a second sandwich before Carrington suggested it was time to return to the classroom for the second part of the briefing session. As the

WAVES took their seat, Sarah raised her hand. Midshipman Proctor smiled and Sarah asked, "Were you surprised when you learned you were going to be working on Japanese codes rather than German?"

"The joke is that there was a poker game among the military leaders and the Navy lost that hand," Midshipman Proctor said dryly. "The people we're working with keep telling us we never saw the code-breaking command at its worst. Immediately after Pearl Harbor, we didn't think we would ever be able to break the Japanese additive structure. Compound that with all the American losses in the Pacific, and morale was really low. Luckily, we had mathematical geniuses who were able to discern patterns in the Japanese cipher structure."

Cynthia shot Meg a quick look when Proctor mentioned mathematics. Meg's previously happily full stomach did a small, uncomfortable lurch. Meg knew very little about the mathematical basis of cryptology and was not sure if she understood the additive numerical structure. She reminded herself Carrington was a zoologist rather than a mathematician and she was training the WAVES, so Meg couldn't be expected to be an expert. Or could she? Meg also thought of Lieutenant Prescott. Hadn't Cynthia said he had a PhD in math? Had he been one of the people who had cracked the additive puzzle?

Proctor continued, "We know the Japanese will change their additives and codes again, but we also know which techniques to use to break them. We know so much more about their habits than we did before."

"Can you tell us more about how you work with the additives?" Meg asked.

"Yes," Cynthia quickly followed up, not waiting to be called on or wanting to be outdone. "What is a typical shift like?"

"Nothing is typical," Proctor laughed. "Codes don't work when they become typical or expected or routine. The Japanese are good at staying one step ahead of their enemy—us!" she emphasized, and the class laughed. "They're especially good at frequently changing the codes and ciphers even though it's a lot of work for them."

As Meg looked out the window, she noted the snow was falling steadily. They needed to be careful walking back or they could slip on the cobbles. Meg forced herself to return her focus to the lecture. She knew what she was learning would help her when she got to her assignment, but she could not help thinking about her Christmas list.

"One of the fun facts I have learned is naval codebooks have lead covers or water-based ink, so if the Navy is worried about enemy capture, they toss the books overboard rather than let them be captured." Proctor giggled gently. "There aren't many codebooks lying around for guidance. Fortunately, we have technology to give us an advantage. We've been using machines to help us. We punch cards with the ciphers from the transmissions and a huge sorting machine helps us to identify frequent patterns. Then we start to crib. We look at the weather and battle action reports and try to back into what the message might be and see if that helps us to break the ciphers we have."

"It sounds painful," Cynthia commented.

"But it's wonderful when we have a breakthrough! And it does work. We're so busy, we always need to work extra hours and extra days. That's why we're here," she told them. "With the creation of the WAVES, it now makes more sense for the female cryptanalysis to be commissioned rather than continuing in their role as civil servants. As officers, we are going to be able to work as many hours as they assign us! Knowing that, I am going to enjoy sleeping at night in a comfortable bed while we're here. And eating more sandwiches. It's almost a vacation compared to how hectic my life has been." Her eyes shone as she said that, and Meg suspected that she missed her work more than she enjoyed the much-lightened schedule.

"There is one more thing I want to mention. You will be working primarily with men. Most of them are smart and respectful. A few of them are not. You have the benefit that you will be going in a group and unlikely to be working alone. Try to keep a buddy with you, especially when you are first getting to know the other officers."

As Proctor finished her presentation, it was time for all the WAVES to say good-bye. Next week was reserved for graduation practice, and, hopefully, uniform inspection.

"Thank you. Now I feel ready to start," Sarah said to the visitors.

"Our assignment is not nearly as much of a mystery now," Meg agreed. "Lieutenant Carrington, it has been wonderful learning from you. I look forward to using some of your teaching approaches when I'm back in the classroom."

Lieutenant Carrington blushed. "I am sure I could learn just as much from you, Midshipman Burke."

"Goody-goody," Cynthia said under her breath to Meg, then turned on her heel and hurried off.

As the others thanked Lieutenant Carrington, Meg hurried to put on her coat. The session had gone longer than she'd expected. It was too late for a snowball fight or to go shopping. Usually the six walked back together, but Cynthia had left without the group. Meg did not like to think of her walking alone in the snow, especially if she were to fall. It could be a dangerously cold wait for Cynthia until the others found her. Meg waved distractedly at the others and rushed out of the building. In the growing dusk, she could barely make out Cynthia walking away from, rather than toward, the USS Northampton.

"Cynthia," she shouted. "Wait up!"

Cynthia turned and from the splotches of red on her cheeks, Meg knew she had been crying again. Meg hurried over to her and put her arm through Cynthia's to guide her in the direction of their quarters.

"Come on. There isn't a path through the snow, and we don't have boots on. Let's get back to the hotel so we can stay warm and dry."

"I don't want to go."

"I know." They walked in near silence for a few minutes. The only sound was an occasional muffled sob from under Cynthia's scarf.

As they turned away from campus and onto the street to the hotel, Cynthia choked out, "You know that could have been me."

"Hmmm," Meg replied noncommittally.

"I was interviewed for the special training my senior year," Cynthia said.

"Were you?" Meg cautiously replied. She did not want to slip and give away the fact that Julie had told her about Cynthia's romantic quandary senior year.

"I told them I was about to be engaged and couldn't do the training. If I hadn't been so proud or so stupid, I could have been one of the cryptologists coming back today." The sobs shook Cynthia's body and Meg drew her close for a moment.

When the sobs calmed, Meg said, "What you need to do now is to concentrate on how good everyone thinks you are at the training we have been doing." Meg squeezed her arm. "You are so good, everyone is putting up with you." Cynthia gave a small chuckle but did not take her arm away from Meg until they entered the USS Northampton.

## 12

D inner was an increasingly boisterous time of day and that night was no exception. As Meg looked around at the smiling faces, she did not see Cynthia. Cynthia had likely gone straight to her room. She was not only avoiding joining the others, but probably did not want to face Meg after her outburst.

The dinner conversation focused on two topics: graduation and Christmas. Lieutenant Roland announced that Mildred McAfee, recently promoted to the rank of captain, was scheduled to arrive at noon the following Friday to inspect and to address the young women during their graduation ceremony. Meg sighed with relief when she heard the news that graduation would take place inside the gymnasium rather than outdoors. The cold did not particularly bother her, but she'd had a few near falls on the cobblestoned pathways and the uneven stairs ubiquitous in the older buildings, which she blamed on her Navy-issued shoes. She was glad to avoid what she thought was a dangerous combination of ice, graduation nerves, and her heeled shoes.

The WAVE training had been designed for a total of four

months—one month as a seaman and three months of training after the women became midshipmen—but it was clear the women had acclimated to the training quickly and that the total training could have been done in twelve rather than sixteen weeks. For this particular group, however, the longer schedule was maintained because their uniforms had been delayed. In the weeks following Thanksgiving, for many, Indoctrination had been reduced to busywork, resulting in bored WAVES. Meg was glad she had her extra training to keep her busy; Vivian was constantly complaining about the extra marching used to fill the time. Julie demonstrated the extra hop-step she had to do while marching in order to keep up with her taller companions for emphasis.

"I'm sure I take fifty percent more steps than you and Cynthia take! I should get extra dessert for all of the extra work I do," Julie complained to Meg.

"I'll give you my dessert tonight," Meg promised. "I don't want you wasting away."

Meg had not attended her college graduation, held when both of her parents were working. She could not justify the additional cost to participate in the ceremony. Instead, the Sunday after Meg received her degree, Father Campbell had announced Meg's accomplishment at Sunday Mass and the congregation had congratulated her. Now, she was intrigued to be part of the ceremony, which she suspected could resemble a Smith or Wellesley event. Because the WAVES already knew their place by height, graduation rehearsal was uncomplicated. They practiced walking into the gymnasium, following the cue to sit or to stand as a group, and to process off the stage.

Graduation day dawned clear and cold; the WAVES were thankful for their heavy gabardine belted coats and marched quickly to the gymnasium in an effort to stay warm. It was a brief but lovely ceremony. In their new uniforms of navy-blue wool, officer's gold buttons, white shirt, navy ties, and gored skirt—some of which were held up with safety pins (after marching so much, many of the young women were not the same size as when they were initially measured at officer intake)—the WAVES were impressive. Captain McAfee reminded them that there was precedence in coeducation for men and women to work successfully together as peers. She urged them to use this model in their new assignments.

"I know this initial class of WAVES officers will make a significant contribution to the war effort," commended the captain. She demonstrated her knowledge and interest in the cohort as she welcomed some of the Wellesley women by name, including Cynthia and Vivian. Cynthia stood up a bit straighter when identified, but Vivian blushed and ducked her head. Meg shook her head slightly as she realized how different the two sisters were. As they neared the end of the alphabet, Meg still had not been called to receive her commission. For a moment, she thought her training was so secret it wasn't recorded in her file and the Navy did not think she had completed enough of her preparation to become an ensign. She reassured herself that Cynthia and the others in the class had been called.

Captain McAfee spoke. "Midshipmen Burke, Duncan, and Williams, please come forward." It was Meg's turn to be surprised. As she moved to the front with the two other WAVES, Captain McAfee continued, "Based on their achievements during training in combination with their professional expertise and experience, these women will be commissioned as lieutenants." When Captain McAfee announced, "Margaret Burke, lieutenant junior grade," and the applause started, Meg felt her cheeks burn and the sea of faces became blurry. She wished her parents were there to see her. Although she could not tell them about what she was doing, luckily, she could share her rank with them. Even though she felt the insignia pinned to her jacket, she had to look at her certificate to believe what she had just heard was true: *Lieutenant (j.g.) Margaret A. Burke*

## 13

Coming after the emotional high of graduation, the WAVES were wistful and sad as they prepared to leave Smith. Laughs were a little too forced and the WAVES desperately tried to maintain their excellent posture, fighting off tears while waiting for the buses to take them to Boston. As they said their good-byes and wished each other Merry Christmas at the Boston train station, the WAVES left their overcoats unbuttoned in spite of the cold so others could see their dark blue fitted suits. They wore their uniforms with pride, receiving both covert and overt admiration from other travelers. Usually preoccupied with her shoes, today Meg was worried about her uniform. She was using a couple of strategically placed, hopefully unnoticeable, safety pins to keep her too-large waistband in place and it did not feel secure. She would need either her mother or Mr. Shaunessy, whose shop was down the street, to alter her uniforms before she left for Washington, DC.

Julie's parents had driven to pick her up at Smith so they could go skiing for a few days before she reported for duty. Both she and Meg had tears in their eyes as they said good-bye. Julie was the only one of the four assigned to go to Ohio. Meg and the others kept reminding her that she was living near a busy air base and the pilots were sure to be impressed with her uniform. Meg realized that in this short time, Julie had become her closest friend. Meg's lip trembled as she hugged her friend good-bye. She wondered if like her, Julie was playing their lights-out conversations in her mind. "My letters will be full of news about making coffee and emptying trash cans," Meg assured Julie. Their forced laughter gave their sadness away.

Ever since Cynthia had told Meg about turning down her initial chance at being part of code training, their relationship had warmed enough that Julie, Cynthia, Vivian, and Meg were again comfortable eating together, but Cynthia was not Julie. Meg was not looking forward to the long train ride without her friend. She looked outside the train window at the buildings dusted with snow to try to clear her head. At least her Christmas shopping was done. Although there were daily newspaper articles about clothing shortages, the Northampton shops had an excellent selection of merchandise, and she had a generous salary to spend on the gifts. Meg found a beautiful, soft blue-gray cashmere scarf to match her mother's eyes and buttery leather gloves for her father and brothers.

As much as Meg wanted to take out the section of the newspaper with the crossword, or simply hide behind the paper, she knew she needed to think about what she could and could not tell her eager family. She could tell them about the hotel, which was turned into a dormitory, and the variety of food served. She could tell them that if it were not for the constant marching, she could have gained a lot of weight. She could tell them about the beautiful buildings at Smith and the picturesque but challenging cobblestone pathways on which she regularly caught her heels. She could tell them she had succeeded in making a naval regulation bed her first time, but skip telling them she had spent that afternoon showing others how to do so. The big challenge was reassuring them of her safety living and working in Washington, DC, without providing specifics about what she was going to do next. She also wondered how her brother Tom felt about his younger sister coming home with her lieutenant's commission.

She knew many of her cohorts were going to tell their families that their first assignment was general clerical duties. Most families could be happy their daughters were serving their country and doing their part. With her mathematical training and their sacrifice for her education, Meg's family wanted and expected more from her. She dreaded their disappointment, even though she knew that, secretly, she was using her skills. Meg anticipated that both of her parents, especially her mother, might question why she was making coffee when she could be teaching math. Meg spent much of the journey writing a list of appropriate rebuttals to the anticipated debate. She worked to tune out Cynthia as she discussed the parties she and Vivian were attending over the holidays, spoken at a volume Meg was sure was higher than necessary.

As they left New England, the snow became less deep and changed from white to gray and then to ice. As they approached New York, it looked grimy, and Meg idly watched the telephone wires looping up and down as the train moved slowly south. They were approaching the station when she had an idea. She thought about her interview before she'd started the cryptology training and the questions asked about her work with radios. As long as she was vague, radio communication was close enough to what she was doing and likely to be much more warmly received than making coffee. For a few moments, she thought about the handsome lieutenant who had conducted the interview and wondered what he would be doing for Christmas.

The train entered the final tunnel and stopped with a lurch. As Meg walked up the tunnel with Cynthia and Vivian, she could see Tom waiting just outside the barrier. She hoped he had the taxi. At the very least, it would be a much easier subway ride with him there to carry her bag.

"Hello, sis!" He bent down to give her a huge hug. "Good to see you. Let me take your bag."

Cynthia and Vivian were frozen in place staring at her brother. Meg tried to look at her brother through non-sisterly eyes. He was tall and lanky, and had twinkling blue eyes as well as the slightly curly, always somewhat disheveled, black hair marking him as part of the Burke clan. When he smiled, Meg thought he looked friendly and approachable, but she did not think he deserved the openmouthed stares Cynthia and Vivian were giving. She reminded herself that they hadn't seen too many men the past few months.

"Meg, are you going to introduce us?" he nudged.

"Tom, may I introduce Ensign Cynthia Collingsworth and Ensign Vivian Collingsworth? Cynthia and Vivian, this is my brother Tom, uh, Thomas Burke."

"Ladies, I mean Ensigns, may I help you with your bags?"

Cynthia had a look on her face Meg had never seen. Meg realized she had described Cynthia to her family as having the unusual ability to look down her nose at Meg while sitting next to her. Meg wondered if Tom had read that letter or remembered this description. Luckily, he appeared to be on his best behavior. Cynthia had tipped her head so far to one side as she looked at Tom while trying to make sure he did not see her looking that her hat looked in danger of falling off. Feeling an unnamed, but not unpleasant tension among the small group, Meg glanced at Tom, but could not catch his eye because he was smiling at his feet.

"This way, ladies—sorry again, Ensigns." As they reached the main floor, Meg took a moment to enjoy the station's Christmas decorations and half listened to her brother. Cynthia and Vivian ignored the decorations and focused on Tom.

"Where to? Are you grabbing a taxi?" Tom asked.

"Yes," Cynthia said. "We live on Lexington near Eighty-second."

"May I give you a ride?" Tom offered.

Oh, her brother was going to pay for this. Meg was never going to hear the end of her brother, the taxi driver, giving the Collingsworth sisters a ride. This story could follow her for the rest of the war, especially if Cynthia were to embellish it. She might describe Tom as either missing teeth or drunk, or possibly both. What had possessed her brother to offer a ride?

A voice she did not recognize said, "That's very kind." Was Cynthia holding back giggles? Why did she sound like that?

"Tell you what, Meg, can you get the group over to our usual corner while I'll go and get the car? I had to park a few blocks away," Tom suggested.

"Sure," Meg said somewhat dubiously, and she rolled her eyes at her brother when he took Cynthia and Vivian's suitcases and left her to carry her own bag. Cynthia and Vivian practically skipped out of the station and Meg called to them, "Left out of the door and straight at the first traffic light."

"Cynthia, slow down! Wait for Meg," Vivian demanded.

Once Meg caught up, the three walked abreast along the sidewalk. As the pedestrians saw their uniforms they not only stared and pointed, but made room for the three women. After crossing at the first intersection, Meg instructed, "One more block north." The trio had barely crossed the street when she saw her brother approaching. As she moved toward the curb, Cynthia protested, "We're waiting for your brother, Meg. Don't try to put us in a cab."

"This *is* my brother," Meg shot back as she stared at Cynthia and watched as her jaw briefly dropped and she fought to return her face to a more neutral expression.

"How convenient," Vivian replied, breaking the silence.

Tom hopped out to get Meg's bag, which he swooped up with a practiced motion, and Meg quickly took the front passenger seat. She wanted to be able to watch her brother's expressions as well as having a barrier between Cynthia and herself. Within moments the bags were stowed in the trunk and they were underway, with Tom coolly negotiating the streets as he headed north. While driving, Tom amused them with a story about an elderly woman he had driven earlier in the morning who had pressed him to give her ideas for Christmas presents for her family. During the fall, Meg had mimicked their instructors, so Cynthia and Vivian were aware of the family talent, but they were completely unprepared for Tom's skill level. It was as though the lady were in the taxi with them, fretting about her choice of gift for her daughter and confiding in her displeasure with her son-in-law's attitude toward the holidays. Meg hoped the earlier passenger was not a friend or even a Collingsworth family member. Vivian was more animated than Meg had ever seen her, laughing so hard she started to cry. Cynthia was more relaxed. In just a few minutes, they were at the Collingsworths' building.

"Meg, why don't you give us your telephone number? Maybe we could get together over the holidays before we go to Washington," Cynthia suggested. "We could go to the Met and have lunch. Or we could go and see *Holiday Inn*. I do love Bing Crosby. Do you have a piece of paper, Tom?"

"Here's my card. Let me write our home number," Tom responded before Meg could answer.

It had started to mist, and Meg decided to stay in the car. As WAVES, they should be able to carry their own bags, she thought. If Tom wanted, he could bring the bags up to the door-man, but it was not his place or responsibility to help. She resented his doing so. Meg tried to look straight ahead and not watch Tom with Cynthia, but could not help herself. As she was trying not to watch, she saw Cynthia leaning forward to shake Tom's hand.

Meg shot her brother an exasperated look as he got in the car.

"I guess you aren't friends," he said.

"Neither one of us goes out of her way to spend time with the other."

"Meg! You're fighting on the same side."

"She has spent most of Indoctrination reminding me that I am not 'her kind,' and my self-confidence could use a break during the holidays."

"Who said keep your friends close and your enemies closer?"

"Sun Tzu."

"Good. You learned the concept in your training. Now you need to do it. You should go to lunch with her. It couldn't hurt you to meet her family if she asks you."

Meg rolled her eyes at her brother and responded, "Yes. I know who her father is. I've heard every day since the end of August who her father is. Not biting."

"Well, no one can accuse you of sucking up." His smile said peace for now, but he reserved the right to bring this topic up at another time.

"Did you really have that woman for a fare this morning?"

"Nope. Made it all up."

She smiled at him. She hated that being a mimic was his only apparent outlet for all his creativity. "What should I know before I walk in?"

"In addition to giving you and William up for the war effort, Ma is saving bacon grease as well as donating several of her pots and pans to the metal collection." Meg looked horrified.

"Don't worry, she still has the Dutch oven. I don't think she could cook without the pot. And you'd better be prepared to be shown off." His tone changed slightly. "I hope for the family's sake having a lieutenant j.g. more than trumps having someone who flunked out as a sickly 4-F."

"Oh Tom, it isn't like that."

"Well, maybe not, but it will be nice for someone else to be the focus of conversation for a while."

The mist turned to rain and as the rain started to come

down more steadily, Tom concentrated on his driving, especially when going over the bridge to Brooklyn. He had barely come to a stop in front of their row house on Troy Avenue when Meg opened the car door and flew up the short set of steps. Her father was waiting near the door and her mother, clothed in one of her numerous aprons, all of which had faded to muted lavender, hurried to take her coat and to hug her.

"We have a lieutenant in the family!" her father said. Tom came through the door with her bag as her father continued, "We're so proud of you." Tom shot her a smile that said, *See, what did I tell you?*

"Sit down, sit down, Meg. You must be exhausted from your journey," her mother fussed. "Actually, don't sit down yet. Take a few steps and turn so we can see your uniform." As Meg followed her mother's direction, Tom let out a quiet whistle.

"Thomas Burke, a gentleman shouldn't do that," his mother scolded him. "But your uniform does look very attractive, Meg. I've seen the pictures in the paper, but the material and design are even more impressive in person. The skirt is beautifully tailored, flattering yet practical with those pockets."

"They should be impressive. It took months to get them," Meg agreed. "I'm hungry and can't wait to eat dinner, but first, before I sit down I need proof we still have the Dutch oven!"

Tom laughed heartily and her father explained, "Your mother and I fought about that pot, but there was no way it was leaving the house. It is part of the family. Almost anything else can go, but not that."

"I looked in the attic and in the basement for scrap metal and bought an extra war bond so Ma couldn't turn it in," Tom added.

"Are you having trouble getting gasoline since the rationing started at the beginning of the month?" Meg asked. "We walked and rode bikes at Smith, so I don't have a sense of the impact."

"I'm in a special category, so it hasn't been a problem." Tom shot his sister a look that said this was not a good dinner topic and changed the subject, asking, "Have you heard Liam Dunne is on a ship somewhere in the Pacific?"

"Yes. He wrote to me as he was leaving," Meg replied.

"You're writing to Liam?" Tom grinned at her.

"There's been a lot going on in the Pacific, what with Guadalcanal and fighting in the Solomon Islands. A letter from home can't hurt, right?" Meg explained.

"I am still not sure that it's really appropriate for women to join the military," her mother said. Meg and Tom exchanged a look. "You could have kept your job teaching math and done your bit for the war by writing to Liam and buying war bonds with your salary."

"Annie, the Navy sent our Meg to Smith College," said her father. "I cannot think of her doing anything more appropriate." He turned his focus to Meg. "Now tell us about going to school in Massachusetts."

"One of my favorite parts of going to Smith was being taught by women with graduate degrees. There were female instructors who had doctoral degrees in zoology and physics. It made me think about what I might be able to do after the war." Meg turned to her mother. "Maybe I could teach at Smith."

"You look very happy and healthy," her mother admitted. "You have wonderful coloring for December. The rest of us turned pale gray in November and we will look like this until March, at least."

"It was all of the marching! In fact, I am going to need some help with my uniforms. We were measured at the end of August and by the time the uniforms came in December, I was a different size. Do you think you can help me take them in?"

"Of course. I'll start on them tonight. Everyone is so excited to see you in your uniform. But first, I made rice pudding to welcome you home, Meg dear. I didn't use the usual amount of sugar, but I found some substitutions."

Sitting with her family at the table, Meg exclaimed, "Mom, this is delicious. I've missed your cooking." Even without the full complement of sugar, her mother's pudding was mouth-watering.

"If you eat enough pudding, you won't have to take in the uniforms," Tom teased.

"Everyone is looking forward to seeing you at Christmas Eve Mass," her mother announced.

"Especially the Dunne family," Tom said under his breath.

Her mother ignored him and continued, "I volunteered you to help get the church ready for the holiday services. I hope you don't mind." Meg had already assumed her mother had signed her up.

Her brother interjected, "We won't have Meg the entire time, Ma. Meg will be going into the city to meet a few of her WAVE friends during the holiday. I think they're going to the Met." Meg glared at her brother.

"Oh, that's nice, Meg. I didn't realize any of the WAVES you met would be in town. I thought you said in your last letter that Julie was going to stay in New England and you couldn't see her before you go to Washington."

"Oh, there were a couple of my fellow officers on the train with me who appreciated a ride from Tom, but I am sure we'll be too busy to get together." Her look dared Tom to keep this particular conversation going.

"In that case, could you help at the Taylors over the break? They're giving a party on the twenty-seventh. I'd appreciate your help," her mother said. Meg panicked. What if Cynthia were there? Or the lieutenant? Tom came to her rescue. "Ma, she's a naval officer. Let her be. She needs to rest up to serve her country."

That night, as Meg climbed into bed, it was both comforting and unfamiliar to be in her bedroom. After weeks of worrying that she could fall out of her bunk, she had gotten used to her narrow bed and the moonlight pouring into her shared room. It was now strange for Meg to sleep alone in a room without Julie. Tonight, she especially missed her. She wondered what Julie might think about the taxi ride and Cynthia's strange behavior with her brother. Meg could hear Julie saying, "You're imagining things! You always think Cynthia is up to something. Relax." Just imagining her friend was with her allowed Meg to start to drift off to sleep, although her last conscious thought was whether Julie would act as silly as Cynthia around Tom.

## 14

While her mother worked at the Taylors', Meg spent the morning at home, cleaning and baking. After living with so many people and a full schedule at Smith, she took a moment to watch the sun shining through the kitchen window, marking a bright rectangle on the faded kitchen linoleum. Her mother had wanted a new floor for ages. One of these years Meg and Tom needed to make sure she got it. Meg made herself a strong cup of tea, using the rose-patterned mug she'd had since childhood, now slightly chipped on the rim near the handle, helping herself to half a teaspoon of sugar, mindful of the rationing but justifying the sugar to celebrate the holidays.

In the afternoon, her chores finished, Meg walked the few short blocks to St. Brigid Church. Normally, the sanctuary felt almost as familiar to her as her own home, but today it felt strange. It was shabbier than she remembered; the roof leak had not been fixed properly during the summer and the water stain over the side altar had grown. The hum of the female Altar Society members' voices stopped as she entered.

"Well, if it isn't Margaret Burke," called out Mrs. Keating.

"Are we allowed to call you Margaret or is it Officer Burke?" asked Mrs. Dooling.

Meg smiled before replying, "Actually, it's Lieutenant Burke, but I'm not on duty. I still prefer Meg. What can I do to help?"

"You can unpack the crèche," Mrs. Dooling directed as she pointed toward a packing crate, and Meg spent the next few minutes happily and carefully unpacking oxen, donkeys, shepherds, numerous sheep, and the Holy Family. From a distance, the figurines looked to be in one piece, but if she examined them closely, several of the sheep and one of the wise men had been carefully glued back together after falling and shattering. Meg touched every piece slowly and carefully before placing it reverently in front of the altar. She put the magi on the side altar to wait until Epiphany to join the main group. She stood up and looked for a broom to sweep up the stay pieces of straw that had fallen from the statues.

Before she reached the utility closet, one of the ladies stopped her, saying, "You know, Meg, someone came to the house and asked about you." The speaker was Mrs. Dunne, who had been her next-door neighbor since the Burke family had moved to Brooklyn and the mother of the sailor about whom Tom had teased her at dinner last night. Mrs. Dunne quietly continued, "Someone from the government asked Mr. Dunne and me about your work habits and whether you drank liquor."

Meg hoped her smile looked natural, even though her stomach had dropped and her heart was pounding. "What did you say?" she asked in what she hoped was a neutral tone.

"Oh, we said you were a lovely girl and you had no time for drinking or parties because you were working so hard to put yourself through college." Mrs. Dunne added with a slight bite to her tone, "I could also confirm you hadn't had any serious romances and weren't engaged." Meg thought Mrs. Dunne was still upset Meg had never fancied Liam.

During their training, Lieutenant Fowler had mentioned

that US Naval Intelligence conducted background interviews to clear the selected WAVES for their additional code-breaking duties. At the time, Meg had thought the process was similar to checking her references when she was hired as a high school teacher and involved calling the school principal for whom she worked and talking to one or two of her Brooklyn College professors; she had not anticipated investigators following up with her neighbors. She wondered how many people Mrs. Dunne told about her interview. Meg quickly thought about what she should say to her. What could she explain? She thought about her training and the constant theme to keep silent and to say nothing. Mrs. Dunne probably wanted another tidbit of material, but Meg needed her to drop the subject.

"Thank you for taking the time to speak with them," she said in her newly found, pleasant but authoritative officer tone. "Where can I find a broom for this straw?" She thought, uncomfortably, that she sounded a little like Cynthia as she redirected the conversation.

Mrs. Brennan announced she had made tea, and the group moved to the hall to celebrate getting the church ready for the holiday services. Once in the hall, Meg was the center of attention. Again, Meg thought about what the group wanted to hear and how she could deflect or minimize her actual training and new assignment. She told them about marching and that, despite the wonderful food, she had gone down a dress size. She talked about waiting for the uniforms and wearing temporary ones, hemmed with safety pins. She had one of the ladies get up and walk on her left so she could show what she was supposed to do when a superior officer walked by. She promised to wear her uniform to church for Christmas so they could see it.

As she walked home, she realized she was unexpectedly tired. Meg was not used to pretending to be someone else. Having her secret assignment was already exhausting. Thank goodness, she thought, she wasn't a spy; she wasn't cut out for keeping secrets or pretending to be someone else. Lost in thought, as she walked into the living room it took a moment to register that Tom was sitting with a telegram in his hand. She felt herself start to grow faint. Her family had only just gotten a letter from William. It sounded as though he was safe, in fact safely bored and in a monotonous routine. Tom jumped up to steady her and reassured her.

"Meg, it isn't William. You've been called to Washington early, before New Year's. You need to leave on the twenty-seventh." His eyes twinkled as he continued, "Cynthia's already telephoned to see if we could pick her up when I take you to the train." Meg was so thankful the telegram was not about William, she did not have the emotional energy needed to wonder why Cynthia was so interested in her brother.

# 15

**M**eg was preoccupied with the fact that she was about to start breaking codes sooner than she planned but could not tell anyone why she was nervous. Especially for her mother's sake, she tried to talk to as many of the neighbors as possible on Christmas at church and accept their congratulations for her naval commission. As she nodded and smiled, Meg wondered if Cynthia and Vivian were the focus of attention at their church and, if so, how were they handling it. She thought, ruefully, that not only were they used to socializing, but also more people at their church probably had a Navy connection, so they were less of a novelty. Several of the young women in the parish admired her uniform and asked how they could become WAVES. Meg congratulated herself that the lipstick she had found while Christmas shopping in Northampton was finally the right one.

Her mother fixed two Cornish game hens, roasted golden brown and surrounded with fresh green peas, which was the perfect-sized meal for the four of them. Meg thought the hens were probably from the Taylors and had no idea where her mother had found fresh rather than canned peas. Because of gasoline rationing, her brother James and his wife could not join them from New Jersey, but the family did have a carefully timed three-minute long-distance call to wish her brother Merry Christmas.

Although it had been a brief visit, the time with her family seemed to have put her parents more at ease about her going to Washington; they were certainly less worried than they had been in August when she left for Smith. Perhaps her reassurance that her duties consisted primarily of radio supply logistics, leaving her plenty of time to continue to attend church and to write them letters, had worked.

Now, early on the morning of the twenty-seventh in her brother's taxi, she asked grumpily, "Remind me again why we are picking up Cynthia?"

"Because she's reporting for duty at the same time you are, and it's better to travel in pairs."

"I could meet her at the station and still travel with her. It isn't as though her family can't afford a taxi. They might even have a driver. I'll never know because I did not get a chance to go to the Met and have lunch with her."

"Maybe. But she needs a friend. Her sister is coming down later and I don't think Cynthia is used to being alone."

"I feel as though you're pairing me up with her so she'll have a maid to travel with," Meg complained.

"If Cynthia starts acting superior, why don't you tell her about how you skipped third grade," Tom counseled before giving her his mischievous grin. "Tell her stories about the boarder who lived with us who we were sure was running alcohol during Prohibition." Having to take in a boarder after the stock market crash was not one of Meg's favorite memories. She glared at Tom.

"Okay then. Tell her about your brother who was a standout on his high school basketball and swim teams. Remember, my voice has been compared to Bing Crosby's."

"I thought it was your ears that have been compared to Bing

Crosby's." She waited for her brother to stop laughing before she spoke again. "She doesn't need me as a friend, Tom. You forget she is bosom buddies with the entire New York City debutante class of 1939."

"I'm sure she needs a real friend. We all need real friends, and you are a good woman to have in your corner." His eyes twinkled. "Doesn't she have a brother?"

"Yes. Two. Both naval officers. One went to Princeton. With one of the Taylors, but I'm afraid to bring up that connection."

"Ah, at least you checked."

Meg giggled before asking, "Why are you so worried about her?"

"I'm worried about you both. Not everyone is overjoyed to have female naval officers, especially ones who are important enough to be called into work early," he said seriously. "I think it's better if the two of you have each other's back. Also, as a newly commissioned officer it couldn't hurt for you to know at least one Navy family."

When they picked Cynthia up Meg tried to see her through her brother's eyes, or at least kinder eyes. Cynthia was quietly talking to Tom, who leaned in to hear her. She said something and he took her arm with one hand and her bag with his other. Meg noted that Cynthia looked uncommonly pale and nervous, as though she had not slept well. Maybe she was hung over, Meg thought unkindly before dismissing the thought from her mind. Meg moved into the backseat and let Cynthia ride up front. Cynthia smiled, weakly, at her.

"All set?" Tom asked, and Cynthia nodded. The post-holiday traffic was light, and it took only minutes to get to the station. Meg noted that Tom kept a reassuring hand on Cynthia's arm during the ride.

"I'm going to drop you off at the cab rank," Tom announced. "Are you both going to be okay with your bags?"

"I think we have to be. We're in charge and responsible for our own gear, right, Ensign?" Meg answered for both.

After stopping and opening the trunk, Tom placed Cynthia's bag in front of her, squeezed her arm lightly, and leaned in to whisper something to her. Whatever it was, Cynthia smiled broadly for the first time that morning.

As Cynthia started to walk into the station, Tom gave Meg a huge hug and said, under his breath, "Meg, remember you are both on the same team. Try to be nice."

The marching and rope climbing was paying off. The suitcases did not seem very heavy, and as they were in uniform, civilians made room for them as they walked toward the tunnels to the tracks. Although the carriages were crowded, the two WAVES found separate seats across from each other. Cynthia was stuck next to a chatty serviceman who could not accept that she was giving him the cold shoulder. Meg knew Cynthia was going to have a terrible headache when they got off the train from his constant prattle. After saying a polite hello, her own seatmate fell quickly asleep. At one point, Meg had to gently move his head from her shoulder and position him back against the seat. Several times Meg thought Cynthia was about to say something to her, but she stayed focused on her book, although she did not turn the pages.

Even though Washington, DC, was fewer than four hours from New York City by train, Meg had never been to the capital. Before the Depression, there might have been the possibility of a school trip to see the monuments, but after the crash, money did not exist for such a trip. Other than taking the train to Tarrytown to work at Camp Andree Clark, she had only taken a few local day trips, such as touring the military academy at West Point and visiting Princeton with her family since it was near where her brother James lived in New Jersey. Although a little nervous, Meg was enjoying looking out the window and watching the clusters of houses, busy factories, and as they moved farther south, farmland. In Philadelphia, the train had a scheduled fifteen-minute stop. As much as Meg wanted to get off and stretch her legs, she knew they could lose their seats if they did. Meg stood in the aisle to improve the circulation in her legs and Cynthia stood with her.

"Meg, why isn't Tom serving in the military?"

"I told you the story on the train to Boston."

"Tell me again. Please," Cynthia pleaded. This was a different Cynthia, Meg thought. Cynthia had never been interested in anything about Meg.

"It's all pretty straightforward. Tom volunteered the day after Pearl Harbor, passed his initial physical, and went to training in Texas. While he was playing a pickup game of basketball he sprained his ankle badly, and when the ankle swelled so horribly that he could not put on his boot, he had to report to sick call. While he was being treated, the doctor heard a heart murmur."

"Did he suspect he had a heart condition?"

"Tom had scarlet fever as a child, but he played basketball in school and was a lifeguard at the city pool. He never knew there was a problem."

"Why a cab?"

"He didn't get his job back at the shipyard. As you've seen, he likes people and people like him. It seems to suit him."

The train started to jerk as it got underway, and the noise prevented Cynthia from saying anything further. Cynthia sank back against the seat and looked as though she might nap. Meg thought about Tom for a few minutes. He had to have had physicals to play basketball. Moreover, he had seen a physician before he became a lifeguard. Why hadn't anyone diagnosed a heart condition then? She could not put her finger on it, but she knew something was not right about the story. Moreover, his worry this morning seemed more than the normal concern for a kid sister and her fellow WAVE. She was missing something. When an answer didn't come to her, she pulled out the *Times* crossword puzzle; she might as well warm up for work.

After Philadelphia, Cynthia appeared to have fallen asleep; Meg was too wound up to nap. She finished the crossword puzzle, then mentally reviewed cipher approaches. What should she do if a colleague asked her to work on a Wheatstone-Playfair cipher? First, she remembered, that cipher was only twenty-five letters with no Z. She would ask for a ruler so she could draw the needed rows and columns for the table in which to place letters. She tried to remember, were the Japanese or Germans using that method to encrypt transmissions? As much as they had studied and prepared, she questioned if she were ready for this assignment.

It might be better if she were working on radio supply logistics, she thought. Both of her parents had to sense she was doing more than that, even with her award-winning reassurances, but, thankfully, had not pushed her on the subject. She suspected that her father had concluded she was doing something with her math skills; why else had she been commissioned as a lieutenant? Moreover, having her leave canceled indicated she was more than a supply officer. She was sure Tom had guessed she had an important role or critical duty. As she felt the train starting to slow down, she reached over to wake Cynthia gently. Then Meg took a deep breath and straightened her uniform. She was about to report for duty.

## 16

Although Meg was used to Grand Central Station, the activity level in Washington's Union Station was unlike any she had ever seen. Not only were there servicemen and servicewomen, but also women dressed for professional civilian jobs as part of the war effort. While she was conscious in New York that there was a war going on, there were still many people doing other types of work, especially in finance. She quickly noted THE business in Washington was the war. War posters alternated with advertisements for every possible type of food or beverage on the station walls. There was a serviceman's canteen rather than just a commercial cafeteria. Meg knew she should be a blasé New Yorker, but she walked agog at the multitude of shoeshine stands, newsstands, and the need for so many people to stand despite the vast waiting room.

She was not watching those around her as she crossed in front of a group of superior officers. Mortified, she apologized. Fortunately, the men seemed more amused than upset. As she and Cynthia walked over to the taxi stand, one of the officers approached and asked if they knew where they were going and if he could help give directions. The combination of the novelty of WAVES, the dashing uniform, and the two women's good looks was a magnet for male attention. Meg was still smarting from her mistake, but after her long nap, Cynthia was back on her game. She said they knew where they were going, but the officer still offered to carry both their bags, which both WAVES politely refused.

As they got in the taxi, Meg deferred to Cynthia, saying, "You know your way around."

Cynthia leaned forward and said to the driver, "Main Navy and Munitions Building." She turned to Meg. "Of course. My uncle ran the Smithsonian. My aunt still lives here."

Whatever hesitation or temerity Cynthia had shown earlier this morning was gone. She was back to what Meg considered Cynthia's usual self: confident, impatient, and slightly haughty.

"It's my first time here," Meg said.

"I can tell," Cynthia said. Meg was relieved that even if Cynthia was interested in her brother, they were not now best friends. The cabbie drove south and turned right on Constitution Avenue. Meg could see the Capitol building in the near distance and exclaimed quietly as they drove past the National Art Gallery and the Smithsonian. Meg had expected the marble and bronze statues from pictures in history books and newspapers. What she had not realized was the impact of so many people like herself reporting for duty in the city. Temporary buildings lined both sides of the Reflecting Pool east of the Lincoln Memorial. Bridges spanned the pool to connect the building complexes. There were rows of offices along Constitution Avenue on what had recently been green parkland. They passed the White House before stopping in front of the gate of US Navy headquarters, a huge, low wooden building that looked like a warehouse next to the Munitions Building. Designed and built as a temporary headquarters for the War Department in 1918, the Navy never anticipated using them during another war.

"This is it," their driver said. Meg had checked three times while on the train that the copy of her orders was in her purse and within easy reach. She assumed Cynthia had done the same. After the driver put their bags on the curb, Cynthia insisted on paying for the journey. Meg decided not to fight her. Tom had driven her twice. They grabbed their bags and walked in unison, as they had done frequently on the Smith campus. As they approached the gate, the guard asked for their papers, without saluting as Meg thought he should, and looked at the orders with surprise. He called to another guard and directed him to escort the two women to the information desk. They were brought to a room that looked somewhat like a bank with a counter of teller windows, but unlike a bank had a water-stained ceiling, faded paint, and discolored linoleum indicating where people waited in line to speak with the seamen at the windows. Cynthia wrinkled her nose and Meg also noted it smelled more like her classroom at the end of a hot spring day than a bank. The two women waited their turn in line behind four sailors. As they stood in line, Meg realized she still needed to memorize which insignia corresponded to which rank.

"Welcome aboard, Ensigns. Sorry. Ensign and Lieutenant. Wow, I did not know women were going to become lieu-tenants," the seaman behind the counter said when they approached. Meg had felt terrible making the mistake of walking on the wrong side of superior officers in the train station, but she had quickly corrected her error and apologized. This young man had not yet saluted and did not seem the least bit concerned about his lack of respect toward them. In fact, while speaking to them, he quickly saluted another man as he got in line behind them.

The seaman continued, "We weren't notified of your assign-ment, so there isn't any room for you."

"What do you mean?" Cynthia's tone more than made up for the simplicity of that question.

"Your last names were on our list of arriving officers, but not that you were assigned to the Communications Center." He gulped nervously. "Or that you were women."

Meg heard grumbling behind them and when she turned around, saw the line was quickly growing.

"What does our being women have to do with anything?" Cynthia pressed.

"Your assigned billet was the BOQ. I can't put you in the BOQ."

Meg thought quickly. They were the first WAVES. There were no bachelor officer quarters for women.

"I need to speak to your superior officer," Meg said. Meg had not even known she was about to say that, but realized when with Cynthia, she was the senior officer and part of her duty was to look out for her officers. Meg and Cynthia did not make eye contact while they waited. Meg wasn't sure what she was going to do next. She felt her stomach rumble.

"I'll go get him, but I'm not sure what he is going to do," the seaman said before leaving his spot at the window.

Meg and Cynthia exchanged looks and Cynthia whispered, "Useless."

"Good afternoon." A chief petty officer appeared in the window. *Still no "ma'am,"* Meg thought. "What seems to be the problem?"

"We have orders to report to the Communications Center at this address. We understood our billet was to be within walking distance of the Communications Center. We need a place to stow our gear and someone to direct us to the Mess," Meg asserted.

"The seaman told you that the Communications Center did not get your orders and we can't billet you at the BOQ."

"Yes. That has all been explained, Chief. Now I need you to tell me what you are going to do to solve the problem. We're here. We need a place to sleep. We need food to eat."

"Yes, let me get to work on that," he said. Meg raised her eyebrows at his reply.

"Yes, let me get to work on that, ma'am," he corrected. Cynthia looked at Meg with some admiration. The chief walked over to a desk and picked up the telephone. When he got off the phone, he walked the length of the counter and opened a door that let him into the general reception area. "Grab your bags and walk with me." Once he saw they were holding their luggage, he gestured toward a window and two scratched wooden chairs that looked as though they had been taken from a classroom. "I've got a place for you to sit and wait with your bags. I've called Communications. They're sending someone down to talk to you."

As soon as he saw the WAVES approach the chairs, he turned on his heel and quickly departed. Meg realized he had tried to make them someone else's problem as soon as possible. Cynthia looked at the chairs with distaste.

"Do you think they will hold us?"

"Only one way to find out," Meg replied. "But sit on the edge. They look as though they might have splinters that would tear our stockings."

Cynthia lowered herself very slowly and carefully. She started as the chair creaked but found that it would hold her weight. She tapped her fingers impatiently on her right leg. Meg lowered herself more quickly and the chair swayed. Thankfully, it also held.

"From what I remember of *The Bluejacket's Manual*, we will be AWOL if we leave at this point." Meg was trying to be funny. She hoped if she said something, Cynthia might respond that she already had a solution to the problem, because Meg didn't have one. Cynthia's brief look of admiration was gone. She frowned at Meg. They both looked up as they heard footsteps approach and saw an officer and a seaman coming toward them.

"Lieutenant Burke, Ensign Collingsworth." Meg recognized the man addressing them as Lieutenant Prescott, the naval officer who had come to Smith to administer the puzzle test and to interview her. Meg thought he looked a little more comfortable in his uniform than when she had last seen him. He also looked exhausted. There were gray circles under his gray-green eyes. Although Lieutenant Prescott had shaved within the past twenty-four hours, Meg suspected it had been late last night rather than early this morning, which made her wonder what sort of schedule he was working. They all saluted.

"I understand there's been a bit of a mix-up. Let me take you to get some coffee and we'll sort this out. Seaman Chambers, could you go and get some visitor passes, please? Also, could you please find a safe place to store the officers' gear? Thank you," Prescott said.

As the seaman left, Cynthia exclaimed, "Robbie, we are so glad to see you."

"Thank you for intervening on our behalf, sir," Meg said with what she hoped was a fraction of Cynthia's emotion.

"It's a long trip to make, especially given the crowds on the trains," he commented.

The seaman quickly returned with two visitors' passes that the WAVES pinned on as he departed with their bags.

Lieutenant Prescott led them through the guarded door leading out of the reception area and down a hallway, catching Meg's eye as he did so. He gave her a small smile. Then he went through an open door, which led into a small meeting room, and confirmed the door was firmly closed behind them.

"I'm sorry about all this. Can I get you some coffee?" Cynthia and Meg both shook their heads.

"I can talk to you a little more here than in the reception area, but it is still not a secure area." He paused and looked at them. They both nodded that they understood what he was saying.

"As you know, we use *communications* as a bit of a euphemism around here. I'm not sure how it happened, but your orders were sent to an actual radio communications department. It's going to take us a day or two to get your files back and to get ready for you. I'm sorry you're missing your holiday leave to hurry up and wait. We can have you come back tomorrow morning and get badged; then you will have time for some sightseeing. The good news is all the museums are open tomorrow and the weather should be good. We'll get you onboard before the first of the year, though. We really need you upstairs."

"Robbie, how was your Christmas?"

Meg marveled that although Cynthia lived in a household ruled by military regulation, she was the first to abandon protocol, especially when it involved a handsome man.

"Brief. Thank you." He looked uncertain about continuing this conversation. "I did have Christmas dinner with my folks. My sister was home from Smith."

"Did you know my brother John has deployed?"

John, Meg remembered, was the brother who had gone to school with the lieutenant.

"Yes. I heard. Sounded like he got the ship he hoped for." He cleared his throat nervously. "Back to the matter at hand. My bad news is we don't have too many options for a place for you to sleep. We're going to have to put you in the enlisted women's barrack. We don't have any female officer facilities."

"That doesn't sound too bad," Meg said helpfully.

He gave her a small smile, and then took a deep breath. "You are going to have to hot bed."

"You've got to be kidding me!" Cynthia exclaimed. "I'm not sharing a bed with anyone, even another officer." Meg shot her a look to say, *Attitude, Ensign*.

"Sorry." He ducked his head as he said this. Meg was glad not to be in his shoes.

"I know how you can make it up to us, Robbie." Cynthia had suddenly perked up and what Meg called "the tone" had returned to her voice.

"How's that?" the lieutenant said with what Meg thought was resignation.

"Make sure we go to the best New Year's party in Washington, DC," Cynthia answered.

Meg felt sorry for the exhausted lieutenant as he forced a smile at her. She could see he wanted to get back to work and clearly needed some sleep.

"I can make sure you get to the one I'm invited to. Will that work?"

"Perfectly," Cynthia replied, and she gave him her "I am going to dazzle you" smile.

"Okay. Let me take you back to Reception. I'm going to have one of the seamen show you where you can get some food and then get some sleep." As they approached the badging area, he gave them a tired smile and turned quickly away before Cynthia could ask him to do something more or complain.

A seaman was waiting for them with their bags. He took them out yet a different door than they had entered or the one they had taken to the conference room. They found themselves in the middle of a courtyard, and he led them down a path and around another building. Meg looked for signs and saw all the buildings were marked with numbers. She hoped she would be able to find her way back the next morning. She smelled the Mess before the seaman pointed it out. Her stomach grumbled in recognition of the aroma of chicken.

"Here we are." He pointed to a doorway. "I can't go into the women's barracks." Meg noted that he left before being dismissed. The Navy textbook read one way, but the practice was quite different. They turned to the temporary plywood building and passed through two sets of doors into a room that looked like a high school gymnasium hastily refitted as living quarters. There were sixty-square-foot cubicles with bunk beds and steel lockers in which to place their belongings. Meg started mentally counting bunks. She and Cynthia exclaimed simultaneously, "Forty-eight beds!" Cynthia went into the communal bathroom, announcing as she returned, "There are still urinals."

"I guess these were going to be for male sailors but reassigned to the arriving WAVES," Meg concluded.

"Where did they put the men? In tents?"

"On the White House lawn," Meg said sarcastically. Had Julie been here, she could have heard from Meg's tone that she was in dangerous need of food, but Cynthia did not know better.

"I didn't expect the USS Northampton," Meg said wistfully.

"But you didn't expect this?" Cynthia finished.

Meg shook her head slowly. "I definitely feel as though we are doing something for the war effort now, don't you?" she asked Cynthia.

"Not quite our normal digs, is it?" Meg thought she must have been hallucinating. Cynthia had answered in a voice that sounded like Julie's.

"Howdy, strangers." It was Julie! Meg threw her arms around her friend. The feeling of dread in her stomach vanished. If Julie was there, it was going to be an adventure.

## 17

"I checked. Lights out is at twenty-two hundred. They don't quite know what to do with a few officers, so they're having us follow the enlisted regulations," Julie continued.

"Wait until my father hears about this," Cynthia said under her breath.

Julie and Meg both glared at her.

"You're not going to get him involved," Meg commanded. Cynthia looked as though she could strike her, but kept her mouth shut and her hands to herself.

"Let's go get something to eat and stretch our legs. We can walk the Mall. We aren't going to be able to sleep in these conditions unless we're exhausted," Julie suggested.

"Good idea. And you can explain why you aren't in Ohio," Meg said.

"For now, I can tell you this. I took the overnight train from Boston with a berth in the sleeper car, but it was one big party, and I arrived this morning, hours before you and without much sleep. Then I got the good news about our accommodations." Meg had to smile at Julie's unemotional dispatch. Julie was as annoyed as Cynthia was, but unlike Cynthia, Meg knew Julie became quieter when upset.

After a meal of chicken, mashed potatoes, and peas, they left to explore. As they walked, Cynthia told Julie about seeing Lieutenant Prescott.

"He's taking us to a New Year's party," Cynthia told her.

"He's *not!*" Julie was amazed. She shot Meg a look that said, *I told you he noticed you.*

"Oh, he is. Cynthia sucker-punched him, so he had no other option. And in a glaring display of insubordination, she calls him by his first name rather than his rank," Meg confirmed.

"I call you by your first name," Julie replied, and Cynthia smirked at her.

"I'll send you both to the brig in a moment," Meg said as she squeezed Julie's arm.

The trio took another quiet lap around the Mall. Meg longed to tell Julie about Cynthia meeting Tom, but that update needed to wait until she had Julie to herself. Instead, she asked,

"Have you told us everything about why you're not in Ohio?"

Julie stopped walking and held her head to one side as she thought about her answer. The two waited for her to speak. Julie looked over both shoulders and around the area before she started walking again and said, "Did the two of you meet Missy Franklin at Smith?"

"Yes," Meg replied, remembering the woman who had described how she was setting up a library of information to help the code-breakers during their special Saturday class. She started laughing.

"What's so funny?" Julie demanded.

"Not exactly radio work," Meg said quietly.

"Well . . ." Julie began.

"But what about Missy?" Cynthia interjected.

"Missy got engaged in December and isn't coming back."

"Oh," Meg and Cynthia said in unison.

"I'm her replacement!" Julie announced. "More about that later. I don't know about you two, but I think I am finally tired enough to sleep." The three turned reluctantly back to the barracks.

Meg slept fitfully on what she thought of as her borrowed bed. As expected, the room was noisy. Although the other inhabitants tried to be quiet, some got up periodically to use the head. In the dim light, at least two women stubbed their toes on a bunk corner. Just as Meg was starting to fall asleep, a group of women assigned to the three-to-eleven watch returned and prepared themselves for bed. She heard a church bell toll one o'clock; exhaustion must have set in sometime after that.

It was still dark when Reveille played, and Meg was still asleep. Julie shook her awake at 0700 so she had time to remake the bed before the next occupant arrived. Meg tried to dress quietly since those who returned around midnight were, hopefully, sound asleep. She put on her uniform by her bunk rather than crowding near one of the few mirrors, happy that she could adjust her now altered uniform and hat by feel as well as tie her sailor's knot with her eyes closed. When she arrived at the head to brush her teeth, she saw she was far back in the line. Mental note: she could not wait until the last minute if she needed the toilet. Luckily, this morning she was not in a rush, but she prepared herself for the fact that on a future morning she could either brush her teeth or make it to breakfast.

A cross-looking Cynthia and a smiling Julie were ahead of her in line. Meg realized Cynthia had hidden the fact that she was also not a morning person better than she had. The sooner they could all get coffee, the better. It occurred to Meg that as officers, they could probably cut in line, but none pulled rank. When she finally got to the sink, Meg did not feel comfortable spending more than a minute brushing her teeth and splashing some water on her face. More cleaning would have to wait for another time, and she walked briskly back to stow her gear in her locker. She started to run down the stairs before she remembered she was in an officer's uniform and needed to present a better example.

Even Cynthia looked less confident than usual; she was unable to do her characteristic look down at Meg this morning. Meg tried the runny porridge. The other two opted for toast. Thankfully, the coffee was hot and strong. As they took their food to a table in a far corner, Meg noted they were the only WAVES officers in the room, which was getting a great deal of attention, both male and female. Her officer insignia on a designer uniform was a powerful visual indicator of who she was expected to be even if she did not have a place to live. Meg was going to need all the caffeine in her cup of coffee in order to cope with the stares.

"I could not believe how many people got up in the middle of the night; there must be something in the water," Cynthia grumbled.

"Maybe they were brushing their teeth and getting ready for the next day," Meg responded. Julie smiled at Meg's early morning humor. She had lived with her long enough to know that Meg was really trying to be funny.

"It's unacceptable. I should not be sharing a bed with an enlisted woman," Cynthia continued.

"Cynthia, we're in the military; it is bound to be uncomfortable," Julie said.

"My brothers have never described their military sleeping accommodations. Maybe they're used to such conditions, especially onboard ship," Cynthia conceded.

"We know from class they hot-bed. But maybe not the officers? Or just the officers with other officers?" Julie wondered.

Cynthia sipped her coffee and did not reply.

"I had an idea in the wee hours of the morning. As I remember, we're eligible to live off base," Meg said. "You remember that lecture, don't you, Julie?" Julie nodded in confirmation. "Let's get our badges and then we'll see if I have a solution."

"Meg, are you going to try to get us off-base housing?" Cynthia asked.

"That's my idea," Meg confirmed.

As they walked, Meg wished she had gone with toast rather than cereal. The cereal was sloshing uncomfortably in her stomach. When the trio entered the badging office, they joined the line under the sign "Badging." After being photographed from the front and the side while holding a sign with her name and the number 3141, a seaman in a perfectly pressed uniform and polished shoes led the WAVES and three other waiting seamen into a room for fingerprinting. Maybe the third time could be the charm to satisfy the Navy's need for her fingerprints, Meg thought to herself, since apparently the ones from Brooklyn and Smith had not traveled with her. She noted this time that the security posters were more serious. In addition to the ubiquitous "loose lips sunk ships," as she rolled her inked fingers across the oak tag of the fingerprint record, she stared at a picture of a deceased soldier who reminded the viewer he was dead because someone had talked.

A seaman was waiting to escort the WAVES to a barren auditorium; the only color was the United States flag on the left with the US Navy flag to its right. There were at least a dozen people, primarily male enlisted as well as two male officers, chatting quietly or looking straight ahead. The room went silent when the WAVES walked in. Meg hoped that she could get over her anxiety when people stared at her. So far, she loved being part of the Navy and liked wearing her uniform but did not like being gawked at. Thankfully, an officer walked in from a side door, and all rose, as if in a courtroom when the judge entered. The officer was in his dress uniform; he had salt-and-pepper hair and twinkling blue eyes. Meg thought he had to be close to her father's age but looked to be in tremendous physical shape. He could easily climb the rope in the gym if tested. He introduced himself as Captain Douglas Lyall McClaren, the commanding officer of the Naval Communications Command.

"It is my pleasure to welcome you to our nation's capital and to the Communications Command," he began. He took a moment to try to make individual eye contact with everyone in the room. "You all have an important role in making sure we are successful in this war, a war we are going to win because of your contribution and your discretion. After completing your loyalty oath, you will be given further instructions specific to your individual assignments. You're all lucky this morning. As my uniform may indicate, my schedule prevents me from staying and telling you stories or lecturing you this morning, but I will make sure you hear from me at another time," he said with a smile. "Good morning." He went back through the same door he had entered, while a young lieutenant went to the front of the room in his place. Meg thought if she had blinked, she could have missed his presentation.

The lieutenant explained, "You will receive a copy of the oath. Please read it carefully and consider what you are signing. Seamen, please pass out the forms and the pens."

A group of enlisted men distributed pens and paper. The only noise was the rustle of paper and the sound of pen caps being removed. Meg scanned the paper quickly. As she signed, Meg swore to defend the United States Constitution against all enemies and that she was making the obligation freely. The second document was a secrecy oath promising not to discuss her work with anyone outside of her official duties. The oath was timeless. During her entire life, the oath prohibited her from ever discussing what she had done. Although they had discussed each document during their training and none of the wording was a surprise, Meg temporarily felt overwhelmed by the significance of what she was doing. Working on ciphers at Smith was nothing more than solving a problem set for school; what she did now was for real.

Another officer, thin, blond, and exuding nervous energy, entered the room and introduced himself as Lieutenant Commander Lewis. Meg knew placing people in their rank and role soon could be second nature, but they had not seen much variety in the insignia at Smith. She tried not to stare as she scanned his uniform to find the gold oak leaf on his collar device. He gestured to the three WAVES.

"Please come with me." He led them into the same room where Lieutenant Prescott had spoken to them the previous day. Meg mentally nicknamed it the "room of doom."

"As you are aware, there was an issue with your orders. Although you received your orders to arrive on twenty-seven December, our copy of the orders indicated your arrival on thirty December. You have almost two days of leave before you report. You have a place to sleep." Cynthia coughed. The officer stopped for a moment to look at her, suspecting but not sure that it was an unnatural cough, and continued, "Go and see the sights. Take pictures of the monuments to send home to your parents and your sweethearts to let them know you are having a good time." Meg thought this was the only part of her experience in Washington, DC, she could faithfully describe to her parents; most of the important details needed to remain inside this building and in her mind. There was a knock on the door.

"Come in," Lewis commanded.

A seaman carried their photo badges. As the WAVES confirmed they had the correct ID cards, the lieutenant commander excused himself, saying, "I'll see you at oh-seven-hundred on the thirtieth."

"I'm happy to escort you to anywhere you need to go," the seaman said, "but with your badge you now have full access to this building, your barrack, and the cafeteria."

"Could you take us to whomever we need to speak to about housing?" Meg inquired.

"Certainly, ma'am," he replied.

He led them back to the intake window where they had started the previous afternoon. The three WAVES rolled their eyes at each other. Cynthia walked purposefully to the window as Meg and Julie followed her. Meg thought as the senior officer she should have led the trio, but she knew that not only did Cynthia know more about the city and possible housing options, but she was far more fearsome than Meg and much more likely to get a result.

The seaman at the housing window looked uncomfortable and swallowed hard a few times as the three approached. Cynthia paused before asking her question. She stared hard at the man until he coughed slightly and saluted.

"Could I speak to someone about housing?" Cynthia asked.

"I'm your housing contact," he replied.

"During our Indoctrination we learned we will receive a housing allowance, which will allow us to live off base. We'll fill out the appropriate paperwork this morning and relocate today. How long will it be before we receive our stipend?"

It was not the first time that Meg marveled at Cynthia's ability to skip the preliminary questions where someone might be inclined to say no. She proceeded as though they had an affirmative answer and only needed to discuss the details. The young man swallowed again before speaking.

"We've not actually processed off-base housing for any WAVES."

"Then we'll be the first. It had to happen sometime. Today is the day," Cynthia responded.

He shuffled a few pieces of paper before answering, "I don't think I have the proper forms."

"I don't think I have the proper forms, *ma'am*," she said archly and continued, "Who does have the proper forms?" Cynthia had a smile on her face but an evil glint in her eye. Julie looked amused; she had seen Cynthia in action for more than four years, but Meg felt the needles of anxiety pierce her growling, empty stomach.

Meg might have turned on her heel and spent the afternoon finding earplugs and eyeshades, but she was the one who had remembered the housing briefing last night. Moreover, the cryptologists who had returned for their shortened officer training talked about living in civilian homes. They had ensured they could return to their hard-found lodgings when becoming officers, so Meg was sure the regulations were in their favor. Unfortunately, she thought the memo with the regulation details probably resided in another building in Washington, DC, or maybe as far away as Northampton, Massachusetts, in WAVES headquarters.

Meg's hunger was making it difficult to follow three things at once. She was thinking primarily about lunch and secondly about waiting in lines. She forced herself to return to the ongoing back-and-forth between Cynthia and the petty officer. The young man left in search of someone who could help them. He returned with an ensign no older than they were. This man saluted and asked how he could help.

"My fellow officers and I are exercising our privilege to live off base. We want to complete the paperwork," Cynthia repeated. Unlike the petty officer, the ensign heard the insistence in Cynthia's voice. He did not like her tone or the sense that she was pushing him around.

"You've been in Washington for about twenty-four hours. You've not had enough time to experience our housing shortage. Let me give you some numbers. Seventy thousand people came here this year. The District is issuing fifteen hundred building permits a month and it still can't keep up with the demand. I can send you to the YMCA at Seventeenth and K, but that is only good for five days. Then you'll have to find another room." All three women stared at him. Meg pulled herself up as straight as she could stand and glared at him.

"Ma'am," he added after an uncomfortable period of silence. "I might be able to find a basement or an attic for one of you, but I am not going to be able to place all of you together. You'll be much better off staying here. Then you won't need to bother taking a bus."

Meg said before she could catch herself, "It is not for you to decide if we should or should not ride the bus, but it is your task to find the paperwork. I am sure you can annotate an existing form to suffice, and Commander Lewis will be happy to sign any authorization." She was not sure of that at all, but she was hungry, and they needed to resolve the issue in the next five minutes or they would have to come back. Julie grinned at her, and even Cynthia looked at her with admiration.

"Why don't you leave your names and I'll reach out to you if anything for three WAVES comes up." They all heard the unspoken caveat, "sometime after this war and maybe after the next one."

Cynthia said, "We already have the house; we just need the form and permission to move our gear."

"You have the house?"

"Yes. We'll provide the address once you find the paperwork."

The ensign knew he was beaten. He found the form and gave it to Cynthia. Cynthia confirmed, "We can move today?"

"Yes. Stop at the Intake window on your way out and give them your updated addresses."

"We're going to your aunt's house?" Meg's voice was half-questioning and half-incredulous. "Is she expecting us?"

"Probably."

"Probably?"

"Mother wrote to Aunt Isobel telling her I was coming and Vivian follows in a week or two." She turned to Meg, "You remember. I've told you about her. Isobel Milbank is my great-aunt, my mother's aunt. She's young to be a great-aunt. Her husband collected things for museums and she collects interesting people. You know the type: gives small but elegant dinner parties for influential friends serving in the presidential administration and at the State Department. She'll probably feel more comfortable knowing that we're living where she can keep an eye on us. I don't know why we didn't plan to do this from the start. Anyway, she liked Julie when she met her at Wellesley celebrations." Cynthia added, "She's an alumna, too."

Meg interjected, "I can understand that she might want her family there, but I'm sure I'm an imposition."

"You are," Cynthia conceded. Meg felt her heart sink. She was going to need eyeshades and earplugs after all. She briefly wondered if there were a way to find out if a Brooklyn College alum might have a room for her, and then realized there probably were few Brooklyn College alums in the District, let alone ones with an empty room. Cynthia interrupted her thoughts. "She likes Austen, though, Meg. Maybe you can appeal to her as a fellow bibliophile."

Julie interrupted, announcing, "I'm starving. We can discuss the details over lunch. Food. Now!"

Over beans, toast, and more wonderfully strong coffee from the Mess, the three decided it made sense for Cynthia to telephone her aunt and see if the WAVES could visit that afternoon. On a full stomach, though, Meg was still uncertain if she could or should be part of the adventure. Cynthia must have seen Meg's concern.

"My aunt's patriotic. I'm going to appeal to her and tell her how proud she'll be to support one of the first female lieutenants, even a one-bar one. If nothing else, I'm sure you can stay there until you find something else. Enjoy your coffee," Cynthia commanded. "I see a telephone box." With a turn of her head, Cynthia was off.

## 18

Cynthia returned to the table with a huge smile on her face. "Let's get our gear, ladies. There is no time like the present. Let's take a cab. My treat."

There was a woman sound asleep in the bed Meg had used the night before, so Meg tried to be as quiet as she could while she retrieved her gear from the locker. Even if she had to sleep under the eaves or in the garage at Aunt Isobel's, Meg already appreciated that she would be the sole occupant of her bed for the near future.

As Julie and Cynthia chatted during the short cab ride, Meg told herself not to act surprised when she saw the house. She had spent a substantial portion of her childhood helping her mother at the Taylors' house, albeit generally taking the back staircase to navigate it. She knew which fork to use; she also knew whether someone was polishing them correctly. Even so, she was impressed with the beauty of the area as they approached Dupont Circle. There was a stunning marble and limestone mansion near the circle, and she felt a wave of panic even though she was certain Cynthia's aunt did not live there.

She looked down an adjoining street and saw handsome

row houses built in Queen Anne style. She could feel more comfortable if she were back in a row house, even if a larger row house than the one on Troy Avenue. Cynthia gestured toward the mansion and told Meg, "That is the Patterson mansion. The Coolidges lived there when the White House was undergoing renovation. The Phillips Collection is down that street." She pointed in the opposite direction. "It will be nice to go there when we have free time."

"Patterson as in the newspaper family who dislikes FDR so much?" Meg asked.

"Yes. That's the one. How did you know that?"

"Sometimes I do the crossword in the *New York Daily News.*" She quickly added, "I only buy it for the puzzle."

"A *Daily News* reader? They shouldn't have let you into the WAVES."

Meg was sure Cynthia was kidding but realized it was yet another fact she should have kept to herself. The taxi had come to a stop in front of a beautiful freestanding Georgian home. Pruned, flowerless rosebushes lined the walkway; Meg hoped to be there in the spring to see the garden in full bloom. The front door opened before they could ring the bell. Standing in the doorway was a tall woman who looked to be in her late fifties or early sixties, with gray hair in a perfect French twist and with possibly the best posture Meg had ever seen. She wore a simple dress Meg was sure was made of silk and probably designed for her. Meg doubted Aunt Isobel shopped at Macy's, or whatever its counterpart was in Washington, DC. She also wore a single opera-length strand of beautifully matched pearls. Meg wondered if those were her wedding pearls.

"Come in, Officers. Please come in out of the cold. There is a fire in the living room. Come straight through. The driver will bring in your bags."

Meg did not think it was that cold but, as a houseguest, she was not going to argue. She could not help thinking about how

Tom could describe their arrival to her family at dinner if he had been the driver bringing the three WAVES to the house. The young women walked through the door into a large hall; Meg imagined the passage holding temporary coat racks filled with gorgeous furs during a party. At the end of the hall, they walked into a spacious living room with a large fireplace at one end and French doors opening onto a patio and then into a garden. The garden had pathways and nooks for cocktail tables. Even though much of the garden was leafless, Meg could tell it bloomed lushly in the spring and summer. Aunt Isobel followed the WAVES into the living room.

Meg extended her hand and said, "I am pleased to meet you. I'm Margaret Burke."

"Oh yes. Cynthia has told me a great deal about you. I understand your family was very kind to Vivian and Cynthia when you were returning from your training in Massachusetts." Meg was surprised Cynthia had mentioned the taxi ride to her aunt. Was her aunt being sarcastic?

Meg plunged forward. "It is terribly kind of you to let me stay here until I can find another billet. I think Cynthia explained the barracks were a bit like summer camp."

"She did." Aunt Isobel smiled. Meg realized she wanted to be able to convey paragraphs of thought and commentary with a single smile the way Aunt Isobel did. She wondered if she could grow into the ability or if one had to have been born with it.

"I had Davis put tea out a little early. I'm sure you girls are hungry." She laughed. "I know I should not call you 'girls.' At least I remembered and said 'officers' in front of the driver, but I'm afraid in this house you will be girls. Please sit down. I want to hear about your training, your travels, and what you will be doing."

Meg looked at the table set with a Wedgwood tea set and a chocolate-covered sponge cake. She thought Aunt Isobel must have good connections with her grocer.

Cynthia asked, "Should I play mother?"

"Yes, dear. That would be lovely," Aunt Isobel replied. Meg started to say something and was glad she had caught herself. Cynthia started pouring cups of tea. Meg had never heard pouring the tea referred to as playing mother.

"Sit, sit," Aunt Isobel repeated. Meg and Julie's eyes met, and Julie sent her a reassuring smile. Julie moved to a seat on the sofa across from Aunt Isobel and indicated to Meg that there was room next to her. Cynthia brought a cup of tea to Meg and then returned with a slice of cake. Meg was not sure how she should hold her tea and eat the cake at the same time. A woman in a black housekeeper's uniform entered with a small table with sides that folded up and cutouts to make handles. Meg remembered the Taylors called it a butler's table. The woman placed it between the two sofas, and Meg watched as Cynthia and her aunt put their cups and plates on the trivets to protect the table.

"Julie and Margaret, may I introduce you to Davis? She runs this house and is my majordomo. The household could simply fall apart if she were not here."

Julie said, "Hello" and Meg said, "Pleased to meet you." Meg wondered if Davis had a family and if Aunt Isobel knew Meg's mother was a Davis.

"Meg goes by Meg rather than Margaret, Aunt Isobel—at least she did at Smith. Are you going to be Margaret now that we are officers?" Cynthia asked.

"I have always been Meg unless my mother is upset with me. Please call me Meg." The fire and lack of sleep were making her drowsy, and she allowed Cynthia to control the conversation as she told her aunt about Indoctrination.

Julie described her need to develop the double-hop step to keep up with the marching exercises. "It didn't help that I had to keep up with Amazons," she joked.

"You're quite tall, Meg. I think the same height as Cynthia,"

Aunt Isobel remarked. "That must make it easier to swap clothes."

Meg groaned inside. She could not imagine Cynthia ever wanting to wear something she owned. "Yes. Cynthia and I were the final pair in the marching line. We were fondly referred to as the 'anchors.'"

"As Cynthia knows, one of my favorite things to do is to bring interesting people together over a meal, although poor Davis has to get more and more creative with the menu as foods disappear from the grocers and the butchers. I expect the telephone is going to start ringing and a few people will call tomorrow afternoon. Having WAVES in the house will be a wonderful attraction."

"Aunt Isobel is being modest," Cynthia interjected. "She gathers more than people; she is eclectic. She and Uncle Charles started collecting Berthe Morisot paintings before anyone had heard of her. And Civil War letters." Cynthia turned to her aunt. "You should have been a librarian or a curator, just like Uncle Charles."

"If I were your age, I probably could have been, but I grew up in an era when I was lucky enough to go to college and my family was able to support my intellectual pursuits. My husband grew from curator to gifted administrator and public servant, but I like to think some of his success came from how I supported him," Isobel responded.

"What is your favorite place to visit, Mrs. Milbank?" Meg asked.

"Oh, Isobel, please. Aunt Isobel if you must, but not Mrs. Milbank." Isobel took a sip of tea and paused. Meg wondered how many places there were from which she had to choose. "This is not what you asked, but my favorite time was soon after Charles and I got married. Charles was traveling for work, but it didn't seem like work. Instead, it was the most wonderful honeymoon. Officially, he was meeting with various European museums and assessing who might be willing to sell pieces of art to the Metropolitan Museum of Art." She smiled as she remembered. "But really, we had our own equivalent of the 'grand tour.' Charles could speak French like a native, but my German and Latin were better, so I helped him study art provenances before his meetings. In addition, I proofed his reports before he sent them. I loved my husband very much, but he did love to use a dozen words where one or two could do." *Just like his niece*, thought Meg.

"I also knew more about ballet and opera, so I could prepare him before we met other cultural attachés when we attended events. It was important that the American representative have as strong a background, or at least appear to, as his European counterparts did. I loved my life of going to museums during the day and to the theater, ballet, symphonies, and opera at night. In 1910, we were in Paris for six months, and our apartment quickly became a gathering place for other young people of all nationalities. It didn't matter what food I served or the liquor we had to drink. The parties were always a success because so many interesting people with innovative ideas surrounded us. I was determined to speak as well as Charles, so I took French lessons and practiced my grammar with some of the best artists in France."

"You should write a book," Julie suggested.

"At the very least, I should take out my diary to remind me of my adventures if you girls are interested in hearing about them," Isobel said. "Next, we went to London for a few months. After the light and excitement of Paris, it was a bit drearier. That is until I was in the British Museum one gray afternoon and I fell in love with the most beautiful, colorful Islamic tiles. From that day on, I had to study everything I could about the tile and mosaic-making processes. I even took Arabic so I could read about the techniques in the primary language." She sighed. "Enough about the past. I'm sure you will need to be available to report for duty, but if you do have some time off, the three of you should be guests of honor at a luncheon for one of my favorite causes, higher education for women. You're all wonderful examples of why we should support female educational programs."

"Aunt Isobel, you aren't competing with the McLean Sunday lunch, are you?" Cynthia said.

"Absolutely not!" her aunt said with force.

Until that moment, Meg thought she had been following the conversation remarkably well, but she was completely lost at the mention of the McLean lunch and the knowing smiles that passed between Cynthia and Julie.

"Oh, Meg. Not to worry," Cynthia said, seeing her quizzical look. "Evalyn Walsh McLean throws lunches for upwards of a hundred people every Sunday at their house on Wisconsin Avenue. She is always in competition with Cissy Patterson and Alice Roosevelt Longworth to see who has the biggest and best parties. It is a place to see and be seen, but not nearly intellectual enough for Aunt Isobel. Aunt Isobel is much more than a continuous round of opera, theater, races, and charity balls. When she talks about inviting a distinguished guest, it's likely to mean the individual is studying an unusual dialect or is taking out a patent on an invention." Cynthia turned to her aunt. "For whom are we dressing tonight? Is your good friend Eleanor expected?"

"That's enough, Cynthia." Meg wondered from Aunt Isobel's tone how well she knew the Roosevelts and, more importantly, did she like them? The mention of the First Lady shook Meg out of her drowsy comfort. Dinners in this household were formal. At Smith, everyone wore her uniform to dinner; she did not have to worry about her meager wardrobe. She knew she did not have the right dress for dinner in this house. Maybe she could eat in the kitchen with the staff.

"I'm sure you all want to bathe and relax a bit before dinner. Are you allowed to wear your uniforms to dinner?" Aunt Isobel asked. "That way I could admire them a bit more." Meg looked up and saw the woman smiling kindly at her. She knew Meg did not have a dress to wear to dinner. She continued, "Cynthia, you are in your usual room. Vivian will be in her room when she arrives. Julie and Meg, I have you in a guest room with twin beds; it has its own full bath. I hope that will work. I believe you were roommates during your training."

"That will be lovely," Meg said quietly.

"It was so strange to sleep in a room alone at Christmas," Julie said. "I had gotten used to falling asleep talking to Meg. Talking to my pillow was not quite the same."

"I hope not," Meg said. The four women laughed.

Davis entered the room. "May I show you to your rooms?" The guest room, painted in light blue with matching blue-and-white comforters, capturing the southern exposure, was warm and inviting. Meg could not believe what a difference twenty-four hours made in their accommodations. Davis indicated bath towels in the bathroom and opened the door to a walk-in closet.

"Oh look," said Julie, "we each have our own side."

After Davis left, and as Julie unpacked, Meg asked, "Aunt Isobel did not seem that surprised to see us, did she?"

"Not really. I assume she knows how difficult it is to get housing. She probably hears about it at every party or get-together she hosts. Besides, she knows Cynthia is never going to share a bunk if she doesn't have to. Why? What are you thinking?"

"I have the sense she was told to watch over us."

"I think you've been reading too many mysteries. Relax. Unpack. Take a bath." Meg tried to follow her advice, but she was intrigued by the idea that the museum acquisitions Uncle Charles and Aunt Isobel were making before World War I were a cover for something else.

## 19

A t dinner the night before, the three WAVES agreed to set the alarm for what seemed like a very lazy, very late eight in the morning. Meg remembered walking up the stairs after dinner but had been so tired, she was not sure if she had brushed her teeth before falling into bed. She was thrilled to be sharing a room again with Julie.

Although she was usually the one who had difficulty waking up, Meg finished dressing a few minutes before Julie and wandered down the stairs. Through an open door, she saw Aunt Isobel in the library writing letters, and Meg tapped lightly. Aunt Isobel looked up and waved her in.

"Aunt Isobel, I wanted to talk to you about my staying here. I'm not sure when we'll start to receive our housing and food allowance, but as soon as I do, I'll make sure you get it. Perhaps I could help with some of the household chores." Meg took a breath and remembered a little bit of humor can go a long way. "Julie will confirm I am a demon with an iron."

"Meg, I appreciate the sentiment, but I have a household staff."

"But we are increasing the household by three, soon four."

"And now I will no longer have to justify why I am keeping my staff on during a war. You are probably not aware but this year at a press conference, the President suggested residents of Washington, DC, should move out of their homes to allow those here as part of the war effort to live in them. Opening my home to naval officers will assuage my guilt. When you do get your allowance, I'm sure Davis will be happy to receive it."

Meg could tell by her tone that Aunt Isobel had ended any conversation on the subject, and yet her smile was extremely kind.

"Thank you," Meg said and smiled back. "I'll leave you to your letters."

Compared to the weather in Northampton, the temperature in Washington, DC, was balmy; the women did not even need their overcoats. They decided walking rather than taking the bus was a good way to maintain the benefit of their months of marching.

Cynthia warned Julie and Meg, "You've got to be careful of the starlings. They're nasty birds who soil anything in their flight path, including sidewalks, parked cars, pedestrians, statues, and the facades of government buildings. Whatever you do, do not look up with your mouth open."

"Cynthia, we have pigeons in New York," Meg retorted.

Cynthia's look said, *Don't say I didn't warn you.*

In New York, Meg always made fun of the tourists as they craned their necks to look at the skyscrapers and was determined not to look like one, but quickly realized the fact that stopping several times a block to read the plaques on the building clearly gave her away. Even if they had not been reading plaques, those around them noticed the three women. They were among the first WAVES officers to arrive in Washington and as they walked, it was the first time many had seen their uniforms in person rather than in a magazine or a newspaper photo. Meg realized she was being stared at more than she was staring.

Meg was glad Cynthia had been willing to go to the National Museum of American History, even though Meg was sure she already knew it well. Meg took a moment to pretend she was sitting at Thomas Jefferson's desk and paid much more attention to the displays for the Morse telegraph and an Alexander Graham Bell telephone than she might have before her WAVES training. She could have spent hours looking at the First Ladies' dresses and promised herself to return when she was alone and not feeling as though she was holding the others back. Meg could not believe how petite many of the First Ladies were and how small their waists were. She sent a silent thank you to the universe that as much as she did not love wearing inch-and-a-half heels as part of her uniform, at least she was not wearing a corset. When she tried to imagine dancing in Helen Taft's dress with its long train, she started laughing as she could only imagine herself tripping, and quickly stopped herself. *WAVES should not chuckle in public*, she told herself. Julie put her arm through hers and said, "Time for lunch. When you start to giggle like that, you need to eat."

As they walked to the museum cafeteria, Julie asked Cynthia and Meg if they had noticed the four officers who were following them. "I was only looking at the gowns," Meg admitted.

Cynthia's jaw dropped. "As observant as you are about some things, Lieutenant Burke, you are hopeless about men. Julie, I think they're working up the courage to ask us to dinner. Where should we go next? The Art Museum? Should we give them room to walk up to us as we are looking at the pictures?"

Apparently, the officers were less interested in the art museum; other than a few school groups, the WAVES had many of the galleries to themselves. Meg spent several minutes looking at *Girl with the Red Hat* by Johannes Vermeer. Although a small painting on a wood panel rather than a canvas, it caught her eye not only because the sitter's clothing intrigued her, but also by the girl's direct gaze. It was impossible to walk past the young woman's opulent blue robe and contrasting luminous red hat. Were the sitter in the present-day United States, Meg felt she would already have joined them as a member of their WAVES cohort. As they left the museum, Meg looked around and did not see any naval officers. She wondered if Julie and Cynthia had been playing a joke on her. Probably there weren't any men following them.

"Let's stop at the bar at the Willard. It is sort of on the way back to Aunt Isobel's," Cynthia suggested as they left the art museum.

"Should we call your aunt and tell her we will be late?" Meg was worried someone was preparing dinner for them. She was not sure about the rules of the house, did not want to cause trouble, and certainly did not want to waste food.

"Oh, we're not expected for dinner," Cynthia said breezily. She took a long look at Meg.

"You're nervous because you've never been to a hotel bar, have you, Margaret Burke?" Cynthia shook from laughing. "The look on your face says it all. Why not?"

"Ensign, I was taught a lady did not enter a bar, especially a hotel bar."

Cynthia stood up slightly on her toes, opening her mouth to speak; Meg held herself rigid as she waited for the next insult. "And your mother would be right, Lieutenant, if you were going into a hotel bar alone, but we're a bunch of college girls out having fun, which is entirely different. We went into hotel bars after football games with our Wellesley chaperone, so it must be okay. If you're worried, you can order a Coke."

"The officers are waiting on the corner to see where we are going next," Julie added. "Don't you think we should finally meet them after they have followed us all day?"

Meg had never been a college girl out having fun but decided if Julie thought it was all right, it must be.

"Let's find a table big enough for them to join us," Cynthia directed.

As she predicted, almost as soon as the WAVES sat down, the officer leading the group asked, "Is there room for us to join you? We're your welcoming committee and want to hear all your Navy stories. Drinks on me. I'm still flush after Navy blanked Army last month." He looked knowingly at the other officers. "I'm going to keep my streak going betting Alabama will beat Boston College on New Year's Day in the Orange Bowl." As they sat and a waiter appeared, the officer said, "A round of whiskeys for the entire table."

Meg said in a small voice, "Could I have a Coke?"

The four men laughed and the leader said to the waiter, "Make hers a double."

Meg felt herself observing and listening to the group rather than trying to be part of the conversation. The "leader," as she identified him, wore the two silver bars of a full lieutenant, and introduced himself loudly as James Osgoode. He was of medium height with dark brown hair and, unlike the other three men, who looked as though they had just walked off an athletic field, the button at his waist was starting to strain. If he were not in uniform, Meg might have thought he was a type of salesman; he did not have the air of an officer. When he said they were all Annapolis men, it was in a tone that Meg felt suggested the WAVES should have already known this. She could hear Cynthia talking about her brother Peter, who had gone to the Naval Academy, to the man next to her. Something was said, but in the din, Meg couldn't hear if the others knew him. She was unable to read the expressions on their faces. When the whiskeys and lone Coke arrived, the men quickly downed their drinks in one sip while Julie and Cynthia both played with their glasses. Julie reluctantly took a small sip when urged to do so; Cynthia spun her glass in half turns.

Osgoode moved next to Meg and she could smell the whiskey on his breath. "You'll quickly learn that there is much marble but very little excitement in Washington. We're short of just about everything: butter, gasoline, meat, cigarettes, and apartments. We've been short of girls, but now the WAVES are here!" He grinned at her. "It's been hard to have a good time in DC. As soon as we get an influx of arrivals, the District makes a new liquor law. The first one was that you couldn't serve alcohol to anyone standing up. Then, they limited bar stools to drinking beer and wine. If you want a real drink, you must sit at a table. At midnight, the bars close and people pour out with nothing to do. Hell of a way to show the military you appreciate their service." Osgoode signaled to the waiter and ordered another round for the table. Meg noted Julie was taking tiny sips of her drink, but after some urging Cynthia had finished her whiskey.

Initially the conversation was quiet, and Meg struggled to hear the others over the noise of the bar, but her companions, especially Osgoode, became louder with each round of drinks. At every opportunity, the men turned the conversation back to the young women.

"Where are you from?" one asked Meg.

"New York City," she replied.

"And why leave such an interesting place to come to Washington? You must have something exciting to do here," he probed.

"How exactly are the WAVES helping their country?" another asked with a wink.

"We spent the past several weeks learning how to stretch out a can of coffee and how to file without getting paper cuts," Cynthia offered.

"Sure you are. C'mon, we're all officers—you can tell us!"

Julie said, "Actually we are part of a new religious branch of the military." The drinks had started to affect the men's cognitive ability and they looked as confused as Meg felt when Julie said it.

"Religious branch?" the man on the other side of Meg asked skeptically.

Cynthia stepped in. "You know how there are chaplains in the Navy?"

"Of course. My uncle was one in the last war."

"Well, now that we have women in the military, we're going to have female officers who are going to be chaplain nuns." The men looked very confused and the WAVES, including Meg, burst out laughing.

After his fourth whiskey, Lieutenant Osgoode became loud enough that the waiter hesitated when he asked for another round but did not deny his request. After he brought their order, Osgoode put his arm around Meg's waist. "You don't become lieutenant, darling, because you make coffee. What do you really do?" Meg shuddered involuntarily as he tightened his arm around her waist.

"My specialty is poisoned coffee, in case of enemy invasion." That sounded ridiculous to Meg, but she could feel Osgoode trying to slip his hand between her blouse and the waistband of her skirt and she panicked. She knew Cynthia thought she was a goody two-shoes and it was true. Meg did not know how to handle this man. She desperately needed to get away from him and out of the bar. With some effort, Meg pulled herself out of his grasp and marched out of the bar into the cold, smoke-free air. A few moments later, Cynthia and Julie were outside with her on either arm.

"What about the bill?" Meg asked.

"Don't worry about the bill," Cynthia said.

"Osgoode's a pig, isn't he?" Julie said vehemently.

"You've never had a guy pull something like that on you?" Cynthia was incredulous.

Meg was near tears and her voice shook. "When could I? I only went to a few dances with lots of chaperones. Usually, I was studying and working. I didn't have a season. I haven't spent much time with men, let alone men who act this way." Meg stopped and took a deep breath. "Tonight is the first time I realized you might learn something valuable as a debutante beyond learning to dance."

"Oh Meg! We're going to have to toughen you up. We're going to work with men like them every day," Cynthia counseled. "Every serviceman—strike that, every man—is going to try to ply us with alcohol and join the national contest to see how far he can get a WAVE to go. For now, you'd better find your best schoolmarm voice until you can find a better way to fight back."

# 20

Although she should have been exhausted from exploring Washington, DC, Meg had trouble falling asleep. She was upset about what had happened in the bar and nervous about her first day at work. As thoughts swirled in her head, she heard a church clock strike one; she was completely unsure where she was when Julie shook her awake at six in the morning.

"C'mon, sleepyhead. We have work to do." Julie shook her by the shoulders.

"I don't think I'm ready for this," Meg replied sleepily.

Moving quietly to not wake Aunt Isobel, Meg and Julie crept downstairs. Cynthia was drinking coffee but not eating.

Davis had put toast and boiled eggs on the sideboard. "Would you like coffee or tea?" she asked.

"Tea would be lovely." Meg thought it was an extra bonus that in addition to living in this beautiful house, in which food was magically available, she was able to get a cup of tea made with boiling water, milk, and at least one sugar cube rather than made with water heated but not boiled and poured onto an already used tea bag. She had a growing list of reasons to be thankful for Aunt Isobel. Although Meg had not minded keeping her clothes ironed and hung in order of length from left to right during Indoctrination, she was grateful she didn't have to worry about surprise inspections to check if her shoes were lined up in order of height or if she had made her bed to regulation.

Meg looked again at Cynthia and saw she was pale. She, too, had not slept well. Meg thought about Tom's suggestion that Meg look out for her. For a moment she again wondered why Tom seemed so interested in Cynthia's well-being.

"We all need to eat something. At least we need to eat some toast. Can you manage an egg, Cynthia? Later this morning you'll be glad you did." Meg tried to follow her own advice and swallowed most of a boiled egg with toast.

Meg did not enjoy her first Washington, DC, bus ride; she did not mind the crowd as much as the curiosity directed toward the WAVES. She thought she might try to walk to work tomorrow, although she realized she needed to get up even earlier to do so. Meg was happy to get off the bus and walk the two short blocks with Julie and Cynthia to report for duty at the Naval Annex on Nebraska Avenue.

Meg noticed the temporary building looked like a bunch of combs lined up end-to-end, with their spine or back on Constitution Avenue, beginning just west of the Washington Monument and stretching to the Lincoln Memorial. They looked even less substantial on the inside.

At the sentry entrance, two Marines guards checked the three WAVES' badges and inspected their purses before directing them to wait for an escort at the reception area. Meg stared at the water-stained ceiling, which creaked every time someone walked above them. When a door down the hall was forcibly closed, the pens on the desk in front of them shook. Meg thought it was lucky the weather was milder here than in New York. A blizzard at home could knock these buildings down.

Exactly at seven, an enlisted man walked in and stood in front of the WAVES and said, "I am here to show you where to report." He showed no interest in chitchat as he led them through numerous corridors and up a flight of stairs. Meg was not sure if she would be able to retrace her steps at the end of the watch.

"Here's your spot, ladies," he said as he let them through a door into what appeared to be a converted attic.

The WAVES exchanged a look. They outranked the young enlisted man who had just called them "ladies." They knew he could never have done that to their male colleagues, but it was quickly becoming clear they could be constantly fighting the small slights rather than focusing on their work.

This morning it was chilly in the building and as Meg glanced around the desks and at the people sitting at them, she saw several wore gloves with the fingers cut out. She guessed that as cold as it was today, it could be insufferably hot in the summer. There was a large group of about twenty people in the room with a mix of civilian clothing, officers' uniforms, and enlisted seaman attire. The din ceased as the WAVES walked in.

"Welcome to the Research Desk." In her brief contact with the field, Meg had grown to love the various euphemisms given to cryptanalytics. She froze as she recognized the voice and, egg or not, her stomach did a somersault when Lieutenant Osgoode walked over to greet them. The conversation around them restarted and Meg watched the expression on Osgoode's face, as well as those of Julie and Cynthia.

Cynthia whispered, "Last night was a test!"

Meg looked around and saw two of the other men from last night. Now she understood why the men had asked them so many times about their work. They were trying to find out if the WAVES had zipped lips and would remain discreet about why they were in Washington, even after a few drinks. Meg also noticed Osgoode looked much the worse for wear this morning. She wondered what, if anything, the lieutenant had told the rest of the team about last night with the WAVES.

"Did we pass last night's test, Lieutenant Osgoode?" Meg said carefully.

Instead of answering her, Osgoode announced, "Our first and last rule is 'Don't talk.' Failure to follow this rule means dismissal. Any questions?"

The three shook their heads "no."

Osgoode barked, "You NEVER talk about what you are doing. Not to your family, your bunkmates, the sentry at the door. You talk to no one about your work other than another individual in this room, and even then only in this secure area. Is that clear?"

Cynthia's voice shook as she responded, "Yes."

"Okay. That's out of the way." He gestured at Cynthia and said, "Ensign, go get me a cup of coffee." He pointed to the corner of the room where a small group was gathered. "The urn is over there."

Cynthia narrowed her eyes, stared back, and remained motionless.

"That's an order, Ensign."

Cynthia's face turned purple and she mumbled, "Yes sir" as she turned neatly on her heel toward the coffee.

"You two. Over to my desk." He guided them to a desk in the corner of the room while indicating chairs placed against the wall. "Grab a seat. I don't know what you learned at the finishing school, but I'm going to tell you what you really need to know."

Julie and Meg learned the chairs were against the wall because several were missing legs. Meg found one with four legs and a heavily taped seat, while Julie's was missing a back, making it more of a stool. They exchanged worried looks as they moved the two chairs closer to his desk. Osgoode stood, pacing in a small oval. Cynthia returned with a mug, which she forcefully put down, without spilling, on the desk. Meg had to admit she was impressed with her technique. Meg was furious at Osgoode's treatment of her friend, even if Cynthia had been the one to suggest going to the bar. Cynthia walked slowly to grab another chair from against the wall and, as she dragged it deliberately toward Julie and Meg, a leg snapped off. She shrugged her shoulders slightly to ask what now.

"I haven't got all day. If there aren't any chairs, you can stand," Osgoode bellowed.

Looking around the immediate area, Meg spied a trash can, quickly got up, confirmed it was empty, and turned it over. Cynthia made brief eye contact with Meg as she lowered herself to sit.

"Are we settled?" Osgoode asked in a slightly exasperated tone, to which Meg clenched her fists to her sides in response. She reminded herself that she was a lieutenant, too.

"We're ready," she said in her teacher voice with a polite smile.

The lieutenant took a few sips of coffee; reading his expression, Meg could see he needed the caffeine to kick in as soon as possible. "Our official title is Navy Communications Security Section. Our code's designation is OP-20-G, but we call ourselves the Research Desk. That is when we call ourselves anything at all." He glared at the WAVES and took another sip of coffee. "You can see we have a blend of military and civilians working here. That's unique. The civilians were part of the civil service before the war." He stopped to take a gulp of coffee. Meg took the advantage of the pause to check on Cynthia, who had been very pale but whose color was now returning to her cheeks. Osgoode cleared his throat. Meg waited anxiously for him to say something about Cynthia, the coffee, or the trash can, but he merely continued his monologue.

"At least you are pretend military." He glanced around the room with what Meg felt was a menacing stare. "You'll have to be better than some of our civilians who quite literally don't seem to realize we are at war and will only work their scheduled hours. This is a military operation and we need everyone to remember that. That will be part of your job. You will need to make sure the civilians are behaving." Meg felt for the civilians, who could not help but hear his harangue. No one seemed to be paying much attention to Osgoode, so she concluded maybe they were familiar with his complaints.

After the mug of coffee, he looked surer on his feet and his gait was steadier. "Time to see how things work around here. We follow a process and you need to understand each step of the method as soon as possible." He began moving slowly, and the women were not sure if he was about to walk or merely resuming his pacing. "C'mon. Come with me, we don't have all day." Rather than scrambling, Meg took the time to get up gracefully, but was perturbed to see Osgoode gawking at her as she did. The three WAVES reluctantly followed as he led them through the room.

"In the building next door," he gestured toward the wall as he started walking toward the other end of the room, "we have radio operators, listening to transmission. They write down the code they hear. When you see three dots rather than a number, that means the operator didn't understand or hear a portion of the code. We train the operators not to guess what they are hearing because if they guess wrong, it affects our ability to break the message. You may see some of the women you went to finishing school within that department soon."

The group of four had reached a hallway on the opposite side of the great room where they had started and Osgoode continued, "The next step is 'write-up,' and this is where we have people prepare the paper copies of the transmission, which we call worksheets. In the classification room, we have people who salvage garbled intercepts. Some messages are tagged routine, others urgent. We have other teams who review all radio traffic that has come in and been decoded, translated, evaluated, and given appropriate priority during the previous twenty-four-hour period. We sort these messages into areas of interest, such as geographical area." Julie, Meg, and Cynthia exchanged overwhelmed looks at the description of this work. Meg thought to herself that she did not think her training had prepared her for such work. She was relieved when Osgoode started walking out of this section, back to the hallway, and into another room. Thankfully, she would not be working on garbled transmissions. Or at least not today.

Osgoode guided them into a room where the sound of machines became louder and said, "Ever since we figured out how the Japanese code machines worked, we've been using special machines to help us do our jobs." Meg saw a few adding machines, with extra keys and components, as well as huge machines that looked similar to the card catalog at the library, only the drawers moved and the cards were fed through the machine rather than staying in the drawer. As she watched, Meg remembered punch cards from their training.

"Didn't the Navy group in Pearl Harbor use the punch card system to help them identify one set of additives?" she asked.

"Be careful of the cables!" Osgoode barked. The WAVES looked down and saw a cable system connecting various machines that looked like a mass of seaweed and was more of a trap for their heels than the uneven cobbles at Smith. Meg noted that the mechanical hum of machines never stopped. She also found herself annoyed that Osgoode hadn't answered her question.

The final part of the tour was a small room filled with wooden file cabinets. They heard the scamper of rodent feet as Osgoode opened the door and turned on the light.

"This is called the Vault. There is no reason why you should be there. You won't be working with the decoded information. Besides, I'm sure none of you will want to go in with the mice." He smiled flirtatiously at Meg. "You can always ask me to hold your hand if you're scared." Not only did Meg clench her fists as he said this, but she vowed that she would get back at him, preferably in front of a large group for the best effect!

"Even the military had to give up their metal files? They are so much more secure," Meg said in her teacher voice. At least she could deflect with her tone, Meg thought.

"You don't miss much, do you? Always thinking. I like a girl who thinks." His grin looked more like a leer. "Metal is better, but they have already been requisitioned and re-melted for other military purposes."

The group returned to the main room, and the very simplicity of the office around them belied what was taking place. The scuffed desks and battered cabinets would have looked shabby even in Meg's public school. Now that she could look around again, Meg noticed a few important features she had missed when they first entered. The telephones in this department had rotary dials, allowing them to make a direct call and bypass a potentially nosey operator. She noticed thin paper strips hung from lines, almost like pieces of clothing on a drying line, which brightened the drab room but were not actually meant for decoration. She realized they helped the analysts to transpose vertical and horizontal codes more easily.

"Ensign Bowen." It took Meg a moment to acknowledge that meant Julie. A woman their age but wearing civilian clothes approached their small group. She extended her hand to Julie. "I'm Laura Martin. I'm a civil servant here and temporarily assigned to help you get up to speed replacing Missy Franklin. We heard you did an entire library degree in just a few months. We have scraps of paper everywhere just waiting for you!"

Julie gave Meg and Cynthia a huge, triumphant smile. "Someone has to make sense of the thousands of pieces of paper flying around here every day. Might as well be me."

"Bet you never guessed that about her when you met her last night," Meg added, making eye contact with Lieutenant Osgoode, who was the first to look away.

"I am going to whisk Ensign Bowen away and help get her started on her project," Miss Martin said, breaking the tension.

With the group reduced to Osgoode, Cynthia, and Meg, Meg was grateful for Cynthia's company. Osgoode cleared his throat, bounced slightly on his feet, and did not suggest sitting down. Rather, he had them standing in front of the desk of a man with several sheets of paper spread out, using a ruler to keep him on the same line across the sheets and, Meg thought, counting under his breath. Osgoode had to be disturbing the man's work, but seemed oblivious to his effect as he commanded, "Now that our process is clear, you need to get to work." Meg and Cynthia exchanged looks. Their cursory tour made their work far from clear.

The lean, slight man dressed in a well-worn suit, who Meg thought was in his late twenties or, possibly, early thirties, looked up and seemed ready to say something to Osgoode, but then abruptly decided against it. He had fine, black hair, which she thought tended to cling to his scalp unless recently washed. He went back to staring resolutely at his paper, but Meg noticed he had not made a mark and his gaze had not moved. He was trying, without success, to ignore them. Lieutenant Osgoode gestured to the man and said, "That's Warren Elliot. Civilian. I think he has been here since before the war. Warren, I want you to train our new officers on what they need to do."

Meg instinctively knew that the only reason Lieutenant Osgoode had called them officers and referred to Warren by his first name was to goad him. Mr. Elliot opened and then closed his mouth again, but not before Meg noticed a turned incisor, which upset otherwise nicely spaced teeth. She guessed that when he smiled, it was with his mouth closed.

"Hello, I'm Margaret. Most people call me Meg." Her voice sounded much braver than she was feeling. Her stomach dropped. Immediately she realized she should have said "Lieutenant Burke." The protocol was much easier in the classroom than it was in person, especially with the mixture of officers, enlisted, and civilians working within feet of each other. She was glad neither the lieutenant nor Mr. Elliot commented on her slip.

Cynthia said, "Ensign Collingsworth," without extending her hand.

Without a smile or any sign of friendliness, he said in a near monotone, "Are you ready to start?"

He got up and walked Cynthia and Meg over to an empty desk against the wall and gestured for them to take a seat. As they sat, he walked away. Meg and Cynthia exchanged glances. Was he leaving them there? Were they supposed to have followed? Soon he returned and handed each of them a ruled yellow pad of paper as well as a pen. "I heard Lieutenant Osgoode review a lot of historical information. Some of it was correct." Meg and Cynthia exchanged a look.

"Cryptography is the language of intelligence. For hundreds of years, diplomats and military leaders could never be sure if their message was going to reach its destination or fall into the wrong hands." He paused for effect. Meg noted that Elliot was like an actor. She would not have looked at him twice in a crowd, but as he spoke passionately about intelligence his skin glowed, and his posture straightened. The man loved his work, she thought.

"We're the wrong hands," Meg said.

Elliot and Cynthia looked at her strangely.

Meg blushed and explained, "The communications fell into our hands."

Elliot looked at her as if seeing a different person than he had met a few minutes earlier. "Not the answer I was expecting." He stared across the room and then said, "What are the four essential skills for cryptanalysis? I'll be back to collect your answers in twenty minutes."

Meg thought this was another test like going to the bar last night, less about knowledge and more about how she reacted and handled the situation. Cynthia was already bent over her pad and writing furiously. Meg found herself nibbling on her lip as she thought about her coursework at Smith. She decided to list that as her first skill. Being familiar with codes and having the skills to learn new ones. She thought about why she had been selected for this assignment and put down two more answers: attention to detail and persistence. She thought about why college-educated individuals, even if they did not speak Japanese, were an asset. She was well read and was able to make connections. Her ability and enjoyment with crossword puzzles reflected both skills. She wrote, "Ability to make inferences." Meg thought of a fifth item but was not sure if it were better to follow directions strictly or to show initiative. As she chewed on her lip, initiative won out. "Luck."

As she turned over her paper, Mr. Elliot returned. As he scanned Cynthia's paper, his face remained impassive and he said, "Hmm." Then he looked at Meg's answers and gave her a long stare. "You're right, of course. It is all about luck, but until you have luck, you must work hard. Go and get lunch. We'll get to work this afternoon."

## 21

---

The WAVES officers were a novelty in the Mess. Several male officers asked if they liked Washington and assured the WAVES they were available as tour guides for the capital's attractions. Meg's stomach was queasy, faced with working with Osgoode and realizing the enormity of the task ahead of them. The complexity of the work described in the classification room had unnerved her, and she could only manage to eat a bowl of soup. Cynthia complained of a headache, but Meg couldn't do any more than give her a sympathetic look. Both women were happy to get back to the comparative quiet of "The Research Desk," although Meg knew she and Cynthia were an object of interest there, albeit more covert. Meg reassured herself that novelty wears off in a few weeks. At least she hoped so.

Mr. Elliot was waiting for them. He did not smile, but nor did he seem to have the same attitude of resentment he'd had earlier. As Meg and Cynthia sat down, he asked in an undertone, "How much do you know about the Battle of Midway and our role in it?"

Meg wondered if the entire day would consist of nothing more than one test after another.

"I know we won the Battle of Midway last spring," Meg said.

"Anything more?" he probed. Meg looked at Cynthia, who shook her head slightly.

"Not really," Meg admitted.

"We could tell by radio traffic that Admiral Yamamoto had his eye on Midway Island. He wanted to have a base closer to Hawaii, making us even more nervous."

"That makes sense," Cynthia agreed.

"What he didn't know is that the naval radio station in Honolulu listened to their radio signals, which they send in a different sort of Morse code based on syllables rather than letters." Elliot tapped his pen on his desk for effect. "Very difficult to understand. Almost a code within itself. That small command worked nonstop to decrypt the transmissions and disseminate Japan's plans, including much of the timetable. The Japanese called the target 'AF,' which US naval commanders knew had to be in the Pacific, but the Pacific covers a lot of territory. It was Rochefort and his group in Hawaii who figured out a way to learn what 'AF' stood for. He suspected it was Midway Island, and Rochefort was able to convince American forces on the island to send out a radio message saying that Midway was running short of fresh water. When his codebreakers intercepted a Japanese message, that 'AF' was running short of fresh water, it confirmed the target." He paused and looked intently at them. Meg was sure he was waiting for her to respond, but she had no idea what he was expecting her to say. She was relieved when he continued speaking.

"We must make sure we are always ahead of them. Since the day war was declared we have been behind. But the Battle of Midway finally made our Navy understand that this type of intelligence gathering is crucial to military operations. Outside of a few people in the Navy, no one will ever know that we will win this war because of our superior code-breaking, not because of anything anyone does on a ship."

Meg did not think Warren was wrong. The decoded transmissions were vital intelligence. The next few hours passed in a blur as they became familiar with the transmission process. Mr. Elliot had Cynthia and Meg draw flow charts of how they thought codes were processed and corrected their steps, filling in with the detailed steps the Research Desk used. He also sang the praises of "good" mechanical pencils and reminded them paper was cheap.

"Use as much paper as you need to if that will help you break the code. Paper isn't rationed for us. Let me know if you need graph paper or cards." He stood up for emphasis as he said, "You must always, always, always put any of your papers, including anything you scribble on, in the burn bag when you finish. There will be a day when you will want to take just one page home with you so you can continue to look at the letters or numbers. You will think, 'If I just look for the pattern while I'm getting ready for bed or when I'm brushing my teeth, I can break it.' You CANNOT do that. The letters and numbers must never leave this room. You can NEVER, ever share anything from this room with any person outside this room. Even if I come up to you in a park in the city and we are the only two people in the park, we can't talk to each other about work."

As he worked himself up lecturing about maintaining secrecy, somewhat uncharitably, Meg thought about how she was going to mimic Mr. Elliot over dinner but quickly caught herself. Any reference to him outside the workspace was out of bounds and broke her secrecy oath. Mr. Elliot continued, "We have put together a departmental training manual of sorts. I'm going to have you study it for the rest of the afternoon and begin your tasking first thing tomorrow."

The training manual turned out to be a collection of papers stored in a loose-leaf binder, which allowed Meg and Cynthia to read at the same time.

After thirty minutes of reading, Meg whispered, "I think it's written in its own code. I can't see how this is going to help."

"If you don't understand it, how do you think I'm doing? It's fourteen forty-five; pretend to read for another fifteen minutes," Cynthia whispered back. "Also, whatever you do, Meg, don't ask Mr. Elliot a question. He might start us on a project that will take us until midnight."

The WAVES hunched over the shared book and did not see two officers approach the desk until there was a slight cough. They rapidly stood and awkwardly saluted.

"Good work. You're already learning to tune the noise out. I'm here to welcome you, officially, aboard. I'm Lieutenant Commander Andrew Lewis. We met briefly at your intake session a few days ago."

Lewis was pencil thin, with piercing blue eyes and short-cropped light blond, almost white hair. Judging simply from his demeanor, Meg was positive he did not suffer fools.

"Today was your training day," he continued. "You should be ready to work first thing tomorrow. For the moment, you'll be on the day shift, but as you know, WAVES can work nights and weekends. We'll get you shifted over as soon as you are up to speed."

"Yes, sir," Meg said, as that seemed to be the only appropriate thing to do.

Next to Commander Lewis was another tall, young man— one she recognized. Although his face was carefully holding a neutral expression, his gray-green eyes were laughing at her uncertainty about how to interact with Lewis.

"Welcome aboard," Lieutenant Prescott said. "Good to see you got settled. Did you enjoy your day of sightseeing? Sorry we were in meetings all day and weren't here to welcome you first thing, but I understand Lieutenant Osgoode and Mr. Elliot have gotten you started. You found the Mess all right?"

"I understand the two of you are experts on how to work the off-base housing protocol, so I'm going to assume you know how to find food," Lewis added grimly. Meg was amazed that he knew about their housing issue and noted he did not appear particularly pleased with how they had asserted themselves, or maybe he had not liked the fact she had used Lewis's name to get the process started.

Cynthia spoke up. "We're still a little lost, sir. Perhaps Lieutenant Prescott could walk us to the gate? All of the corridors look the same." Meg felt they had just been reprimanded and could not believe Cynthia had made such a request. Meg looked down at the floor, avoiding eye contact as she felt her own cheeks burning, even though she had not been the one to ask.

Before the lieutenant could reply, Commander Lewis said, "Send them with Elliot. We have work to do." He turned and barked, "Elliot! Elliot, guide our new WAVES back to the entry!"

The lieutenant gave them a quick smile and quietly said, "See you tomorrow," before falling in step with the commander.

As Mr. Elliot came over to escort them, Cynthia announced, "We'd better practice finding our way out during the day. If we get lost, someone will find us. It will prepare us for working nights. We'll see you tomorrow." She turned to Meg and said, "Let's go find Julie."

Julie was in another room, connected to the main workroom and lined with files. She looked exhausted and brightened when the two WAVES told her their shift was over and it was time to go home. As they exited the gate, the sun was still out and Meg suggested walking home. She knew they could talk about their day while walking as long as they avoided specifics. More importantly, Meg could avoid being stuck on the crowded bus. She carefully worded her first statement once they were past the gate.

"Cynthia and I had our one and only day of training, which

wasn't that helpful. I need a guide to keep all of the personalities straight. How about you, Julie?"

"Oh, I had a great day. There are months of organizing to be done. All the . . ." She quickly caught herself. "There's a lot of focus on completing the project but not filing, so I have my work cut out for me. It's so strange to have three—*three*—people waiting for me to give them direction. I think I have the right idea about how to run things. I guess we'll see."

Meg squeezed her friend's arm to assure her that she would do well. "So, Cynthia." Meg turned to the other woman. "I think it is time to put your strengths to use."

"My strengths?" Cynthia looked at her in confusion. Meg never spoke to her like that.

"Our fearless leader. Time to use your connections to find out why he is miserably deskbound, literally pulling his hair out. He doesn't seem very personable, but he has already been promoted several times to lieutenant commander and is heading a vital project. There has to be a story there."

"You figured out all of that in the three sentences he spoke to us?" Cynthia responded.

"I was paying attention to him and what he was saying, rather than the dashing Lieutenant Prescott."

"Do you know what I think?" Julie interrupted when she saw Cynthia's hurt expression.

"What do you think?" Meg's voice was teasing.

"My guess is that the dashing Robbie Prescott has been assigned to him as his deputy to help soften his edges," Julie said, ignoring Meg's teasing. "Bet he was happy to see you today, Meg," she added with a glint in her eye.

## 22

As the WAVES sat down for dinner, Meg felt faint from the aroma of beef stew. She noted the huge chunks of meat and several vegetables in addition to potatoes. Moreover, there was a butter dish next to a loaf of crusty bread. This might have been a birthday dinner in her Brooklyn household rather than an ordinary weeknight meal. Aunt Isobel was dressed in a formal knee-length dress, wearing her ever-present string of pearls, while the WAVES continued to wear their uniforms to dinner rather than changing.

Aunt Isobel smiled. "I know I can't ask you what you have been doing, but I can tell you have been busy. You all look as though you have put in a full day of work. You should go to bed early and get some rest. Tomorrow will be a busy day and night. We have all been invited to a New Year's Eve party. Let Davis know if you need your dress uniforms pressed or your pumps shined."

"It will be the first time I've spent any length of time in my pumps," Meg disclosed. "I hope they fit well, or I'll be miserable."

"We've also been invited to a party," Cynthia said. "I don't think we can attend your party, Aunt Isobel. You know the rule: dance with the first person who asks you even if you want to dance with the second."

Meg had forgotten about that conversation with Lieutenant Prescott in the "Room of Doom." It seemed like a lifetime ago, even though it had been just a few days. Meg smiled inwardly as she listened to aunt and niece. She knew the niece really wanted to go to the party with the first person who asked her, even if she had cajoled the officer in question into making the invitation.

"I think you will decide to attend my party. The party organizer is married to your commanding officer." Aunt Isobel paused. "My understanding is there will be any number of young men there. The hostess was quite adamant that I should bring my WAVES."

"Sorry, Aunt Isobel. We already have plans," Cynthia repeated.

"Cynthia, you can't hold him to it, especially since this is an official invitation," Julie said.

"Of course I will. I'll remind him tomorrow at work. Just think who might be there," Cynthia responded.

Meg wondered why she was constantly reminding Cynthia, who had grown up in a naval family, of naval protocol. "I think, Ensign," she smiled to try to soften the effect, "we need to go to the CO's party. Lieutenant Prescott was probably just being polite the other day. Besides, it is quite possible the commander is making the poor lieutenant the watch officer so the commander can go to a party."

"Lieutenant Prescott, as in Robbie Prescott?" Aunt Isobel arched an eyebrow.

"Yes," confirmed Cynthia.

"We are no longer at cross-purposes. I know his parents will be at the party and his mother has already told me how much she is looking forward to seeing you. She reminded me that the last time she had seen you . . ."

"I still had braces on my teeth and fell off the rope swing into the lake," Cynthia finished for her. "I'm looking forward to hearing the story repeated several times." She rolled her eyes at Julie and Meg.

Isobel glared at her niece in a clear reprimand and continued as if she had not been interrupted, "Mrs. McClaren stressed proper attire is your dress uniform with white gloves and dress pumps." She smiled, a smile that Meg already recognized meant the subject was now closed.

"I have more news," Isobel continued. "Vivian will be joining us next week. She received her orders today."

"It will be good to have her here," Meg said, filling the unexpected silence while looking at Cynthia, who was now pouting.

Once upstairs, Meg confided in Julie, "I don't want to go to the official party either. I can't imagine what I'm going to talk about. We can't talk about work. There are only so many times I can make the comment that winters are so much milder in Washington, DC, compared to New York City. I'll put myself to sleep with my boring comments. I thought we were going to a party with the lieutenant and two dozen of his closest teammates. Are they teammates? Boatmates? *Boatmates* doesn't sound right. Julie, do you row with teammates?"

Julie giggled. "I think *teammates* is fine. It is a crew team. Can you imagine going to one of their parties?"

"I can hear my mother saying 'no' to that! Seriously, though, I'm not sure that my presence is really needed at this party. You and Cynthia will know some of the people there, but everyone will be a stranger to me."

Julie shot her a disapproving look. "Lieutenant, you're normally so bright, but you have a mental block about the social component that is part of your rank. There's a reason the Navy is the President's favorite service. The Navy follows social etiquette and knows how to throw a good party. You learned that in Indoctrination. For now, you are on duty even when you are off duty. Just look at it as a job responsibility to go to parties and dinners and put your best foot forward. Especially as a lieutenant. It's what you have to do."

Meg sighed. "Help me come up with small talk. What am I supposed to say?"

"Start asking people questions about themselves. You're lucky. Almost no one is from Washington, so it's fine to ask them about where they grew up. You like baseball. Ask them about which baseball team they follow. Right now, everyone much prefers talking about the WAVES and our 'darling' uniforms than our losses in the Pacific. Think of it as helping morale. Go to the party tomorrow night and do your duty." She stopped and smiled at Meg to let her know she did know these situations were tough for her. "Besides, I'm sure the food is going to be good. Mrs. McClaren is undoubtedly like Aunt Isobel. She knows how to work with the ration stamps and has Navy supplies as well. Even if we come back the minute after midnight, we need to go. You never know." Julie paused for effect. "You might meet someone."

Meg shook her head. "Doubtful," she retorted.

Julie would not be dissuaded. "You talked to one of the officers at the bar—not Osgoode. Another officer. Lyall. I didn't catch his last name. He seemed nice. I saw him today at work, when I was sorting papers. He brought me a few boxes and seemed happy to chitchat. He'll probably be there. Get some sleep. It will seem better in the morning."

"There is something else I need to tell you about."

Julie propped herself up on her pillow. "Is this a lights-on or a lights-off discussion?"

"Much easier as a lights-off discussion."

Meg turned off the lights, stepped out of her slippers, and tucked herself slowly into bed before she spoke. "I think Cynthia likes my brother Tom."

Meg could hear Julie exhale. "Oh Meg, I thought you were going to tell me something awful, like one of your parents was sick or that you were going to resign your commission."

"I think Cynthia liking my brother *is* pretty awful." Julie's giggle turned into laughter and left both gasping for air, trying to catch their breath.

"At least I thought she liked my brother, but now she seems to be back to liking Robbie Prescott."

"You mean *your* lieutenant."

Ignoring her comment, Meg continued, "My brother Tom picked us up at Grand Central with his cab. I thought Cynthia was going to make snide comments, but instead she and Vivian could hardly keep their eyes inside their heads. It was awful," Meg said forlornly.

"It was awful because there were women flirting with your brother? Because you don't like to think of your brother liking women? Or because it was Cynthia."

"All of those things, but especially because it's Cynthia. She doesn't think I'm evolved enough to be in the Navy, even if I were enlisted. How could she like my brother?"

"Why don't you let me meet him and then I can tell you?" Meg could sense Julie smiling in the dark.

"I tried to warn Tom," Meg continued. "I don't want Cynthia to hurt him. Do you know what he told me?"

"You should be friends with her?"

"Exactly. How did you know?"

"Because you should be."

"She hates me."

"She doesn't hate you. She is jealous of you."

"Hardly." Meg paused. "How could she be jealous?"

"You are bright, attractive, self-confident, a born leader, and are from a loving family. In comparison, her father is still upset at her about her making such a mess of things that he had to send away his assistant, which may or may not have had ramifications for his own career. Her parents probably have Isobel watching her to try to keep her out of trouble. If the Prescotts are good family friends, Robbie may be under orders to keep an eye on her. By the way, since you are clueless about these things, she's only flirting with Robbie to annoy you. He surely knows her history with the naval officer. That's the kind of gossip that travels quickly."

"So now that the Navy is out, she has moved on to cab drivers."

"That's it in a nutshell. Cute cab drivers, at least."

Meg sighed. Although she soon heard Julie's even breathing, it took her much longer to fall asleep. She had expected Julie to tell her she was imagining that Cynthia was interested in her brother rather than confirm her suspicions. Eventually, her exhaustion from her busy day overcame her.


AFTER A GOOD NIGHT'S SLEEP, Meg was still reluctant to attend the party, but she realized this was part of her job and much safer than military duty for so many people, including her brother William serving somewhere in the Pacific Ocean.

Although the weather was colder than it had been, the trio agreed to walk rather than take the bus, and the brisk walk felt good. Cynthia was still pouting; both she and Julie were quiet for most of the walk, so Meg enjoyed walking without active commentary. The WAVES arrived at the outdoor sentry post and when Meg presented her badge and opened her purse for inspection, she felt as though she was starting to catch on to her new routine.

As Meg moved to sit at the desk where she and Cynthia had sat the previous day, she was a bundle of nerves and did not notice several pairs of appreciative eyes glancing at her trim waist and light-footed walk. One of the officers she'd met at the Willard bar came over to the two women as they sat down. Over six feet tall, with blond hair and caramel-colored eyes, he looked as though he could be as comfortable walking off a tennis court as he was wearing his uniform. Meg had noticed that every male officer she had met in the department, except for Osgoode, was tall and looked as though he played at least two or three sports. It was not impossible, she thought, that being a multi-sport athlete was a Naval Academy requirement. She could not remember this officer's name and tried to look furtively at his name tag.

"Don't get too comfortable. This won't be your place for too much longer."

Meg and Cynthia exchanged worried looks. Meg didn't think their first day had been that bad. Were they being reassigned already?

He grinned at them. "Not you specifically. Had you going, didn't I? We've outgrown the command building and the entire department is moving. My name is John Boller, by the way. I go by Jack. Except for Elliot and Commander Lewis, most of us who work in this room on this part of the project are on a first-name basis." He smiled. "It was noisy in the bar the other night and I didn't hear your names."

Meg and Cynthia introduced themselves.

Another officer from the Willard, the one who had an uncle who was a military chaplain, joined the trio.

"Jack, that is probably secret information. I'm Lyall, or Li, or Wolf. Any of them work when you want to talk." He smiled at Meg.

"Wolf?" Meg asked in confusion.

"He's a wolf in sheep's clothes." Meg felt like she was drowning on land and shot Jack a look of desperation.

"Annapolis's mascot is a sheep and Lyall is Scottish for wolf, so at school we started calling him a wolf in sheep's clothing. Li is the very opposite of a wolf," Jack teased.

Meg did remember Lyall trying to talk to her about baseball. He was a little taller than Jack, probably six foot three, with dirty-blond hair, which Meg was sure was much lighter in the summer, and gray eyes. When he smiled, he had a dimple on his right cheek, which made her want to smile back. She did not think he had finished growing; he looked like her own brother William before he had finally filled out in his early twenties. For years, her brother had feet that looked too big for his body and her mother had to take in his clothes, otherwise they looked as though they were falling off him. This man's uniform had been tailored for his thin frame but could not hide his youth. Although she had tried to forget the end of the evening, she remembered Lyall had looked very concerned as Osgoode became increasingly inebriated.

Jack continued, "We're moving to a girls' college. We all think it has to do with you."

"Me?" Cynthia asked. *Here we go*, thought Meg. Had Cynthia's father been involved in the procurement?

"We need more female heads and the Navy probably thinks you cannot survive in a warehouse. We're all hoping we get better facilities than we have now."

Cynthia's face looked like a punctured balloon.

"A school?" Meg was amazed. "How could having a school be useful?"

"Not just any school," Jack continued. "The Navy is taking over Mount Vernon Seminary."

Meg gave him a quizzical look.

"It's a posh finishing school," Lyall said. "From Annapolis to a finishing school. How are we going to explain that when we're up for promotion?" The two men laughed uncomfortably. Mr. Elliot walked over to his desk during the exchange and had a frown on his face as he took his seat.

"One of the quickest decisions I've ever seen the Navy make." Jack raised an eyebrow.

"You're not kidding," Lyall confirmed. "As I heard the story, the Navy decided it wanted the school for its brick buildings and classrooms. It's probably worth five million dollars, but the Navy got it for a little over a million."

Jack let out a low whistle.

"Glad I'm not one of the students," Lyall continued. "They left for the Christmas break and now they are coming back to school held on the second floor of a Garfunkel's department store. Can you imagine?"

Jack pretended to flounce a skirt and said in a high voice, "It is for the war effort." The two men laughed.

"It is THE finishing school for well-connected daughters of senators and other important government men. But it's in northwest Washington in Tenleytown; it isn't close to all the war department buildings." Cynthia had rebounded.

"Still not going to help our careers, even if it is THE school?" Lyall mimicked Cynthia's voice and she blushed. Meg knew they should start to get to work but saw that Mr. Elliot had gotten up from his desk to get a cup of coffee. It appeared they had a few more minutes to talk.

"Oh." Meg ignored the flirting. "So, we will be near the National Cathedral and American University. Aren't there a number of embassies around there?"

"My, you are the smart one, aren't you? Yes, there are. Do you like going to the embassy parties too?" asked Jack as Lyall smiled at her.

"I didn't know about the parties. I was just getting a feel for where we're going." It was now her turn to blush.

Cynthia coughed lightly. "We had some training yesterday," she said. "Are we ready to start?"

"About that. We were expecting Emily Proctor back from WAVE training. Did you meet her?" Jack inquired.

"We did," Meg confirmed as Cynthia nodded. "She talked to us about working almost nonstop to help identify additives."

"Emily has the gift of identifying patterns. I think her eyes are different than the rest of ours," Lyall commented.

"She was going to train you, but she has been reassigned to a project in San Diego. Very hush-hush, just like this one. Can you imagine palm trees and wearing shorts in January? Some people have all the luck," Jack said.

"Instead," Lyall said, "We're going to show you how to do our work." He grinned and turned to Mr. Elliot, who had returned to his desk. "Elliot, I'm going to get them looking at some recent transmissions, okay?" Warren stared stonily at Lyall, but silently passed him a box filled with small slips of paper.

"We know you were selected for your strong mathematical or language skills, which we are now going to put to use," Lyall began.

"Not me," Cynthia said. "I don't have strong math skills, but she does." She inclined her head toward Meg. "She's a math teacher."

Lyall turned to Meg with a smile. "Then you will be good at this. Maybe you can explain it to your partner if she doesn't understand my directions."

"Correct me if I'm wrong," Meg said. "In order to create their code, the Japanese assigned a numerical value to every word or syllable that was likely to be used in a transmission. We have broken that part, right? We have a codebook, or at least know many of their codes."

"Full marks," said Lyall.

"It was more than finishing school," Cynthia added, with a glare.

"The tricky part," Lyall continued, ignoring her annoyance, "is the second step, when the Japanese attach the additives. And we are talking about *thousands* of additives."

"How long do we have?" Meg asked nervously.

He put the box on their desk and smiled kindly. "You aren't responsible for actually cracking the additive algorithms. That's what the math professors do." Lyall adopted a mock serious voice as if he were an announcer and said, "Our highly trained academicians determine the mathematical underpinnings of cipher creation." Using his regular voice, he continued, "They find where the random really isn't random. Robbie's really good at it when Lewis lets him do some work instead of putting out fires for him."

Jack said, "It took the 'professors' more than a month to figure out the current set of additives the Japanese are using."

"Not just the professors, Jack," Lyall said. "We occasionally figure something out."

"Speak for yourself."

"Okay. I've never really helped to crack anything," Lyall admitted. "Actually, all we recent Annapolis grads are good at is subtracting numbers from the transmissions. We are marking time until we're sent to sea." He gestured toward Elliot. "Guys like him provide the continuity. We're on a strict rotation, which limits our shore duty to two years. Just about the time we catch on to what's going on around here, we'll leave for our mandatory sea duty. Osgoode has a math background and had his tour extended to keep working on the codes. He isn't happy about it."

*One mystery solved*, thought Meg.

"Could you walk me through working on one of these slips from start to finish? Then you can get back to what you need to be doing," Meg said.

"Great idea!" Jack responded. "You can see firsthand how we are decoding transmissions as rapidly as possible." He grinned at her. "It is now up to you to make sure we're ahead of the Imperial Navy's next move."

As Jack took over the instruction, he explained, "We need the two of you to learn to sort the transmission slips by country. Most of ours are from Japan, so you will start to use that country code the most. We also get messages from Germany or some of the neutral countries, such as Portugal, when a transmission is incorrectly forwarded to us." He looked specifically at Meg. "Maybe you can translate the messages from the Irish Republic." Meg felt her cheeks burn. Jack continued, "There's a list of country codes in the binder. The second code is the station. That's longer and there are more of them, but you gals know about patterns and only a few stations account for most of the messages. After a little while, you'll just need to look up the ones from what we call a 'quiet station,' which just means we don't get a lot of communication from them."

Meg and Cynthia gathered speed throughout the morning and by lunchtime, they did not need to look at the code list any longer. After lunch, they asked for another box and competed to see who could sort through more documents.

Later in the afternoon, Meg was stretching her shoulders and Cynthia had stepped away to get a cup of coffee, when Lieutenant Prescott walked over to their desk and said, "I understand I'll see you at the party tonight."

"Cynthia's furious you didn't tell us the other day the entire command was invited."

"She heard what she wanted to hear. I told you I could get you an invitation to the same party I was going to, and I did." He smiled at her. "I have a question for you."

"Yes?"

"I feel as though I've met you before."

"What a line." Meg returned his smile.

"No, really. It's been bothering me since I interviewed you at Smith. I think I must have met you at a Princeton dance? Maybe at a football weekend? Could I have gone to school with a brother?"

"I'm sure you did not go to school with any of my brothers," she said lightly but felt her stomach do somersaults as she remembered where she had met him. During college, Meg had been working at one of the Taylors' parties when a lady had spun into the punch table where Meg was stationed. The force of the crash launched the bowl in the air, showering Meg in sticky liquid and surrounding her in broken glass when it shattered against the floor. Meg realized the lieutenant was the young man, with beautiful gray-green eyes, who had helped her to pick up the sticky and broken glass pieces.

"I'm sure we've never met. I'd remember if we had," Meg said politely but firmly.

"If you say so." He seemed unconvinced but not willing to push the issue. "See you tonight," he said as he walked away.

"What did the lieutenant want?" Cynthia asked.

"He was telling me that until we can get through four boxes a day, we can't move on to the next task."

"Really? Then why are you blushing?"

## 23

To save energy for dancing at the party, the WAVES decided to take the crowded bus home even though it would get them there later than they would have liked. The entire ride, Meg worried about how long she had until the lieutenant remembered the circumstances of their first meeting. If Cynthia didn't think she belonged in the WAVES, what was it going to be like when the entire Research Desk knew that she had worked as a maid? In fact, if she had not been called in early, she might have been working at the Taylors' after-Christmas party before reporting for duty. Meg still was not used to combining the different parts of her life, especially the changes in lifestyle associated with being a military officer.

Meg saw that Davis had laid her other uniform, handsomely steamed, on her bed. Her white shirt had never been so perfectly pressed, and the navy tie was starched so that it might stand up on its own. Meg could see her reflection in her new black pumps, designated for an occasion such as tonight. As her stomach sank, she realized she was going to have to find another place to live. She was not the type of person who could have another individual wait on her. Tonight, she could ask the other partygoers where they lived and, with any luck, have a lead on another billet by midnight. She walked into the bathroom and started to battle her curls back into a mini chignon as she thought about where she might move. Surely, she thought, the Navy could find a room for one WAVE officer. Her reflection in the mirror frowned at her.

Julie knocked on the door and came into the bathroom to share the mirror as they put on lipstick. "You look almost human, Meg," she teased.

"As do you," Meg retorted.

The young women took a moment to look at their reflections with their gored white wood-blend skirt, accentuating their trim waists and flaring out closer to their knees. The design flattered both women even though they were at least six inches different in height and Julie curvier than Meg's lean frame.

When they arrived downstairs, Cynthia and Aunt Isobel were waiting with their uniform gabardine belted coats and white gloves. Aunt Isobel was wearing a beautiful sable coat and her pearls. Meg thought once again about how she wanted one day to have Isobel's elegance. Isobel never seemed to worry about how she looked and was always so well dressed. Meg was sure Cynthia would someday have the same style; however, her pushiness might prevent her from having the same grace.

The night was the coldest it had been since the WAVES arrived in Washington and they were glad for their coats. The ride took only a few minutes. Although the city was mainly in blackout, the moon provided enough illumination for Meg to see white colonnades on several of the houses. They soon arrived at her commanding officer's house, which was larger and more imposing than Isobel's. Meg had assumed it was a Navy property but wondered for a moment if it were possibly a family home. As the driver pulled into the semicircular drive, Meg could see by the number of parked cars that it was an enormous party, although the blackout curtains threw things into shadow. Early arrivals had parked their cars on the edge of the drive, forcing cars trying to drop guests off to inch carefully past. With so few lights, the women kept tripping on the path to the front door.

"We look as though we're drunk," laughed Meg. She realized Aunt Isobel might be struggling and lightly took her arm to guide her in through the door. As they entered the lighted vestibule, she saw a startled look on Isobel's face and realized she had overstepped by grabbing her arm. Already nervous about the party, she looked for an escape route; she desperately wanted to find a place to hide.

Before she could depart, she had several social responsibilities. Captain McClaren and his wife approached, greeting Aunt Isobel. Isobel introduced her houseguests, saying, "I believe you have met my niece, Ensign Cynthia Collingsworth. May I introduce Lieutenant Margaret Burke and Ensign Julie Bowen?"

"So pleased to meet all of you." Their host saluted while their hostess nodded in greeting.

"Lieutenant Burke, how does the command compare with teaching high school math? Do the officers behave better than your students?" the captain asked.

It was only a second or two, but Meg felt as though it was a good minute before she was able to respond. She would never have imagined her CO knew a thing about her. "Far better-behaved, sir. Thank you for asking." Meg did not think it sounded like her, but at least she had kept her voice steady.

"Please go in. I think you will recognize some familiar faces. They're probably all near the punch bowl."

Meg nodded and smiled before pressing into the crowded room. The architect had designed the house for entertaining and the current guest of honor in the drawing room was the ten-foot-tall Christmas tree, decorated with small white lights and red bows. Each bow was tied precisely, as suited a naval household. As she was estimating the tree had at least 250 bows as well as small anchor ornaments, she felt a hand on her elbow.

"Hello. I'm happy to see you here." Meg was surprised by her tutor from the morning smiling at her. Suddenly it clicked. Lieutenant Lyall McClaren. He laughed at her expression as she made the connection.

Meg grasped desperately for something to say. "It's a beautiful tree. Did you help tie the bows?" Why had she said that?

Lyall chuckled. "I did growing up, but I had a good excuse to get out of it this year. I think my sister helped my mother. Have you met Mandy?" Suddenly, there was a slightly shorter, female version of Lyall standing next to her.

"I'm so glad to meet you. I'd like to join the WAVES. The uniforms are gorgeous. What's it like? What do you do?" Mandy's words spilled out of her as she bobbed on her feet. Meg marveled at how the entire family had such enthusiasm.

"I work on logistics," Meg said with a smile. Finding a good one-word answer for the public when asked what she did was the first thing she had done well this evening. She was glad she could not see Aunt Isobel. Her eyes were still smarting from the mistake of grabbing her arm.

"I'm a freshman at Goucher, studying art history, but I really would like to leave school and join the WAVES."

"You can't be an officer unless you have your degree, so you should stay in school until then. There are plenty of other ways to help the war effort while you go to school," Meg lectured, realizing she was using her teacher voice.

"That's what Pops says. I thought he was making it up. But if you say so, it must be true." Mandy gave her a big smile. "Nice to meet you," she said, and wandered off to a group of young men who were waiting for her.

"Right answer, Lieutenant. My parents barely got her into college. She can't leave now." He grabbed her arm and turned her toward the other side of the room. "Let's get something to drink."

As they approached the drinks table, Meg saw Lieutenant Prescott on punch bowl duty.

"Am I allowed to call you Meg tonight?" he asked as she approached the bowl. "What can I get you to drink? Punch or lemonade?" His eyes met hers as she started to ask for punch, and she could tell by his expression that he had just remembered where they had met before.

She felt bile start to fill her mouth, swallowed, and mumbled, "Sorry, not thirsty." She knew she had been rude to both Lieutenants Prescott and McClaren, but she needed to get as far away from them as fast as possible. As she made her way through the crowded, noisy room, she felt like she was walking on the dreaded balance beam during a long-ago physical education class as her sweaty feet slipped on the lacquered wood. *One foot in front of the other*, she told herself. *One foot in front of the other.* Thankfully, on the opposite side of the room, she found an alcove leading to an enclosed patio whose windows were lined with blackout drapes. In this area it was quite a bit colder, raising goose bumps on her arms, but from here, she could peek around the corner and watch undisturbed as the single male officers flirted with the many young women not in uniform whom she assumed were a combination of civil servants, family friends, and perhaps Mandy's classmates.

Meg watched Julie smiling broadly as she danced with Jack Boller. In spite of the strange circumstances of meeting at the Willard Hotel bar, Julie and Jack seemed to be enjoying getting to know each other better. She could see Cynthia happily dancing with Lieutenant Prescott. At one point, a middle-aged couple approached them and as the officer and Cynthia greeted them, Meg felt sure it was Prescott's parents. The man looked exactly like the lieutenant but with grayer hair. Her heart started to race again, and she felt a pulse throbbing in her temple as she thought about Lieutenant Prescott. He had probably already started telling people she had been a servant. She needed to find somewhere to live, not with Cynthia and Isobel, quickly.

"Hey Meg, do you know how to dance to this one?" Meg was at first startled but then had to smile. Being with Lieutenant McClaren was a little like being followed by an enthusiastic puppy. Or, maybe like spending time with a younger brother, she thought, although he had to be close to her age. Maybe even a year older. "I know all the hiding places in this house. You're going to have to do better than this to escape."

"I give up," she said.

"Good."

As he danced with her, he said, "It's funny, I had you picked as a snob. I didn't realize you were shy."

Once she started dancing, the ratio of men to women insured she had a constant partner. Meg danced with Lieutenant Boller a few times when he tore himself away from Julie and then several times again with Lyall, as well as some other officers she had not yet met at work. She even danced with the extremely awkward Commander Lewis, who talked about the weather. Meg found herself starting to enjoy the party. She was surprised when the bandleader announced it was almost midnight, and recognizing curfew, time for the last dance.

Meg felt an arm around her shoulder and came face-to-face with an inebriated Lieutenant Osgoode. Her stomach sank, but she reminded herself he couldn't be too obnoxious when surrounded by others. His voice slurred a little as he said, "You're stuck with me." Meg was mortified, as she could feel his hand moving down her back to try to clasp her buttocks. She found if she inserted a small extra half step as she danced, she could keep her partner just enough off balance to keep him from getting too close. Meg was focusing so hard on this dance pattern, she was surprised when Lieutenant Prescott cut in. Osgoode looked annoyed but moved away to let Prescott take Meg's hands.

"Did you really think you weren't going to dance with me this evening?" Lieutenant Prescott asked.

"Um, well, no," she sputtered. He pulled her closer and thankfully, she had only to dance and not to talk.

He whispered in her ear, "Cynthia sent me over. She said Osgoode isn't your cup of tea." The music finished and she tried to pull away, but not before he pulled her close, squeezed her hand, and grinned at her. "Thank you for the dance, Meg. I wish you could call me Robbie. We both love baseball. We should be friends." He smiled kindly at her and although she was sure he would publicly give her a hard time about being a Dodgers fan, it was hard to imagine him teasing her about being a servant.

Cynthia approached the pair and interrupted before Meg could respond, asking, "Could you find Aunt Isobel? I know where Julie is."

"Sure. I'll look for your aunt. Why don't you and Julie get our coats?" Meg suggested. As she smiled at Lieutenant Prescott, he winked back at her. Meg found Aunt Isobel getting her coat and she nervously approached. She started, "I think I—"

Aunt Isobel interrupted, "I need your arm again, Meg. I'm tired and I don't want to trip in front of all these people." She squeezed Meg's arm and Meg realized her earlier look had been one of surprise, not distaste. Cynthia and Julie joined the pair.

When the group approached the door, the captain said, "Lieutenant, I heard you told my daughter she needed to stay in school if she is going to join the WAVES. Thank you." He smiled at Meg. "Hopefully, she'll listen to you since she doesn't want to listen to me."

Mrs. McClaren, added, "Lieutenant Burke, I hope you had a good time, and that we'll see you again soon," as she smiled at her.

"It was a lovely party. Thank you." Meg waited until they were on the driveway to let her breath out.

"I think you were a hit," said Aunt Isobel. Meg realized she had not asked one person about an alternative billet, and she was just as glad she hadn't.

## 24

———

The next morning dawned cloudless and the WAVES decided to walk to work. They could not talk about their work during their walk, but Meg appreciated the chance to "wake up" and not be as grouchy by the time they entered the security gate.

The topic of the New Year's Eve party came up as soon as they were on the sidewalk in front of Isobel's.

"Meg, where were you?" Cynthia inquired. "Aunt Isobel was going to introduce you to the Prescotts and couldn't find you. It was rude, if you ask me."

Meg rolled her eyes at being called rude but said nothing.

"No one asked you, Cynthia, and I can answer that," Julie replied on Meg's behalf. "The question is, is Lyall a good kisser?"

Meg burst out laughing to cover her embarrassment. "I don't know," she said honestly. "I talked to his sister. Lyall told me about the Christmas tree decorations, but no kiss."

"Sure there wasn't," Cynthia said mockingly.

"He certainly looked at you as if he wanted to kiss you," Julie observed.

"Tell us about who you danced with, Cynthia," Meg requested, knowing Cynthia would talk about partners and dance styles until they got to work. Meg let this go on for several minutes until she needed a change in subject.

"Enough about you, Cynthia. Julie, tell us more about Jack," Meg commanded.

"Um . . ." The normally loquacious Julie was at a loss for words and had turned bright crimson. "He's from Kansas and had never seen the ocean before he took the train to report to Annapolis."

"Having seen the ocean is an important quality in a man," Meg teased.

"He's good-looking, an officer, and he can dance—what more is there to say?" Cynthia asked.

"Exactly. There is no more to say," Julie replied. The WAVES had reached the security gate and she was anxious to bring the conversation to a close.

A week after the party, Vivian arrived at Aunt Isobel's. She traveled with a trunk rather than a suitcase, delivering requested books for her aunt from an antiquarian bookshop in New York as well as more clothing for Cynthia.

"Cynthia, why do you need more dresses?" Julie inquired. "We wear our uniforms for everything anyway. What social plans do you have that we don't know about?"

"It doesn't hurt to be prepared," Cynthia replied archly.

Meg watched as Julie studied her friend for several moments before Julie said, "I hope you know what you are up to." Cynthia scowled at her in reply.

Once in Washington, DC, Vivian had immediately been assigned to work with the group organizing the move to Mount Vernon and within only a few days became an expert. Since numerous newspaper articles had been published about the move, Vivian was the only one of the four who could talk about what she did when she was outside the command. Although it sounded simple enough to move the offices, she pointed out not only how many boxes and people it was going to take to complete the task but also that it had many logistical challenges. Since there was a shortage of available moving supplies, the move would be conducted in phases; as soon as one department began to unpack at the new site, the containers would be conveyed to a department at the old site so they could box their items.

On a mid-January morning, Lieutenant Osgoode approached Cynthia and Meg as he did daily when they arrived and said, "Remember, as you conduct your work, you must maintain absolute secrecy in what you are doing."

Meg thought it ironic that he was the officer who issued the daily blanket secrecy warning given his behavior at the Willard bar. She was still surprised there had been no further mention of that night from Lieutenant Osgoode. Maybe, she thought, he could not remember what had happened or he might be in trouble for drinking with them as he had. He had never apologized for his behavior toward her.

"Yes sir," Cynthia and Meg said in unison. Generally, Osgoode let them get to work at that point, but today he hung around their desks.

"Anything interesting? Have you come across any unusual stations when sorting messages?" The Research Department was currently in what they called a "sweet spot." They had the additives and could decode the Japanese transmissions. All of their efforts were directed to the process of decoding. Meg and Cynthia were sorting transmissions for origin location as rapidly as they could so that they could go to Lieutenants Boller and McClaren for transposition.

"Mine have all originated from carriers in Japan," Meg answered simply. She did not like him standing around.

"I had one from Portugal yesterday," Cynthia said. "I had to look up the station. It was one in Lisbon. The message was short. Only a few sets of numbers."

"Lisbon?" Warren Elliot had quietly walked up behind the trio.

"Paper shuffler," Osgoode mocked under his breath.

Elliot sneered and responded, "Never underestimate using paper as a weapon in the military." Meg and Cynthia frowned at each other.

"Cynthia, maybe you could find the transmission since it is unusual," Meg suggested.

"Did I hear Lisbon?" Lyall had joined the group. "Give me the transmission and I'll start transposing it."

"Bet you I can do it faster," Osgoode taunted.

"Are you a gambling man?" Meg asked, surprised when Osgoode challenged Lyall.

Osgoode laughed. "Only when I know I'll win. By the way, I won big with my bet on the Orange Bowl. 'Bama beat Boston College."

Cynthia had started sorting through the folders on her desk and as Meg joined her to help search, Cynthia asked, "Should I have pointed it out sooner?"

"It's unusual," Mr. Elliot answered before Meg could say anything. "And perhaps something we can understand and use. All of us know more about Europe than the Far East."

"Here it is," Cynthia said with relief as she handed the slip of paper to Lyall.

Lyall sat at Meg's desk, and she marveled at his proficiency and speed. The Japanese were encoding their message using columnar transposition, which involved writing the code groups out horizontally but transmitting them vertically. Her head swam as she watched Lyall transposing the message columns back to horizontal rows.

He put down his pencil with a flourish and looked at Elliot. "Do you want to do the math or should I?"

Normally, Warren Elliot did the arithmetic, stripping the codes of their additive numbers.

"Here's the right additive page," Elliot replied. He'd stuck his thumb on the proper page and passed the book to Lyall. "You can do it. It's nice to see you do something other than sharpen pencils for a change."

Rather than looking hurt, Lyall gave him a huge smile and replied, "Pencils are my specialty. I earned the knife skills badge in Boy Scouts."

Meg stifled a giggle and she saw Cynthia grinning.

As the others looked on, Lyall ran quickly down the list of numbers and wrote the corresponding alteration.

"That's all I can do," he confirmed. "Time to send it to the 'professors.'"

Meg had seen the people in the far corner of the large room whom their group called the "Office of College Professors." Many of the code analysts were PhDs trained as mathematicians, physicists, and linguists. Everyone knew that the "professors" were critical to breaking the two-part codes. Since the additives were currently known, Meg had only observed a fairly relaxed group of reservists called up from their civilian professions who were working on rote translation of messages using a known code. She could imagine their personalities and the atmosphere around them took on a horrible intensity when they were grasping at rows of numbers and desperately trying to identify some sort of pattern or assign reason to the numerical figures.

"Come with me," Lyall urged Cynthia and Meg. "I don't think you have seen the final part of the process."

As the trio began to stroll over to the corner, Commander Lewis and Lieutenant Prescott entered the room and stopped them.

"What's going on?" Prescott asked.

"Why does it take the three of you to walk over a slip of paper?" Lewis asked.

"Collingsworth noticed a message from Lisbon. I transposed it and thought the WAVES should see how it's decoded," Lyall replied.

Meg interpreted Lewis's lack of response as passive affirmation and was surprised that he and Prescott joined the growing party approaching the "professors."

"So many of you. This must be important," a short man with silver hair said, greeting the group. If she substituted a tweed jacket for the tan uniform, Meg could easily imagine him as one of her math professors. The "professor" teased Lyall, "Good thing you have us around, Lieutenant; you career officers can't deconstruct messages."

The "professor" grabbed his codebook and in a few minutes handed the piece of paper to Lewis, raising his eyebrows expectantly as he said, "Was this what you were expecting?"

Meg glanced at the sheet and saw in careful block letters:

AGENT    IN    PLACE.    INITIAL    INFORMATION TRANSFERRED.

Lewis and Prescott exchanged a long look. Meg thought about her training at Smith. At Indoctrination, the objective had been to figure out the cipher and to put numbers or letters into some sort of meaningful language. She had not thought about what would happen when the message was ambiguous and the enemy's intention not self-evident.

"Prescott, my office. NOW!" Lewis demanded, and the two men walked off in lockstep.

"Glad it made sense to them," Cynthia said with a toss of her head.

Although the office door blocked the actual words of Lewis's tirade, Meg could easily discern that he was not happy about the recently decoded message. Lyall was staring at the door as if it held the answer to why there had been such an emotional reaction to six words.

"Well, I'd better get back to work," he announced to the WAVES. "Those messages are not going to transpose themselves."

"And we'd better sort so you have something to do," Meg agreed.

As Meg and Cynthia headed back to their desks in the opposite part of the room, Cynthia whispered, "Why don't we go down the hall and grab a cup of coffee with Julie? I think Lewis woke up on the wrong side of the bed. We should give him some space."

Walking into the room that she had mentally named "Julie's Lair," Meg could not believe her roommate's progress.

"Julie, everything is put away." She looked around admiringly. "Where did you put all the boxes of overflowing paper?"

"It's only 'sort of' organized," Julie confessed. "We sorted everything by country and placed it in segregated file cabinets. The volume is overwhelming. There are more than twenty thousand messages a month."

Cynthia whistled.

"I'm impressed. Did one of your brothers teach you to do that?" Meg asked. "Why didn't you ever use that at Indoctrination?"

"Not ladylike, I guess," Cynthia replied, but Meg noted she was flushed with pleasure at the compliment.

"Definitely not ladylike," Julie confirmed, "But I agree, very impressive!" Julie turned to gesture at the files and closed boxes. "Once we move, I need to file things chronologically and do more refining of the filing system, but I couldn't think when surrounded with complete chaos. The timetable for the move has me second-guessing what to do next."

"What do you mean?" Cynthia asked.

"I'm sure boxes will be dropped and any system I design will need to be reapplied. I want to get to work, but I don't want to waste too much time doing something we will end up doing again. I also want the information to be available now," Julie replied.

"You're right about needing to have the information at hand. We haven't stopped working on codes because of the move, so you can't put the communications in storage," Meg agreed.

"Actually, she could put the older messages in storage," Cynthia objected. "They're never going to get to those until maybe after the war."

"I don't want them out of sight. There is so much focus on breaking code, sometimes I think the rest of you forget about the messages. It's not just flimsy slips of paper. They provide important intelligence," Julie said.

"In fact," Cynthia lowered her voice to a whisper, "one of those pieces of paper this morning said 'agent in place.'"

"Really? Intriguing." Julie looked surprised.

Cynthia continued in her normal voice, "Just goes to show anything's possible. For example, a girl who got a 'C' in high school trig gets to work with the smart people." The three WAVES laughed.

"By the way," Julie had a twinkle in her eye as she looked at Meg, "Lieutenant Prescott has already come in and pulled a few older transmissions he thought could help him understand something he was working on. He came back with a few of the 'professors,' who asked me to show them the system."

"Did Jack get a special tutorial?" Meg asked. Julie's blush was the only answer Meg needed.

"Has Commander Lewis seen your progress yet?" Cynthia asked.

"He stopped by and asked me if I had burned all the communications because I didn't want to do the work," Julie replied.

Meg giggled. They were quickly learning their commander had a fairly short fuse and an extremely acerbic wit. This morning's strong reaction to the decoded message was not the first time she had seen an emotional outburst. In her first weeks on duty, Meg had witnessed Lewis's almost fanatical devotion to his position. He frequently worked more than fifteen hours a day and was known to sometimes sleep in his office. His stooped frame suggested he had taken on the responsibility of the war single-handedly. Meg was thankful it was Prescott rather than she who had to work closely with him.

"Lewis also said," Julie continued, "women were more suited to the housekeeping of code-breaking."

"Oh, Julie," Meg commiserated even as she was impressed with how calmly and matter-of-factly Julie was taking on the responsibility and leadership for a task that probably still needed an official Navy title and code.

"I know. On the other hand," Julie smiled, "he did tell me that as soon as a few enlisted women were available, they could be assigned permanently to me so I could direct their work. You met the wonderful civil servant who initially joined me, but I only had her for a week. I had to give her back, along with the three enlisted men who were helping me get the papers into the drawers."

Julie put her hands on her hips as if she were about to scold them. "Not that I'm not happy to see you, but why aren't you doing whatever it is that you do?"

"Lewis stormed into his office and I, for one, am hiding. Besides, we are more than a day ahead of Lyall and Jack transposing," Cynthia replied. She looked around the room and continued, "Not that you don't need help, Julie, but they need more people who can transpose," and looked at Meg as she said *transpose*.

Changing the subject, Meg wondered aloud, "I've yet to figure out why Lewis is in charge. He doesn't seem to work on the codes very often and doesn't seem to enjoy or have the experience managing people."

"My bet is on the rumor that he was a divinity scholar who was good at translating Bible texts," Julie suggested.

"You think he is short-tempered because he wants to be back in the library with his ancient scrolls?" Meg asked. She turned to Cynthia. "Can't you call a brother and find out what the story is?" Cynthia only shrugged her shoulders.

"We should get back," Cynthia replied.

## 25

———

Within three weeks of her arrival in Washington, DC, Meg was adept at organizing communications by station and by type. Meg was ready to do more. She remembered her Indoctrination training and Lieutenant Carrington starting every lesson by having them count the frequency of letters, symbols, or numbers in their transmission. Meg started to sort not only by station number, but also by messages with similar patterns, adding brief notes to outline the patterns she had observed. When she completed her work, she started using graph paper to rearrange the transmission from its vertical order to horizontal order. Meg was proud of her neatly organized folders of communications prepared for the next group to subtract the additives.

"It's time for you to join the analysts and stop sorting their work," Cynthia told her.

"I am not sure if I'm ready yet. This isn't like teaching. If, at the end of the period or the end of the day, I felt like I hadn't gotten through to the students, I could always come back and start again the next day. I might have to reteach a class or identify a few students to stay in at lunch so I could coach them, but no one was going to get hurt because they didn't understand a math concept the first day. When I see things that say 'Secret' and 'Top Secret' on them, I find it not only a bit strange but also frightening. There's such a small margin of error in what we're doing."

"The margin of error for you is tiny!" Cynthia retorted. "The transmission has already been sent. The sorters performed the initial triage and decided to send the message. If you can figure anything out, you're value added. I think you're ready. You've already noted a couple of patterns the cryptologists said probably weren't coincidences. Meg, I am going to be sorting the entire war, but you can pick out the signal from the noise. Don't feel you have to keep me company."

Meg did not tell Cynthia the real cause of her reluctance to move from sorting to analysis. Butterflies filled her stomach when she wondered whether she, a novice high school trigonometry teacher, could have anything to contribute to the work of brilliant people, with credentials from the best universities in the world. Especially when Lieutenant Prescott, and possibly others, knew about her domestic employment. It felt much safer to sort and to volunteer to pack as the February moving date grew closer.

While she was lost in thought, Lyall rushed, or Meg thought bounded, over to their desks, interrupting her meditation.

"Hey Meg, Cynthia. Lewis is back from a meeting. He's calling us all together for a brief."

They exchanged glances.

"Just because Commander Lewis has told us to gather immediately doesn't have to be bad news," Meg said quickly.

"Maybe he finally got our specific move time," Lyall said, trying to mirror Meg's upbeat tone.

Unlike other departments in the building, the Research Desk still did not have an official move date.

"Or maybe he'll compare us all to apes," Cynthia concluded pessimistically.

As Meg, Lyall, and Cynthia moved closer to the group of desks near Lewis's office, they saw the commander pacing among the desks, completing a circle, turning, then retracing his steps in the other direction. Feeling the tension, the officers sat quietly, staring at their desks, occasionally stealing frightened glances at each other. Finally, he erupted. "This is not a university lounge! I'm tired of you sitting around and drinking coffee as if you are discussing an academic problem. We have a war to win. You've got to increase the volume of messages you are processing. No one goes to lunch until I have an uncoded transmission from each of you."

As he stomped off and slammed his door, the group remained seated. They were drained and had not had a day off since before the New Year. The remaining officers looked at Lieutenant Prescott for confirmation that they needed to skip lunch. He shrugged his shoulders. "Give it a few hours. He'll calm down." Prescott sighed. "At least he usually does."

"Maybe he could take a look around," Osgoode grumbled. "With all these new arrivals we don't have the space we need. We're using the same desks for three eight-hour shifts, so the desks never get clean. We can't let the janitors in, so we burn our own trash. I thought the WAVES were supposed to come in and clean, but they are just adding to the mess." Osgoode stopped to glare at Meg specifically as he said that before continuing, "And Lewis wonders why we aren't getting anything done." Meg felt her face flush as she stole a glance at Julie, who was looking pointedly at the floor.

Cynthia spoke up. "If you think the dirty desks are the problem, let me point out some real problems: the lack of fresh air, the noisy heater, about-to-burst-boiler, poor lighting, and the horrible toilet facilities." Cynthia turned to glare at Osgoode. "Try walking as far as we do every time we want to use the head."

"Much of that should change once we move," Lieutenant

Prescott responded. "I know it's a tough situation, but we are going to eliminate a lot of those issues in just a few weeks."

Meg said softly, "People are our critical resource."

"What do you mean, Lieutenant Burke?" Lieutenant Prescott asked.

"We do our best work when the Japanese get tired and we can exploit their mistakes. We need to make sure we aren't so tired that we are making mistakes that the Japanese can benefit from. We have to keep our spirits up."

"What do you suggest?"

Meg tried to use her best schoolteacher voice. "We need a field trip."

Lyall called out, "Dinosaur bones."

Prescott sighed. "Osgoode, McClaren, Collingsworth, Bowen, and Burke. You've got two hours to get some fresh air. I'll let the rest of you go later this afternoon. Walk quickly so I can count it as P.T. Hurry. I'm giving you a five-minute head start before I go in and tell the commander I released you."

As the group left, Meg saw Mr. Elliot, sitting at his desk scowling at the group. She realized Lieutenant Prescott hadn't even thought of releasing him.

The group did not make it to the Natural History Museum. As they started to walk the Mall, they found a hot dog vendor and after an early lunch in the fresh air, felt ready to go back.

"I wonder if Robbie is in the Brig," Lyall joked as they went up the stairs to their corner of the building.

"Not helpful. You really don't have a brain," said Cynthia. "Although," she turned to Lyall and lowered her voice, "make sure you keep Thursday evening free. My aunt is giving a dinner. I've already invited Jack and Robbie."

Lyall smiled. "What about . . .?" He jerked his head in Osgoode's direction.

"No," Cynthia replied. Meg had not heard about the dinner and for a moment wondered why.

Lieutenant Prescott was waiting for them when they walked

in, looking pale and as though he had a terrible headache. She knew Lewis had vented his frustration about the group's lack of progress for some time to his assistant. She hoped Lewis's complaints had been about how slow the work was progressing in general rather than directed specifically at the lieutenant.

"Lieutenant Burke, I want you to come with me," Prescott announced.

"Sure," Meg replied, and gave him a smile of encouragement.

"I'm going to have you start working on transposing the water transport transmissions." As they walked toward Elliot's desk, he said in an undertone, "I reminded Lewis of your math background and your test scores."

Meg, looking at him with concern, said, "I never studied cryptology."

"Neither did I, but it is not stopping me, is it?" He laughed in a timbre more resentful than humorous. It did nothing to relieve her anxiety.

He stopped laughing when he saw Meg's face. "Don't worry. You're more than ready to do some analysis work. From the notes I've seen, it looks like you're already doing seventy-five percent of your new tasking. Besides, the idea isn't for you to start identifying algorithms; I'm just moving some people around to see if we can use our resources better."

"If you think I'm ready, I'm happy to give it a try." Although her stomach was madly flip-flopping with nerves, she tried to give Robbie a smile to indicate her thanks. She started to reach out to put her hand on his arm and caught herself. Instead, she asked, "Is Mr. Elliot going to be okay with me branching out to work on this? What will he be doing?"

"What he is always doing: overseeing the technical aspects of code-breaking."

It was on the tip of Meg's tongue to ask, "Which is?" but she saw Robbie's wan face and instead suggested to him, "Maybe a cup of coffee would help. Do you want me to get some for you? Can you take a moment to eat something?"

He shook his head and said, "Just continue to check in with Elliot so he thinks he's overseeing your work." More loudly, he said, "Think of this as your call up from the Minor Leagues, Burke. Make the Dodgers proud." As he gave her a parting smile, some color shot into his pale face.

"Mr. Elliot, I was just speaking with Lieutenant Prescott and . . ." Meg had barely started speaking when Mr. Elliot interjected, "And you are going to go and work with Lieutenants Boller and McClaren."

"I think it's temporary," Meg stammered apologetically in reply.

"And here I am to whisk her away," Lyall interrupted, and took her arm at her elbow to guide her toward his desk in the other corner of the room. It was closer to the bank of windows, and with the extra light she could see the profusion of cobwebs and water stains at the corner of the ceiling. Once seated, Lyall mimed putting glasses on and adjusting them so that he was looking over them.

He began in a donnish tone, "Let's review what you learned. You've demonstrated some skills, but much of your training may have atrophied while you've been sorting transmissions."

Meg started to giggle, in spite of her nerves.

"No. No laughing," he continued in the same tone. "This is *very* serious business." He pulled a piece of graph paper out of his desk drawer. Holding it a few inches above the desk, he let it drift to the table while saying, "Lieutenant Burke, I present our Rosetta Stone." Meg was shaking as she tried desperately not to lose control laughing.

"See? It's not going to be as bad as you think," Lyall said reassuringly in his regular voice. "Remember, your primary job is to transpose columns of transmission to rows. Once you get over the mechanics of transposition, you will start to notice when you see frequent repeats; you should circle them using red pencil. In Japanese there are frequently occurring pairs of vowels such as *o-o, u-u, a-i,* and *e-i.* If you circle them, it makes the 'professors'' jobs easier."

After her quick tutoring session, Meg was working on transposing her first real communication. At first, she saw a sea of four-digit numbers, but after taking a deep breath she found drawing arrows helped her transpose the numbers. Once rewritten, she noted a few digits that seemed to repeat or to be in the same place in multiple messages. She assumed the repeats might be things like wind velocity and directions, as well as air and water temperature. Once she relaxed, Meg found the exercise was a repeat of what they had learned and practiced while they were still at Smith and, perhaps, a little easier since she just had to worry about moving the numbers rather than decoding them.

The next morning at breakfast, Cynthia spilled coffee on her uniform and told Meg and Julie to leave without her; she and Vivian would take the bus. As she entered the workspace, Meg was relieved to see that Lieutenant Osgoode was not waiting for them at her desk. In fact, she and Warren Elliot had their part of the room to themselves. It was eerily quiet.

As Meg sipped her coffee and tried desperately to wake up, Elliot startled her by saying, "Before the war, I led a department."

Carefully, in an even tone, she asked, "Could I hear more about how you became part of code-breaking?" She quickly followed up by saying, "That is, only if you want to tell me."

"I was recruited from the Department of Agriculture, where we were using statistical analysis to model crop rotation best practices. The government started looking for people with a math background and suggested I apply to OP-20-G. I did. Especially when we were all code-breakers. What did you do before the war?"

"I taught high school math," Meg replied.

"First in your family to go to college?"

"Yes."

"Me, too. I finished a year at Georgetown, but college is expensive."

"It is," she agreed. "I was lucky. Two of my brothers helped so I could finish."

"I don't have any brothers to help." He smiled ruefully. "My father grew up on a farm in Maryland." Meg nodded, hoping if she did not say anything, he might continue sharing his background. She had watched Aunt Isobel use this technique during dinner and thought maybe thoughtful silence could work for her.

"During World War I, my father reported to Washington, DC, when called up, but the war was over before he deployed. He gained plumbing skills as part of his training and decided to stay here. He met my mother, who had recently emigrated, at church here in DC."

"I thought you were Black Irish, like me," she said, pointing to her hair.

"Nope. Mine is from my mother," he said, smiling at her. Meg noticed for the first time that when he didn't have a frown on his face, he really wasn't that bad-looking.

"My father understood pipes. He could identify where the problem was in any system more quickly than the man with whom he apprenticed."

Meg said kindly, but truthfully, "He probably could help us find patterns here, couldn't he?" She was embarrassed when she saw tears in Warren's eyes after she said that. "Two of my brothers were electricians at the shipyard before the war. It was good work. Did you ever think about being a plumber?"

"I worked with my father during the summers. It was hot, smelly, dirty work, but we were always busy. One of the truths about DC is there is never enough housing for all the people who are drawn here. People are always piecing together buildings; everyone is desperate for a place to live, so the buildings are shoddy." He paused and smiled. "There was always plenty of business and my father started to dream. He wanted me to go to college. Probably like your folks," he added.

Meg nodded.

"Unfortunately, just after I started at Georgetown, my father had a heart attack. There was no way for me to keep the business going. I didn't have the skill or the love for the trade my father had. I also couldn't stay in school. One of my professors suggested the civil servant exam, and here I am."

"Here we are," Meg agreed.

"The civil service is the only way someone like me could get this position. It's on merit. I took a test and showed I was qualified for the position. Government managers could only hire from the list. I couldn't be here if I needed a favor." Meg silently agreed with him. "Did you pass a test to get your teaching position?" Warren asked.

"I knew the principal," Meg replied.

He was silent for a moment. "You're wondering why I am not in uniform?"

"Not really," she said. "Two of my brothers failed the medical. We have terrible eyes in my family."

"Not you, though."

"True, not me. I must have gotten my mother's eyes, the way you got your mother's hair." She thought of Tom and wondered who he might be driving at this moment. Was he still tracking the European and Pacific battles, using pushpins on his world map? She hoped he talked to some interesting people while he was driving today. She wished there were a way he could join her on this project. She was convinced he could see patterns that she could not even imagine existed. She was so busy thinking about Tom, she had not been listening closely to Warren explain about his flat feet and why that disqualified him for military service.

"It was just as well because I did not play sports in school beyond a few mandatory gym classes I willed myself to pass. I had no idea how I was going to get through boot camp." She realized she must have been making the correct responses because Warren was still talking. "We practice singing on Thursday evening and we need more singers," he continued. "Do you sing in your home parish?" *Sing. Parish. Church choir. If only I could put clues together like that using only half my brain, I could easily translate these communications,* she thought.

"No. I didn't sing at home. My schedule was packed with school and more school." Meg regretted saying that as soon as it left her mouth. Warren had just told her about having to leave school.

"Could you come to practice this week? It's just down the street."

"Sure." It was the last thing she wanted to do, but she felt she should go at least once as an apology.

"Great. We can get something to eat at the cafeteria after work on Thursday and walk to practice together."

The conversation had happened so quickly, Meg was not sure how she felt about missing Cynthia's dinner party featuring the officers from her command.

## 26

That night, Davis served a hearty bean soup and crusty bread. She apologized, saying, "Today is a meatless day." Inwardly, Meg rejoiced. This was the first meal she felt her family might eat and she felt truly at home for the first time since she'd moved to Washington, DC.

Vivian was telling them the latest about her work to organize the move.

"I have color-coded different equipment moves so that we'll be moving like equipment with like equipment. People really liked that idea." Vivian smiled broadly, and Meg could see how much her confidence had grown in the short period of not being constantly in Cynthia's shadow. "We can't move soon enough. We need the room," Vivian continued. "In my workspace we have people sitting on upturned wastebaskets."

"Is it too much to hope that at a former girls' school we might have a few more bathrooms?" Julie added. "I don't mean to be indelicate, but it's a challenge, especially with the amount of coffee we're all guzzling. We've taken to going to the men's head and taking turns being lookouts so we can use their facilities. We could spend the entire day just walking to and from the few women's heads."

"Meg," Vivian said, "there's an indoor pool at the school and they're going to keep it open for officers."

"Did you ask if that included female officers?" Julie asked. "Based on our first night on duty, when we learned that bachelor office quarters did not extend to female officers, my bet is all locker rooms will be male."

"I'll ask tomorrow," Vivian promised. "I might even get points for showing initiative."

"Meg, dear, did you swim in college?" Aunt Isobel asked.

Meg laughed. "No. My mother let my older brothers take me on the subway to Manhattan Beach. My brother Tom was a lifeguard at the city pool, and I taught Girl Scouts to swim at camp, but no collegiate swimmers in my family."

"Manhattan Beach?" Aunt Isobel asked. "I've not heard of it."

"And that is the charm," said Meg, smiling. "Near Brighton Beach and Coney Island but not nearly as popular. It's much easier to swim without a crowd. When the beach is busy, I can only bob in the water."

Cynthia asked her aunt, "Do you think we will get to the Maine house this summer?"

"I think that depends on whether you all can get enough leave at the same time. I can certainly have it opened."

Cynthia turned to Meg. "I dare you to swim in the water!" Meg looked confused.

"It's very cold," Aunt Isobel clarified. "Most people briefly wade rather than swim."

"I can't imagine we could all get enough leave at the same time," Julie said. "They're staggering the leave for the female civil servants who are becoming officers. I think we were brought on to work all summer so the others can get leave."

"Probably true," conceded Cynthia. "But it's fun to dream of a lobster bake. Yum."

"Once you have had your first DC summer, you will all want to get away to the beach. Unfortunately," Isobel continued, "George Washington chose the location of our country's capital very badly. Washington, DC, is comprised of a fair amount of land below sea level. We don't have nearly the malaria problem we once had, but the climate is damp and, especially when it's warm, uncomfortable. The British Foreign Office has classified the District as a hardship post." Isobel paused and smiled. "British diplomats get extra pay when they are assigned here. The ambassador is allowed to wear khaki shorts, knee socks, high-top brown shoes, and a pith helmet—the same uniform he wears in Southeast Asia and central Africa—if he wishes. "Most of the time, however, he suffers with the Americans and wears a coat, tie, and long pants."

"When Vivian and I were younger, I remember playing a lot of cards out on the screened porch. The air was so wet that the cards stuck," Cynthia said.

Julie looked alarmed. "They'll have to give us our summer uniforms."

"If they don't, they will have a number of passed-out WAVES," Cynthia agreed.

"Oh, they will," Isobel confirmed. "The day the uniforms change to summer wear is a big deal around here. Especially for the Navy. I think there is a special ceremony. Cynthia, Vivian—you might know better than I."

"By the way, Aunt Isobel, we should have an additional four from work for dinner on Thursday. I have confirmed Lieutenants Prescott, McClaren, and Boller. Osgoode will be here as well. I couldn't figure out a way to ask the others without asking him," Cynthia reported.

"Knowing Osgoode, he can't stretch his thirty-dollar monthly meal allowance. I'm sure he was glad to be invited to dinner," Vivian commented.

"Good. Lieutenant Prescott's parents will be here as well. That is one of the reasons we are having bean soup tonight—I

want to make sure we have enough meat to eat," said Aunt
Isobel.

"Unfortunately, I am not going to be able to join you. I have
choir practice on Thursdays," Meg announced.

"Since when do you have choir practice, Meg?" Cynthia
demanded.

"Warren Elliot asked me if I could go with him today."
Cynthia choked on her coffee and Julie laughed.

"Your comedic timing is improving, Meg!" Julie exclaimed.

"I'm not kidding. He asked me to go to choir practice with
him and I couldn't think of a good reason why not. Usually, at
home, I'm involved in something at my parish, and I should be
doing something here."

As the others laughed, Aunt Isobel said, "That is very laud-
able, Meg. Of course you should do that. You're also welcome to
invite Lieutenant Elliot to join us for dinner instead of going to
choir."

"He's Mr. Elliot, Aunt Isobel. Bright enough but 4-F and the
command punching bag. Meg shouldn't be spending her time
with him." Cynthia started to laugh again.

"Cynthia, be glad Meg is gracious about the company she
keeps. Meg, I do hope you can make it back for dessert on
Thursday. Since all of the officers are joining us, I will invite a
friend of my late husband. He and his wife lived in Japan and I
am sure you should find the evening fascinating. He is one of
the few people I know who has some understanding of
Japanese culture." She continued, "Shall we retire to the
library?"

Meg had grown to love evenings spent in the library. The
room had walls of creamy yellow displaying selected Impres-
sionist prints by Monet, Pissarro, and Morisot that Isobel and
Charles had found during their time in Paris, as well as several
bookcases with glazed glass doors holding classics from the last
century and recently published books, including art books in
German, French, and Italian. The wood of the French writing

desk gleamed in the firelight and when the lid of the desk was open, Meg could see the thick, embossed writing paper Aunt Isobel used for her daily correspondence. That evening, while the others were knitting or reading magazines, Meg tried to read news about the war in the Pacific. She looked for names of ships and commanding officers, and skipped to the weather page to see what the weather was like in Tokyo, even if the report was a day or two old. She was grateful Aunt Isobel subscribed to both Washington newspapers and the *New York Times* so she could read as much information about the Pacific theater as she could.

Meg knew that as good as she was at finding patterns and counting repeated numbers, she knew very little about military intelligence. That is what the "professors" were far more likely to know and to use to guide their decryption work. The war could long be over before Meg had the knowledge of those well-established academics, but she appreciated that Aunt Isobel was doing everything she could to help her succeed by subscribing to newspapers and inviting scholars to dinner. She could not help but wonder what Lieutenants McClaren or Prescott heard at their parents' parties or dinners, which might have given them an edge as they did their work. She knew from the Taylors' house that after a few drinks, people were likely to share information they should keep secret. She was sure the same thing happened in Washington. Now that she knew the Prescotts were coming as well as someone with expertise in Japan, she was not as happy about missing the dinner; she wanted to learn what the lieutenant's parents were like. She got up and started looking at the titles in the bookcase in front of her without really seeing them.

Julie called out, "Are you going to read something for us, Meg?"

"Do you want me to?"

"How about *Little Women*?" Cynthia asked. "I want to hear your interpretation of Jo."

"Why Jo?"

"Because you're independent like Jo," Cynthia replied.

"I've never really liked her."

"Why not? I would have thought she was one of your favorite characters." Julie sat forward on the sofa and looked with surprise at Meg.

"Maybe it's because I'm not a writer, but I never could understand her holing up in the attic away from people. More importantly, I couldn't understand her choice of men. Her eventual husband, Friedrich Bhaer, could have been Mr. March with a German accent. Sort of creepy if you think about it."

Julie and Vivian both made faces as they considered the likeness.

"You think Jo should have married Laurie?" Vivian asked.

"Of course she should have," Meg confirmed. "I would have married Laurie in an instant if he had asked. But then again, I always liked the section when Amy is with Aunt March in Europe, terribly homesick, and Laurie is hit by a lightning bolt: Amy, not Jo, was the right sister for him."

"I knew it. You're looking for a rich husband, just like Amy!" Cynthia exclaimed. "That's why you joined the WAVES."

Meg felt her face flush and she forced herself to answer evenly, "No. I just don't see myself as Jo."

"Girls, I think it is time for bed," Aunt Isobel commanded.

Once the lights were off, Meg allowed the tears to fall silently. She was not sure if she was crying from exhaustion, frustration, or fury.

Julie's voice reached out through the dark. "Meg, I'm reminding you Cynthia is jealous of you. Her aunt tolerates her because she is her family, but Aunt Isobel likes you because you are Meg. Cynthia must find a way to show us she's in charge because she knows you lead as easily as you breathe." The springs creaked as Julie rearranged herself on the bed. "Just checking, but you made up the part about Warren, right? You're not really going to choir practice with him?"

"I am going. I made a slip of the tongue and said something graceless. When he asked about choir practice, I said yes as an apology. Besides, I should get involved in a parish here. I've felt guilty about neglecting that part of my life."

"You're going to leave both Lieutenants Prescott and McClaren to Cynthia?"

"Yup. No one will be able to accuse me of trying to marry up if I stick with Warren."

## 27

Meg hoped in vain that Thursday might be a snow day. While eating breakfast and watching the sunrise in a cloudless sky, she realized that if she was going to get out of choir practice with Warren, it was not going to be because of the weather. Choir was not the only thing annoying her. She had grabbed a letter on the hall table in her brother's handwriting only to discover it was addressed to Cynthia. As the WAVES walked to work, Meg tried but could not think of one good reason why Tom should be writing to Cynthia, which in combination with Cynthia talking about tonight's dinner made the idea of going to choir more and more depressing.

As Meg sat down at her desk, she decided she was going to focus on inverting the list of numbers in front of her and worked for more than an hour to process a folder of Japanese carrier transmissions, dulling a half dozen pencils in the process. When she got up to use the pencil sharpener across the room, Warren followed her.

"I'm looking forward to choir tonight." He paused and waited for her to say something. Meg thought he was expecting her to agree with him or, perhaps, make a declaration of her faith. Instead, she responded sincerely but succinctly, "I gave my word I would attend."

When she returned to her desk, and saw heads snap back to looking at desk blotters, she realized most of the working group had been watching the exchange. The "professors" probably thought it was cute. She knew Lyall had not been goofing around with her as much since Cynthia told him Meg was missing dinner to go to choir with Warren. When she got back to her desk, she looked at the list of numbers with such focus they appeared to jump off the paper.

As agreed, she and Warren stopped by the cafeteria to eat before walking to the church. Warren wanted to pay for her sandwich and coffee, but Meg insisted she needed to use her own dining allowance. For most of the meal, Warren talked about the music the choir sang at Christmas; she realized they had little in common other than work, which they could not discuss. Meg had only to say, "I see" and "yes" when there was a lull in the conversation, which, after staring at numbers all day and a headache she could not shake, was the extent of her conversational capacity.

"I think we'd better get started if we're going to be on time," Warren finally concluded. As they exited the gate, he asked, "Are your family regular churchgoers?" Meg laughed heartily but stopped abruptly when she saw Warren's hurt expression. She gave him a gentle smile.

"You couldn't know. I don't talk about it and you didn't grow up with me. People joke that my mother has better attendance at our church than our parish priest does. Every Sunday morning and every holy day of obligation all the Burkes—father, mother, three boys, and one girl—were in a pew wearing their Sunday best." Out of the corner of her eye, she could see Warren's frown was gone, replaced with a slight smile, so she kept going. "My brothers were altar boys and I've been helping to clean the church since I could handle a dust rag."

"You don't talk about your family or who you are at work."

"Just like you, I'm trying to get the job done. Talking about my personal life could only be a distraction. Besides, there really isn't that much to talk about. I haven't traveled. No one wants to hear about how I listen to baseball games and do crosswords."

"I'm sure there is much more to your life than crossword puzzles."

"You're right. Crosswords and grading math homework." Laughing gently, she looked down the block and, thankfully, saw the church. Meg was ready for the conversation to end.

"How do you feel about the job? I mean especially since you're Irish. Does it ever bother you that you are helping the British?" Warren's question asked in public, on a busy sidewalk, shocked her. She made herself take an extra breath, forcing oxygen to her brain before answering. This felt like a subtler test than when Lieutenant Osgoode tried to ply the WAVES with alcohol weeks earlier, but she reminded herself that she was good at tests.

"As an American," she emphasized, "I'm happy to make coffee and help with filing so our servicemen can do their jobs."

Warren frowned at her answer but did not have time to ask further questions as they entered St. Patrick's. With its familiar scent, a combination of candles, incense, and more than a hint of musty air, Meg immediately felt at home. She stood for a moment looking at the pamphlets in the vestibule advertising different religious societies, reporting on overseas missionary work, and soliciting war relief funding. She laughed at herself when she noted the pamphlets were alphabetized by organizational name. *Burke, this is not code-breaking*, she told herself sternly. Although she had never attended this particular church, she realized she could probably guess where everything was. Compared to the past several weeks in Washington, DC, she did not have to pretend here. Tonight, she was not a visitor in a foreign land where she knew nothing of the local customs. She found the vigil candle and genuflected.

Obligations completed, she looked up and saw the dozen or so choir members milling near the side of the altar. She and Warren were easily twenty and maybe thirty years younger than most of the singers. Warren was one of only three males, including the choir director, in attendance. Groaning inwardly, Meg walked deliberatively over to the expectant group. Warren quickly sidled next to her before she could introduce herself. He stood up straight and had a smile on his lips.

"Let me introduce Lieutenant Burke, who is joining us from New York City."

As Meg moved to take her place, she heard whispers about her "dashing uniform" but quickly forgot the awkwardness once the choir began warm-up exercises. For a few minutes, her mind was free of everything but the notes she was singing. It was like swimming for her, without getting her hair wet. Unlike swimming, where she knew she was talented, she was only a passable singer, but she could easily hide her shortcomings within the collective tone of the group. Or so she hoped. Unfortunately, but not surprisingly, the choir was not very good. Every song but one was slightly flat. The recessional hymn was sharp. She thought of the dinner party at Aunt Isobel's as they reviewed several bars of music yet again, because two of the singers were starting too early, and she sighed inwardly. She was not sure if it was rude to mimic the singing to her housemates. Could they appreciate the joke? By the time the director, Mr. Kelly, announced a break, her headache was back and she was no longer mentally joking about the situation.

As the group milled around, a woman barely five feet tall, with gray, curly hair and a once bright flowered dress now faded to muted circles of color said, "I'm Jane. We used to have cookies or cake during the break. With rationing, we only have black coffee." She smiled. "It's probably better for our waistlines." She looked admiringly at Meg. "Even at your age, I'm not sure I could have fit in a uniform like that."

"The design helps a lot," Meg assured her. "But the Navy cafeteria food is quite good. I must watch how much I am eating. We do so much sitting, I feel as though I'm not getting enough exercise." As she smiled at the group, she noticed that the men had not joined them. Warren was in deep conversation with one of them. Although the men were speaking quietly, she heard a phrase now and then and realized they were not speaking English. Meg wondered if they were speaking Spanish. The women were ignoring both men in such a way that Meg thought the pair's conversation was likely part of the weekly ritual. Meg was intrigued.

She walked purposefully to the pair, pivoted slightly toward the other man, and the conversation stopped abruptly as she extended her hand and said, "We haven't met yet. I'm Meg Burke."

The man turned a deep shade of red and put his hand to his mouth as he started to cough. When Meg realized he was not going to shake her hand, she drew it back and looked quizzically at Warren. Warren nervously cleared his throat and his voice broke a little as he said, "The break is over. It's time to get back."

Meg spent the second half of practice half singing and half wondering why the two men had acted so strangely. At eight o'clock, practice finished and Warren said, "Lieutenant Burke, I'll give you a ride home." Warren had a car? How had he gotten it to the church? Why didn't he bring the car to work? Did she want to be alone with Warren in a car? As Meg was trying to think what to do, she heard, "Mr. Elliot, may I catch a ride as well? I know you're going in my general direction."

"Of course, Jane." Meg could hear the disappointment in Warren's polite reply. Meg did not realize she had been holding her breath until she started to let it out. *Thank goodness.* Tonight, she was okay and she could work on her strategy to avoid a ride next time, if there was a next time. Warren led them to a small church parking lot, where an older, but well-maintained Chevrolet sedan stood, explaining, "I don't drive every day. Between my gas ration and the parking issues at the Navy building, it makes more sense for me to take the bus. On Thursdays I drive, park the car at the church, and it is waiting after practice."

"I'm sorry I didn't get a chance to meet the other tenor," Meg said to Warren.

"Oh. Yeah. Francisco. Francisco Avila. He's shy."

"He's a quiet man," Jane confirmed. "The only sound we ever hear out of him is his singing. He's a waiter at one of the hotels and helps around the church. Light maintenance. That sort of thing. He emigrated from Lisbon just before the war." She turned to Meg. "Mr. Avila is probably so tired of talking at the end of the day that he is happy to just be quiet."

Meg thought that if he were so worn out by people, he shouldn't volunteer to sing in a choir, but she was happy to have someone else making the small talk.

"Tell me your street address," Warren said to Meg. "I'll stop and walk you in."

"Oh, please don't stop. I don't want to waste any of your gas ration. Just drop me at the next corner and you won't have to turn the engine off. You can keep going to Jane's house."

"She's a smart girl, Mr. Elliot—you should listen to her," Jane agreed.

After a brief stop at the corner, Meg thanked Warren for the ride, gratefully shut the car door behind her, and relaxed her face. Her facial muscles hurt from the smile she had forced for most of the evening. As she approached the house, it was dim because of the drawn curtains, but she could hear laughter. The dinner guests were still there. The tears she'd felt during choir practice reappeared, stinging her eyes. She guessed, correctly, that the side gate was open and quietly eased in through the kitchen door. Davis looked up in surprise, then smiled at her and said in a low voice, "St. Patrick's choir is terrible, isn't it?"

"You'll have no argument from me on that subject," she whispered back. The kitchen door opened and Aunt Isobel walked in.

"Just in time, Meg. We're having coffee in the library and you can join us." She looked closely at her.

"I most certainly need that cup of coffee!" Meg replied.

Isobel smiled kindly when she saw Meg's face. "More of a good deed than you bargained for?"

"Definitely. Almost a penance."

"Will the evening still count as penance if I tell you there is a slice of cake with your name on it?"

"I'll take my chances," Meg said with a smile.

As Meg entered the room, Lyall, Jack, Robbie, Osgoode, and another man she did not know stood to greet her. Meg moved toward this man, who was slight, with graying brown hair, a goatee, and wire-framed glasses. He wore a dark tweed jacket and a tie embroidered with shields. He extended his hand to her. "Professor John Knowles." He had a slight accent. It was slightly harsher than an English accent but sounded similar. She knew it was not Scottish or Irish.

"Lieutenant Margaret Burke," she said in reply.

"We've been having a wonderful evening learning about Professor Knowles's various academic posts," Robbie explained to Meg.

"Mainly I've been explaining how a man born in South Africa became an international academic gypsy," Knowles confirmed. *That explains the accent*, Meg thought. He said to Meg, "Do sit down and join us."

"Why don't you take my place, Meg?" Lyall offered. "I'll move to the piano bench." Although a generous offer, Lyall was sitting next to Osgoode and Meg did not want to be anywhere near him, especially since she could see Julie frowning and holding herself rigidly on Osgoode's other side.

"Let me take the bench," Meg insisted. "I can't eat my slice of cake if I'm on the sofa." As she settled on the bench, she quickly scanned the room and confirmed that both Robbie's parents and Mrs. Knowles were missing.

Professor Knowles looked directly in Meg's direction as he said, "I was talking about how difficult it is to learn Japanese."

Meg nodded in agreement since she had a mouth full of cake.

"In day-to-day interaction, even the Japanese can be stymied by the fact that there are so many homonyms in the language."

"How do they get around it?" Jack asked.

"It is perfectly acceptable socially to pull out a small notebook and pen and write the character for clarification," Knowles explained.

"Perhaps I should carry a small notebook and whip it out at work when I don't understand what is going on," Julie suggested. The group laughed.

"Is it really Japanese or is it Chinese?" Cynthia asked. "I thought the Japanese used Chinese ideographs." Cynthia had prepared for this guest, Meg thought.

"Yes and no," Knowles replied. "The two languages have more than half of their characters in common, but Japanese and Chinese have diverged and evolved so that each nation has its own writing system."

"I don't anticipate becoming fluent in either anytime soon," Lyall confessed, and the others laughed.

"It's been a lovely evening, Isobel, but I should start back while I still have a hope of catching a bus," Knowles announced.

"It has been," Isobel confirmed. "I hope you will join us again." She looked around the room before continuing, "I hope to see you all again soon."

During the general commotion of putting on coats as the men got ready to leave, Meg noted Julie unnecessarily helping

Jack with his coat. Lyall bounded over to Meg. "Glad you made it. I'm sorry you missed dinner—it was really good. Knowles was fascinating. I wish he could have lectured at the Academy. We might all have learned a little more about Japan."

"So true," Meg agreed as Lyall reached out and clasped her hands in his. Meg looked up to see Cynthia staring at the two of them. "Better get going," Meg urged. "You don't want to miss your bus."

Lyall grinned at her broadly as he called back to her, "See you tomorrow."

Meg quickly retreated to the library to help pick up the remaining coffee cups and ashtrays and avoid Cynthia's commentary. To her surprise when she opened the door, she saw Robbie gathering dishes.

"You shouldn't be doing that," Meg gently scolded. "You're a guest."

"It doesn't mean I can't help," he said quietly. "It will go more quickly if we work together."

"Fair enough," she assented as she grabbed a tray from the side table.

"Sorry my parents weren't here to meet you."

"Are they okay?"

"My father had a meeting at the last minute, and I think my mother felt like she might be the odd person out," he replied. From the little she knew about the Prescotts, she thought that unlikely.

"And Mrs. Knowles?"

"At home with a sick child."

"What was the most important thing I missed?"

"He emphasized how little Americans understand Japanese culture. We already know that, but what reinforced it for me were his examples of the Japanese cultural focus on doing things for the group in contrast to our more likely default to the individual."

She was stacking the cups when she felt Robbie move next to her, almost as if he were about to start to dance with her.

"Do you buy that he is an academic?" he whispered.

"As much as you're an academic," she whispered back.

"Oh, here you are," Isobel exclaimed, and Meg and Robbie jumped apart. "Robbie. You don't have to help with the dishes."

"Sure I do. Especially if it gives me a few more minutes to talk to Meg," he replied flirtatiously.

Meg looked over at Isobel and was surprised to see her grinning.

"I'll leave you to it," Isobel responded and quietly left the room.

## 28

At the Research Desk the next morning, there was no discussion of the previous night's activities. Lieutenant Commander Lewis gathered the group for an impromptu meeting about the Communications Command's timeline to depart for the new location.

"We'll relocate at the beginning of February," he announced. "I can only hope our transfer will go better than the Pentagon's."

"You know what the guard said to the woman going into labor at the Pentagon?" Osgoode chimed in. The group looked at him. "He said to the woman, 'You should not have come in your condition.'" Osgoode paused for effect. "And she replied, 'I wasn't in this condition when I came in.'" There was silence. "The building's so big she got lost for nine months. You don't get it? You guys have no sense of humor."

Meg could tell Lewis had been about to put Osgoode in charge of the move, but now hesitated. Lewis looked at Julie and said, "Ensigns Bowen and Collingsworth, you're in charge." Meg was surprised and relieved not to be included.

"Thank you, Commander," Julie said with a smile. Turning

to the groups, she said, "I've studied military history and I promise this move will not be anyone's Waterloo." Jack beamed at Julie as the group broke into widespread laughter.

Within a day, Julie and Cynthia had created a plan and a timeline. Cynthia readily adapted to her role as stern taskmaster. She was well equipped to frighten the enlisted personnel tasked with the actual packing and physical transportation of the machines. Meg wished Captain McAfee could see the two WAVES at work. Not only were they amazing tacticians, but they were also doing exactly that for which the WAVES were designed. They were freeing men to work on other tasks. The Research Desk was among the first to move and the Navy assigned extra Marines to move their heavy equipment. It was driven in a special convoy up Massachusetts Avenue in the middle of the night.

Although Meg did not feel she was a critical member of the "cipher caper," as Lyall referred to their work, especially since she was working on weather reports rather than fleet code, she was on the list of individuals for the first phase of the move. While her three housemates remained at the main building as part of the cleanup detail, the plan was for her to take the bus to work by herself. She looked forward to the opportunity to do crossword puzzles as well as to work in a building with a reliable heating system.

On February 7, 1943, she reported to her new duty station, referred to as the Annex, near the intersection of Massachusetts and Nebraska Avenues. It was picturesque and expansive, occupying nearly forty acres. From the site, she could see the new Pentagon building in Virginia as well as Fort Meade in Maryland. The buildings were constructed of red brick and had lovely Georgian features including cloisters, but the newly erected six-foot-high chain-link fence and Marine guards indicated it was a secure military compound rather than a college. Later, Meg learned that many of the Marines assigned to Naval Communications Command Annex guard duty had seen traumatic duty at locations such as Guadalcanal. The Marines considered this duty an opportunity for them to recuperate after some of the horrors they had experienced during that campaign.

Much like the brand-new Pentagon, the Navy found themselves outgrowing the campus's capacity from the day they moved in. In response to the never-ending requests for space, large Quonset huts appeared almost daily, their half-cylinders of corrugated galvanized steel marring the campus's graceful landscaping. Every time Meg saw Barrack D, the huge housing facility for WAVES, which had eighty-four bunks on a deck, she silently thanked Aunt Isobel, yet again, for taking them in.

Meg loved her new desk, located in the former chemistry department, whose walls were decorated with unused gas piping, which had once powered Bunsen burners and smelled faintly of carbolic acid. Even better was the ability to swim, as the pool was open to female officers. As she predicted, the one locker room was for the men, but there was another large restroom with a shower for the few female swimmers. Although she had been working on code for only a little more than a month, she found the work strangely physically demanding. Her shoulders were constantly tight and sore. As many times as she tried to correct her posture, she slipped back into a hunched position over her work. It was as if she were instinctively trying to protect or shield the communication slips. She grew tense as the stacks of paper next to her grew. Now, when her shoulders became too tense, she could swim.

She usually went to the pool after work, since she could hide her still-wet hair under her hat during the bus ride home much more easily than when she was bareheaded during work. One afternoon, as she finished a set of laps and tugged her swim cap straight, she heard a familiar voice she could not place say, "You're putting your head back in the water too late. Your face should be back in the water as your right arm is starting to come out. It will cut down on your drag and you won't be as drained. Of course, until you get used to doing it, you'll feel as though you are drowning." The Navy was not stinting on chlorine, and she was having trouble making out the speaker through her burning eyes.

"Why don't you give it a try?" he suggested. "You're going to have to breathe more quickly. You'll feel panicked but work past it."

"Aye, aye, sir." Her timing was off on the first length and she was still breathing as she put her head in. She spluttered and coughed to get the water out, forced to tread water mid-lap so she could breathe, but on the return length, she found her rhythm. She was not going faster yet, but with practice, she could be. The other swimmer was waiting when she finished the lap. After she blinked a few times, she realized it was her CO, Captain McClaren.

"I thought you were going to drink the entire pool. The lifeguard was getting ready to jump in." Meg flushed, but she knew he was teasing. "Could you feel how it will make a difference over several laps?"

"Yes sir. I could feel more pull when my face was already in the water. I can't waste too much time getting a breath, can I?"

"You keep at it. I expect improvement the next time I see you."

The pool was not the only benefit. In just a few weeks, the Annex was not only bustling with activity but also provided some of the services missing in their previous location. Hot Shoppes, known for its milkshakes and sundaes, took over the gymnasium and ran the Mess Hall. Since coming to DC, Meg had developed the habit of skipping lunch. It was a natural tendency when she became engrossed in her work, but it was dangerous for those around her when her blood sugar fell dramatically and she became almost combative. The new proximity of the Mess encouraged her to eat. In fact, Meg was either going to have to do a great deal of swimming or limit herself very strictly as to how many sundaes she could have.

Although now a much longer distance from Isobel's, Meg tried to walk to work in the morning and ride the bus home in the afternoon. One rainy, cold morning in mid-February, when her housemates were still at the old command tying up loose ends, she overslept and was running late. There was a crowd at the bus stop. Even though people frequently stopped their cars and offered uniformed service members a ride to work, Meg was not only uneasy about accepting one alone but thought it unlikely to get an offer. She was walking briskly as the light rain changed to a downpour. The elegant, uniform Federal architectural style of Washington, DC, was more esthetically pleasing than the more eclectic New York collection of nooks and awnings. However, it was less helpful to the pedestrian trying to stay dry.

When a dark Buick with a military tag stopped and the driver leaned over to open the door, Meg was conflicted. As she stood getting drenched and running late, she went against her sixth sense and decided to get in. The male officer driving was a pleasant-looking man with a head full of well-cut gray hair, very white teeth, and a nondescript raincoat covering his uniform. She had not realized how chilly she was until the warmth of the heat pouring out of the vent in front of her hit her face. She realized her fingers were numb and her toes had been curling in her shoes against the cold.

After they had both saluted, he said, "Good morning, Lieutenant. Where are you going?"

"I'm going to the Communications Annex on Massachusetts, sir."

"Very convenient, I'm headed in that direction. What do you do there?"

"I'm unpacking boxes. I'm glad on a day like today to be in the new building. At the old building, on a rainy day, I might oversee identifying leaks."

"What do you do when it's not raining, or you aren't unpacking?"

"Logistics," she said with a smile. "I make sure everyone has paper and pencils. I'm very good at replacing typewriter ribbons. In fact, ribbon replacement is my specialty." The driver grinned at her.

It was not a long car ride and soon he said, "Well, here we are." The man's raincoat sleeve rose as he reached over to open the car door, and she saw his sleeves had bands of thick gold. She was sure he saw her gulp. She had been riding with an admiral. Yet another test. Hopefully, she had passed.

"Thank you for the ride, sir," she said as she saluted.

"Of course. I didn't want you to be late for your watch." And he saluted back.

Meg rushed into the women's head, readjusted her hat, and applied lipstick, hoping she looked prepared for work. She was not the least bit surprised when she arrived at her desk to hear Lieutenant Commander Lewis calling them together for a meeting. As the group rapidly gathered, the man who had given her a ride strode quickly into the room. He took a moment to scan the group, and Meg was sure she saw a momentary smile when he saw her among the analysts.

"This morning I have the honor of introducing Rear Admiral Van Orden to Code OP-20-G," Commander Lewis said. Meg noted that not only did Lewis seem nervous, which did not surprise her, but even Lieutenant Prescott looked uncomfortable with the visit from their distinguished guest.

"At ease," the admiral began. "I know that you are all extremely busy, but I want to take a moment to recognize the dedication and skill of one of your colleagues, Lieutenant James Osgoode, who identified additives after studying over twenty-five hundred Station Tokyo communications to trace similarities in transmission patterns." There was loud applause, as well as a few cheers of "Go Navy" from the Annapolis graduates. Until that moment, Meg had been unaware of Osgoode's intellect or gift with numbers and patterns.

## 29

W ith the move to the Annex, Meg no longer had to worry about Warren's offers to drive her home after choir. He, too, was now strictly a bus rider. Nevertheless, attending choir continued to feel like an obligation rather than a hobby. Meg wondered what her brother Tom would do. She decided he would apply his energy to finding out more about the mysterious male singer, Francisco Avila. During practice she noticed Avila taking copious notes on his musical score. They all took some notes, such as when to over-annunciate or phonetically spell a foreign phrase difficult to pronounce correctly, but to her eye, he was writing short stories on his music sheets. Meg decided to ask him about how he marked his music to break the ice and walked up to him before he started his regular conversation with Warren.

"Mr. Avila, I never remember the symbol I am supposed to use to remember to take a breath before a long passage. Could you show me how you mark your music? I'm sure there is a better way for me to do this."

He quickly gathered his papers without making sure they were in order and thrust them into a folder. "Not yours."

"I know they're not mine; I was asking for your help with *my* music."

"Not important," he said.

"Lieutenant Burke, leave him alone." Warren had come up behind her and had a commanding tone in his voice she had not heard before.

"Of course," she agreed. To Warren she said, "I was asking for help."

"No, you weren't. You were goading him."

Meg pointedly avoided eye contact with Warren for the remainder of the practice. As she rode home on the bus that night, she was annoyed that Warren had rebuked her for an offense she did not feel she had committed. Meg put it down to Warren being upset because she was showing an interest, albeit not a romantic one, in another man.

DURING THE LAST week of February, Cynthia and Julie joined Meg and Vivian at the new site, and Meg was happy to take breaks to sit with them rather than always working next to Warren. "Girls, we've got to try the sundaes," Cynthia insisted.

"You're going to have to join Meg in the pool if you eat too many of these," Julie warned.

"I will happily walk to and from work for these," Vivian said with a smile. "Aunt Isobel feeds us so well, I can't complain. But I have missed ice cream."

Julie burned off her sundaes in a frenzy of activity, as she threw herself into organizing her boxed communication files. Thrilled with her assigned space, which had formerly served as a library, Julie proposed implementing a cross-referencing system rather than just storing the files neatly. When she first suggested the idea to Commander Lewis, he responded, "I'm not sure it is worth the time."

"Sir, let me apply it to the past two months' transmissions rather than the entire depository to test if it is helpful. If not, we haven't lost that much time." She looked at him earnestly and with such enthusiasm for slips of paper that he could not say no.

"Okay. You can have Collingsworth to help you. You've got a week."

Cynthia walked unenthusiastically toward the library, while rolling her eyes at Lewis's retreating figure. She sat down at a table and started sorting the pieces of paper. After a few minutes, Meg heard her call to Julie.

"Julie, I can't read what these messages say, but I can tell they are the same thing. Does anyone look at the addresses or the date and time stamp and check for duplicates? How many times do we have the analysts transposing duplicates?"

"I don't know how they're sorted before they're processed. I can only tell how I want to organize them after they are decoded. Why don't you ask Lieutenant Prescott?"

"I'm always happy to talk to Robbie," Cynthia replied. Meg watched as Cynthia walked quickly, almost skipping, as she went in search of the lieutenant. She brought him back to the library area and showed him why she thought several duplicate transmissions had been processed.

He whistled under his breath. "Sometimes we can't see the forest for the trees," he admitted. "We'll need personnel sorting the messages by date and time as well as address before we send them to the analysts to reduce duplication. We've been replicating a fair amount of effort." Looking at Julie, he said, "You may never have such an important finding. This is your time to ask Lewis for what you want. More workers? Keeping Cynthia? Both?"

"Both," Julie said with a smile. "I asked for a typist and a file clerk when I first arrived. When I was working with the librarian at Smith last fall to develop an organizational plan, we identified three people as a bare minimum for the project. With Cynthia, we can do great things." She smiled at her friend, who was strangely quiet in the face of her important discovery.

"If I call a meeting, Ensign, are you ready to brief the group?" Prescott asked.

"Absolutely." Julie grinned.

As Meg walked with her down the hall from the library to the main decryption area, she marveled at her friend's self-confidence. Meg knew that in a similar situation, she would be a bundle of nerves. Instead, Julie appeared to be looking forward to talking to the group. Julie waited calmly as the group assembled and began once the commander joined them.

Julie spoke rapidly but clearly, determined not to waste their time.

"You all know that I have been working to organize the communication transmission slips after you've finished the transposition and decoding. Today, Ensign Collingsworth noted several duplicate messages have been processed, which wastes your time. Starting today, a process will be implemented to sort by date and time stamp in addition to the station. Second, Ensign Collingsworth and I are going to begin cross-referencing the messages so you can look them up by coding station and time. We've all heard the stories about how you code-breakers have a sixth sense or magic ability to pull out a pattern among stacks of printout. Hopefully this system will make the magic even stronger."

Meg saw Lewis nodding his head. After the brief she was not only going to tell Julie she appeared to have their boss's respect, but also that Jack beamed nonstop at her during her report. Meg wondered what Captain McAfee would have said if she had been there to witness Julie's brief.

## 30

In addition to Cynthia, the Research Desk's first enlisted woman was assigned to type and file for Julie's project. The cross-referencing was a massive undertaking, but the "professors" were soon relying on the ease and precision of being able to look at previously decoded transmissions to provide context for new ones. Commander Lewis had uncharacteristically praised Julie, saying, "One of the challenges to any intelligence organization is that it is usually overwhelmed with all the information that is coming in and it is poorly organized. Ensign, your system is helping us to understand what we know, which is desperately needed."

"I thought my new enlisted woman was going to pass out when I went over the security procedures," Julie quietly confessed to Meg. Because Julie had started leaving early in the morning and was staying late to set up files and organize code slips, Meg had started to take a coffee break mid-morning in "Julie's Library" to catch up with her friend. This pause had the additional benefit of making sure she stepped away from Warren every morning. "Meg, did we look that worried when we started?"

"Probably even more." Meg quietly chuckled. "I remember thinking Cynthia was going to pass out and I assume I looked just as scared. My stomach was doing flip-flops; it was a few weeks after we arrived in Washington before I could eat a full meal. It's amazing to think that was only two months ago. A year ago, I'd just been made head of the math department, but that feels like a lifetime ago." Meg sighed, slowly stretching out her legs and shrugging her shoulders.

"What's upsetting you, Meg? I know you enjoy the work."

Meg raised and lowered her eyebrows noncommittedly and raised her shoulders slightly.

"Warren?" Julie asked.

"Not Warren exactly, but Warren plus choir, I guess. I wonder if the censors think I'm using some sort of elaborate code in my letters to my family. I describe choir practice in detail, since it's one of the few things I can talk about. I even comment on which hymns I know and which ones are new. My letters are unbelievably boring."

"You think you are making someone work as hard reading your letters as you are looking for patterns?" Julie laughed.

"Ironically, I might be." Meg shook her head slightly as she pictured someone with a sharp pencil bent over a desk with a copy of one of her letters, counting the frequency of letters.

"My mother's relief that I'm going to church was palpable in her most recent letter," Meg told Julie. "She's worried I'm going to forget who I am if I wear this uniform for too long."

"Does she worry about your brother, the one who is ship-board?" Julie asked.

"No. At least not in the same way. But he's a son, and more importantly surrounded by men from the neighborhood, or at least from neighborhoods like ours." Julie's eyebrows went up ever so slightly as Meg looked pointedly at her. "I'm not quite sure what my mother thinks about the fact that I live with Isobel rather than work for her."

"Okay. So, lots of positive points for choir for making your mother happy." Julie made a tick in an imaginary box in the air. "I must admit I don't like that it meets on Thursday. That's the one night the shops are open late, and it's fun to walk through the department stores and window-shop even if we don't have enough coupons to buy anything. As the weather gets warmer there will be concerts on Thursday night, which you won't be able to go to."

Meg frowned. "All true." In her best FDR impression, she said, "But war is a sacrifice."

Julie laughed until there were tears in her eyes, but her voice was serious when she counseled Meg, "You need to be careful that you are not completely out of sight or you'll be out of mind. The officers are starting to forget you are one of us. Although I don't think Robbie quite has yet." She grinned. "Neither has Lyall if it comes to it, but," she shook her finger at Meg, "you aren't giving them any encouragement either."

Meg continued as if she had not heard Julie's last comment. "Also, there is a choir member who gives me the willies."

"The willies. Is that some sort of weird Irish condition?"

"Makes my spine tingle, but not in a good way."

"You feel uncomfortable around him, but you don't know why?"

"Exactly. He doesn't seem to enjoy singing. He only talks to Warren, and then only in a language I don't know. He's from Lisbon, so I guess it's Portuguese. It might be Spanish." She paused slightly. "It isn't Japanese."

They both laughed.

"Officers, good to see the library is being used." Lieutenant Prescott interrupted their conversation. "Busy day, Lieutenant Burke?" Meg felt herself blush as she wordlessly nodded.

"The library appears to have a magnetic draw for personnel," Robbie said as his eyes twinkled. "As you were."

Both women watched him walk down the hall before Julie asked, "Still feeling blue, Meg?"

"Not as blue," Meg said with a smile. "But I'd better get back to work."

Meg had barely sat down at her desk and was organizing her piles of messages when Lyall brought a chair over and sat across from her, asking, "What are you working on today?"

"Leftovers," she said with a grin.

"Are you going to share?"

"Only if you want slightly shriveled communications that have been in the ice box for a few days," Meg replied.

"I'm always game. Tell me more," Lyall instructed.

"Most of the group, including you, works on Fleet Code, which is the naval warship encryption system."

"You sound like a teacher. Pretend I'm one of the smart students and you can skip a few of the details," Lyall suggested, and Meg chuckled.

"Alright. But stop me if you get confused," she said with a grin. "Then I will switch back to speaking more slowly." He laughed as she moved a pile of communications from the side of her desk to the center so Lyall could see them, before she continued, "Mr. Elliot and I are working with the water transport code communications, which use a different encryption system. This type of communication is a 'catch-all' for messages from supply ships to people in the fishing fleet. They send messages about sailing times, their noon positions, cargoes, and climatic conditions. I read *a lot* about the rain."

"It may be a 'catch-all,' but those are important details. Those are the sort of details that allow us to flesh out the tiny blips on the RADAR screen to understand if they are convoys or warships," Lyall concluded.

Meg nodded her head in agreement and said, "And the code has been easier to transpose quickly."

"How so?" he asked.

"I haven't taken the time to track it, but it feels as though eighty percent of the messages are about the weather, especially warnings of heavy rain and storm fronts. I noticed the same repeating patterns. When typhoon season starts in May, it will be interesting if the weather messaging illustrates patterns and help us break code the next time the Japanese change the additives," Meg explained.

"Does Robbie know about this?" Lyall asked.

"Do I know about what?" Lieutenant Prescott interrupted. Meg hadn't noticed his approach while focused on explaining the situation to Lyall.

"McClaren seems to feel it is important, so I'd better get a brief right now," Prescott ordered.

Meg looked at him to acknowledge his request and was relieved to note Prescott was barely keeping a straight face. He was playing around.

"It might be easier if I could show you rather than just telling you," she said. Prescott pulled up a chair and sat down next to her, while Lyall remained across the desk from the pair. The room was chilly and Prescott was close enough she could feel his body heat as she organized papers in front of her. She gripped her pen to steady her nerves.

"Do you need me to explain what the lieutenant is doing?" Elliot had gotten up from his desk and joined the growing group at Meg's.

"By all means. You should be part of this brief too. But Lieutenant Burke should start the presentation, as I want to hear her ideas."

She looked up from her papers to see Elliot frowning and rocking slightly on his feet, but Prescott was smiling at her, encouraging her to go on.

"My analysis work is a little different from most of the group's. I concentrate on the water transport communications, which are largely weather reports and certainly have a more limited vocabulary than the Fleet Code. I start working on a transmission the same way the other analysts do. I look down a vertical column and use the current additive to subtract numbers. I then rewrite the numbers horizontally." She stopped and took a deep breath. "But the complexity of the additives is sometimes a little much for the radioman on a fishing boat or a convoy ship. Occasionally, they forget and just send the message, so when an additive doesn't seem to be working, I go back and check if the message is uncoded."

Lyall interrupted, "Didn't you decode a birth announcement last week?"

"That's right!" She smiled in remembrance. "That was a fun message! I've gotten so used to things being complicated, I was surprised that when I used just the code, without any additives, it said, 'Kiko had twins.'"

"Probably the person sending it to the new father was in such a hurry, he forgot to do the extra encryption," Robbie concluded. His eyes twinkled at her as he called out to Lewis, who was walking back to his office from the coffee urn. "Come and hear what Lieutenant Burke is doing with the water transport communications."

As Lewis walked over, Elliot grunted, turned, and walked back to his desk. The springs of his chair squealed as he plopped in the chair dramatically. *Just ignore him*, Meg said to herself.

"Are the fishermen catching anything, Lieutenant?" Lewis asked with a smile. Meg was always taken aback by how much a smile transformed her extremely uptight boss into a real person.

"Honestly, they don't talk much about their catch. I hadn't really thought about that." She paused for just a moment. "But we do know they are fed up with the 'curtains of rain' and that they are 'drenched.' Thankfully, the fishermen are more human than the Imperial Navy." Lewis looked at her quizzically.

"How are they more human?" he asked.

Meg replied, "We know the Imperial Navy uses machines to help encode their fleet communications and to prevent 'silly' mistakes by doing a lot of the adding and subtracting having to do with the additives for the cipher clerks. But the fishing boat doesn't have a machine. If the day's catch is bad or the fisherman had a fight with his wife, his mind is not going to be on communication code. He is not a radio officer. Recently, I translated a birth announcement written in straight code rather than with additives. They are infrequent, but we do get communications without additives. When the fishing fleet makes mistakes, I always give it to the 'professors' to see if it might match anything they are working on. The 'professors' live for mistakes like these because it allows them to test their algorithms and assumptions."

Robbie broke in, "Lieutenant Burke was also explaining that the water transport groups tend to send the same formulaic weather messages or information about their location. She is working with a smaller vocabulary than with Fleet Code."

"That makes some sense." Lewis looked at Meg and continued, "So you have been able to trace patterns more easily?"

"Exactly, sir. There are only so many words for wind, speed, and swells. I don't know if I should call it a crib exactly, but I marked the frequency of numbers we were seeing and then substituted words such as *arashi*, which means 'storm,' or *hakuu*, which means 'rain shower.' Another word I see a lot is *Shōgo*, which means 'midday.'"

"To confirm, Lieutenant Burke, you have been able to decode messages from the water transport system?" Lewis asked.

"Yes sir," Meg said. "With Mr. Elliot's mentoring, of course. If it were not for the work he does on the Fleet Code, I would not have understood how to approach the problem."

"Um-hum," Lewis replied somewhat absently, and started to turn to walk back to his office before stopping. "Good work, Lieutenant. Really good work."

Lyall waited until Lewis was out of earshot before saying, "High praise indeed, Lieutenant. Let me take you to lunch."

"Lewis has an important brief this afternoon, Meg. You just

saved his bacon. He should be buying you dinner," Robbie stated.

"But she would rather dine with me," Lyall countered with a saucy grin. "Wouldn't you, Meg?"

"Yes. Lunch. Sounds good." Meg could feel her face was bright red as she replied, but she was also really pleased to have her work recognized. And it would be fun to go to lunch with Lyall.

"Have a good time. You've earned it," Robbie agreed. He gave her another smile, but Meg noted not the one she usually received that lit up his face. Instead, this was his polite, perfunctory smile. He was not as happy about her discovery as she would have thought. As Meg and Lyall got up to go to lunch, she thought she saw Robbie and Warren exchange a look, but quickly dismissed the thought, focusing instead on getting a sundae to celebrate.

# 31

On Saturday afternoon, Aunt Isobel's house hummed with activity. Isobel had invited several of the officers, including Captain McClaren and his wife, as well as Dr. and Mrs. Prescott, to a cocktail party, purposefully scheduling it on a Saturday so Meg could be there rather than joining late from choir practice. Cocktail parties, Aunt Isobel had explained one night at dinner, were the war-friendly solution for socializing. With food rationing, preparing a dinner, or even a lunch, for company had become challenging. Liquor, however, remained plentiful, and the cocktail party could be an unstructured event from five to seven thirty in the evening. There was no need for seats; people could easily stand with their cocktails in one hand and cigarettes in the other. Meg thought there was the potential for an overheated, smoky room, but could see the appeal of such a party during the spring in Isobel's lovely garden. At Isobel's direction, Meg had invited Warren, but he had declined almost before she had finished asking him.

Davis already kept an immaculate house, but today she was waging war on what Meg was sure was nonexistent dirt and scowling at the windows as if she had missed a spot. Meg retreated to her bedroom to press her uniform and polish her shoes before Davis could do it for her and found Julie with curlers in her hair, sorting stockings.

"You might want to give Cynthia some room," Julie suggested.

"Has she joined Davis on the war against cobwebs?" Meg responded.

Julie laughed. "No. She is a little upset." Julie added, "At you. Robbie said something about his parents looking forward to meeting you and, well, you know Cynthia."

"Why did the lieutenant say that to her?"

"Why indeed?" Julie smiled. "Just give her space. And maybe don't be immediately impressive. Wait until everyone has had at least one drink. Especially Cynthia."

Meg rolled her eyes. "Maybe I should use the opportunity to ask her why my brother continues to write to her?"

"Do you really need an answer to that?" Julie countered.

"But why does she write back?"

"Again. Do you really need me to answer that?" Julie replied as Meg threw a curler at her.

Rather than admit she was nervous about the party, Meg tried to fade into the background. A few minutes before the guests arrived, Isobel found Meg in the pantry helping Davis to wipe down glasses.

"To the library," Isobel commanded.

"Davis needs a hand," Meg countered. "Davis has wiped all those glasses every day this week. To the library," Isobel repeated.

Meg carefully put down the highball glass she had in her hands and silently followed Isobel to the library, where Cynthia, Julie, and Vivian were sitting on the sofa and laughing. The doorbell rang. A moment later, Davis showed the three McClarens in.

"Always the first," Mrs. McClaren apologized. "As you know, we keep naval time."

"Promptness is politeness," Isobel said with a welcoming smile. "Especially since I know I can put you in charge of drinks, Lieutenant," she said as she smiled at Lyall.

"Of course," Lyall said. "The one thing I can be reliably counted on to do well." He grinned at Isobel and then his parents. "What can I fix for you, Mrs. Milbank?"

"A whiskey sour, please," Isobel answered.

"Mother. Father. The usual?" Once she had quickly greeted her CO and his wife, Meg retreated to a corner of the library, where she was willing herself to fade into the bookshelves while noting that the McClarens' usual was a gin martini with a lemon twist.

As the doorbell rang again, Lyall called, "Meg, you're next." She reluctantly left her corner and walked over to the bar. "What do you want? A Coke?" he teased.

"You remember that?"

"Of course. You looked at Osgoode as if he had horns growing out of his head when he ordered the whiskey." Out of the corner of her eye, she could see Robbie Prescott and two people in civilian clothes enter the room.

"The Prescotts are here. Why don't you fix their drinks first?"

He stared at her, started to say something, and fell silent as Meg retreated to her corner. Cynthia got up from the sofa to greet the new arrivals. Mrs. Prescott hugged Isobel Milbank, while Dr. Prescott kissed Cynthia on her cheek.

A few minutes later Jack arrived, and after politely greeting their hostess and his CO, made a beeline for Lyall and the bar. Soon the crowd at the bar included Julie and Vivian; all tried to come up with the name of a drink Lyall did not know how to fix.

"Jack, I need you to take over. I have a drink to deliver," Lyall announced.

Lyall came over to Meg's corner with a drink in hand. "A whiskey sour. Mrs. Milbank drinks them, so you should feel it is a drink for a lady." Meg smiled. He certainly understood how uncomfortable she was at parties. Perhaps even more than Julie did. "I took your dreaded whiskey and added some lemon juice and sugar. Normally, I put in some egg white, but I am not going to use up Mrs. Milbank's eggs after I have used her sugar ration."

"Thanks."

"Sip it," he warned. "It doesn't taste strong, but I promise you it is, especially since you don't usually drink."

"Roger that." She smiled again and saw that Lyall's parents had walked over to join them.

"Lieutenant. Good to see you on dry land."

"Sir. It's nice to see you and Mrs. McClaren."

"Are you as happy as my husband is to have the pool at the new location?" Mrs. McClaren asked.

"I'm a much happier person when I can swim," Meg replied.

"So is he. And so am I," his wife confided.

Meg felt a slight tap on her elbow. "Lieutenant Burke, I don't think you had a chance to meet my parents at New Year's." Robbie and his parents were now in what was becoming Meg's very crowded corner. She turned and found herself at exactly eye level with a beautiful, tall woman wearing a forest-green silk dress, her dark brown hair in a perfect chignon, smiling with the same green-gray eyes as her son. Next to her stood an older version of Robbie Prescott.

"Dr. and Mrs. Prescott, may I introduce Lieutenant Margaret Burke?" Robbie said in a formal voice that made her stomach tense until she saw he was smiling at her.

Meg extended her hand and said, "Very nice to meet you. Please call me Meg."

"Well, then, you must call me Ellen," his mother said, but Meg knew she could not. As she shook Robbie's father's hand, she knew her hand was clammy; Dr. Prescott was certainly aware of how nervous she was.

"Robbie told us you were a math teacher in your civilian life," Mrs. Prescott said. "Is your war work as interesting?"

"What she really wants to know is, are the Navy men better behaved than your students?" Dr. Prescott interrupted. "I can tell you kindergarteners are better behaved than some of the government officials I work with. So, my bet is your former work was more civilized. But was it more interesting?" His eyes twinkled as he waited for her to answer.

"You can't compare the Secretary of the Treasury to a kindergartener, Robert," Aunt Isobel interrupted. Meg hadn't noticed her approach. She had only taken a few sips of her drink. Lyall was right. It must be much stronger than it tasted.

Mrs. McClaren smiled at Meg and said, "Your current role may be easier than if you were teaching. I have been reading that the teachers in the District have had to take on extra war duties. The school board ordered them to serve as wardens to protect the schools. Every night a teacher is assigned to sleep overnight in an unheated building."

"The irony is that they usually don't have a key to the principal's office, which is where the telephone is," Mrs. Prescott interjected. "Those poor women are getting a horrible night of sleep and they couldn't do a thing to help even if they wanted to without a phone." She shook her head. "The organization of the civilian response has been less than efficient." She turned to Isobel. "Do you remember the first meeting we went to for the Civilian Defense Committee?"

"I do," said Isobel. "They expected a couple hundred people, at most, to attend and almost three thousand were there. They underestimated the residents' fear of sabotage and enemy attack. When you declare war on a country, you are by extension attacking its capital city. I think we all feel under attack."

Meg heard laughter from the bar and wondered how she could move toward the safety of Julie and Vivian and away from her commanding officer and the Prescotts, whose verbal repartee she struggled to keep up with.

Mrs. Prescott continued, "They gave direction to volunteers in Dupont Circle that conflicted with those being given other groups." She changed her voice to a low, officious tone and started pacing slightly, tossing an imaginary baton. "'You are getting these directions today. Be aware, they may be changed tomorrow. In a few days or a week, they may be changed back to the original directions. It is not your duty to question. It is your duty to do.'"

"I'm going to bring you in to run my next meeting," Captain McClaren said. "You definitely could be a communications officer!" Mrs. Prescott laughed.

"Well," interjected Robbie. "Could the problem be that the former dean of Harvard Law School is running the Office of Civilian Defense? He can only communicate the theory rather than the practice of what people should do. You can't trust Harvard men to run anything."

His father laughed. "Alright, son. You've gotten in your requisite put-down of Harvard for the evening. Now you can let it go." Everyone else laughed, so Meg joined in, very quietly. When she had worked at the Taylor's house she had heard similar banter, but she had never known the individuals the others were talking about. She was certainly not expected to participate. For a moment she desperately wished for her maid's uniform, which would make her invisible. Being part of the party was much harder than working on Japanese codes.

Aunt Isobel turned toward Meg. "The District is experiencing growing pains. Before Congress installed air-conditioning in 1938, they adjourned in May, or at least no later than June. Congress was only in session for about five months. The professional politicians spent more of the year in their home states. Now Congress is in session all year and we have people leaving their private banking jobs in the North," she smiled fondly at Dr. Prescott, "to work in the federal administration and tell us how to live our lives. It is hard to believe but, before the war, on summer days, government employees had lounged on the White House lawns eating picnic lunches out of paper sacks."

"Meg, does Warren ever tell you about doing that?" Cynthia asked.

"Warren?" Dr. Prescott asked.

"I work alongside several civil servants who have been part of the federal government for several years as part of my logistics work. One of them is named Warren," Meg replied in what she hoped was a bland tone before shooting a look at Cynthia. She saw that Robbie was also glaring at Cynthia. If she didn't pay attention to Meg's warning, hopefully Robbie's look should silence her.

"I wish there were more civil servants who were familiar with the District's traffic patterns organizing and running transportation in the District," Captain McClaren said, graciously moving the conversation to safer territory. "Especially since our command moved away from the Mall. It's really challenging getting everyone from where they're lodging to report to work. For as slow as the buses are during the day, they are nonexistent at night. Almost a third of my people are reporting at night. Even if they could afford a cab, there aren't cabs to take. And yet it could have been worse. At one point, before the Navy bought the school, there was talk of our moving out near Fort Meade. As bad as the public transportation system is in the District, our people would have to have cars out there."

"I'm thankful we have our car," Ellen confessed.

"And, to be honest, my special gas ration," her husband agreed.

"I think the trolley cars they have brought out of retirement are beautiful, not practical but beautiful." As she voluntarily joined the conversation, Meg realized she now understood the saying "liquid courage." "It's like visiting a museum on my way home from work when I ride in one of the wooden cars with the clerestory windows."

"But a historic car almost always indicates we have a new driver who isn't going to know the route and where to stop." Vivian had moved with Julie from the bar to join the group. "We constantly have new motormen from out of town who don't know the streets. At the intersection switching points, often we have to tell them which way the car is supposed to go. Sometimes I think I should drive the trolley! I know the area better than most of the drivers."

"You know, Ensign Collingsworth, that's not a bad idea. It could be fabulous PR for the Navy if the WAVES could get the transportation system organized and running on time," Mrs. McClaren agreed.

"But a loss of some of my best people," her husband added. Vivian flushed at the compliment.

"I am trying to be rational about my commute," Julie added. "I'm never sure of the better approach. Will I have enough ration tickets for shoes if I walk? It's often faster than the trolley or bus stuck in traffic, or do I save my shoes and get paralyzed in traffic?" Julie smiled at Robbie. "What does your mathematical model say?"

"Sleep in your office," Robbie answered.

"You could move into the barracks next to the command," Captain McClaren suggested.

"Hot bedding?" Cynthia shuddered. "No thank you."

"That temporary solution didn't go over too well," Robbie commented.

"It was awful," Cynthia confirmed.

"Not a Girl Scout, Ensign Collingsworth?" the captain asked.

"Oh no. Not me," she replied.

"Doug, do you really think we should have the military step

in and run the District's transportation?" Dr. Prescott asked Captain McClaren.

"Robert, I thought it was your job to make sure the federal government in one form or another eventually does run everything," the captain retorted. The elder Dr. Prescott feigned chagrin. Everyone laughed, even Meg, although a beat later than the others. This was a foreign language for her.

"You're lucky to still have staff, Isobel. It is difficult to keep servants since the war pays so well," Mrs. McClaren commented.

"If we have reached the 'I can't keep servants' conversation,' it must be time to go. Time to make our excuses," said her husband.

"I wish I could offer you dinner," Isobel lamented. "Even chicken is hard to come by these days and never as tasty as before the war."

"Don't be silly, Isobel. No one is throwing dinner parties these days," Ellen reassured her.

Robbie shot the other young men a look. "Mrs. Milbank, the other officers, save the Captain of course, and I need to take our leave. We've got to get back to some work since we took early leave," he said politely.

"That's right," said Lyall, taking the cue.

As the men thanked Isobel for her hospitality and said good-bye, the two older couples quickly followed. In a matter of minutes, the once bustling room was silent. The WAVES and Isobel sat quietly on the sofas. Meg thought Cynthia looked disappointed and upset. Meg looked across the sofa at Julie, who was smiling.

"They liked you," Julie said.

"Yes, they did," Isobel confirmed. "Of course, the McClarens already knew you were a delight, but the Prescotts—Ellen in particular—thought you were charming."

"Meg said ten words this afternoon, Aunt Isobel. How could

she have made any impression, let alone a good impression?" Cynthia said churlishly.

"The important thing, Cynthia, is Meg said the right ten words," her aunt replied.

Julie beamed at Meg from her place on the sofa.

## 32

Meg was happy to be out of the crumbling War Office building and in her new surroundings at the Annex, but there were daily reminders that the facility was still more a school than a naval communications hub. Immediately after moving in, the Navy discovered the existing circuitry could not handle the new electrical demands, which far surpassed the student and faculty needs. Although electricians were working in three eight-hour shifts to add circuitry, there were still times, especially during the day shift, when everyone plugged in machines and the resulting demand blew out several circuits, leaving them without the real-time communication transmission feed and no overhead lights. This morning was cloudy and the room was gloomy with only window illumination. When it was clear that the lights were not coming back on quickly, Meg gathered her bag and announced, "This is a good day for me to go to the library."

Sometimes Commander Lewis sent one of the WAVES, most often Cynthia, to the Library of Congress to look up geographical information about areas in which there were current conflicts. Now that Cynthia was helping Julie, Lewis sometimes sent Meg. It was a task she looked forward to as she enjoyed the research, the walk to the library, and the library facilities.

"It's my turn to look up maritime rosters and look at pictures in the Tokyo paper," she said happily.

"Only ten weeks and you're already fluent in Japanese? Amazing!" Lyall grinned at her.

"It's raining; you'll get soaked," Jack protested.

"I've got an umbrella and I need the walk," Meg replied.

"With those ankles, I'm sure you will get a ride the moment you exit the gate and walk toward the bus stop. What was the Navy thinking? You all should have been issued trousers," Osgoode remarked.

When Meg looked out the window and saw how hard it was raining, she decided against her library outing, put her bag back in the drawer, and got up to distribute the coffee from the urn before it cooled off without electricity for the heating element. When she returned to the group with a carafe of coffee, she saw Lieutenant Prescott had visited the Mess Hall and brought back a pitcher of milk. She was convinced he knew about a secret passageway or had a special entrance at the cafeteria where milk awaited him.

Once she moved around the workspace pouring coffee, an impromptu party started. The number of snacks people were hoarding in their desks surprised her. Jack brought out crackers. Cynthia had a package of Hydrox cookies. Meg saw a bottle of whiskey passed around at desk drawer level, discreetly poured into coffee, and shook her head "no," but she did grab a cookie and moved her chair to the outskirts of the rapidly forming circle of chairs. Julie sat down next to her.

"Meg, by chance did you grab some of the fishing transmissions from their files this morning?" she asked, adding, "It's okay if you did."

"No. The lights were off when I got here. I haven't done anything but serve coffee. Why?"

"Some of the files were in the wrong place this morning. It's probably nothing. I'm glad that the transmissions are useful, and I want them to be easy to access, but I want to make sure only the people who should have access are using them." Julie frowned.

"Should you tell Commander Lewis or maybe Lieutenant Prescott?" Meg suggested.

"If it happens again, I will. This time it was probably just me being preoccupied and not noticing what I'd done," Julie said.

"Good morning," Lyall said to Julie, who smiled as he sat down on the other side of Meg.

Most of the group was arguing about a pre-war football game. Given who was doing the arguing, Meg realized it had probably been between Princeton and Navy. Cynthia was debating heatedly about a play and to Meg it sounded as if she was winning; she remembered as much as the men and understood the strategy. Meg let her fingers warm up on the mug and let her mind wander a bit, especially as the conversation turned to reliving the highlights of the 1942 Army-Navy game in which Navy had shut out Army at Annapolis. Travel restrictions required playing the game at the Naval Academy rather than the usual, neutral, site in Philadelphia, with third- and fourth-year naval cadets assigned to cheer for Army to reduce the home-field advantage.

She realized she had stopped paying attention when Lyall jabbed her. "You're from New York. I'm sure you went to Princeton all the time," he said conversationally.

"Not all the time, but I've been there."

"Did you go to house parties? I don't know how any of the students passed their exams after a weekend-long spring party before finals. I'd have flunked if I had gone to a civilian college. Too many distractions. Did you ever see Robbie at house parties?" he pressed.

Meg chuckled softly and avoided Cynthia's look of disbelief.

Lieutenant McClaren needed to improve his ability to place people socially if he were to advance as far as his father. "No house parties and no football games. I've only been there once, while visiting family who live near the university. We walked through the campus one Sunday afternoon before the war. I remember the architecture was magnificent and there was a beautiful garden in the center of the campus, which was blooming because it was spring. There were arches everywhere. In fact, there was a group singing in one of the arches. It was lovely."

"One of the many tourists. How I hated you." Meg was surprised Robbie could hear her talking to Lyall. "There was nothing worse than not wanting to study on Sunday afternoon and watching all the people walking around campus, laughing and chatting. Used to drive me crazy."

"I'm sorry we disturbed your studies, but surely you didn't mind the student singers practicing. The singing and the arrangement of the music were really beautiful. Did you sing?"

"What you saw was called an 'arch sing.' The acoustics in the arches are wonderful for *a capella* singing. But I never sang. No time with crew." He shrugged his shoulders. "I don't have the voice, either." Robbie gave her a long look after he finished. Meg wondered what he was thinking. He had never said anything to her about recognizing her from working at the Taylors'. As far as she knew, he had never mentioned it to anyone else.

"When you graduated did you think you could be code-breaking?" Lyall asked Robbie.

"Not really. I knew there was going to be a war in Europe, but at first I told myself we were not going to get involved. Once I knew we could be involved, I thought the government might want me to run models for the central banking system, but as a civilian. I could have taken math classes related to cryptology, but I took the ones that focused on economic modeling. What about you? Were you prepping at the Academy to break codes?"

"We trained to serve on a ship or help run a base." Jack joined the conversation. "Not to sit at a desk and have our fellow officers think we're sitting out the war. I've always liked math and puzzles, but I can't wait to get aboard a ship. My classmates are at sea, rising through the ranks. I'm stuck here, and the next promotion board is going to laugh at my desk job. My mother's happy, though." They all laughed.

"Next Thursday night the National Gallery is going to have musicians in the Rotunda. We should all go," Cynthia said as she looked directly at Robbie.

"That sounds fun," Lyall said.

"I'm in." Lieutenant Osgoode was never one to miss a party.

"Sounds great. We could share a couple of cabs," Robbie added. "Of course, that is if we can find the cabs."

Jack looked at Julie. "You and Vivian are coming, right?"

"Of course," Julie responded.

Osgoode asked, "What about you, Lieutenant Burke?"

"It sounds like a nice outing, but I have choir practice on Thursday nights." If anyone but Osgoode had spoken to her, Meg thought, she should have said yes.

From his desk, Warren caught her eye. He had been listening to every word and had two pink circles on his cheeks. He was the only one among them being purposefully excluded. Her sympathy for Warren, even if misplaced, was sending her to practice rather than the concert.

At that moment, the lights came on. Almost instantaneously, Commander Lewis hurried in. "The electricity is back on. The machines are back up. Let's get to work, people. Enough socializing."

Meg grabbed the coffee cups and went to the small galley to wash them. Robbie followed her, carrying some of the remaining spoons and trash. As she turned on the water to fill the sink, he stood close to her to dry the dishes and said under the noise of the faucet, "You should come on Thursday. It will be fun. You know the choir isn't going to fire you if you don't go to a few practices."

"Lieutenant, I will be at choir practice for two reasons. One, I gave my word. Two, as an officer assigned to this command, I'm obligated to support the group's morale. If I go with Mr. Elliot, it might be good for the department's spirits."

"What do you mean?" he said quizzically. She had his attention.

"Think, Lieutenant Prescott. Pretend we're looking at one of your mathematical models and examining the variables. One variable is a civilian man with tremendous experience with ciphers and code-breaking, another variable is that he is constantly being put down."

"I don't put him down."

"You don't overtly put him down, but you don't stop anyone else from giving him a hard time. Every day he listens to the officers complaining about how being here is hurting their naval careers and how they are just itching to leave and to do something to really help the war effort, when codes and ciphers are his career. Now there are even female officers who are held in higher esteem than he is. The other day I briefed you, not him."

"It was your work," Prescott protested.

"Even so," she said slowly. "It can't be easy to be in his shoes. He's about our age. If he were in uniform, he'd be part of the team. Instead, he is even more of an outsider than I."

"Is that how you see yourself? As an outsider?"

"Every day I tell myself I must be good at what I do. Otherwise, how could I have overcome the two strikes against me?" She stopped abruptly. She had just said far too much; she knew the lieutenant was familiar enough with her background to put everything she had said into context. "Please leave the dishes to me."

But he did not walk off. He stayed, drying silently next to her.

## 33

lthough only a few days into Lent, the six weeks of quiet reflection before Easter, the choir began to practice for Easter Mass. The cheer and happiness of the songs contrasted strongly with the quiet reflectiveness of the Lenten church season and Meg's mood. While on duty, she had watched and waited for Warren to leave so she could eat in the cafeteria alone.

Tonight she could barely sing. She kept thinking about Julie and the others at the concert, wishing she had agreed to go rather than attend the unending practice. Meg thought she was going to scream every time the group went flat during the recessional song. During the break, Meg stood on the periphery, watching Warren talking to Avila in the muted light of the sacristy. She often wondered what they spoke about so intently. Cast in shadows in the poor lighting, they looked like characters in a grainy newsreel rather than fellow choir members. Even though she did not want to talk to Warren, she found herself inexplicably annoyed that after she had sacrificed going to the concert for him, he wasn't even talking to her. Meg looked at her watch as practice ended, sure that they had gone at least a half an hour beyond the normal session. Instead, they had ended three minutes early.

While many of the choir members took their music home with them, Meg put her songbooks in the closet that had cubbies for music folders as well as their robes in order of size, from smallest at the left to largest on the right. Tonight, the closet was chaos, with several robes jammed in and cardboard boxes stacked on the closet floor. As she bent down to store her music, she noticed a thin briefcase. She had not noticed any of the singers carrying one, and thought it was a strange item to find in the closet. She was so focused on closing the closet door, which involved leaning against it to get it to shut, that she did not notice Warren walk up behind her and jumped when he said, "Do you have plans for Easter, Miss Burke?"

Rather than answer, she said, "There's a briefcase in there. Is it yours?"

"No. If we both lean on the door, it should close," he suggested.

Once they closed the closet, Warren gently grabbed her arm and guided her toward the main part of the church. He stopped as they reached the altar and, in a tone Meg might almost have called flirtatious, said, "You didn't answer my question. What are you doing for Easter?"

She laughed. "Singing with the choir, of course."

"And after Mass?"

Meg thought quickly and realized she did not have a good answer to his question. Her mother had asked if she could come home for Easter weekend and had been disappointed, but not surprised, when Meg responded that her schedule meant she couldn't get home. Her military life was so different from her family life that she had not been thinking about the upcoming Holy Day as a holiday. She was sure that Aunt Isobel would be able to obtain lamb or ham for Easter dinner and provide a delicious meal for the WAVES as well as several guests. Did Warren want an invitation? Should she invite him?

"I'm having dinner with Mrs. Milbank. I'm sure she would want you to join us."

"Oh." Warren sighed. "My mother wanted me to ask you if you would like to join us for Easter dinner." Meg was dumbfounded, even though she realized she should not be. "Perhaps you could change your plans?" he suggested.

"That's very kind of her, but I do have plans." Meg gulped nervously and choked out, "I'm sorry. I'd better catch my bus, or it will be another hour until the next one." She stammered, "Good night." Warren's bus came from the opposite direction and her bus used a stop across the street, which prevented any need to wait with him. She moved briskly and focused on the traffic to avoid looking across the street and catching his eye. Thankfully, for once, she did not have to wait long for the bus. Dazed, she found a seat and realized the last thing in the world she wanted to do was go to Easter dinner at Warren's and was grateful she had thought quickly how to turn down the invitation. As the bus lurched through its route, she was hit with a powerful, sudden wave of homesickness. She wanted to go to Easter dinner with her family in Brooklyn even if it meant dusting her entire house, cleaning the church, and working the punch bowl at the Taylors'. She knew that it wasn't possible to join them and was glad at least she was at Isobel's.

Going through the side gate and opening the kitchen door, she entered a quiet house; it could be at least another hour before the others returned home from the concert. Aunt Isobel must have heard her footsteps in the hall and called to Meg from the library. Meg had noted bulbs starting to push up in gardens during her short walk from the bus stop to the house; spring was on the way, but she was sure there was a fire in the library, as much for atmosphere as for warmth. Meg sat down on the chair opposite Isobel as the older woman put a marker in her book.

"You don't have to be part of the choir," Aunt Isobel said.

Meg sighed. "I was going to tell the director this evening

that Easter had to be my last day. I got sidetracked before I could resign." Isobel raised her eyebrows slightly.

"Warren's mother invited me to Easter dinner." Meg paused before adding, "I told him I had plans here I couldn't change."

"Which is true. I'm pleased you'll be joining me for Easter dinner." She smiled at Meg. "I know it's difficult going so long without seeing your family."

Meg nodded silently.

Isobel continued, "It isn't going to get any easier to put him off, Meg."

Meg sighed deeply, got up, lightly touched Aunt Isobel's arm, and went upstairs to bed. She had almost drifted off to sleep when she heard the other women come home. Cynthia was humming Vivaldi. She had certainly had a good time. Meg turned in bed toward the wall and put a pillow over her head and feigned sleep before Julie walked in. She did not want to hear about the concert tonight.

The next morning it was warm enough to walk without coats, and the soft air tickled her cheeks rather than stinging with cold. Normally the WAVES had to be vigilant about what they said to each other in public, often catching themselves before talking about a problem or a situation that needed to stay within their office walls. Today all the discussion was about the night before and strictly unclassified. The three concert-going WAVES had a terrific time.

"You *have* to go with us next time," Julie insisted. "If you refuse to come, I'm going to carry you."

"I'll help," Vivian said. Cynthia frowned at her sister, but Vivian ignored her. "As the weather gets nicer, the opera is going to play outside. In addition to selling outdoor seats, the opera encourages people to anchor on the Potomac in boats, listening under the stars." Vivian added, "You must go with us, Meg. Won't the choir take the summer off? It does at our church. Summer is the best time to go to church. No choir and a short sermon."

Meg agreed, "You're absolutely right. I needed to go to last night's rehearsal, but I won't miss any more concerts."

"Well done. Good decision, Lieutenant. You're starting to make your own decisions rather than having them made for you," Julie confirmed.

Meg continued, "On that subject. I got an Easter dinner invitation last night. I fibbed and said I already had an invitation. You know, I was raised to accept the first invitation but I really didn't want to, and I figured it was understood I could have dinner at Isobel's. Still, it was a little unnerving to learn his mother was inviting me for Easter." She knew the WAVES knew who it was from without mentioning names.

"You shouldn't be *that* surprised, Meg," Cynthia said. "You encourage him."

"Cynthia, that isn't fair. Meg doesn't encourage anyone. Lyall asked me several times last night if Meg had ever talked about him and I could honestly tell him 'no.' He looked so dejected I had to tell him that she doesn't talk about anyone. Poor thing. He really missed you last night, Meg," Julie said.

"Meg, I'm glad you'll be with us for Easter," Vivian said. "Every time she has mentioned Easter to me, Auntie has had that gleam in her eye, which means she is up to something."

"What do you think she's planning?" Cynthia asked.

"I assume she's going to figure out a way to feed some of our favorite officers and their families Easter dinner." As soon as Vivian said it, Meg realized that was exactly what Isobel was doing.

Inside the security gate, Vivian was the first to leave the group, and she waved to them as she entered her work area. As they approached their section, Julie said, "Meg, why don't you stop by later? You'll need a change of scenery. You might even want to work in our room today."

"I'm going to go hide behind a screen of graph paper. I'll be all right. I'm made of strong stuff, but I'll stop by mid-morning," Meg confirmed.

Warren almost smiled as Meg walked over to their shared desks and then croaked out a tortured "good morning." Meg averted her eyes as she responded, "Good morning," and then focused pointedly on the reams of paper in front of her. By 10 a.m., the tension became unbearable. When Meg walked into the library, she found the normally smiling Julie frowning at the large microfilm machine in the corner of the room.

"Maybe you should walk away," Meg suggested. "You look as though you might hurt it."

"That machine has become the bane of my existence," Julie said feelingly. "I want to kick it or worse. It's so heavy, though, I'd probably be the one to get hurt."

"Is it broken?"

"The machine isn't broken, but the plan is."

"What plan?"

"You know I am supposed to do two different things. The first is to impose order on the communication records," Julie explained.

"You've done that. Some of your colleagues might suggest there is even a little too much order," Meg said wryly.

"I'm going to take that as a compliment." Julie smiled.

"As you should." Meg grinned at her.

Julie became serious. "Every month I get rolls of microfilm. We have operatives obtaining images of technical documents and periodicals still available in Lisbon, Stockholm, and Dublin. Most of the rolls come from Lisbon since it's a crossroads for both the Allies and Axis. There is still Axis information floating around, if you know where to look for it."

"Do they walk around pretending to be tourists wanting to take pictures?" Meg asked incredulously.

Julie shrugged her shoulders. "We have agents pretending to be librarians acquiring books."

"Librarians?"

"I guess the cover of museum curator was blown in the last war," Julie replied.

Meg laughed heartily before asking, "Do you think we will ever know what Charles and Isobel were up to in Europe?"

"So many secrets have already gone to the grave and I cannot imagine Isobel giving anything away, even under torture," Julie said before continuing, "I have a huge number of images I'm supposed to review and 'look for clues.' Cynthia has been helping me. Not surprisingly, she's better at it than I am. The thing is, what we are working on doesn't seem to relate to any of the work you are doing at this command. If we had Tokyo newspapers or society magazines, maybe we could find something to help the code-breakers. Although neither Cynthia nor I read Japanese, so we could miss a lot of clues. I'm frustrated and in a bad mood."

"Do you give the information to anyone?"

"I make an outline report for Commander Lewis every week, but he never says anything about it. Robbie sometimes thanks me for my work. I assume he has skimmed it once or twice, but he doesn't care either." Julie sighed.

"We both need a break."

"We all need a break," Julie agreed.

# 34

The next morning it was raining, and Meg was once again grateful for her utilitarian Haverstock with its generous hood. The WAVES had briefly thought about taking the bus but knew the rain would only make it even more crowded than usual. Walking was the best option. With their hoods up as they walked, it was difficult to talk to each other, which was probably just as well. As far as Meg was concerned, the topic of her near miss of going to Easter dinner with Warren had been thoroughly exhausted, although Cynthia was delighted to continue to discuss it.

One of the drawbacks of the Annex was that the building complex was located on a small plateau and elevated from the street entrance. When it rained, water streamed down the incline toward the security gate and the sentries. At any sight of rain, Meg had learned to chance not wearing nylons during her commute, which meant she was technically out of uniform were she to be inspected, but it also meant she could walk barefoot through the streaming water. Once up the incline, she could put on her nylons and her relatively dry shoes within one of the discreet porticos of the building. She had watched several other women taking this approach before adopting it as her own. Most of the women were walking from the barracks across the street, however, and were not taking the same chance of being out of uniform as she was on public transportation. Her male counterparts adapted to the situation by putting their socks on the radiator to dry. If ever reprimanded, she was going to point out that her approach was much less pungent than her colleagues'. Meg looked at her feet and realized she had on her stockings. She could not take her shoes off and made a mental note that she needed to stuff them with paper and put them near the radiator when she got near her desk.

The room was abuzz with conversation when Cynthia, Julie, and Meg walked in and saw Jack and Lyall talking. Lyall bounded up to the trio and exclaimed, "We're waiting for confirmation, but it looks like the Navy has captured a Japanese destroyer."

"Isn't that great news? Won't we get a copy of their code-book?" Cynthia said.

"If only it were that simple." Jack explained that earlier in the year, a steel trunk buried in a streambed by retreating Japanese radio operators on a Pacific island had been recovered by American soldiers. A group of experts had painstakingly dried pages to preserve a portion of the codebook. As far as the Americans knew, the Japanese were unaware that their code had been found.

"We'll get a copy, but in this case, unlike with the trunk, the Japanese know we have the copy. This is such bad news," Lyall said glumly. "The Japanese will reset their code and we'll have to start over again."

"So, we're back to square one with Fleet Command additives?" Meg said.

"I'm afraid so." Lyall sounded despondent and his lanky body slouched as he stood.

"Gather up. Gather up." Commander Lewis sounded uncharacteristically calm as he announced, "You can all take the rest of the watch off and get some rest. We'll begin again tomorrow." Following the short directive, Lewis walked briskly to his office. Meg waited for the door to slam, but he merely shut it normally.

"Something is off with the commander," she noted.

"I think he's frustrated. Just like the rest of us," Julie observed.

"Usually, he is a loud frustrated rather than a quiet frustrated," Meg said.

"What will we do with our free day?" Lyall asked. "It's raining; otherwise, we could go to the zoo."

"Sleep," said Cynthia.

"That's not like you, Cynthia," Robbie teased as he joined the group. Meg was surprised. Lewis must have also released Lieutenant Prescott. Something was really wrong with Lewis.

Julie looked out the window. "It looks like the rain is letting up. How far away is the zoo?"

"About a mile," Jack replied.

Lyall looked skeptical. "Closer to two."

"We should walk," Julie said. "I was in great shape after all the marching during Indoctrination but we're sitting way too much. That and too many milkshakes downstairs. I'm kidding myself when I say I need the calcium. I'm getting a lot more than calcium."

"Meg, you coming?" Lyall asked.

Uncharacteristically, Cynthia urged her to come. "Won't you please come? We need you to keep us in line and to tell us stories about the animals using your animal voices."

"Animal voices?" Lyall asked.

"She is a terrific mimic," Julie answered.

"How come we don't know any of this?" Lyall probed.

"Because Lieutenant Burke is always doing twice as much work as the rest of you and not fooling around," Robbie said, coming to her defense.

"Actually, the water transport reports probably haven't

changed yet. I could stay and do some work," Meg confessed, but she regretted saying it as soon as the words left her mouth.

"Nope. More important that you clear your mind too. I am ordering you to join this field trip," Robbie commanded.

"Okay," Meg acquiesced. "But only if you promise we can feed peanuts to the elephants. I used to go to the Bronx Zoo with my brothers and I could spend hours watching the elephants."

"Right after we see the tigers," Robbie promised.

"Of course we'll let you feed the elephants," Cynthia confirmed. "Let's go." *What is Cynthia up to today?* Meg thought.

Out of the corner of her eye, Meg could see Warren shuffling papers in his corner. She knew she should ask him to join them but could not make herself do it.

As they left the Annex and started along Massachusetts Avenue toward the zoo, Meg confessed, "It might not be a good idea to have the seven of us walking around during a workday. I'm a little worried the public will think we're up to no good or that we should be at work."

"Yes, Mother. If you're going to be like that, go back to work," Cynthia told her. Meg felt more comfortable with this Cynthia.

"Margaret Burke, I've never met someone who can worry as well as you do. You could make a living worrying about little things," Lyall said.

"You sound like my mother. Especially when you call me Margaret." Meg blushed and looked at her feet. He put his arm loosely around her shoulder and said, "I'm kidding with you. C'mon. Having fun is like anything else. You have to practice to get good at it."

"Let's get going, then." As she started to walk brusquely, Lyall was forced to quickly pull away his arm.

Meg couldn't believe that there could be a better animal home than her beloved Bronx Zoo, but quickly appreciated that the National Zoo had far more luxurious and spacious grounds for the animals and was a horticulturalist's delight, with tags indicating rare plant species throughout. Stopping first at the tigers, who were pacing and sizing each other up, she shivered a little as one of them pounced on the other when it got too close.

Lyall put his arm around her again. "Don't be scared," he whispered in her ear. It felt nice to have his arm around her and let herself enjoy it for a few moments before Robbie called, "Okay. Time for the elephants."

The moment passed and Lyall bounded away, imitating the tiger's stealthy walk before he pounced on a startled Jack. As they moved away from the tigers, Meg observed that Julie and Jack were lost in conversation with each other. She was happy for her friend, especially as Jack was possibly Julie's biggest cheerleader and even more supportive of her work than Meg. He happily provided the context of naval procedure when Julie lacked military knowledge and often had suggestions for either how to get around the rules or how to make the rules work in her favor. Cynthia and Robbie had different body language. The two were often together, but ever since the cocktail party, she noticed their interactions had become at best companionable rather than flirtatious.

Lyall called out, "I'm getting peanuts from the kiosk. Who else wants some?"

"I do," Meg replied. "I mean, the elephants want me to get peanuts for them." The group laughed. "Let me help you carry them."

"The elephants are lucky the peanuts are not rationed," Julie said.

"American crop," Jack suggested.

"Isn't sugar American? How about Wisconsin cows making butter?" Cynthia countered.

As she passed out small brown paper bags of unshelled peanuts, Meg was surprised to hear Robbie say, "Meg, how is your swimming going?" She had not hidden that she swam, but she had not made a big deal about it, either.

"It's nice to have the pool at work. More convenient than when I was teaching. Swimming really helps to get the stiffness out of my shoulders after a day of work."

"Word on the street is that you are really good," Lyall said.

"My skill level is at best recreational."

"That's not what I hear," he countered.

"Okay, then. When they allow female frogmen, I'll try out," Meg promised. The group laughed.

The afternoon passed quickly with a great deal of banter, including Meg mimicking several of the animals. She compared a pacing panther to their Commander Lewis, which left the group in hysterics.

"I think we had better head home while we might still get a seat on the bus and before Meg is put in the brig," Julie commanded.

"Why don't we all go to dinner?" Jack asked.

"Yes! Let's," Lyall agreed.

"What do you say?" Robbie asked Cynthia while quickly glancing at Meg. Cynthia, Julie, and Meg looked at each other.

"Sounds good. Where should we go?" Julie asked.

"Maybe the Willard Hotel," Meg quipped. The entire group laughed.

"Aunt Isobel expects us for dinner. You'll need to ask another time," Cynthia said firmly. "It is time for us to go." Meg and Julie exchanged a glance. Cynthia's tone indicated it would be an unpleasant fight if they were to push. Meg could see Jack and Robbie exchanging a look, which she assumed was surrender.

"We'll at least walk you to the bus stop," Lyall told them. The officers waited politely, but there was little conversation. It was as if the joy of the afternoon were a balloon that had been punctured by Cynthia's refusal. Meg was sure the others were as grateful as she when a bus approached after only a few minutes wait.

Since most people were still at work and they were traveling in the opposite direction of most of those working the evening or swing shift, the WAVES were able to get seats together and there were only a few passengers to see the officers waving goodbye. One of the middle-aged women wearing her hotel staff uniform smiled at Meg and said, "Nice to get that attention, isn't it?"

Once seated, Julie hissed at Cynthia, "Why did you say 'no' to dinner, Cynthia? Aunt Isobel wouldn't mind. In fact, she would be pleased. We had plenty of time to telephone and say we would be out before Davis started dinner. I know I would have enjoyed it and I think Meg would have too."

"We don't want the men to start thinking our calendar is open. Let them think we might have a few suitors," Cynthia replied.

"Cynthia, we spend almost every waking moment with those men. They know we don't have time to meet anyone else," Julie responded. "What has gotten into you?"

Cynthia ignored Julie and turned to Meg. "What do you think of Lyall?"

"I don't really think about Lyall," Meg said, but her flush gave her away.

"He likes you," Cynthia confirmed.

"I think he likes that I don't tease him as much as the rest of you do. That's probably the only reason he likes me," Meg explained. Julie looked at her skeptically.

"I thought it was clear during Indoctrination," Meg continued, "unless you already had a sweetheart, you were not encouraged to find one. Besides, it could be complicated, even more complicated than just dating a fellow officer. He's the CO's son."

"And you're Catholic, so it would never be serious, but you could have fun for a while. He'll ship out soon enough and that will be the end of that. You aren't officer's wife material, so no harm done," Cynthia said matter-of-factly.

"Cynthia, you can be heartless at times," Julie said with disbelief in her voice. Steering the conversation in a new direction, she asked, "What I want to know, Meg, is how does he know about your swimming?" Julie said.

"His father swims. He's been coaching me a little." Julie and Cynthia looked at her in surprise.

"When were you going to tell us you've been swimming with the CO?" Julie asked.

"When you asked me directly, as you just did," Meg replied curtly.

"And you, Julie? What do you think of Jack?" Cynthia had moved on to tease Julie.

"Probably about the same thing you think about Robbie," Julie retorted.

"Oh, I doubt it," Cynthia countered.

"Cynthia, I saw you with Robbie and his parents at Isobel's. Even I could tell that you are very comfortable with his family and they already know Isobel well," Meg said.

"Maybe a little too comfortable," Cynthia said with a frown. Thankfully, the bus pulled up to their stop at that point.

As they walked toward the house, Meg changed the subject away from discussion of the officers. "It's Friday, so we'll be having fish for dinner. It's very nice Aunt Isobel is serving fish on Fridays. It makes following Lent a great deal easier for me."

"She does it because she wants to support the Chesapeake Bay fishermen, you know. It's nice you appreciate it, though." Walking through the front door, Cynthia turned again to Julie.

"Do you think about being an officer's wife, Julie? Jack needs just a little encouragement to give you a ring."

"Maybe, at some point," Julie admitted. "But I really like what I'm doing now. Before the war, I couldn't imagine doing anything beyond being a school librarian for a few years, then getting married. This is a huge adventure! I want it to continue for a while. Also, I'm not sure this is the time to get married. Jack will be deployed sooner rather than later; it's almost two years since they graduated." She looked at Meg. "So will Lyall. Robbie won't be, though, will he? He's a reservist and was called for special duty, so he will be here for the duration of the war." She shot a quick look at Meg before looking back at Cynthia.

Aunt Isobel walked into the hall and stopped in surprise. "My goodness, you're home early. Is everything alright?" All three WAVES hesitated. "Say no more." Aunt Isobel waved her hand across her mouth to indicate silence. "Let me see if Davis can put together tea for us."

"Oh, please don't trouble. We're not expecting it," Meg said.

"Just proved my earlier point, Meg." Cynthia looked pleased with herself. "I'm not sure that you have much of a future as an officer, let alone as an officer's wife. You need to be more commanding. Instead, you worry about everyone and try to do everything yourself. You're always identifying more with the servants than with the officers. If you're going to advance in the Navy, and in life, you need to change how you present yourself."

Aunt Isobel saw Meg's eyes flick toward the staircase, plotting an escape to their bedroom. Cynthia's comment about servants figuratively punched her in the stomach.

Isobel gently put a hand on Meg's arm and led her into the library. "Everyone will feel better when they have had something to eat."

Davis brought in a table with sandwiches and two cakes—more confirmation to Meg that Davis was buying food on the black market. No matter how good she was with substitutions, no one could manage two cakes and tea with their sugar ration.

"Why are you talking about being an officer's wife? Has one of you received a proposal?" Aunt Isobel's eyes twinkled.

"Lyall McClaren is crazy about Meg, and Cynthia is making trouble rather than letting Meg enjoy the attention," Julie said.

"Honestly, Cynthia! Meg is better officer's wife material than you are," she said forcefully, and then gasped. "Oh Cynthia, I didn't mean it like that." Cynthia started to sob, and Julie rushed to throw her arms around her friend.

Isobel looked alarmed. "This isn't a conversation for tea; this is a conversation for whiskey." Julie sat on the sofa with her arm around Cynthia as Isobel rang the bell. When Davis arrived, Isobel asked her to fix a tray of whiskey sours and then fixed her gaze on Meg and said, "Meg, do you like this young man?"

"I honestly have no idea. I haven't let myself think about whether I do or don't like him. I didn't join the Navy because I wanted to find a husband. I joined the Navy so I could say I had spent part of my life outside of Brooklyn. I know I'm never going to travel the way you did, Aunt Isobel, or the way Julie and Cynthia will, but I thought at least I could see more of the country and meet people who are not just like me."

Davis returned and quietly put a silver tray with four glasses on the table. Meg gratefully grabbed a glass and took a small sip. Davis made a better whiskey sour than Lyall did; Meg remembered Lyall's warning as she told herself to sip slowly.

"I admit when I applied to join the WAVES, I didn't realize that there would be so many unspoken rules and had no idea of the Navy's emphasis on who you are and where you went to school." She stopped and took a breath. "If I had really thought about it, I should have understood that my being Catholic might be an enormous limitation." She turned to Cynthia. "I did not grow up in a family who knows military protocol the way you do. The more I'm exposed to how the Navy works and learn the unwritten rules, the less I understand why my application was accepted." She paused. "I haven't told anyone, not even my family, but I applied to be in the Women's Army Corps, in May 1942. And was promptly rejected." Three sets of eyes looked at her in surprise.

Cynthia said under her breath, "Why, I wonder?"

Meg said to Cynthia, "I think my background is much more suited to the Army, but it was the status-conscious Navy who took me, and here I am."

"But you still haven't told us. Do you like Lyall?" Cynthia pressed. Her slightly puffy eyes were the only indication she had just been crying.

"Cynthia, whether I like him or not doesn't matter. I know being associated with me could ruin his career chances. I didn't attend a Seven Sisters college. My religion is a liability. Honestly, I'm not trying to lead him on, but you saw him today, he's so enthusiastic when I'm just being friendly." She paused. "I'll give you this: I could easily like him. He's a good man and much brighter than any of you seem to realize. I don't want to lead him on, though. Going forward, I will draw a clearer line." She sighed. "It's better for him if I pull back from socializing with the group outside of work." She looked directly at Cynthia. "I won't be leading him on if I always say 'no' to drinks or to dinner with the group."

"Does it have to be that black and white?" Isobel inquired.

"I can only work with clear guidelines," Meg replied.

"Meg, I think you are being a little extreme. Besides, doesn't Lyall have any say in the matter? As you said, he is bright, and it isn't any secret you are Catholic. Maybe he has decided that at this point it isn't an issue. After all, it isn't an issue for anyone in this room," Julie responded.

"But we aren't going to marry her," Cynthia interjected.

Meg heard Julie let out a small gasp.

To Meg's surprise, she started laughing. As soon as she started, the others joined in.

"So I guess I continue to be an expert in the logistics of procuring typewriters and stationery for the US Navy and let the chips fall where they may," Meg said. The whiskey had hit her bloodstream and made her feel brave.

"Exactly, Meg. You don't have to play with Lyall as Cynthia suggested on the bus. No one is saying you have to marry him, but you could go to a USO dance with him or dinner without anyone being too worried. It could be fun," Julie proposed.

"I agree with Julie," Isobel confirmed. "Lyall has a good head on his shoulders."

Meg turned to Cynthia and asked, "Let's hear more about your plans, Cynthia. Do you think you could contribute more to the war effort if you were to marry an officer and guide his career, helping his promotions because of your dinner parties and social connections, or doing whatever it is you do as part of the WAVES?"

"Oh, definitely the dinner parties. You haven't seen me in action, but I can throw a wonderful party. Maybe I can rescue the heartbroken Lyall when he finally gives up on you." Cynthia smirked.

"Cynthia, do you really want Lyall? Or is it his connections? I thought you were quite happy to seek Robbie's well-placed affections. Or is it just a game?" Julie asked. The front door closed and Vivian walked into the library, looking confused to see the whiskey glasses.

"What's going on? What did I miss?" she asked with a smile.

Her aunt answered, "We are participating in a debate. Resolved: Being an officer's wife contributes more to the war effort than being in the WAVES. Cynthia is for and Meg is against."

Vivian said, "You mean Meg is for and Cynthia is against."

"No, dear."

"Oh, I'm pretty sure Cynthia will marry a civilian rather than an officer."

Cynthia shot Vivian a look that immediately silenced her, but Meg wondered if that civilian could be her brother.

## 35

Two weeks after the trip to the zoo, Meg slogged up the hill to the Annex. Although they had fun during their field trip, the crushing schedule of working on the code and additives had tempered the camaraderie present when they visited the animals. Meg hoped with a change in the seasons, there might be the chance to get outside, together, again. Spring came more quickly to the District than to New York. The Navy had notified the men that they should switch to their summer uniforms in mid-April, which was only two weeks away. There was no word when the WAVES might get their summer uniforms, let alone be allowed to wear them, but Meg said a small prayer that it would be soon. Her current wool-based uniform was becoming unbearably hot. The rain drummed down as she walked up Massachusetts Avenue; she had checked the sky before leaving Isobel's and decided this was a good morning to chance commuting bare-legged. The aroma of the Research Desk as she entered the main room indicated she was one of the few to have thought ahead. The stench of overripe socks steam-drying on the radiators augmented the palpable tension in the work area.

In the main work area, Jack, Lyall, and Osgoode had moved the tables to give themselves room for a makeshift batter's box. Lyall was pitching crumpled paper balls while Jack caught, or rather stood where a catcher would crouch. Osgoode couldn't hit the pitched paper balls with the ruler he was using as a bat, but Jack couldn't catch them, either.

"Are you being called up?" Meg asked Lyall as she smiled, ignoring Warren's scornful look indicating she should not pay them any attention.

"Major League Baseball isn't that desperate," came Robbie's voice from behind her. "C'mon, guys, what gives?"

"Nothing. The 'professors' don't have anything. We don't have anything to transpose. My head is swimming from punching cards with the numbers from the transmissions we're getting, and I can't get the little dots from the cards out of my shoes and my uniform," Lyall explained.

Ever since the American capture of the Japanese destroyer and implementation of the new Japanese additives, the Research Desk had yet to unearth the new system. Other departments of the Navy had become used to their daily intelligence report using decrypted information. Even though it had been less than a month since the ship was captured and the codes changed, the Command was under tremendous pressure to decrypt the latest pattern. How they did their work might still not be widely understood or appreciated, but the information that resulted, especially after the US success at Midway, was now key to military operations.

"Sorry, guys. I'm suspending play because of rain," Robbie announced.

Lyall groaned. "Robbie, let us play around for a little while. See if it clears our head, or our vision, or something."

"I've just come from a briefing with the 'professors' and they're playing additive hangman; if you're looking for a diversion, make it a word game," Robbie suggested.

"Lieutenant Prescott, can I get a chalkboard?" Meg asked

Robbie, using his formal title. She still felt uncomfortable using his first name outside work; when on duty she always used, at a minimum, the officer's rank.

"Lieutenant Prescott, can I get a chalkboard?" Osgoode said sotto voce. "You're such a teacher's pet."

"Actually, she *is* the teacher," Lyall snapped.

As both men glared at each other, Robbie rubbed his temples before saying, "Osgoode, go and get the chalkboard from Ensign Bowen's office."

"But . . ."

"Just go do it."

Osgoode frowned but left to comply.

"What are you thinking, Lieutenant Burke?" Robbie always smiled slightly when he addressed her formally. Meg wasn't sure why.

"Nothing, other than maybe writing on the board will help us as a group to see a pattern we aren't seeing on paper. Sometimes when a student is having trouble with a proof, it is easier to do it on the chalkboard than at his seat."

"Or more terrifying," Osgoode said as he brought the board in. "Makes the students so scared they freeze. I'm sure you're known for being a mean teacher."

"Bet Meg's known for being a pushover," Jack said.

Meg turned on her heel, facing Osgoode, and in her best teacher voice said, "If you had been in my class, you would have had my undivided attention."

"Oh, if you were the teacher, I would have enjoyed the attention." Osgoode flashed her his saucy grin.

Feeling her face flushing, Meg debated whether she should get coffee to give herself a moment to calm down. Concluding she might pour the coffee on Osgoode, she took a deep breath instead. As she looked at Robbie, she saw his face was almost as red as hers felt.

"I've got better things to do than play school," Osgoode declared.

"Like?" Robbie retorted.

"Getting another commendation for my code-breaking ability, unlike some Columbia PhDs I know."

Robbie shook his head but didn't order him to stay.

"So, Meg, what's the game plan?" Lyall asked. "Break it down for us. If you were teaching us how to break apart an additive, what would you tell the students?"

"Not a bad idea, McClaren. You may be smarter than you look." Robbie turned to Meg. "How would you teach this lecture, Dr. Burke?"

*Dr. Burke.* Thinking of how much she wanted to emulate Lieutenant Carrington teaching them coding, Meg tried to stand a little straighter even as her heart started pounding; it was not the first time she was thankful that a stick of chalk stuck to a clammy hand.

"Okay. We know that since 1938, the Japanese Navy, JN, frequently changes its code on at least a quarterly rotation, and sometimes more frequently. As much as it is a production for us to break it, it is intensive work for them to change it. Luckily most humans are at least a little lazy, look for shortcuts, and make mistakes. All these facts work in our favor. Let's start with what is most familiar to you: JN-25."

She wrote *JN-25* at the top of the chalkboard, with the definition, *Main Code*, and put a big star next to it with a flourish. She smiled at the trio. "We—I mean other analysts, not me—have been able to break versions of JN-25, including the one that decoded messages before the attack at Midway. That's important. We've studied their code, found weaknesses, and broken it before."

As she was speaking, Warren silently joined the group. He put his chair behind Lyall's and watched Meg.

"Mr. Elliot and I have been working with some of the other ciphers," she gestured toward Warren in acknowledgment that he was now part of the group, "which are less complex and changed less often. For example, JN-166 is the naval air and weather code."

She added *JN-166* to the board and said as she wrote underneath that heading, "We see frequent use of words such as *rain, storm, storm front, downpour, deluge, blustery, gust, peaks, wave height,* and *typhoon*."

"You're right, Meg," Jack agreed. "Off the top of my head I know rain is 7745, wave 2374, and gust is 8992 because we see them several times a day."

"The dreaded 8992," Lyall joked.

Meg moved to the far side of the board and wrote *JN-167 merchant ship code* and smiled at the group. "I find these words the most interesting. We see *convoy sailing time*; *noon positions*; *cargoes*; *barges*; *container ship*; *fishing boat*; *tanker*; and *trawler*."

"I understand that we know several words and their additives because we broke the code from two other communication systems. But how is that going to help us with JN-25?" Jack asked.

Meg smiled. "This is my idea. It's such a huge undertaking to update the additives, and I am assuming the Japanese were not expecting their ship to be captured a few weeks ago. They had to quickly substitute the new additives. If I were them, I would adapt something they already had rather than starting fresh. I thought you could help me test my hypothesis if we looked at some JN-25 messages that should have some weather or transport information. Maybe we can use frequently transmitted patterns to help us back into the current additives."

Meg stopped to check the quartet's reactions. Warren looked down at his feet, Jack was sketching something on his notepad, and Lyall smiled at her. Robbie was raking his fingers through his hair, staring at a distant point across the room, and seemed not to have noticed she had stopped talking.

"What do—" she continued.

"The Japanese do love their formalities," Robbie interrupted.

"If I were the radio operator, especially if I'm under pressure, I would get annoyed with having to transmit 'I have the honor to inform Your Excellency' rather than 'Captain" or 'Admiral.' But, to your point, Lieutenant Burke, we have used the frequently repeated stylized titles and the Imperial Navy's tendency to repeat messages using a formal template to help us pull transmissions apart before. In fact, that's what the 'professors' are playing hangman with right now. Why don't you and Elliot pull some of your transmissions out, especially the weather ones? Jack and Lyall, you work with them to tabulate frequencies, okay? I'm going to go tell the 'professors' what you are up to. Maybe they can help identify some likely code chains and we can do a more focused run on the IBM machines." He smiled at the group. "And I can tell Lewis we have an idea. Hopefully, he'll stop kicking his desk if he thinks we aren't completely stuck." As he walked away, he turned and said over his shoulder, "Thank you all."

Lyall grinned. "He liked your idea enough to take it to the 'professors' and Lewis."

"Maybe. Of course, if it doesn't work, Lewis knows it was my idea." She pretended to shudder.

"Oh, it's a compliment, Dr. Burke." Lyall emphasized 'Dr. Burke' the same way Robbie had. "You'll be one of them someday."

Warren stood up, stepping closer to Lyall. "Don't tease her, Lieutenant. She does good work. There is no need for you to make fun of her."

"I wasn't making fun of her. Why shouldn't Meg become a professor? She's brilliant and she's good at teaching. Besides, people like her."

"You know why," Elliot continued.

"No. Actually, I don't." He turned to Meg. "Sorry, Meg. Not sure what Elliot is on about."

"Don't worry about it." She bit her lip slightly and wondered for an instant if she should explain why it was unlikely she would ever go to graduate school before dismissing the idea. "Let's just get to work, okay? Could you move the foul lines," she pointed at the desks moved earlier this morning to delineate the batter's box, "together so that we can spread the transmissions out?" For the next few hours, they focused on looking for possible similarities in transmissions.

Julie interrupted the nearly silent scratching of pens against paper later that afternoon. "Is anyone having lunch today?"

"Oh," Jack said, looking at his watch. "I was supposed to meet you for lunch, wasn't I?"

"It's not the first time I have lost out to a list of numbers," Julie chuckled. "But seriously, I think all of you need food!"

"I know I do," Lyall agreed.

"Meg?"

"I think I am on to something; why don't you go without me," she replied. Julie rolled her eyes back at her.

"C'mon. Get something to eat with us. You can drink a milkshake quickly, if you really are in that much of a hurry," Lyall suggested.

Meg groaned. "I gave them up for Lent."

"Okay. A tuna sandwich, then," Julie suggested.

"But I've made a list of some shared text..." Meg responded.

"Which will be waiting when we all get back," Julie answered, undeterred.

"Can I get you something, Mr. Elliot?" Meg asked. Warren shook his head and frowned at the papers on his desk.

"You tried," Julie said under her breath to Meg. "You're awfully good about trying to include him."

Arriving at the Mess Hall, the other three joined the ever-present line for ice cream. Tuna was not as popular an option and Meg quickly got her sandwich. As she looked for a place to sit, Robbie beckoned to her. As she got closer, she realized Osgoode was sitting with him.

"Oh. Actually, there are four of us." She looked at the two men, who both seemed agitated. "Are you sure you want company?"

"Plenty of room for all of us," Osgoode said, patting the seat next to him. Osgoode was giving Meg what she had started calling his oily smile and Robbie looked as though he needed to take out a scull for a long row to get rid of his pent-up frustration. "Thanks, Osgoode," Lyall said, sliding between him and Meg.

"Did your chalkboard trick work, Burke?" Osgoode asked.

Using her biggest, fakest smile, she turned to him and said, "Let's not talk about that over lunch." She gave him a warning look. "Definitely not here."

"So, who is up for going dancing?" Jack asked, changing the subject. He turned to Meg, adding, "Not on a Thursday."

Meg couldn't help but smile. She wasn't sure if Julie had insisted he say that, but even if she had, it was nice to be included. She remembered Julie suggesting a dance during their conversation about the officers in Isobel's library.

"Where's the best place to go dancing?" Julie asked Osgoode. Meg raised her eyebrow in surprise. Was Julie going to go anywhere Osgoode might suggest?

"The Casino Royal Night Club on Fourteenth and H Street," Osgoode replied.

"Are you kidding?" Jack questioned. "Polluted air. Bad bands. Lots of fights."

"I was in a briefing last week to discuss the issue of the recently increased number of servicemen arrested there," Robbie interjected.

"Oh, to have your job, Robbie. Good to see that math PhD put to good use." Osgoode smirked.

"Yeah. So many nights burning the midnight oil only to review drunk-and-disorderly statistics," Robbie agreed and shook his head thoughtfully. "Anyway, I thought this was kind of interesting. One of the Morale and Welfare officers was saying the Casino Royal has had so many inter-service brawls that now, as soon as a fistfight starts, they lower the house lights …"

"Probably not that high to begin with..." Osgoode interjected.

Robbie ignored him and continued, "And they turn a spotlight on a very large American flag. They even have a fan positioned to make the flag flutter. Then they have the band play the 'Star-Spangled Banner.' Apparently, their appeal to patriotism works pretty well and generally calms things down."

"They're lucky they weren't part of the raid in March," Osgoode said with a smile.

Meg wished Cynthia were here to see that she knew Osgoode was talking about a huge DC police raid on several houses of prostitution that spring.

"There are ladies present, Osgoode," Robbie said in a cautionary tone.

"There were ladies present at the raid, Prescott. What world do you live in?"

Meg noted, for at least the second time that day, Robbie blushed horribly at something Osgoode said.

"So, I'm going to try this again," Jack said determinedly. "We need to go dancing. It will use a different part of our brains. Maybe we could go to an embassy party. Lyall, you're the most likely person to have been to an embassy party."

Lyall shook his head. "I've been to a party at the White House," Osgoode whistled quietly as Lyall continued, "but not an embassy." Julie smiled across the table at Meg as Lyall explained, "President Roosevelt has the US Marine Band play at diplomatic receptions. My father knows the Marine bandleader, so we were invited once. Going made up for the hassle of putting on the dress uniform. It was something else. We're at war, but the Marine Band was dressed in their scarlet-and-gold uniforms, and diplomats wearing white shirts and red sashes holding all their medals were dancing as if they didn't have a care in the world. It was surreal."

"I don't think we're going to get an invitation to the White House this week," Meg interjected.

The group laughed.

"Probably not," Lyall agreed and smiled at her.

"Do enemy diplomats go to each other's parties?" Julie asked.

"Maybe not to each other's, but the State Department has maintained its diplomatic lists. They still invite people who have remained at their embassies in Washington. I assume some countries are trying to maintain a tepid relationship with each other, even those on opposing sides. Sooner or later, post-war, they're going to want to be able to speak to each other again," Robbie answered. Meg looked at Robbie with some surprise, which he acknowledged with a slight shrug. She wondered if he went to some of the parties with his parents. With someone else?

"How do we get invited?" Julie asked. "Is there food? Drinks? What happens at the parties? Just dancing?"

"There's a lot of intrigue," Robbie interjected.

"Are you really a math professor or is that a cover?" Osgoode remarked.

"Just a math professor, but I read the newspaper," Robbie responded in a tone suggesting Osgoode did not but should. "There are all sorts of stories of diplomats using the gossip they pick up at parties for their intelligence reports."

"I'm sure it can't be that hard to go," said Lyall.

Julie laughed. "You always say something is going to be easy, Lyall. It's seldom as easy as you think it is."

"This should be. Hell, it should be easier than what we do every day," Lyall replied. "We'll walk down Embassy Row after work and we're bound to see an embassy with people and cars entering and leaving. Even I'm smart enough to see that means there's an embassy party. See? Easy."

"I'm not sure we should go in uniform," Jack said.

"But I thought we were always supposed to be in uniform while on active duty, even if we're getting married," Meg fretted.

"You're thinking of getting married, Burke? Who's the lucky

guy?" Osgoode asked, and Meg blushed furiously.

"Lieutenant Burke's right," Robbie confirmed, ignoring Osgoode.

"Technically, couldn't we say we're not on active duty if we are not on duty?" Jack suggested.

Robbie shrugged his shoulders noncommittally. "It doesn't really work that way."

"I say the girls put on a good dress after work and we'll change into dark suits. It would make for a really nice change," Jack urged.

"Won't we need an invitation?" Meg asked.

"Or do they put names on a list?" Julie added.

"We bluff," Osgoode suggested. "You say something vague to whomever is at the door. You say you are with Senator Lodge or Senator Taft, who is going to be there in a few minutes. Or, we could tell the truth and say we are with Secretary Prescott."

Robbie glared at him. "My father is not a secretary and we should leave him out of this. Honestly, the more I think about it, I'm not sure it is such a good idea for us to be going."

Osgoode smirked and continued, "Senator Taft, then. I'm sure the crowd from the other embassies won't say anything. They won't know who we are, but they will be afraid that they should, so they'll never say anything."

"You're probably right," Robbie reluctantly agreed.

"Besides, there will be a bar and a band inside. If we're lucky, the band will be good and the buffet plentiful," Osgoode added.

"Can everyone be ready to go by this Friday?" Jack pressed. Meg looked with alarm at Julie, who knew she had nothing to wear.

"Absolutely," Julie said. "I can't wait. I know Cynthia and Vivian are going to want to come too."

"Okay. That's settled, then. We'll *all* be ready on Friday," Jack concluded.

Robbie glanced at Meg as Jack said "all" before he

commanded, "Back to work."

Meg signaled to Julie to wait a moment so they could walk back together. As soon as the men left the table, she moaned, "I can't go. I don't have anything to wear."

"If Cynthia won't loan you something, I am sure Isobel will. Davis would make you a dress if you asked her. The dress really isn't the problem, is it?"

"No," said Meg in a quiet voice.

"Maybe they will have to spotlight the embassy flag and play their anthem to keep the men from fighting over you," Julie said with a smile. "C'mon, we have work to do."

For the remainder of the week, Meg and Warren worked on decoding weather and shipping fleet messages to provide port entry requests, daily merchant and fishing ship positions, and the weather. The "professors" focused on their search for commonly repeated text, without success.

Meg could ignore some of the group's strain, but it was difficult to overlook Warren mumbling for her benefit "yet again an officer has stolen my ideas." She waited until Robbie was alone while getting coffee at the communal urn and grabbed her mug.

"Lieutenant, could you help me with something?"

"Gladly." He looked surprised and his smile indicated he was pleased. "What can I do for you?"

"You've got to talk to Mr. Elliot."

"Oh." As quickly as his face had broken into a smile, his serious expression was back. "About what?"

"He's really upset that the 'professors' are using his ideas. If he can't work on looking for the common patterns, can you at least mention it was his idea at the next meeting? Maybe sit down with him to assure him his ideas are useful, and that Lewis knows he's doing good work?"

"It was your idea and Lewis knows you are doing good

work," Robbie said evenly.

"I think it would help," Meg pressed.

He looked at her skeptically, and she knew he wouldn't say anything or reach out to Warren. "Ready for Friday?" he asked.

"Not really. I'm not sure we should be going and I'm pretty sure you don't, either," she answered curtly.

"I guess I'm going to take a chance and let the chips fall where they may." He grinned at her. "Don't you think it will be nice to go to a party for a change? Don't you miss dancing?"

"I guess," she said, and turned to walk back to her seat, but not before catching a glimpse of his hurt expression.

For the rest of the week, walking to work and during meals at Isobel's, all conversation was about going to Embassy Row on Friday. Cynthia and Vivian modeled dresses for Julie on Wednesday night, but they kept changing their minds about what they were going to wear. Meg had made Julie promise that she would not say anything about her not having a dress. During the fashion show, Meg skimmed the newspaper and avoided the conversation until Vivian called out,

"What are you wearing, Meg?" Sweet Vivian never wanted Meg to be left out.

"Yes. Why don't you put on what you are wearing?" Cynthia said slyly. "I'm sure I have a necklace you could borrow, but I need to know what you're wearing so I can pick the right one."

"Oh." Meg pretended to be surprised. "I thought you knew I wasn't going. It's a Friday during Lent."

Aunt Isobel glanced at Meg and arched an eyebrow. Meg wondered, not for the first time, if that was a talent you were born with or if it could be learned.

"It's not Good Friday," Julie said simply.

"Yeah. There is no reason not to go—just don't eat meat," Cynthia said with a smirk.

"Time to get ready for bed, girls," Isobel commanded while looking sternly at Cynthia. "Go. Now. If you are going out on Friday, you need extra sleep."

Meg avoided Isobel's eyes as she said, "Good night."

Julie waited until after the lights were off. "You know, Meg, I think you are being a bit of a coward not going. Vivian is close enough in size that she has something you can borrow if you're going to refuse to ask Cynthia. Besides, Vivian would love to help you figure out how to wear it."

Meg felt tears sting her eyes as Julie very noisily turned over, indicating she was going to sleep.


MEG WAS AWAKE BEFORE DAWN, dressed quietly, and tiptoed out of her room. Downstairs, Davis was up and boiling water on the stove. She looked surprised to see Meg.

"No breakfast for me this morning—I'm going to swim before work." Meg forced a smile onto her face and slipped quietly out the kitchen door. Walking brusquely, she realized her actions this morning only reinforced Julie thinking she was a coward. She reminded herself, with a hungry and sinking stomach, that she had choir tonight.

At work, Meg tried to ignore Julie's hurt look when Julie came in to say good morning to Jack. She drew her papers around her and tried to block out the banter, the chatter, and the grumbling in the room. Lyall and Robbie must have sensed her mood because they left her alone all day. Even Warren seemed to grumble less, or at least more quietly than usual. Waiting until the others left after the afternoon change in watch, Meg gratefully ordered two tuna sandwiches in the Mess and ate for the first time that day. Deciding it was now light enough at night to walk, she skipped the bus, not realizing she had seriously miscalculated the time it would take to walk to the church on the crowded streets. Moreover, her uniform was heavy for walking in the spring weather, and she was enervated as she opened the heavy vestibule door. The smell of incense assaulted her nose and the processional hymn her ears. She had missed the warm-up. As she walked in late for the first time since she had joined the choir, Mr. Kelly, the director, drew up the small pointer that he used as a baton and stopped practice.

"Nice of you to join us, Miss Burke."

"Lieutenant."

"Lieutenant?"

"Lieutenant Burke. My title is Lieutenant Burke."

Meg glared at the shocked choir director. The other members sat stunned in their chairs. Meg couldn't hear anyone breathe.

Finally, Warren cleared his throat and said, "We've got a lot to cover this evening, don't we?"

"Of course," the director stammered. He was still reeling from Meg's correction. "We do indeed."

The choir moved listlessly through the music from the first part of the Mass and Meg pretended that she did not notice the other members covertly staring at her, wondering why she had made such an outburst.

"I think it is time for a break." Mr. Kelly put down his pointer and waited for a moment before turning to approach Meg.

Before he could reach her, Warren was at her side. "I've got to talk to you. Not here. In the vestibule." He guided her by the arm and out of the sanctuary. "What was that about?"

"What was what about?"

"Telling Mr. Kelly to use your title. You're not on duty."

Meg tossed her head slightly. "You're right. I'm not. But I am in uniform. It's my title."

"You have a thin skin."

"*I* have a thin skin? You're one to talk." Before she could stop, she blurted, "You're sure everyone at the Command is out to get you."

Warren looked at her sadly. "They are, or at least some of the officers are."

Kelly stormed into the vestibule. "Mr. Elliot. Lieutenant."

He made her title sound like a curse word. "I'd like to resume practice." Warren and Meg wordlessly followed the director back into the room.

Meg could feel her fellow choristers continue to glance discreetly at her and she imagined she had a magic cloak deflecting their looks. As soon as she sang the last note, she gathered her music, placed it in the closet, and left without a word to the rest of the group.

During the bus ride home, she replayed the different parts of her day. Her first big mistake had been not eating breakfast. Her second was not talking to Julie. She walked slowly from her stop to Isobel's house. She was trying to put off facing the others for as long as she could. Thankfully, no one was in the kitchen, and she crept up the back stairs. Julie was in bed reading. She did not say a word but glanced over at Meg's bed. A pressed green dress was lying on the bedspread. Meg started to cry.

"I told them not to do it, but Vivian and Davis insisted."

Meg's tears turned to sobs. Julie jumped out of bed and rushed to hug her.

"I've had the worst day." Meg hiccupped and struggled for breath. Julie let her cry until she could speak again.

"Tell me what happened."

Meg recounted not eating, being late to choir rehearsal, insisting on her title, and the encounter with Warren.

"Good work."

"Good work?" Meg asked.

"You are a lieutenant. It's not a secret and it is your rank. If there were a male lieutenant singing, the others would use his title. Maybe you were a little pushy, but who cares? You're not going back after Easter. Telling Warren he has a thin skin was exactly right."

"I'm sorry."

"I know you are. Turn off the lights and let's get some sleep."

# 36

The next morning, Meg barely noticed the walk as they chatted about the night's plans. The WAVES brought their extra bags of dresses and shoes, which they planned to stash with Julie and Cynthia in the library.

"Do you think the guards will have a problem with our bags? I hadn't thought about that until now," Meg asked.

"There you go, Meg. If it sounds like fun, you must worry," Cynthia lamented.

Meg was about to correct Cynthia and say something when she thought about Warren's comment about her thin skin. She would not admit it to him, but he wasn't entirely wrong.

"I don't think the guards will have a problem," Julie said. "If they expected to see documents or letters in our bag, but only see clothes, I think the worst that is going to happen is they will blush."

Meg took a deep breath. "Vivian. Thanks for loaning me your dress. I'm really excited to go dancing tonight."

"I'm so glad you're going, Meg. So is at least one other officer." Vivian smiled, while Cynthia looked at Meg in astonishment.

The day dragged; Meg kept putting her watch to her ear to make sure it was still ticking. Warren was ignoring her, which was fine for today but might be problematic if it were to continue. They were no further along with identifying new additives, so she could not lose herself in transposing, which was mentally taxing and would make the minutes pass more quickly. At 1730, the sound of five chairs scraping away from the desk startled Warren, and he looked questioningly at the officers as they moved as a group and walked toward Julie's department. Meg knew he wondered what they were up to.

"Where is Vivian meeting us?" Osgoode asked.

"At the gate," Julie answered. "The WAVES are going to duck into Barrack D to change. There's even a coat check where they'll hold our bags. We will need to come back tomorrow to pick them up. Where are you changing?"

"The swim locker room. We can use the lockers there. I checked," Lyall responded.

"Look at you. Doing recon," Jack teased Lyall.

Meeting at the gate, the four women hurried over to the barrack to dress.

"It took us hours to get dressed for a college dance," Vivian observed. "And now we can get ready in minutes."

"I bet the men will be even more appreciative than they were in college." Julie's eyes sparkled.

"Speak for yourself," Cynthia muttered. "Meg, you've got to cling to Lyall or Osgoode is going to eat you alive."

"It's okay. My going with Osgoode will be a kind of penance. While he's at the bar, maybe I'll dance with a diplomat. Maybe I'll dance with a spy." She smiled wickedly. "Besides, Vivian should dance with Lyall so I can stick to my promise not to lead him on. Vivian is so sweet, she'll be gentle with Lyall and he will have a great time."

Meg pretended not to notice Robbie flush when she and the others joined them. All four WAVES ignored Osgoode's wolf whistle. Meg couldn't help but notice that Lyall looked far more substantial and handsome in his suit than his Navy uniform. She also noticed dark gray was a better color on Robbie than tan. Initially, neither the men nor the women spoke. It was as if they were strangers since they were out of uniform.

"Shall we start?" Meg suggested gently as they began walking down Massachusetts Avenue toward the bus that would take them to Embassy Row. Once on the bus, still no one spoke as they looked shyly at each other. When Lyall observed, "Looks like there are lots of people and cars at the Portuguese Embassy," Jack pulled the bus cord. As Meg stood up, Lyall moved to put an arm around her waist to steady her and did not let go until they were off the bus.

Once on the sidewalk, they formed a small scrum before starting the short walk to the embassy. Julie exclaimed, "A party at a neutral country's embassy. That should be interesting. Who do you think we will meet?"

Meg glanced at Robbie and caught him looking apprehensive, which puzzled her. She had met few people who were as comfortable in their skin as Lieutenant Prescott. Under his breath, Robbie quickly warned the others, "Remember, don't mention your position. If someone says they've seen you in uniform, you sharpen pencils, make coffee—you know the drill. Guys, we oversee housing assignments, if pressed. Don't volunteer anything. Got it? Turn the conversation on the other person if they follow up. Ask them if they know of any apartments for let or if anyone has an extra room to rent."

Cynthia put her arm through Robbie's. "C'mon. We're here to have fun." Meg gave Vivian a slight push so she was next to Lyall, while Meg took the surprised Osgoode's arm as they lined up to enter.

After having prepared their story of knowing the senators, Meg was disappointed the door attendant did not ask who they were or where they were from. He welcomed them, saying, "*Olá*," and directed them to the large main room decorated with green, red, and yellow, the colors of the Portuguese flag. Osgoode made a beeline for the bar, while the rest of the group congregated and tried not to stare as they got their bearings.

"No one has sashes on," Meg said to Lyall.

"All the better not to get stuck while dancing," Julie remarked. "As much as you worry, Meg, I've been sort of concerned about that." They all laughed.

"More wine than booze at the bar," Osgoode whined when he returned.

"And you are surprised?" Cynthia said with disdain. Meg relaxed. It was nice when Cynthia picked on someone else.

Meg turned to Osgood. "Shall we dance?"

"*I'm* supposed to ask *you*," Osgoode spluttered.

"But I'm the one who's asking."

He flushed. As Meg had anticipated, a mostly sober Osgoode was a much less troublesome dancer than an inebriated one, and she stayed with him until she was sure Vivian and Lyall had a chance to dance.

"I'm going to go and get a drink," he said, before leaving her alone.

"Yes. You should do that," she agreed to his departing back.

Meg was happy to find a place along the wall to stand and watch the band. The music was unlike any she had ever heard. She watched as a musician played a large bass drum by hitting only one side of the skin, emitting a low, deep sound. Another musician held a square drum with the thumbs of both of his hands and the pointer of his right hand, using his remaining fingers to tap the instrument. The final percussion instrument was constructed from a skin stretched over a jug and made a sound when the player rubbed it with a stick. More familiar, but still different from anything she had seen up close, was a twelve-string guitar, as well as a five-string guitar whose sound hole was in the shape of two hearts. Even though she was completely unacquainted with the music, she could not help but tap her foot.

"Any similarities to Irish folk music?" It hadn't taken Lyall long to notice she was no longer with Osgoode and to join her.

"Good question. I'm not as much of an expert on my heritage as I probably should be. I really can't tell you."

"No Irish dancing lessons?"

"Nope. Strictly ballroom dancing taught in the high school gym."

"And here you are." He smiled.

"And here I am," she agreed.

He took her in his arm and propelled her out onto the floor.

"Where's Vivian?" Meg asked.

"Dancing with someone she met through her command." Lyall looked amused. "Hasn't she been telling you about the dreamy lieutenant she works with?" Meg shook her head.

"Totally unaware she had met someone."

"Really?" Lyall looked surprised. "I picture you all sitting in your robes before bed, drinking cocoa and ranking us."

"Do you really think we'd waste time doing that?" she teased.

"Probably not, but a guy can hope. Then again, I'm probably at the bottom of the ranking, so maybe it is just as well you don't. I'll tell you what you should do, though. Talk to Cynthia. I know I shouldn't say this, but that girl blows hot and cold. Poor Robbie. Cynthia doesn't want to dance and is pouting. She's asking to go home. But that doesn't mean we can't have fun." He grinned and abruptly twirled her, catching her just before she propelled out of his reach.

She held on to him tightly to get her balance. "I'm so sorry. The last spin left me dizzy."

"That was the general idea."

"To make me dizzy?"

"Yes, if it will get you to hold onto me."

"How many drinks have you had?"

"Maybe one or two more than usual. It's for cultural purposes. You know, becoming more familiar with foreign wines. Osgoode told me it would clear my mind. And, as you know, we all need our minds to be clear."

"I haven't had a drink, but I think something must have gone to my head." She smiled at him.

"About time," he said, pulling her closer. As he turned her, she looked at the band and noted it had grown after the first few dances. She quickly scanned the group, looking again at the unusual instruments. She stopped abruptly when she saw the drummer in the far corner, partially hidden in shadow.

"Lyall. I think I see Warren Elliot playing the drums. In the way back? I didn't see him before. Look! Am I right?"

Lyall gently pulled her into his arms so she was forced to start to dance again. Briefly, he looked over her shoulder at the stage. "I can't see the drummer, but does it really matter? Stop thinking about work. Please." He pulled her tighter as he murmured, "No work talk, Meg." In silent response, she rested her head on his shoulder and closed her eyes. She did not need to be able to see to follow his lead as they danced slowly. For a few moments, Meg thought of nothing other than how pleasant the music was and how comfortable it was to be in Lyall's arms.

"Lieutenant, mind if I cut in?" It took Meg a moment to process it was Robbie's voice, and she opened her eyes as Lyall's body stiffened.

"Yes, Prescott, I do mind," Lyall said forcefully.

Robbie gave him a look that indicated it was rather more a command than a suggestion.

"Alright. One dance," Lyall griped. He huffed as he walked purposefully off the floor toward the bar.

Meg was immediately more alert as the music changed to a waltz and adjusted to following Robbie's rather than Lyall's lead. While comfortably silent with Lyall, she felt she needed to speak to Robbie.

"Robbie, did you notice the drummer in the back corner?"

"The one who is either Elliot or his twin?" Prescott responded.

"Exactly. What do you think is going on?"

"You tell me. You probably know him better than any of the rest of us do."

"It makes some sense, I guess, that Warren could be here. He talks to someone named Francisco Avila at choir every week who's a refugee from Lisbon. Avila works at a hotel. I forget which one, but I am sure I could find out. In fact, I wouldn't be surprised to see Avila here tonight."

"Have you seen him here tonight?" Robbie asked. In the dim light of the dance floor, Meg could just make out the worried expression on Robbie's face, and she could feel tension in his arms. Robbie was trying very hard to keep his questions conversational, but Meg was sure running into Warren Elliot this evening was a problem for him.

"No. I haven't seen him," Meg responded. She gave him a big smile. "But I haven't been looking for him, either." Robbie spun her around in response to her comment and Meg caught a glimpse of Cynthia. Rather than glaring at Meg as she expected, Cynthia was clutching her abdomen and looked to be in a great deal of pain. Meg tapped Robbie's shoulder and pulled back from his chest.

"Cynthia looks miserable. We should probably get her home."

"Yeah," he said flatly. "The party is almost over anyway."

## 37

The event at the embassy had ended with Meg organizing a cab to Isobel's to get Cynthia home, rather than going to another party or to a bar. She had been right to suggest they take her home; Cynthia had acute food poisoning all weekend, which she blamed on stew she had as a late lunch before they went to the party. She had been sick enough to miss work and to stay in her room most of the weekend, emerging on Sunday evening to eat some toast while the others had dinner. Although Vivian had the weekend off, in the absence of progress on the additive Meg and Julie had reported on both Saturday and Sunday, after first retrieving the quartets' uniforms from Barrack D.

Meg liked to arrive early. She could talk to people on the night watch before they left the command. Their insights often helped her get started on the day's activity. Sometimes, Meg sat down at a desk where the seat was still warm and took up where another analyst had been puzzling all night. There might be brief notes in the margin or tick marks with different letter combinations her predecessor had tried. If she arrived early enough, there was the faint smell of paper smoke competing with cigarette smoke. The janitors were not allowed in at night, and some of the enlisted personnel were in charge of burning the trash in an incinerator that had been rigged using a vent in what had been a chemistry lab.

The Monday following the party at the embassy, Meg stopped in the galley for a cup of coffee. This was the first day of wearing their summer uniforms, which were white and lighter in weight, complemented by white shoes. In addition to the white and pink cherry blossoms bursting throughout the city, the change in wardrobe was a much needed pick-me-up. It had been three weeks since the Japanese had changed the additives, and the group had yet to have a significant break in understanding the latest additive code system.

As she walked pass the "professors'" area, she saw they were reanalyzing the most frequent combinations of code to see if that might provide a clue. She noticed that Lieutenant Prescott, or rather Robbie as she was now trying to think of him, looked as though he had not slept last night. Had he come in during the night shift to put in some extra time to identify a breakthrough? Meg noted his perfunctory good morning. He did not linger over his greeting as he often did, and she sensed he was annoyed with her.

Meg was rotating her shoulders and then propping her feet against the modesty panel at the front of the desk to get an entire body stretch when Commander Lewis barked, "All hands. Now!" Meg was surprised. It was too early for their usual group meeting. Without thinking, she glanced over at Robbie, who shook his head slightly. He looked as surprised as she.

Lewis's face was red and he was pacing in the work area while staring at the small clusters of personnel standing and leaning against the desks. "I want everyone to raise their left hand. Does everyone know which hand is his left hand?" Although he was trying to keep calm, Meg realized he was teetering on the edge of throwing a tantrum. The air was tense.

She wondered if others were breathing as shallowly as herself. She hoped he would not be pushed past his point of no return. She hesitantly put her hand up, as she was close enough to him so that he could slap it.

"Good. Very nice, everyone. Now could you please show me your right hand? Great. Full marks. Looks like everyone knows their left from their right." He turned and stood with mere inches separating him from Elliot. "So, Mr. Elliot, do you want to explain why I have a memo from the guard office that you wore your badge on the wrong side Friday morning?" Lewis had overemphasized *mister* and released spittle as he said the *s*. He glared menacingly. "Do you not know your left from your right? Do you think this is funny? Do you think naval rules and regulations are stupid? Do you think just because you can't be a sailor you do not have to follow rules?"

It was so quiet, Meg could hear the blinds gently bumping up against the window in the gentle breeze. Someone on her left let his breath out slowly. Meg looked up from where she had been staring at the floor, afraid to make eye contact with Lewis. She saw Warren's face was a color between red and purple, his eyes bulging, and both his hands clenched tightly in fists. For a moment, she thought Warren might attack the commander.

"Go home, Elliot. You have the rest of the day to figure out your left from your right. You're on the night watch from now on." Lewis abruptly turned, walked to his office, and slammed the door. The group was silent as the noise reverberated through the room. Slowly, the group dispersed and returned to their desks without speaking.

Meg sat down and tried to study the transmission in front of her. She quickly looked at the numbers and worked backward to see if it fit one of the code groups with which they were working. This approach had become instinctual, but this morning she could not make sense of the message. The commander's outburst had rattled her. But that was only part of the issue. The transmission was unlike the codes with which she had been working this week. She was staring at the transmission and tapping her pencil against her cheek, when she heard liquid being poured. She looked up and saw Lieutenant Prescott had a container of milk and her coffee was now a nice tan rather than black.

"Thanks."

"Do you think you can stare it into submission?" Robbie asked. Some, but not all, of the playfulness had returned to his tone.

"If only I could," she replied.

"I give you the better odds in the fight."

"Something is off; I can't put my finger on it. I think it's the transmission, but it could also be the fact that it has been a strange morning." Meg dropped her voice to a whisper. "Did you tell Lewis we saw Warren playing the drums at the party?"

"I did. It isn't necessarily a crime to be playing Portuguese music, but I was a little uncomfortable with someone who's working with highly classified information clearly doing more than visiting another government's embassy. Lewis didn't thank me for telling him." Robbie's fingers raked his hair, which Meg had learned was always a sign he was under pressure. He continued, "Especially since I could only tell him we saw Elliot playing the drums but we didn't see anything I would call suspicious."

"We?"

He flushed. "I told him the eight of us were there."

"Ah." Before she could stop herself, she whispered, "What if he had been bartending? Would you have said anything then?" Now it was her turn to feel herself flush.

He smiled at her. "If Elliot had a civilian job at a civilian party during peacetime, there would be no reason for me to say anything to anyone." He paused and said softly, "Ever."

"Oh." Looking into Robbie's eyes, she saw that her one simple syllable conveyed a tremendous amount of information.

Robbie cleared his throat slightly. "You don't need Elliot to keep you on track, do you? Every time I check in with the two of you, I feel as though you're the one leading. I guess for now you report to me. Will that work?"

"Not really, Lieutenant," she said with a smirk. He grinned at her and walked off. She replayed their conversation a few times in her mind; it was a while before she could focus on the transmission.

LATER THAT WEEK was her first time at choir practice since Warren moved to nights. Meg wasn't sure if Warren was going to be there or if he would be speaking to her. She worked on the *Washington Post*'s crossword puzzle, proud of herself for knowing "hated bird," eight letters, was *starling*.

When she had arrived a few minutes early before the choristers, she waited in the vestibule, noticing, not for the first time, some of the church information pamphlets were out of their normal alphabetical order. The Knights of Columbus were in the top left slot and she had started to move them to their rightful place in a middle slot when Francisco Avila rushed in.

"Don't touch. Don't touch," he hissed.

"I was just trying to help," she explained as Jane walked in.

"Well, hello, dear. How are you?" Jane greeted her. "Are you alright? I have some crackers with me. You have your hungry look."

"Yes. Thank you. I'll gladly eat them. I'm famished this evening." As Meg and Jane walked in, Jane continued, "I love your new uniform. Much better suited for the warm weather. It is truly spring and warm enough for me to plant my seedlings. I'm going to have a huge crop of tomatoes this summer. We'll eat well!" Meg sat at Jane's side and although she could not see Avila, she did not stop thinking about him. Why had he been so upset? Did he struggle to organize the pamphlets because he had difficulty with English? Should she care if they were out of alphabetical order if they were not messy?

Warren walked in a moment before practice started and Meg wondered if he had driven there. His glare at her indicated she did not have to fend off a ride home. Meg spent the rest of the evening lip-synching and wondering what Warren and Avila said to each other until it was time to catch her bus. Warren still needed to wait on the other side of the street for his bus and tonight, Meg noticed another man in business attire, which was out of place at this time of night in this part of town. The man was tall, as tall as Robbie, she thought, and similarly to Robbie carried himself like an athlete, almost as if on springs as he walked toward Warren and the bus stop. Warren's bus came first, and she watched as the man jogged across the street behind the departing bus to join her at the stop.

"I'm new to Washington. Still learning the routes. Just realized I was at the wrong stop," he explained in response to Meg's quizzical expression. His hat was pulled low over his face, so Meg could not make out his hair length or color.

"It takes a while to figure it out," she agreed and was happy to see their bus was approaching. Meg took a seat at the front, near the driver, and took her crossword out. The few times she allowed herself to look up, she knew the man was staring at her. She did not want to catch his eye and definitely did not want to have a conversation with him. *Probably not used to the WAVE uniform if he is new to Washington*, she reassured herself. She was glad to be the only person getting off near Isobel's and quickly walked home.

The next morning, while walking to work, Meg thought about her strange encounter with Mr. Avila. She knew she had been hungry and on edge about seeing Warren for the first time since he had been dressed down at work, but thought that there was something very odd about Avila's behavior. She told herself to put it out of her mind as she sat down at her desk.

She had a much bigger mystery to figure out while studying the transmissions. She tapped her pencil in a brusque rhythm for several minutes until she cried out, jumped up, and hurried to Julie's library.

Julie smiled welcomingly. "What can I do for you?"

"Julie, what is the Japanese word for tungsten?"

"Tungsten?" Julie asked.

"Used in light bulb filaments," Meg explained.

"Not surprisingly," Julie grinned, "I don't know off the top of my head, but let's find it." She grabbed one of the Japanese lexicons. "Looks like in romaji it is *tangusuten*. It's fairly close to the English. Does that help?"

"Have you seen anything in the news about a shortage of tungsten?"

"In the British papers," Cynthia chimed in. It had taken a few days for her to recover from her food poisoning, but Meg was happy to hear the sardonic tone, which indicated Cynthia was feeling much better. Meg allowed herself half a moment to be surprised that she was reading the British papers. The Cynthia she met at Smith only read the society page, but that was before Cynthia had found her métier supporting the archive project. "I think we had an intelligence report indicating raw materials have become an issue for the Japanese."

"We may have just received a gift," Meg said as she turned, smiled at the other two WAVES, and hurried back to the other analysts. She signaled to Lyall and Robbie to come and join her at her desk.

"I think I just found something. Let me run it past you and you can see what you think."

The three sat down and Meg dropped her voice to a whisper.

"This message is dated yesterday, but I could not put it in its group. None of the headers looks right. That is, until you realize someone was tired. The radioman sent the message in plain code without an additive. This part of the message indicates his ship's position at noon." She pointed at 6253 and 1441, which were the current codes for latitude and longitude.

"So far so good," Lyall said, encouragingly.

"So, in addition to the position, it's talking about a critical shipment. I just checked with Julie. She has seen a few reports talking about the Japanese lack of raw materials in general and Cynthia was aware of news in a British paper that specifically mentioned tungsten. Let's assume one of the middle words, an unfamiliar pattern, is *tungsten* or the romaji *tangusuten* and see if that helps people to unlock a pattern."

"What is going on here, Prescott?" inquired the commander. Commander Lewis had approached the group unnoticed.

"I am going to let Lieutenant Burke explain," Robbie replied.

Meg repeated what she noted in the transmission as well as the background information she had obtained from the library desk.

"Ensign Collingsworth, come in here!" Lewis shouted, his voice easily carrying to the other room. Cynthia walked quickly into the room. "Go to the big library and look for anything you can find about tungsten, especially shortages in the Far East.

"Lieutenant Burke, I want you to go and explain what you just told me to the 'professors,'" Lewis commanded.

"Lyall," Meg said quietly. "Could you grab one of the chalkboards for me?"

"Some people have security blankets; you have a security chalkboard?" he teased.

"Exactly." She smiled.

Although she had worked in the same group as the "professors" for several months, she had only ever exchanged a few casual words with any of them. Certainly, she had never spoken to them about code-breaking. Meg could feel her heart beating and her hands getting sweaty. She couldn't allow herself to get nervous.

"This morning I was working on a message, and I felt as

though it had not been through the additive step." She wrote 4821 on the board. "If we take the pure code the Japanese have been using and assume no additive, this corresponds to *tangusuten*, or the romaji for *tungsten*."

"Why tungsten?" one of the men asked.

"That's where it gets interesting," Lewis replied. "Apparently there is a shortage and there is a concern about where they are going to get more. I have Ensign Collingsworth getting more information from the Library of Congress."

Meg felt six pairs of eyes staring at her until she realized the group was looking intently at the chalkboard rather than at her.

After a few moments, another "professor" stood up and started writing 8974. "We've seen this combination, which is unfamiliar, repeated in several messages this week. Let's assume it's *tungsten* and back into the additive from that. We can work with this. Well done, Lieutenant. Very imaginative."

During Indoctrination, her instructors taught Meg that successful code-breaking often came down to diagnostics, but there was also the ability to see the whole rather than just the parts. She had just learned how thrilling it was to discern part of an underlying system of disguise. She felt as though she had joined a club.

## 38

A few days later, Robbie asked Meg to join him in the Mess for a mid-morning cup of coffee. As they sat down, Meg began, "I'm glad to have a chance to talk with you." He smiled at her, and she felt herself blush.

In the momentary silence that followed, surprising herself, she said, "I've noticed several strange things going on."

He looked astonished. Meg was sure that was not what he expected her to say, but he moved closer to her and leaned in slightly as he said, "Are you sure it's not a touch of spring fever? Maybe a full moon?"

She smiled back. "With my lack of sleep, I'm probably imagining things."

"Even without your lack of sleep you imagine things, which is why you worry." His voice took on a softer lilt and he looked concerned. "What's concerning you?"

"When I walk into church for choir practice there is a brochure holder. It holds pamphlets you can take home if you want to learn more about joining the altar society or donate to a missionary society. Most of the time they are more or less arranged in alphabetical order."

"What do you mean, alphabetical order?"

"By the name of the group. Altar and Rosary, Bereavement, Catechism, et cetera. Some weeks, before practice, the Knights of Columbus is first." She could tell he was desperately trying not to laugh.

"But not every time?"

"No. Not every week. Sometimes it's two weeks in a row. This last time it was three weeks before it was in the first slot again. And it was out of order when I went to choir last week."

"Could it be that the person who fills the slots has a Knights of Columbus connection and wants to make sure they're in the best place?"

"Probably." She frowned.

"You're losing sleep over church brochures?" Robbie asked, choking back a laugh.

"Our mysterious choir member, Mr. Avila, got upset as I attempted to straighten the brochures at the last at practice."

"What did he do?"

"He shouted at me to leave them alone."

"So, leave them alone. Let someone else clean up the church. Go help Julie with her filing if you have a particular need to organize paper."

She took another sip of her coffee. "It's not just that. I feel as though I am being followed."

"Of course you are. Any woman in this town who is in an officer's uniform is followed. Strike that. Just about every woman in this town is followed. You probably also get whistles and catcalls. Annoying, but probably not life threatening. In fact, an everyday occurrence with Osgoode. I would think you were almost immune at this point. Didn't the same thing happen when you walked to work in Brooklyn?"

"Infrequently. I could blend in when walking in my neighborhood or commuting to school. I had a teaching colleague who followed me for a time. But it's not that sort of following. I think I've only noticed when the person has made a mistake or gotten careless. I don't think I'm supposed to notice him. It generally happens when I'm going to church, but not always. I swam after work the other day, so I wasn't walking with the others, and I saw him again. He's always wearing a slightly ratty homburg and takes short strides for a man who is about six feet tall. When I sped up, he sped up. I slowed down abruptly, and when I turned to see if he was still following me, he quickly leaned into a doorway."

"Hmm. Only when you are alone?" Robbie teased.

"I know you don't think the pamphlets are serious, but being followed has me a little unnerved." She looked down at the table before looking him in the eye. "It really feels like someone is watching me rather than trying to pick me up. Believe it or not, I do know the difference."

"I believe that you do know the difference," he said more seriously.

"Once I reached Isobel's, he walked casually up to the next block and turned left, as though he were just enjoying looking at the neighborhood. Do you think there are people following us from the Annex because they want to find out what we're doing?"

"It could be. There are so many military personnel walking around, it's hard to tell if any of them are being followed. I would not have thought that a WAVE would be a prime target, but I'm concerned you've noticed it when you're alone."

"We have also started getting telephone calls in the middle of the night and when Cynthia or Aunt Isobel answers, there is no one there. Aunt Isobel is getting annoyed."

Robbie smiled. "With the four of you in that house, of course you are getting telephone calls. I'm less concerned to hear that."

"In the middle of the night?"

"That is when liquid courage kicks in, Lieutenant Burke," he said in a serious tone.

"Robbie, don't you ever have a feeling something isn't right?

You may have an explanation for everything I've said, but I know something is off."

"I'm trying to make you not worry any more than you are already." He looked at her earnestly. "But I do understand that you're unnerved. I think the best thing to do is to make sure you are always walking with Julie or Cynthia. If you're going to swim, make sure you're taking the bus. No walking alone, especially not in the early morning or at night. Let me know if you see the guy with the hat again." Then he chuckled. "But I am interested in your church pamphlets moving around. Can you draw some pictures the next time it happens? Maybe number them before and after so I understand exactly the pattern in which they are moved."

Meg made a face at him. "Any word on how Elliot is doing on nights?" she asked to change the subject.

"Like you, I try to get in early some mornings and overlap with him. He doesn't seem to be up to much. Never anything of significance to report. Moving to nights has taken away any vestiges of esprit de corps he once had, such as it was. Why do you ask?"

"Not here," she said quickly and paused before continuing. "Let me think about how I can say this. Maybe I can tell you."

He looked at her quizzically. She thought for a moment about how to describe the problem without talking about their work. "We're still working on the same project. He works on it at night, and I work on it during the day. Some mornings I have trouble finding what I've been working on the day before."

"Do you think he's hiding the work?"

"Not exactly." She tried to think of the correct explanation. "It's not being filed in the right place. I don't know if the communications are being put in the right place."

"Probably he's just trying to make your life a little more difficult by being a bit sloppy. You know how stuff moves around in our office. But if you are truly missing work, you should let me know."

"Speaking of work, we should get back," Meg said with a smile.

"We should. Try not to worry and make sure you aren't alone." He held her chair and briefly put his other hand on the small of her back as she got up. Meg felt like she was almost floating as they returned to their workspace but was quickly shocked back to reality by the elevated noise level and frenzy of activity.

"Robbie. Meg. We need two more sets of eyes to double-check this," Lyall called to them.

"What are we looking at?" Robbie asked.

"Or for?" Meg added.

"Looks like we have a message about Admiral Yamamoto's travel schedule," Lyall replied.

"*The* Admiral Yamamoto?" Robbie asked.

"Yup. Harvard graduate, playboy, gambler, and the US Navy's nemesis," Lyall confirmed.

Lewis shouted at Lyall from across the room, "Quiet, McClaren!" He walked across the room to the trio before continuing in a lower voice, "You shouldn't have told them that before Prescott had a chance to transpose and decode the message."

"Give me the additives and the message," Meg said. "I know the least about this type of message and almost never work with JN-25. I'll have to brute-force the transposition, so I'm the least likely to read something into it."

"True. Thank you, Lieutenant," the commander said as he passed her the materials.

"Should you have someone on the night shift who doesn't know what we are looking at double-check?" Robbie asked.

"We don't have time to wait for Elliot to look at this. You look at it, too, and see what you think," Lewis said.

Forty minutes later, Meg knocked on the commander's door. Realizing she had never been in his office, she quickly scanned the walls and saw not only a bachelor's degree in engineering from Purdue but also a law degree from the University of Chicago. Lewis answered the question he could read on her face. "Patent law."

She couldn't stop herself from saying, "That explains so much." She quickly added, "Sir," and flushed, expecting a reprimand. Instead, Lewis quietly chuckled.

"I guess it probably does." He sat up straighter before continuing, "What did you find?"

"I could decode 'the honorable Admiral Yamamoto' as well as 'April 18,' 'naval base,' and 'Solomon Island.' I could spend hours on the name of the base, but I don't think we have hours. The base name starts with a B, but that portion did not make sense. Does Ensign Bowen have a list of possible bases?"

"She does. Looks like Bougainville, but don't tell Prescott until he's worked with it." There was a knock on the door. "Speak of the devil," Lewis said.

Robbie walked into the office and closed the door behind him before he let out a low whistle. "Lieutenant Burke is faster than I am. I'm doing too much admin and not spending enough time decoding. I'm out of practice."

"What did you get?" Lewis said sharply. His tone said "compare scores later."

"Naval base starting with a B, I would say Burgundville, but I think I am off a letter or two, in the Solomon Islands on 18 April."

"I had four of the 'professors' run it as well as you two. You all got roughly the same thing. There is only one base, Bougainville, that fits for length. The 'professors' could back into the name once they had it." He pounded the desk. "We've got the additive and we've got a hell of a message." He paced silently for a moment. "I'm not sure if I should pass it on."

"You're only passing on vetted information," Robbie said. Meg watched a silent conversation take place between the two men, who seemed to have completely forgotten she was there.

After a pause, Robbie continued as if both had been debating aloud, "Someone else will make the decision."

"And it could tip off the Japanese about all the good work we're doing."

"Let it be someone else's decision. Go congratulate the team for a job well done."

Meg seldom thought about what happened once they decoded the information and what was done with the intelligence that was passing through their command. Her anxiety and concern were generally limited to whether she could break the code, not what the code said. Finally, she understood why Lewis had a habit of kicking table legs.

## 39

The commander gathered the group together, thanked them for their good work on the travel message, and released them from the watch a few minutes early. Lyall bounded over to Meg and suggested, "Let's go get an ice cream."

"Great idea," Cynthia said from over Meg's shoulder.

"Did I hear 'ice cream'?" Julie asked.

"Oh. Yeah. Sure," Lyall replied. Meg was sure he had not meant it to be a group invitation.

"I'm going to take the extra time to get in a swim," Meg told the others. She had no intention of swimming. Rather, she wanted a few moments alone to think about her conversation in the Mess with Robbie. She would tell Julie parts of it later, but she did not want to share with the other WAVES only to have Cynthia say something to break the spell Meg felt she was under. Meg deliciously replayed the conversation in her mind as she walked home slowly, distractedly looking at shop windows without really seeing them.

She found herself in front of a bookstore a few blocks away from the Annex with the name "Crosby's" written in script on the burgundy awning. She had assumed the bookstore had relied on Mount Vernon for its customers but as she walked closer, she realized that this was not a shop that catered to the daughters of the rich. The shop, like the rest of the stores on the block, still needed to take down their storm windows and touch up their trim after the winter. She hesitated before deciding since she had come this far, she might as well walk in. She could, Meg thought, certainly treat herself to a book.

The door handle needed polishing and it left a grimy mark on her white gloves. A small bell on the door announced her arrival. Although it was a bright day outside, it took Meg's eyes a few minutes to adjust to the gloom inside. Not only did the dirt on the windows cut down on the ambient light, but the store was filled with rows of bookcases, crammed floor to ceiling, allowing for very little illumination to travel across the interior.

A middle-aged man whose military cut was now more gray than sandy blond wore a dark blue cardigan with darned elbows and sat at what looked to be a repurposed bar chair so he was at the same level as the cash register.

"Hello," Meg said, and tried not to start when she realized one of the man's eyes moved as he looked at her WAVES uniform appreciatively, while the other did not.

"Lost my other eye during the Great War," he said simply.

Meg wasn't sure how to respond. The only thing she could think to say was, "Are you Mr. Crosby?"

"I'm *a* Mr. Crosby. Hardly the only one, am I? Wish I had the money of the Crosby in Hollywood." He sighed. "And the women too, I guess." He turned slightly to his left side to let his good eye focus on her. "What are you looking for?"

"An Agatha Christie."

"An Agatha Christie," he repeated and sighed. "Well, they will be with the other mysteries in the far corner." He gestured across the shop toward the back. "I sell them because I must. People always have used copies to spare after the summer or if they take a trip. Of course, not so many now that people aren't taking trips."

As Meg looked toward the far corner, she saw that a curtain blocked more than one side of the store. Her fingers started to tingle and her stomach did its familiar but unwelcome flip-flops. She had not realized what sort of bookstore this was. Still, she had come this far and pivoted neatly to the unshrouded side of the store.

"I'll go check them out." Her heart started beating more quickly as she walked toward the corner. She reassured herself that she was not in any real danger and could tell an unusual story at dinner tonight. She was already thinking about how to best mimic Mr. Crosby.

As she started looking at the spines of the books to locate "Christie," she heard the bell on the door tinkle. She was comforted that another person was in the shop and felt her shoulders relaxing as she gently pulled a few of the books out of the dark shelves and into the slightly better light to look at titles and authors. There were just enough books by authors with last names starting with *A* or *B* that she needed to crouch down to look at the bottom rows. Unexpectedly, she saw feet coming toward her and bolted up quickly, feeling light-headed. As she grabbed the bookshelf for balance, Mr. Crosby said, "You might want to try Ngaio Marsh."

"Who?" she asked in confusion. As she did so, down the corridor of bookshelves, she saw the other shopper. He looked like Francisco Avila!

Mr. Crosby moved slightly so that he was blocking her sight line across the store. "If you like Agatha Christie you should try Ngaio Marsh. Marsh is from New Zealand, but you would think she was English. She writes about a nice gentleman detective who solves crimes for the London Metropolitan Police, when he is not going to house parties and having a new suit custom made."

Meg agreed, "That does sound like a book I would like."

"You might as well start with the first one." He moved over to the adjoining bookcase and handed her a book entitled *A Man Lay Dead*.

"Thank you," Meg responded. She looked across the store and saw the other customer was near the door. "I don't want to keep you from your other customer."

"Oh, him. He never buys, just browses," Crosby said loudly.

A moment later the bell tinkled, and Meg heard the door close. Crosby walked with her to the register. "Military discount. A nickel for the book."

As Meg reached into her purse, he lay the book on the edge of the cash register. "I only wrap books that you would be embarrassed to read on the bus. No bag for this one."

"Right," Meg said simply as she flushed. "Thank you."

As she opened the door, Mr. Crosby called out, "I hope you come back for the next book."

*Not on your life*, she thought as she walked down the street. Turning the corner toward her bus stop, she saw the bus just pulling away. Even if she were a runner and not in her work heels, she would not catch up. She resigned herself to walking home.

Meg shook off her visit to the seedy bookstore and reassured herself the only reason she thought the other customer looked like Avila was because of her earlier conversation with Robbie. As she continued walking, she let her thoughts return to how it had felt to have Robbie put his hand on the small of her back. He was taller than she and it felt good to stand next to him. She felt protected. Meg moved forward in a pleasant haze of thought, not looking at the other pedestrians until she stopped at a traffic light. As she looked around, on the edge of the group of the dozen or so people, she thought she saw the man who had ridden the bus with her the other night. This man certainly had the same tall stature. He didn't wear a hat so she could see his dirty blond hair. He had the unusual gait of almost bouncing as he walked, which she had noticed the other night. In her mind she named him Mr. X. For a moment, their eyes met before he nimbly moved behind another man as the light changed and Meg lost him among the surge of pedestrians.

Meg scolded herself. *Get a grip, Margaret Burke!* Her heart was pounding, and all pleasant thoughts of Robbie were gone. Rather, she thought about telling him her concerns about being followed. She now thought there were two men keeping her in their sights. For the rest of the walk home, she continued to stop abruptly to look for anyone shadowing her.

The smell of beef stew welcomed her. Her mouth watered with the thought of the accompanying hard-crusted white bread, which had a soft interior that acted as a sponge for any gravy stew remaining on her plate. Meg's stomach rumbled as she crossed the threshold and saw Julie and Isobel chatting in the vestibule.

"There you are!" Julie exclaimed. "We're waiting for you."

Meg looked at her watch and saw it was after six. As the days were getting longer, she could no longer tell time by the amount of sunlight.

"My apologies. I got sidetracked and had an adventure."

"Go wash quickly," Isobel. "I can't wait to hear."

Meg rushed upstairs to take off her grimy gloves and start them soaking in the sink. As she hurried downstairs, she wondered how much detail she should include about the bookstore. Might Isobel be upset?

Meg let everyone take a few bites of stew before she said, "I think I wandered into a Washington, DC, institution this afternoon." Isobel arched her eyebrow as Meg continued, "I was looking for an Agatha Christie and—"

"Crosby's!" Isobel exclaimed.

"Crosby's," Meg confirmed.

"Oh no. Did you really have no idea, Meg?" Isobel asked.

"Not until I was far enough in the store to see the curtains. If I had any doubt, it was erased when Mr. Crosby said he wouldn't wrap my mystery. I guess he sells regular books as a front?" Meg directed her question to Isobel.

"You were in an adult bookstore. Margaret Burke! What were you thinking?" Cynthia exclaimed.

"You know me, Cynthia. I'm clueless about so many things. Since the bookstore was close to Mount Vernon, I thought it targeted the students and was struggling since the school shut down."

"Honestly, Meg. You're the one from New York." Cynthia frowned at her.

Isobel made a noise that was between chuckling and choking. When she finally regained her composure, she merely said, "Join the Navy and see the world."

## 40

"Miss Meg. Miss Meg. You need to wake up." Meg looked groggily around the bedroom she shared with Julie. The illuminated alarm clock faintly glowed 4:15. Meg could not understand why Davis was shaking her gently.

"You're needed on the telephone," Davis urged.

That statement woke Meg up. Davis had said *telephone*, rather than *telegram*, she thought sleepily. Still, Meg hurried to grab her robe. Aunt Isobel was holding the telephone receiver and frowning at a picture on the library wall as Meg entered the room.

"Lieutenant Burke has joined me. I will put her on," Isobel said.

"Hello?" Meg said tentatively.

"Lieutenant Burke, it's Commander Lewis. I need you at work immediately."

"Why?" Although still waking up, Meg quickly realized that was the wrong thing to say. "Why, sir?" she corrected herself.

"I'll explain when you arrive, Lieutenant." Meg put down

the phone and saw Isobel's worried expression, which did nothing to calm her own anxiety.

"Do you have any idea what is going on?" Isobel asked.

"None."

"I'm going to have George drive you," Isobel announced, and Meg nodded in agreement.

"I'll go upstairs and get dressed," she said sleepily.

Julie was awake and sitting up in bed. "What's going on?"

"Absolutely no idea," Meg said as she pulled a white blouse over her head.

"You don't think it has to do with going to the bookstore?" Julie asked.

Meg shrugged her shoulders. She was holding several bobby pins in her mouth to pin back her hair. She realized on top of everything else that morning, she needed a haircut. Her potential infractions were quickly compounding.

Once the bobby pins were out of her mouth and into her hair, Meg replied, "That might get a dressing-down similar to the one Lewis gave Warren, but I don't think they would call me in the middle of the night. Or would they?"

"You're right, Meg. Good thinking. It must have to do with your work. It must be some sort of emergency." Julie jumped out of bed to give the quivering Meg a big hug. "You'll do fine," she said to comfort her friend.

As George drove her hurriedly to the Annex, Meg's stomach grumbled. As much as she wanted to believe Lewis needed her to look at a code pattern, she knew that wasn't why he called.

"When should I pick you up, Miss Meg?" George asked as they approached the front gate. Even though she was consumed with nerves, Meg took a moment to look at the building she had only ever seen in daylight. With few lights, curtained windows, and surrounded by many trees, the building took on an abandoned, even haunted exterior.

"I'm not sure when I'll be finished. I'll take the bus back. Thank you for getting up so early," Meg replied.

"You'll be fine, Miss Meg, whatever it is," George said sympathetically. Meg gave him a quick wave and turned to face the impassive sentry who stood under a spotlight. Coming from the dark car, she was startled by this patch of bright light and hesitated for a moment to acclimate.

"I need to see your badge, ma'am," he requested.

"Of course." She grabbed the badge pinned to her uniform and handed it to the guard. As he examined it carefully, Meg noted the spring humidity and constant use had made it dog-eared. In addition to worrying about her appearance, this might be another issue. She forced herself to take a breath.

"Your badge is no longer valid," he declared and quietly whistled. Another sentry marched from inside the Annex to the gate and stood next to Meg.

"Escort the lieutenant to Reception."

Meg held her hand out to retrieve her badge.

"No, ma'am. You don't get this back. Go with the guard to Reception."

As she entered the building, she saw Commander Lewis waiting just inside the door; he stood even straighter when she walked in. After she saluted, she said, "Sorry for the delay, sir, I just learned I need a new badge." The escort handed Lewis her badge.

"I'll take your badge for now, Lieutenant. You won't need it for the next couple of hours," Lewis replied.

Her stomach sank and she felt like her heart might have stopped for a moment. She was in trouble, although she had no idea what she had done.

"You're, dismissed Seaman. I'll escort Lieutenant Burke," Lewis said to the man as he gently touched Meg's elbow to guide her through the hall. Halfway down the passage, Lewis stopped in front of a brown door with no name plate, turned the knob, and ushered her into a room with a table, four chairs, and no window. It reminded Meg of the room at the first installation when Robbie, or Lieutenant Prescott as she had thought of him then, had told Cynthia and Meg they would need to sleep in the barracks. She hadn't wanted to cry then, but she felt like she was about to burst into tears now.

"Take a seat, Lieutenant. There are two investigative officers who are going to be asking you some questions." Lewis started to say something else and then stopped. In addition to being ever so slightly disheveled from dressing quickly, he looked sad. Even disappointed, Meg thought.

"I don't know what this is about, sir," Meg said.

"You don't?" he sounded surprised. "You really don't?" he added. He looked at her for what felt like minutes to Meg but was probably not more than twenty seconds and said, "Don't say any more than you have to, okay, Lieutenant? Keep your answers brief." He gave her a look that might almost have been a brief smile as she stood at attention and saluted before he left the room.

Meg looked around the room and noted a mirror she had not seen when she first entered. She supposed that was the two-way mirror she had read about in crime stories. She heard the door open and was not sure whom to expect. Two new seamen entered the room. Both were young; either might have been one of her students last spring. The first to enter kept his face impassive and stared at a point on the opposite wall, but the other immediately started staring at the gold buttons on her uniform. Meg wondered if she were the first WAVE officer he had seen in person.

The seaman staring at her uniform asked, "Would you like coffee?"

"Yes. Thank you," she replied. He turned on his heel and left the room with only a small squeak of his sole on the polished floor.

Without her badge and in a room without windows, she felt she should not insist on "ma'am." In fact, she realized the other seaman was in the room to guard her, or at the very least watch her. She took a seat in one of the chairs and when she moved slightly, the chair rocked onto the shorter leg, leaving her unbalanced. As she righted herself, she wondered which paint factory had the contract to make the not quite blue and not quite green, not quite gray paint used in every depressing public building in the United States. Were the desks ever pristine or did they leave the factory scuffed? Was furniture scuffer a job title? If she could think about these details, she could control the sob threatening to escape from her chest.

After a knock on the door, the seaman in the room opened it a crack to confirm it was his colleague while also watching Meg to make sure she did not rush to escape. The seaman carried coffee poured into a cup from the receptacle attached to a water dispenser, which was not designed for hot liquids. Meg started to drink the weak cup of coffee quickly before the heat dissolved the paper cup in which she'd received it. It was not the hearty Navy brew she had grown accustomed to. She looked around her and realized she should slow down. There was no reason to be worried if her coffee cup dissolved. At worst, it would add a ring to multiple blemishes on the table.

She had purposefully selected a chair in a position from which she would not be looking directly into the mirror. Still, she could not resist turning her neck, and her reflection surprised her. She had worried that she looked disheveled, but surprisingly, she looked reasonably kempt in her uniform. Rather, she saw her pale face with huge circles under her eyes, accentuated by the fact that she had forgotten to put on any lipstick as she hurried this morning.

While she was lost in thought, the door flew open and two men in civilian clothes entered with an officer wearing Judge Advocate General Corps insignia and the name tag Marshall. When she saw the JAG officer, she felt as though someone was sitting on her chest. If a representative from the branch of military justice was here, she was in serious trouble. This meant a possible court-martial for an infraction of military law. She quickly saluted before clutching the table for support. Her ears were ringing and she was having difficulty controlling her shaking hands. Six adults filled the available space around the table, adding to Meg's growing sense of panic.

"At ease, Lieutenant," the officer said, but it was perfunctory. Meg would not be at ease.

Meg felt like she should say good morning or introduce herself, but this was not a normal social situation.

"You're excused," the officer said to the seamen. The two young men hurried out of the room and away from the JAG officer. The room was still crowded, but with only four people Meg was no longer worried she would faint.

"Sit," one of the men said, and as Meg sat, she looked at them carefully. The two men in civilian clothes were unshaven and also had circles under their eyes. The shorter of the two men's poorly cut suit had not been pressed in ages and his sleeves were too short. As he sat down and his sleeves rode up, Meg could see where his cuffs were beginning to fray. He either had financial problems or did not care about his appearance, or both. The other man was medium height and better dressed. His gray suit was offset by a blue tie punctuated with small red dots. He looked familiar. As soon as she mentally put a black homburg on him, Meg recognized him as the first man she had noticed following her.

Both men put their briefcases on the table and went through what Meg thought was an overly elaborate show of opening their bags and extracting manila files filled with white and yellow papers. She was sure that even with their shuffling they could hear her heart beating with a rhythm so rapid and so strong, she felt it might escape from her chest. Once several files were selected, both men closed their cases with loud clicks. One put his case on the floor to his right and the other to his left.

The shorter man said, "We have some questions to ask you and it is important that you answer them truthfully." He stopped and looked at Meg with an expression similar to the one she had seen on her principal's face as the educator disciplined two students who denied cheating. This man's look told her that no matter what she said, he was sure she had done something very wrong. He continued, "Are you a Democrat or a Republican?"

"Democrat."

"Were you ever a member of a worker's union?" he continued.

"No."

"Would you join a worker's union?"

Meg shook her head.

"I need you to say that out loud so we can both record your response."

"No."

"Have you ever been or are you now a member of the Communist Party?"

"No."

"Have you ever supported the German American Fund?"

"No." Meg tried to keep the exasperation out of her voice. She remembered Lewis's advice and tried to say as little as possible in a polite tone. In her exhaustion, however, she felt a flicker of irritation. She had answered these questions multiple times during the application process and again as part of Indoctrination before she began code training. There was no need to ask her these questions. Her answers were already on file.

"What sort of clubs do your parents belong to?"

"None." Now Meg fought to contain an angry chuckle in response to the question. When did her parents have time for clubs?

"Why are two of your brothers not currently serving in the military?" asked the taller man. After having been silent so far, his deeply resonant voice startled Meg, even though she should have expected the question, and she felt the chair tilt as she reacted. She took a moment to calm herself as she regained her balance.

"My eldest brother, James Burke, has 4-F status because of cataracts in both eyes. My youngest brother, Thomas Burke, is also 4-F because of a heart condition discovered by a Navy physician during his training after he volunteered for naval service on December 8, 1941." The two men exchanged a look.

The shorter one asked, "Have you ever done the wrong thing for the right reasons?"

"I told a friend her haircut looked wonderful when she really looked awful." After finishing her response, she immediately realized that was the sort of answer Lewis had warned her against making.

The two men shifted in their chairs before the taller man said, "Miss Burke, do you deny that you have a weekly rendezvous with Warren Elliot on Thursday evenings and have been doing so since January of this year?"

A faint gasp escaped from Meg before she could stop herself. In just a few seconds, she regained control and said in as calm a tone as she could manage, "I've never met Mr. Elliot for a rendezvous." She took a moment to look directly at the taller man and then at the shorter man and finally at the JAG officer before continuing, "On Thursdays and Sundays, I sing in a church choir with Mr. Elliot with more than a dozen elderly chaperones in attendance."

There were a few moments of silence before the shorter man asked, "Lieutenant Burke, describe the nature of your relationship with Warren Elliot."

"Perhaps we can use another word since I don't have a relationship with Mr. Elliot. Rather, he is my colleague. I interact with him as I work on tasks assigned by my superior officer, Commander Lewis, which include filing paperwork, sharpening pencils, and making coffee," Meg responded.

"And yet you spend your Thursday nights and Sunday mornings with Mr. Elliot, which is outside of your duty hours."

"I do spend Thursday nights and Sunday mornings attending St. Patrick's Church. Mr. Elliot is one of many people attending church," she said simply. Meg hoped her clear, brief answers indicated she had done nothing wrong.

The JAG officer shifted in his seat, pulled himself up to a perfectly straight posture, and said, "Are you aware of the consequences, including you likely facing court-martial, for making contact with individuals who are trying to overthrow the United States?"

Even though Meg wanted to jump up and down and shout as loudly as she could that they were wrong, she forced herself to take a few extra breaths before answering. She needed the mental equivalent of a quick break hanging on the edge of the pool deck to catch her breath and collect herself. Meg realized they thought she was conducting some sort of intelligence work. It was not clear to her if they thought she was helping Warren or he was helping her. She knew she was not spying. Did that mean Warren was? Had she been set up to look like she was passing secrets? Her mother said that there is always a way to get out of any problem; you just had to find it. Meg was going to need an advocate. Currently, there was only one person in the room who might take that role. She turned to the JAG officer.

"Sir, my understanding is that your role as a JAG officer is to both prosecute and defend military personnel. Are you here to advocate on my behalf?"

"Currently, I am here to observe and ensure your questioning follows established guidelines. You are under formal naval investigation, but you have not been charged. If you are charged, then you will be assigned an advocate."

For now, Meg needed to help herself. What would Cynthia do in her shoes? Certainly, she would stick up for herself, Meg thought. But in these circumstances, could she be as abrasive as Cynthia could be? It would be best to start subtly. The first thing, Meg decided, was to try to emulate Cynthia's affect in which she appeared to look down her nose at people, even people who were taller than she, while projecting she was the only person in the room who mattered. Meg imagined she was Cynthia and tried to look down her nose at the others. Once she did that, at least her reflection in the mirror had better posture. While striking this pose, Meg thought, perhaps if she reminded the others, in calm, polite tones, how little contact she had with anyone other than her coworkers, housemates, and some elderly ladies at church, they would realize she wasn't spying. She held herself up and tried to look down her nose as she cleared her throat gently. In response, the two men readjusted themselves from leaning in on the table and into an upright position with their backs against their chairs.

Meg gestured slightly at the taller man and said, "Since I know you have been carefully following me for many weeks, maybe months, I want to confirm the things you have seen me do and make sure they are recorded in this interview. I report for duty. I go to church. I swim several times a week, frequently with my CO." She noted the surprised expression on the JAG officer's face. "I live in Isobel Milbank's house as a boarder. I am sure you have seen how I try to take a different bus than Mr. Elliot and talk almost exclusively to the female members of the choir."

"We know you're doing more than just talking to the women at choir," the shorter man said curtly. He opened a file folder that had been on the table and took out a stack of papers. Meg could see, even upside down, they were photostats of letters to her parents, which of course included talk about choir. Her stomach sank as she remembered Julie joking that her choir descriptions were cryptic messages.

"We know you are using a type of code as you list the hymns," the taller man said.

It had been a long time since Meg had been this angry or this frustrated, even at Cynthia. Cynthia made her think of Isobel. She wished Isobel were with her. Meg would have already gotten out of the situation if Isobel had been here to advise her. Since she wasn't, Meg tried her best to emulate Isobel's noncommittal expression and calm voice.

"This is a list of the hymns we have been singing the past few months at St. Patrick's. I am sure that Mr. Kelly, the choir director, could verify these songs. He keeps a record of what we sing and the day on which we sing it."

None of the three men said anything for several moments, and Meg hoped they were thinking about her earnest justification for the lawfulness of what they had seen her do. She watched, hopefully, as the two suited men exchanged looks.

The shorter man readjusted himself in his chair and straightened his papers. "You've been quick with the explanations, Lieutenant," he emphasized *Lieutenant* as if it were a false title, "but how are you going to explain these?"

He slowly and deliberately separated individual eight-by-ten-inch glossy photographs from a stack and placed them across the table. Meg saw an image of her in the forefront of the picture, walking on the Mall. When she looked more closely at a face circled with a red grease pencil, she realized it was Avila's. There were similar pictures where she was the main subject of the photo and Avila was in the crowd, including one taken near Crosby's bookstore. In a few, Elliot or Avila were the focus, and she was a circled face in the crowd. One picture captured Warren, Meg, and Francisco leaving choir. Meg didn't remember ever leaving in a group, but she could see that the picture made them look like they were together. Most of the pictures showed her walking home from work and were taken only a few blocks from Isobel's house, confirming her suspicions she had been followed. As she looked closely at some of the other red circles, she noted in the photographs the tall man who had ridden on the bus with his hat pulled over his face and who she had thought she'd seen while walking home after going to the bookstore. Who could he be? Why was he circled? Wasn't he working with the man in the black hat who was currently interviewing her? There was also a picture of Vivian, Cynthia, and Meg getting into Tom's cab near Grand Central Station in December. Of all the things she had seen or been asked this morning, this picture with her brother was the most interesting and the most surprising.

"We've been logging your activity," the taller man said with a satisfied grin. "We know you are working with a foreign national and we know what you are up to."

The shorter man clasped his hands in front of himself on the table and leaned forward toward Meg. "We know you are a spy!"

## 41

M eg's stomach sank and she could feel her face flush. A spy! She resumed gripping the table so the others would not see how badly her hands were shaking. She wished she could calmly make eye contact with the three men and show she was not intimidated. Instead, she was completely focused on fighting back the tears that were waiting to stream from her eyes. As the door opened, she readied herself to have the seamen put some sort of restraints on her and lead her away, and one tear dropped onto her cheek from her right eye.

Robbie Prescott rushed into the room and raked his short, dark hair with his fingers as he looked quickly at Meg and then at the three men. He frowned when he saw her distress before his eyes darted to the pictures on the table. The taller man rapidly gathered the photos into a pile as soon as he saw Robbie staring at them. Both Meg and the JAG officer rose to salute Robbie and Meg shakily sat back down. The shorter man exclaimed, "Who are you?"

"I'm Lieutenant Robert Prescott, Commander Lewis's attaché. I'm here on his behalf to see why Lieutenant Burke has yet to report for duty. We've a great deal of work to accomplish today, and Lieutenant Burke is an integral part of the process. I'm here to take her back to the Command with me."

"You can't be here," said the shorter man.

"I'm pretty sure I can be here." Robbie drew out each word and Meg could tell he was barely keeping his anger in check. "As I said, I represent Commander Lewis and Lieutenant Burke reports directly to Commander Lewis. When you told the commander you needed Lieutenant Burke to verify a few of her background statements first thing this morning, you indicated it was a brief administrative review. You've had plenty of time to conduct your recordkeeping, and now I need her to get to work."

Even if there had been an empty chair, Meg was sure that Robbie would have continued to stand. With his broad shoulders, height, and carefully modulated tone, he was the most commanding presence in the room.

"Actually, you can't be in here, Lieutenant Prescott," the JAG officer stated. "You need to leave."

Although seated, Meg felt as though she were falling toward the floor. Her ears were ringing again, and she had trouble breathing. If Robbie could not stay and help her, what was she going to do?

The JAG officer continued, "You aren't regular Navy, so you probably are not aware of the jurisdiction Naval Intelligence has in these matters. If you don't leave in the next few seconds, I'm going to call security and you will find yourself in a similar room trying to explain why you should not face a disciplinary hearing. GO!"

Meg saw Robbie hesitate as he looked speculatively at the officer's impassive face. Robbie opened his mouth and then quickly closed it before saying anything. He glanced briefly at Meg before he saluted perfunctorily and closed the door with force.

The taller man cleared his throat slightly before saying,

"We have a few things we need to do before we resume this conversation." Meg noted he said *conversation* as if it had quotes around it. Even she knew they were not having a conversation at this point.

He continued, "We don't have any custody areas fitted for women since you are the first naval woman we have had to detain. You'll have to wait here until we are ready to talk to you again. One of the seamen will keep an eye on you."

Meg turned to the JAG officer and she felt her face flush bright red as she asked, "What about my access to the head?"

The three men were momentarily silenced and looked at each other in confusion until the shorter man said, "You'll be escorted by a seaman."

"You can't have a man take her," the JAG officer countered.

"We don't have any seawomen. We don't have female security," the taller man responded. "What do you want us to do?"

"You will have to have a seaman escort the lieutenant to the door and wait outside," the officer replied.

"What if she gets away?" the shorter man said.

"I know," his colleague suggested. "Take her up to the third floor so she cannot easily jump out the window."

"May I have permission? Now!" Meg did not disguise the urgency in her voice.

The shorter man opened the door and a seaman Meg had not yet seen entered. Meg realized whoever had been on duty when she arrived had been replaced by those on the day watch. The seaman looked surprised to see Meg and flushed when directed to "take her to the head."

Either the suggestion to go to the third floor had been a joke or it had not been conveyed as part of the instructions as Meg was led to the end of the hall. The seaman looked uncomfortably at a spot on the linoleum as he said, "Please be quick, ma'am. I don't want to have to come in."

Although she wanted to enjoy her moment of solitude, she had no desire to find out the consequences of taking too long.

She rapidly used the toilet but took an extra moment to splash cold water on her face. Grabbing a paper towel, she continued to mop her face while leaving and stashed the towel in her pocket in case her tears returned.

"I'm going to trust you to walk back with me, ma'am," the seaman said quietly.

"Of course," Meg responded. She had no desire for anyone to see her in restraints.

The room was as inhospitable as before. The seaman took a seat in one corner and Meg moved to the opposite side. He whistled tunelessly under his breath as Meg tried to think of the various possibilities of what might happen next. How long could they keep her? Would they feed her? Would they tell someone she was here? She reassured herself that Robbie and Lewis knew she was there. Isobel would be worried when she did not come back. Her colleagues had to have noticed she was not at work. What excuses were Robbie and Lewis giving for her absence? Would Isobel call someone? She realized Isobel calling someone was probably her best bet.

Suddenly the seaman stood up. "I can't think of any reason we can't have a newspaper in here." Meg's stomach gurgled loudly as he moved toward the door. His eyebrows shot up at the volume of the noise. Meg looked at the marred table and wondered if she should start to scratch a message. Moments later, the seaman returned with a folded copy of the *Washington Post*. He unfolded it carefully to expose two apples. "I thought you might like these."

"Thank you," Meg said gratefully.

"Do you want a section of the paper?"

"Would it be okay to work on the crossword puzzle?" Meg asked.

"Sure. I never even try. I can't spell. Here's a pen."

Meg slowly ate one of the apples as she tried to focus on the puzzle. She would save the other apple for later. Although the apple had a few bruises, in her hunger, it was the best apple she had tasted in years. With a little food in her stomach, she found herself nodding off and jerked herself awake. The early wake-up and several surges of adrenaline during the long morning had left her exhausted. She decided there was no reason not to take a nap, so she put her arms down on the table to make a pillow for her head and drifted off into a fitful sleep.

## 42

M eg was dreaming that she was a passenger in a crowded train carriage and woke with a start as the door opened noisily, accompanied by loud voices and heavy footsteps. Her fingers flew to her hair to try to finger-comb it into place and she adjusted her jacket as she stood up, preparing to salute whoever was entering the room.

Captain McClaren strode in with the JAG officer, the two men from earlier in the morning following behind him. As Meg saluted, she noticed McClaren's wet hair as well as a patch of damp on his uniform. She was pretty sure her CO had left the pool in a hurry before drying off. McClaren turned to the seaman and said, "Bring another chair in and go and get some coffee for all of us."

The seaman quickly grabbed the newspaper, pen, and remaining apple. Although Meg might have wanted to eat the apple later, she appreciated that he pretended it was his. With the added chair, the group formed a crowded huddle around the table.

"Sit. Sit," McClaren directed.

He frowned as he watched the four take a seat. Meg sat on

the edge of her chair and fought to control her tapping right foot from betraying her extreme anxiety while trying to look calmly at the others. She noted that, unlike Robbie, McClaren appeared to have permission to be in the room. She knew he outranked the others, but she was not sure if this mattered where Naval Intelligence were involved.

He turned toward the two suited men. "What are your names?"

"Evans," said the shorter one.

"Laing," said the taller. Meg thought Laing was probably Catholic. With his background, he should have known how to check the hymns mentioned in her letters and confirm there was nothing suspicious about them.

"Ah," McClaren replied. Meg knew that McClaren had just said a great deal with that one syllable as the JAG officer quickly interjected, "You were briefed last week."

"Not adequately briefed, Lieutenant Marshall. No one discussed Lieutenant Burke as a person of interest."

There was a knock on the door, and the conversation ceased as the seaman came in with a tray carrying five large mugs filled with steaming black coffee, which he carefully put on the table, saluted, and quietly left the room.

Meg gratefully wrapped her fingers around the mug, comforted by the warmth coming through the ceramic. This time the coffee was much stronger, and Meg reassured herself that if they were using mugs, no one thought she was a risk of throwing her mug at someone's face or breaking it to slit her wrists. Even black, the coffee helped her to feel slightly more human and gave her a moment to organize her thoughts.

"Now that everyone has some coffee in them, I'm going to go step by step through the security concerns Lieutenant Burke has been raising for months and where her concerns overlap with your efforts," McClaren began. Meg was thankful she had formally reported her concerns about being followed to Robbie, even if he had brushed them off and told her not to worry. Based upon McClaren's remark, it sounded as though Robbie had filed a report, which had led to some sort of briefing.

"What concerns?" the short man said. Meg reminded herself he now had a name—Evans.

In the silence that followed as they waited for McClaren to speak again, Meg looked at the table and scuffed floorboards. She had another thought, which made sense but made her feel numb: Robbie's attention wasn't because he was flirting with her but because he was keeping an eye on her. If she had been identified as a security threat and they thought she was passing information, Robbie might have been assigned to oversee her activities both at work and while off duty. She did not want to look at the men who had been questioning her and was afraid that if she were to make eye contact with the CO, she would weep.

"Lieutenant Burke, are you with us?" Captain McClaren asked as he looked intently at her. Meg had been sitting as motionless as possible in an unconscious attempt to have the others forget she was there.

"Yes sir. I apologize." Meg thought he had to see her exhaustion and, possibly, her bewilderment at being in this situation, sitting across from and answering questions from a man whom she generally saw only while she was swimming laps or at a party.

"Lieutenant," McClaren continued, "let's begin by talking about what you do at Naval Communications Command?"

"Sir?"

"What sort of work have you been doing since you arrived in January?"

"I sharpen pencils, make coffee, file, and change typewriter ribbons."

The captain chuckled and the two suited men frowned. For the first time since early this morning, Meg felt it was possible that the day would not end badly. "Is that what you have been writing in your letters home?" McClaren asked.

Meg smiled. "I add a sentence or two about the Senators baseball team and try to make sure I mention I went to church. Apparently, I have included too much information about the songs we are singing," she added wryly. "There are copies of the letters on the table, sir, if you would like to see them."

McClaren snorted quietly as he skimmed the photostats. "Definitely too much about the hymns," he confirmed. "But you're not a Senators fan?"

"No sir. I root for the Dodgers."

He nodded, confirming her answer made sense before continuing, "Tell me more about your specific activities since you arrived in Washington, DC, and reported for duty."

For a moment, while talking about her family and baseball, her heartbeat had slowed down and she had ceased to feel like a suspect, but now her pulse quickened as she scrambled to think what she could say about her work. She had been cautioned time and time again that she was to say absolutely nothing when she was not in her secure area.

"Sir, as you know, I can only speak about my work with my colleagues in my duty area," Meg replied.

"By extension, I am your colleague, and I am giving you permission to discuss your work, at least broadly, during this interview."

Meg noted he said *interview*, not *interrogation*.

"We want to talk about why she has been written up in several reports," Evans interjected.

The CO gave him a scathing look. "I'll ask the questions in the order I want to ask the questions." His tone indicated that he had better not be interrupted again. He turned slightly in his chair and looked at Evans and Laing. "Point of clarification: Lieutenant Burke has been *mentioned* in reports. Not written up. There's an enormous difference between mentioned rather than being written up."

Meg swallowed and took a deep breath as McClaren turned back to face her and continued. "Lieutenant Prescott wrote a formal report capturing a conversation in which you stated the house in which you live has been repeatedly receiving early-morning anonymous telephone calls and hang-ups. Perhaps, more concerningly, you thought you were being followed. Is this true, Lieutenant?"

"Yes sir," Meg replied. She raised her head and looked her CO in the eye as she said, "In fact, one of the men who was following me is currently sitting at this table with us. Today I learned his name is Laing." She heard the JAG officer stifling a giggle.

McClaren shook his head slowly at Laing. "We've even put you in civilian clothing and she spotted you?" The CO picked up his mug and placed it slightly to the right of where it had been. He did this a second time before clearing his throat and saying, "Lieutenant Burke's work and contribution to our command has been exemplary." Indicating the two suited men, he said, "We do have a problem, but it is not with Lieutenant Burke. The three of you are excused. I need to speak to the lieutenant alone so she is free to speak about her work. As she noted, she can't with you in the room."

Evans and Laing exchanged a look as Lieutenant Marshall saluted. Meg thought the door might have been described as having been slammed rather than closed. The room felt much larger once Evans, Laing, and the JAG officer were gone.

Once the door was closed, McClaren glared at Meg and said, "You've got a hell of a lot of explaining to do."

"Sir?"

"I'm here because Prescott got into the pool to interrupt my swim and to tell me Naval Investigative Services was interrogating you. He was beside himself."

"He got in the pool?"

"Prescott didn't know what else to do. His operation is going off the tracks. Lewis told him you were called in early this morning and you had no idea why you were being brought in. When you didn't return after a few hours, Lewis and Prescott put their heads together. The only thing they could think of was to get me involved. I don't want to be involved in this, Lieutenant."

"Sir, I don't know what *this* is."

"You don't?"

"I really don't. I just know that there have been some strange things taking place around me." She quickly added, "Which I formally reported to Lieutenant Prescott, sir."

"The problem is that you have been formally included in reports to the Investigative Service," he paused. "In both good and bad ways."

"What is the good, sir?" Meg asked.

"Commander Lewis reports you are regularly instrumental in code-breaking. Specifically, he reported you helped to deconstruct the structure of a cipher, which resulted in decoding several critical communications."

"I am part of a team who are doing good work, sir. There are many others who deserve a commendation."

"You love the work, don't you?"

"It is the most interesting and challenging thing I've ever done." She stopped herself, remembering Lewis's advice was still applicable to talking to her CO.

"And yet, another person with whom you work, Lieutenant Osgoode, also reported you to Naval Investigative Service. He described three different times he had seen you talking intently to Warren Elliot outside of the command space, beginning when we were at that old building, in a way that could be construed as being suspicious. Why would he say that, Lieutenant?"

"Because since day one when I made it clear to Lieutenant Osgoode that I thought he was a cad, Osgoode has resented me and been jealous of the work I do. Osgoode probably saw me having dinner with Mr. Elliot before going to choir and thought, out of spite, reporting me would be a way to get back at me. I think it is a stretch to say Mr. Elliot and I were talking intently, but that's a subjective call, isn't it, sir?" Meg added.

"I agree it is a subjective call and his report should have quickly fizzled out."

Meg shook her head. "I thought it was bad when he tried to get me drunk. This is so much worse."

"You're right," McClaren agreed. "This is not a minor infraction. Especially since once Investigative Service started looking into it, they found that you and Elliot have frequent contact with a foreign national, right?"

"Yes. I do, sir." Meg looked down at the table and flushed as McClaren sighed loudly. She continued, "Evans and Laing didn't mention this to you earlier, but they asked me several questions about one of the few male singers who attend choir practice. His name is Francisco Avila. I was told he works as a waiter. I learned, secondhand, he emigrated from Lisbon before the war started. He and Mr. Elliott spend most of the break speaking in what I now know to be Portuguese. He never talks to anyone else. I am not sure why he is there. Evans and Laing had him circled in their surveillance pictures. Even though we've barely spoken a word to each other, he was in several pictures Laing and Evans had of me. Including some when I was walking home from work."

"Lieutenant, I know you told Prescott about your concerns, but I need to get a better sense of what is going on. I need details. When did this start? I need you to tell me everything you can think of," McClaren ordered.

Meg took a deep breath and tried to shake off her exhaustion. "When I first arrived at the 'Research Desk,' Ensign Cynthia Collingsworth and I trained with Mr. Elliott." Meg paused and took a sip of coffee before continuing. "Cynthia moved on to other duties, but I have continued to work with Mr. Elliot on transport code, which is mostly weather transmissions and ship movement."

"Neither subject sounds suspicious."

"It certainly isn't glamorous," Meg agreed before she continued. "The strange part is that shortly after we moved to the Annex, files started going missing. Usually, we find the files a few days later in a strange place. They have not disappeared, they just weren't where they should be when we needed them."

"Is this still going on?" he asked.

"Yes. At first, we thought files were rearranged as we unpacked, but it has continued. It happened as recently as yesterday."

"How do you notice things are out of place?"

"Because my housemate is the librarian and is exacting in her filing."

"She is that," McClaren acknowledged. "Could it be someone on her team?"

"It could be," Meg said slowly. "The odd thing is that it is only ever weather reports. I put them away and take them out from the same place every day. Mr. Elliot does the same."

She paused and looked her CO in the eye. "Ensign Bowen can tell someone had been in the library overnight. In fact, rather than being hidden, recently a stack of weather reports was left on her desk." Meg stopped to think before continuing, "The misplaced files make no sense. They are probably the least secret information we have in the command. Unless..."

"Unless?"

"Someone wants to make it look like Mr. Elliot and I are doing something wrong."

"I agree. It seems odd, but it is hardly conclusive evidence of a problem. Tell me more about singing with the choir and how you think that might fit into what is going on."

She shook her head slightly as she said, "I thought singing in the choir would help my family worry less about my living away from home, but it has been an ongoing challenge, especially the transportation to and from church since we moved to the Annex. My plan is to sing until Easter and then resign."

"And it is uncomfortable because Mr. Elliot has a crush on you?"

"He might have had at one point, but I don't think he does now," she said.

"What about Avila?"

"Only Mr. Elliot can really answer that question. At most I can say his presence is unusual, mysterious perhaps. He makes me uncomfortable, but I don't have a concrete reason to say that. I can give you feelings, not facts."

McClaren tilted back in his chair, and he looked up at the ceiling for almost a minute. When he tilted forward, he started to fiddle with his coffee mug again, making several rings. Meg wondered what he was thinking and if McClaren moved cups at home when he was making a decision.

"Here's the problem, Meg," McClaren said as he took his hands off the mug. "As you know, the code changed recently and we've all been playing catch-up."

"Yes sir. It changed after we captured a Japanese ship a few weeks ago."

"Yes and no. We couldn't recover the code from the ship and the Japanese know it. The real reason the code changed was that someone told the Japanese military attaché in Lisbon that we are able to break their code."

"Lisbon. Oh." Meg drew out the one-syllable word as some of the past several hours began to make more sense.

"The Japanese changed their code in response. Unlike at the start of the war, we know enough now about how they structure their process and our IBM machines have gotten faster at figuring out the next version, but still we lost a vital source of information for about a month."

"So someone from our command may have leaked information about our coding success." She paused.

"I know it wasn't you, Lieutenant Burke. The problem is that we have been feeding information to Avila."

Meg's jaw dropped in surprise and McClaren looked grim.

"Obviously, *we* didn't tell Avila that we have been able to break the Japanese code. Prescott has been feeding Avila slightly altered information through Elliot about the challenges of the additives and how we cannot keep up with the communication volume to pass along to Avila's contacts in Lisbon. Avila is part of a much larger network watching what we are doing. We're using doctored information, in an attempt to expose whoever is running Avila. Prescott thought you might be able to pick something up if you were at the church."

"Really?" Meg knew she should not be surprised. Of course, Prescott was using her. He of all people knew that as a servant, she had experience blending into the background and listening to conversations without drawing attention to herself. He could count on her to notice when things were out of place. Even so, she felt like she had been punched in the stomach. Prescott had manipulated her attraction to him.

McClaren continued, "It turned out your being at church hasn't given us any leads, but being followed to and from church has brought us new intelligence."

Meg suddenly felt as though she had solved a math equation. "Now it looks as though Mr. Elliot is passing more than his prepared messages to Mr. Avila."

McClaren tilted his head to one side before answering, "That's one explanation."

"Or it is someone else?"

"It could be. I don't know."

Meg watched her commanding officer's face. She could see him weighing his words before speaking again.

"I'm going to have to ask you to do something you do not want to do and frankly something I don't really want you to do." Her heart constricted. He was reassigning her. She bit her lip and willed herself not to cry in front of the CO. "I am going to have to ask you to take on some additional duties, which bring some danger."

She felt her eyebrows shoot up. "Sir?"

"I'm going to promote you to watch commander and put you on nights with Elliot. We've already put a few women in this role and you're an ideal candidate for the promotion. You can take on more of a leadership role and will be in the right place to watch Elliot. I know you may feel this is awkward, but you're the person least likely to raise his suspicions if you start working with him on the same shift. Because you're with other people, you shouldn't be in any extra danger, but I'm still uncomfortable with the circumstances."

"I'm not sure that I understand, sir. Wouldn't the best thing be to get rid of Mr. Elliot if you think he is sharing secrets?"

"You don't read many spy novels, do you?" She shook her head. McClaren continued, "We're not sure what Elliot is up to and we know Avila is not the mastermind. We need both men if we are going to discover the real organizers. If we can get a better sense of what Elliot is normally up to, it will help us to figure out when he's doing something that isn't normal. Being the watch commander will give you some authority if you find yourself in a situation where you need to use it. But I don't want you to be officious and spook Elliot. Just keep doing what you are doing so well: observing and blending in. Your ability to balance being both inconspicuous and a leader is an unusual one. At some point, when both of us aren't solving the crisis at hand, we should talk about how you are going to continue to develop this skill. For now, your legend is to keep being who you are."

"Legend, sir?"

"A spy's claimed background or biography. Usually, I would give you a report and documents and tell you to memorize details until they become second nature. In this case, it is not that complicated or detailed. You are just expanding an existing backstory that has already overlapped. There are so many overlaps it is hard to think it is coincidence, but we need more information. You and Elliot are working on the same set of transmissions. You both go to choir. You both pull files that are showing up in the wrong places. You were all at the same embassy party." He stopped after mentioning the party.

Meg sat up straighter in her chair and waited to be scolded.

"Lyall should have known better than to go to that party." McClaren shook his head. "Prescott definitely knew better."

Meg quickly interjected, "What am I looking for?"

He smiled. "Ideally, while walking into choir you would see Elliot put a brown envelope in a church pew and watch it get picked up by someone wearing a trench coat who would then send it from an embassy by diplomatic pouch to Europe or elsewhere." He stopped to make sure she saw he was kidding. "But it's not going to be that easy. Although if you see chalk marks on mailboxes or walls at work, do let me know." He winked at her. "Do what you do best: ask the men around you questions about themselves and try not to answer any questions about yourself."

"Is that all?" Meg asked.

"You'll need to continue to go to choir after Easter. I know it's uncomfortable, inconvenient, and tedious, but something is going on at that church."

"It shouldn't be a problem. I'm a welcome participant. I just need a schedule with Thursday nights off." She paused. "And Mr. Elliot will need the same schedule. Why would we both have the same night off?"

"Leave that to me. I'll figure out a reason."

After the long and emotional meeting, Meg was practically asleep on her feet. The CO called to one of the seamen to arrange for transportation to take Meg home. The driver looked surprised to realize he was conveying a member of the WAVES rather than a high-ranking officer and even more surprised when Meg fell asleep as soon as the car started. He shook her gently awake when they reached Aunt Isobel's.

Isobel and Davis were waiting in the entry hall and opened the door before she was at the threshold.

Isobel threw her arms around Meg as she walked in the door and as she released her, asked, "Are you alright, my dear?"

"Nothing twenty-four hours of sleep won't cure," Meg replied. "I'm not back on duty until tomorrow night. I'm going to sleep until then."

As Aunt Isobel accepted this explanation and didn't comment on her leaving before dawn and not returning eight hours later, Meg wondered, not for the first time, what Isobel's husband had really done and whether Isobel had ever worked with him. Her last thought before she fell asleep was to wonder why Evans and Laing had a picture of Tom picking her, Cynthia, and Julie up, but she was asleep before she thought of an explanation.

## 43

L ater that afternoon, rather than after the wished-for twenty-four hours, Meg awoke to the sound of the front door opening and closing. The other WAVES were home. Meg quickly put on her robe and flew down the stairs. As she burst into the library, Julie rushed to give Meg a hug.

"Are you okay?" Julie asked.

"Are you in trouble, Meg?" Cynthia pressed. Aunt Isobel threw a cautionary look at her niece.

"Sort of. I've been reassigned to work nights," Meg answered. "Who knows, it may be more comfortable to work nights during the summer."

"Do you ever get mad, Meg?" Cynthia asked.

"Frequently. And generally, with you." Everyone laughed.

"We will dine early tonight. Meg still needs some time to recover and to adjust her sleep schedule," Aunt Isobel suggested.

"When do you need to be at work?" Vivian inquired.

"Eleven, starting tomorrow," Meg replied.

"How are you going to get there?" Cynthia asked.

"I'm going to take the bus. I'll sit or stand near the driver."

"Perhaps after this week. For the first few days, George will drive you," Isobel said firmly.

The next morning, Meg got up with the other WAVES and had a cup of tea, before returning to bed for a few more hours of sleep. She could not remember the last time she had slept this late in the morning. A little after ten, her body and the sun would not let her sleep anymore. She dressed in civilian clothes and went downstairs. Davis looked surprised when Meg came into the kitchen. Meg realized she did not know what happened at the house during the day. She was going to be in the household's way if she was home and trying to sleep during the day. She needed to come up with a plan.

Davis asked, "Tea?"

"Yes. But I'll make it," Meg answered.

"You sit. You still look exhausted."

"I'll be okay." But she did remain seated. "I slept well last night, but I didn't realize how tired I was."

Davis brought a mug of tea and a plate. Meg burst into tears when she saw it was soda bread.

"I'm sorry, but I'm so homesick. It sneaks up on me sometimes and there's nothing I can do."

"Of course you are."

"My mother taught me to make soda bread." Meg tried but failed to smile. "She also says there are few problems that cannot be solved with a cup of tea."

"She's right of course." Davis passed her a butter dish before asking, "How long are you going to be on nights?" Meg shrugged her shoulders. Davis continued, "I don't know how quickly we can get thicker curtains for your room. The other wing of the house hides the early morning sunshine, so we've never had ones that were that thick, but that's not going to be enough if you're sleeping midday. If you'll help me, I can stitch some towels to the back of the curtains, and that should work for now."

After they finished their tea, Davis said, "Let's go get those curtains. Thankfully, it's a sunny day. I'll wash them and put them out in the sun to dry before we attach the towels. You should nap while they dry."

"I don't want to take you away from whatever you were going to do today," Meg protested.

"This is exactly what I need to do today," Davis replied. Meg surprised herself. As she lay down, she did not think she would be able to sleep, but a few hours later, Davis gently shook her awake and Meg joined her in the kitchen. Davis brought out a pile of towels and her sewing kit. "Do you use a thimble?"

Meg shook her head. "It drives my mother crazy, but no."

As the two women sat in the kitchen alcove, Meg listened to stories about Davis's trip from Ireland to Boston. Davis was pregnant during the voyage, and it had been an agonizing journey of seasickness and pregnancy nausea. She told Meg one of the ladies in first class had noticed her distress and had insisted Davis was one of her maids, allowing her out of the close air of steerage and into the fresh air a few afternoons.

"Being in the sun and getting in the fresh air were the only things that saved me. Now my 'baby' is somewhere in Europe fighting." Although Davis did not say so, Meg was sure the lady was Aunt Isobel.

"I wasn't there, of course," Meg laughed, "but my parents sailed from Cobh in 1909 with my brother James, who was two. My mother's a worrier, so she must have spent every waking and sleeping moment afraid my brother James would toddle overboard."

"How many are there in your family?"

"My two parents and three older brothers. My parents were lucky. My father's brother was already in New York, and they were able to live with them. I can't imagine nine people in the walk-up, but we are all still here. In fact, we all still speak to each other."

"That doesn't always happen."

"I think the crowding gave everyone the impetus to help my mother and father find jobs. My father has poor eyesight, so it was an enormous favor when someone in the parish helped him find a job as an elevator operator at a hotel in Manhattan. My father has a great memory for voices and is very discreet— two critical skills, especially if you can't see well.

My mother started as a maid with a family who has been very kind to her. She's their housekeeper now. The family entertains a great deal, and I learned how to help with parties and around the house."

"Being with a family who respects the work you do makes a huge difference. But you already knew that," Davis said. She smiled knowingly at Meg. "Did all of you go to college?"

"We are all readers and have always liked math. School was surprisingly easy for all of us. In fact, I skipped third grade. All of my brothers did well in high school and should have been able to go to college, but . . ." She left unsaid the need for the boys to bring in money, especially during the Depression. "I'm lucky my family spoils me." Meg continued, "When I was teaching, I liked to tell them at dinner about what happened that day at school and stories about my students doing well. My two younger brothers, especially, and my parents sacrificed a great deal to make sure I could go to college. It was the least I could do to let them see their help made a difference not only for me but for other people."

"What do they think about you being in the WAVES?"

"They're mainly positive. It was nice to be able to share my experiences at Smith with them. They loved the stories about our living at the hotel and my walking in the same worn spots in the staircases as Smith students going to class. They were so proud I could be part of that, even in the small way that I was."

"Do you tell them about singing at St. Patrick's?" Davis asked.

"Yes and no. I've told them, but it's not the best subject. Some of the people are such characters and no matter how hard I try to be kind, my descriptions make fun of them. I feel it is almost sinful to talk about it." Davis laughed. Meg realized she had seen Davis smile but never laugh.

Meg was surprised at how quickly they finished the project and when they rehung the curtains, the room was nearly dark although the afternoon was brightly sunny. As they walked down the stairs, Meg said, "Thank you."

"It is always nice to work with a good seamstress. Miss Isobel is in the library, writing letters. You should go in and talk to her while I get dinner started."

Meg went into the library. Aunt Isobel looked up. "All set?"

"Davis was wonderful. She lined the curtains with towels, so I'll have a hope of sleeping during the day. Yet again, I am putting your household out. Unfortunately, my new assignment is going to affect all of you, although I'll try to limit its impact."

"Dare I ask what happened?"

"There's a situation and I'm being asked to keep an eye on it."

"My guess, and it is a guess, is that you have made an impression at work. Your leadership needs to move some of the WAVES to nights. Does any of that resonate, my dear?"

"A little." Meg gave her a small smile.

"It will be tough on you to not be with your friends. That is the unfortunate part, but as you were saying the other night, you have a job to do."

"Exactly," Meg said somewhat ruefully.

"At least you now have every good reason to stop singing in the choir. You need to be able to grab sleep whenever you can."

"It turns out I'm not quite ready to give up choir."

Isobel gave her a long look. Raising her eyebrow, she said, "Your devotion does you credit."

"Thank you," Meg said meekly. Isobel wasn't the least bit fooled. Would Warren be?

"George will be ready to take you to work at ten thirty."

"I appreciate it. But only for the first few nights," Meg said forcefully. Perhaps too forcefully. She quickly followed with, "You can't spend your entire gas ration on me." Isobel laughed.

At dinner, Meg ate ravenously, making up for almost two days of missed meals, a combination of her interview and her sleeping schedule. Having food in her mouth was also a good excuse to not have to speak with her fellow WAVES, who she could tell wanted to ask her questions but could not since Aunt Isobel's house was not a secure location.

The sentry looked surprised when Meg showed her badge to enter the Annex at 2250 hours. Meg realized there were still very few female officers and even fewer working at night. She wondered how many people at the Annex had heard she was now on the late watch.

"You're working nights?"

"I am."

"Hmm." Meg wondered if this was a "good" hmm or a "what is the Navy coming to that they are putting women on nights" hmm.

She smiled and returned his salute. Since she frequently did not get a salute, she decided to think positively about her night starting well.

As Meg reached her workspace, she was surprised by the cloud of cigarette smoke. She disliked cigarette smoke and was grateful there were few smokers on the day watch. She reasoned the later watches probably smoked more, in part, to keep themselves awake. Hopefully, no one would object if Meg opened a few windows since it was a mild night. She also smelled burnt coffee. She went to the galley and found an empty carafe on the burner. She took a deep breath and told herself if she cleaned the carafe and made the coffee herself, she would know it was fresh.

As others started to arrive for overnight duty, Meg introduced herself to those she had not met already during the night-to-day-shift change. She hadn't had a chance to check who was assigned to the night watch and how many people to expect. Most of the enlisted men did not seem that surprised to see her and got to work without direction. They joked with each other as they brought boxes back and forth from the printing office and started to sort the messages by location, as Cynthia and Meg had once done to prepare for the day watch. The overall atmosphere, Meg noted, was less tense than during the day and she did not anticipate management issues. The one noncommissioned officer present told her she had just replaced him as the senior officer on the watch.

"This is yours," he said as he handed over the logbook; she would now be responsible for the watch report. Meg rolled her eyes inwardly. One of her additional duties. She also noted that Warren had not yet arrived. With fewer analysts at night, Meg decided she would find a corner in which to spread out and from which she could discreetly observe. Within a few minutes, she was happily surrounded by piles of paper, graph paper, and cross wordings.

She heard a bell toll the half hour and realized Warren was still not there. Unfamiliar with her new role, she had neglected to take attendance when the watch started and moved now to find the list of assigned names. After confirming all but Warren were there, Meg noted she would not like the element of babysitting assigned to her new role. She was back to work in her corner when Warren walked in at 2355. She made a notation in the logbook and got up to speak to him.

"Mr. Elliot, your watch starts at twenty-three hundred hours. You were not present when the watch commenced."

"The bus I normally take runs at a reduced schedule after ten o'clock."

Meg felt some sympathy. Where would she be without Aunt Isobel's houseman?

"I trust you will find an alternative transportation option before tomorrow's watch. I have marked your tardiness in the log."

"You could take it out if you wanted to." Warren's tone suggested he was daring her.

"The seamen have already brought in a few boxes of transmissions. There is more than enough to keep us both busy." She turned so she did not have to see his reaction.

Without the noise from the accustomed number of people or machines, Meg found herself initially able to concentrate better, but at three thirty, hit the wall of exhaustion. She got up to take a walk, thinking if she got some fresh air, that would help her wake up.

"Do you know what helps keep me awake, ma'am?" asked one of the seamen.

"Coffee?" Meg replied.

"Freshly made grits."

"At three thirty in the morning?"

"Now is the best time to eat Mess grits. Heavenly when they're fresh," he assured her.

She wasn't brave enough to try the grits, but she did get a hard-boiled egg and some toast from the Mess, thankful it was open at all hours. She realized she was going to have to figure out what she was eating and when if she were going successfully adjust to this new schedule and keep her figure. As she returned to her desk, she saw Warren was dozing at his. She contemplated writing this infraction in the log and decided the tardy was enough for one day. She noted she had not been able to do anything toward her additional assignment. As far as she could see, Warren had not completed any of his assigned work, let alone participated in any nefarious activities.

Lost in thought, she did not notice the faint light starting to come through the windows. She focused on drafting a schedule that would combine watching Warren, still doing her work, and maintaining cover from her closest friends and coworkers regarding this additional assignment. She started when she realized there was someone standing next to her desk.

"Here's some coffee. Don't worry. It's fresh." Robbie and his supply of milk had come to her rescue. She reminded herself it was just good cover for him keeping tabs on her.

"What time is it?" she asked dispassionately.

"Five forty-five. I figured I'd have to wake you up and then I'd go for a swim. Good on you for being awake."

"Most of the group seems pretty with it, but Warren isn't. He dozed most of the night."

"Did you put it in the logbook?"

"I put in that he was late."

"Welcome to the joys of being watch officer."

"Shouldn't I have gotten a small ceremony, or at least a formal announcement?" she said as she thought, *Two can play this game, especially now that I know what you are up to.*

"I'll see if I can get you a doughnut downstairs to celebrate. By the way, I think Lewis will be in early to check that everything is under control. I'll go and wake Elliot so he can be angry at me rather than you," Robbie offered.

"He won't dare show that he is angry with you. But you're right, I'm a different story." Meg watched as Robbie walked over to Warren's desk. It was hard to reconcile the Lieutenant Prescott who was maneuvering her to go to choir with Warren and using her as a distraction with the one who had come in early to help her. Which one was the real Prescott? Was it possible that he could be both?

Robbie walked over, shook Warren awake, and told him to clean himself up in preparation for Commander Lewis's arrival. Then he walked back to Meg's desk.

"Did you know you sing while you work?"

"No. Loudly?"

"Under your breath. I never noticed it before. Probably it was never quiet enough for me to hear it." Robbie smiled. Meg started to smile back but stopped herself.

"I was looking at the weather codes and trying to make sense of the volume patterns. We can see when there is bad weather, but the volume does not always correlate with the weather intensity. It seems to happen on a weekly basis. I was trying to figure out if there is an increase in transmission volume as my new project." She sighed. "Although at the end of the day, I am not sure what the fluctuations would tell us. Probably nothing."

"You never know," he said encouragingly. "I don't think anyone is going to fight you for it. The 'professors' are focusing on the fleet code since we are back to having most of the additive pattern. Elliot is working on the actual weather communications rather than the statistics or the transmission patterns. He could benefit from your assistance, but I think you can work on transmission patterns independently for a little while. Just make sure you let someone on the day watch know if you notice any ominous silences or any sudden appearances of new stations, okay?" Robbie looked over his shoulder and gestured toward the commander's office. "There's Lewis. You should tell him about Warren before it becomes a big deal."

Meg got up and knocked on Lewis's office door. He nodded for her to come in.

"Commander, there is an incident in the logbook. Mr. Elliot was more than thirty minutes late for duty. I counseled Mr. Elliot and suggested he explore other means of transportation."

"Did you use your schoolteacher voice?" Meg could not tell if he was joking or serious. Lewis had very little facial expression at the best of times.

"Probably. It comes naturally at this point."

Lewis started laughing, astonishing Meg. "I appreciate you making the transition. As you can see, the night watch has some good men, and they're working hard. We need them to be more organized and have them do more than move papers around. These eight hours are valuable hours in the communication cycle. You're the right person to supervise the seamen. I think you can teach them to do more as well as continue your analysis. Well done, Watch Commander."

Cynthia and Julie arrived as she walked out of his office.

"How'd it go?" Julie asked.

"You look exhausted," Cynthia noted.

"I'm tired. But I made it through the first night."

Meg quickly found a bus going to Dupont Circle. There were far fewer people headed in her direction at that time of day and she found a seat. Once home, she quickly fell into bed. She would have been able to sleep even without the towels sewn into the curtains.

## 44

Holy Week arrived as Meg had barely adjusted to sleeping during the day and now found herself at church more than usual for additional rehearsal sessions. She did not see Warren do anything out of the ordinary other than perhaps talking less than he usually did to Avila. She noted Warren looked especially tired and wondered what he might be doing during the day, other than sleeping.

Meg went for a walk on the Saturday before Easter with the thought of buying flowers for Aunt Isobel, and she needed to go several places before she found flowers she liked enough to bring back. Meg came in through the kitchen door so she could find a vase in which to arrange the flowers and Davis announced, "You have a visitor. He's in the library." She was not expecting a visitor. In fact, she had never had visitors. Who could it be? Warren? Her heart sank; she hoped not. Lyall? Maybe. Robbie? She was not sure how she felt about that. As she opened the door, Aunt Isobel blocked her view, but she would know the voice of the person speaking to her anywhere.

"Tom!" She ran into the room. He caught her in a bear hug, and she squeezed him back.

"Is everything okay? William? James? Mother and Father?"

"Everything's fine. Mrs. Milbank wrote to Mother a few weeks ago to suggest since you couldn't get away to join us, I should come for Easter and see how you were doing. This way I can assure Ma you really did go to Easter Mass. I hear you're working nights, but I'll be here for a few days, so maybe you can find some time to show me around the city a bit." Meg sank silently into the sofa. "Are you okay, Meg?" Tom asked.

"Just surprised. Very, very surprised." Meg smiled at Aunt Isobel. She would have liked to give Isobel the same bear hug that she had just gotten from her brother.

"We're going to have a quiet dinner tonight in order to pace ourselves for tomorrow," Isobel announced. "It's warm enough to have cocktails in the garden before dinner. I'm so glad you don't work tonight, Meg."

"I do work tomorrow evening, but I'm not going to think about that now," Meg agreed. "There's always coffee tomorrow. Tom, while I'm dressing for dinner, you should ask Aunt Isobel about the tiles you're going to see in the garden. She made some of them," she added.

Meg went upstairs to change for dinner and as soon as she shut the door, Julie pounced on her. "Your brother's gorgeous! I understand why Cynthia noticed him at Christmas."

"I guess. To me, he's just my brother Tom. Of course, he is a great conversationalist. He can talk to anyone and he does not constantly blush or look at his feet when he does."

"He must have a million girls after him," Julie said.

"If he does, he doesn't bring them to dinner or let my mother know about them."

"Surely he tells you about them," Julie insisted. Meg shook her head.

"Occasionally I used to go with Tom, whoever was his date, and his friend Liam to a church dance or into the city. I've never been aware of anyone special. Then again, I didn't know Tom was coming to visit. I may not be your best source about my brother's romantic life."

Since Tom was the only man at dinner, Aunt Isobel insisted he take the host's position at the table. Meg did not ask where Tom had gotten the suit he was wearing. She felt a little like Cynthia; Meg was having trouble not staring at her own unbelievably debonair brother. She had never seen him in such an outfit before and thought it might be Aunt Isobel's late husband's. As Meg knew, Davis was capable of tremendous alterations in very little time.

"How is the war affecting life in New York, Tom?" Aunt Isobel asked.

"I imagine much the same as it is here. We all noticed last month when the sale of butter and oils stopped for a week. Everyone from my father to my fares is complaining about the freeze on prices and wages. It's not an effective freeze because it encourages the black market."

"You should be sure to tell Robbie's father that tomorrow at dinner," Cynthia recommended. "It would be good for him to hear from someone who lives in the real world."

"Robbie? Father?" puzzled Tom.

"One of tomorrow's guests had a guiding role in this month's freezes," Isobel clarified.

"Right. I'll be ready to share my experiences." Tom raised his eyebrows at Meg and continued. "I'm the only one here who can comment on another particular wartime regulation. I like cuffless trousers. I can't believe it saves that much fabric, but they are much easier to iron."

"You know how to press your pants?" Vivian asked.

"Yes," Tom said simply.

"Have you had any problems getting enough gasoline for your taxi?" Julie asked.

"No problems. I'm in a special category, but it seems to me that it is only being rationed for those who really don't have a pressing need to drive."

"It kept the Army from coming to root for their cadets at the Army-Navy game last fall," Vivian noted.

"As I said, no *pressing* need to drive. Don't ya know there's a war on!" he added, capturing the same tone as the jingle played to remind shoppers to tighten their belts. Soon the entire table was gasping for air from laughing so hard.

"You're an even better mimic than your sister. Meg said so, but we didn't believe her," Vivian told Tom.

"Our older brothers used to talk about how there were taxi drivers who knew where the speakeasies were," Cynthia interjected. "I've heard now there are drivers who know where to take you to find gas stations who will sell extra gas without coupons and butchers who are holding back steaks."

"I wouldn't have a clue," he answered quickly. Just a little too quickly, Meg thought. "I spend the day driving people from the train station to their appointments. Basically, I have taken the place of all the chauffeurs who could earn more money working at a war plant than driving a car for someone else." He turned to Meg and said, "By the way, Liam Dunne was home on leave a few weeks ago and wanted me to be sure to say 'hi.'"

"Who is Liam Dunne?" Cynthia demanded.

"Sis! You haven't told them about your intended?"

She glared at her brother. "He's not my intended!"

"Does he know that?"

She faced the rest of the table. "There really isn't that much to tell about Liam. He was a few years ahead of me in school. Tom's year. He and Tom were altar boys at the same time. Liam worked at the shipyard with Tom and William before he volunteered."

Cynthia turned to Meg and asked, "Those are all good reasons why we should know about him."

"I can't believe it." Tom shook his head. "Liam told me Meg writes faithfully to him. You're not stringing him along, are you, sis?"

"Of course not. As his *superior officer*," she looked at her brother for emphasis before continuing, "I'm writing the occasional perfectly bland patriotic letters to a young man serving his country. It's just a nice thing to do, isn't it, to write letters back to people who are far away from home when other people send them?" Out of the corner of her eye, she could see Cynthia blushing while Tom smiled evilly at his sister. He did not want her to discuss that he and Cynthia were pen pals. Vivian looked at Julie to see if she understood what was going on; Isobel looked amused.

"Liam should have known Meg was out of his league when she skipped third grade, but he *and* his mother still hope," Tom concluded.

"Margaret Burke, you are a snob!" Cynthia exclaimed.

"Oh Cynthia, you of all people cannot call Meg a snob," Julie said, and the table broke out in laughter.

After the group retired to the library for coffee, Cynthia sat down next to Tom. Meg had to look away to keep from laughing when Cynthia started talking about the Yankees' season. Tom took the bait and started talking about the Dodgers. He listed the number of Dodgers who had left the team to serve in the military.

"It is hardly fair to call what they are playing 'baseball,'" Cynthia said.

"Exactly. I know they're playing to keep our spirits up, but it doesn't really count, does it?" Tom observed. "Most of the players they're using would barely have played high school ball, let alone been welcomed in the Minor Leagues. It's a travesty to see such poor play."

Meg looked around the room to see if anyone was as astonished as she was. Cynthia read sections of the newspaper at Julie's direction to find relevant information for the code-breakers, but she certainly did not spend any time reading the sports scores. It occurred to Meg that Cynthia had studied for her brother's visit. But, that would mean Cynthia knew he was coming. Did everyone else know he was going to visit?

Meg was apparently the only person concerned or particularly interested in the fact that Cynthia and her brother talked to each other nonstop for forty minutes. From her angle, Meg could see that the two were sitting close enough together that they did not quite touch unless one of them leaned in during the conversation to make a point, which became increasingly frequent as their conversation continued. Meg looked over to see what Aunt Isobel thought of this. Isobel was talking to Vivian about her cousin who had just announced her engagement and did not appear to notice her other niece. Julie was asking questions about planning a wartime wedding and seemed oblivious.

Meg reached the point where she could not keep watching her brother and Cynthia. "I'm still not on a good sleep cycle. I'm afraid I must excuse myself and go to bed," she announced.

## 45

As Meg and Tom came downstairs the next morning, Aunt Isobel asked, "Would you like a ride from George to church? It's no trouble. Especially since it's just a few blocks away."

"We'll be fine walking," Tom assured her. "It gives me a few moments to play tourist, and I know my sister needs the exercise." Meg rolled her eyes at her brother, but Aunt Isobel seemed to find his behavior charming.

At church, Meg quickly seated her brother in the congregation and flew to the side door to put on a robe and join the choir. Warren looked over a few times to frown at her, and Avila looked away anytime he thought Meg was looking at him. Meg could see Tom in the congregation smiling as the songs were alternately flat and sharp, and she anticipated a less than glowing review of the music.

Tom waited at the side exit for Meg and when Avila exited, she could see him look furtively at Tom before scurrying away. Meg did not see Warren after the service and thought he must have left from another door.

It was a sunny, dry day and since there was plenty of time

until the guests were scheduled to arrive at Isobel's, Meg took Tom by way of the White House so he could look through the fence at the Rose Garden. She did not ask about Cynthia and Tom did not mention her.

As they walked past the White House and turned right on 17th Street to return to Dupont Circle, Tom asked, "What did you do to the guy in the choir, Meg? Break his heart? Every time he looked at you this morning during Mass, I thought he was going to cry."

"Yes. But not purposefully. It's complicated."

"Right. And you can't tell me?"

"I can't tell you. Sorry." She sighed, and Tom gave her arm a squeeze before she continued, "I can tell you, or maybe even warn you, that there will be a number of officers with whom I work at dinner and, of course, the WAVES you've met. Aunt Isobel tends to collect guests. I'm not entirely sure who is on the guest list and who is coming."

"Should I expect someone who is fairly high up at Treasury?" Tom asked.

"Yes, someone who is high up at Treasury, whose son I work with. And my commanding officer and his wife as well as their son. My CO's a captain for now, but I am sure he'll soon be an admiral."

"Are we going to start to read about you in the society pages?"

"I would guess you before me."

She thought that might have provoked Tom, but he remained silent on the topic of Cynthia. There were not as many people out walking on Easter as there were on a normal weekday morning and as they crossed the street, Meg thought she saw the man who had ridden on the bus with her after choir and who she had seen after going to the bookstore, whom she referred to as Mr. "X" to differentiate him from Mr. "Hat," as she still called Laing.

"Tom, am I imagining things or is the man in the dark blue suit following us?"

"I noticed him and assumed he was another one of the brokenhearted, checking me out." Tom looked at her warily. "Why do you think you are being followed, Meg?"

"It's happened a bit this spring and I've seen this guy before."

"Does anyone else know about this?"

"Know about what?"

Tom let out an exasperated sigh. "That there are men in suits following you." She shrugged. "Maybe you should say something. Maybe tell your watch officer?" Tom suggested. Meg was surprised by his level of concern.

"I am."

"You are?"

"The watch officer."

"You were promoted for making coffee?"

"Yes. Just like you're unfit for service."

"I hope this morning has shown you that this is an observation you should keep to yourself." Tom gave her the same look that used to mean "don't tell Mother," as they arrived at Aunt Isobel's house.

Tom and Meg went out to the garden to join the guests. Julie was talking to Jack while Vivian was taking Lyall on a tour of the garden. Aunt Isobel was sitting at a table with Robbie and his parents. The four stood as Meg and Tom walked in. Meg wondered, briefly, where Cynthia was.

Aunt Isobel began the introductions. "Dr. and Mrs. Prescott, may I introduce Lieutenant Margaret Burke's brother, Thomas?"

"Tom, please."

As Meg said hello to the Prescotts, she couldn't hear what Robbie said to Tom, but could see they were already joking with each other. For not the first time, she wished she could be more like her brother. Robbie and Tom pulled chairs over to the table so Meg and Tom could join the group. Meg sank thankfully into her chair to relax. Tom was clearly at ease with the hostess and guests; the dreaded Easter choir performance was over. Isobel's guests did not lack opinions, so Meg knew she could listen and relax. The senior Dr. Prescott was talking about the reaction to price and wage freezes. Meg waited for Cynthia to interrupt and to put Tom on the spot, but there was no sign of Cynthia. Seeing Robbie and Lyall with their fathers made Meg realize both men seldom mentioned their families at work; Robbie had once acknowledged his father's position, but only after Osgoode had brought it up. Meg realized that since Indoctrination, Cynthia had also curtailed her name-dropping. Was it because they were living with her mother's family? Had Robbie and Lyall set a good example of downplaying family connections?

As if Cynthia knew Meg was thinking about her, a radiant young woman Meg hardly recognized as her generally acerbic housemate appeared in the garden just as Davis announced dinner. Cynthia took Tom's arm as the group walked into the house. Meg could not believe her eyes when she saw the food on the table. She had no idea where Davis found asparagus or a ham big enough for all of them. Meg took two rolls, just so she could eat the butter. Aunt Isobel asked Tom to carve and after Isobel offered grace, they began their delicious meal. Every few minutes Meg snuck a glance at Tom's end of the table and saw Cynthia beaming at him.

The conversation flowed freely and focused on current events. Although Meg knew all her fellow code-breakers were on their guard not to say something off-limits, there were no awkward pauses, especially since no topic, other than code-breaking, was taboo during meals at Aunt Isobel's house.

Meg anticipated there would be vigorous debate about FDR and the government but was surprised when a column written by Mrs. Roosevelt became the focus of the conversation.

"Did anyone see Mrs. Roosevelt's 'My Day' column last

week about equal pay for equal work?" Cynthia asked from the other end of the table.

"Here we go," Lyall said quietly closer to Meg.

"I thought it was about a situation in Kansas," Jack said.

Julie sent him a scathing look. "The specific example was about a woman who worked in the same office in Kansas for over fifteen years, but the lack of equal pay can be found all over this country."

"For example, Meg does the same work that you do, Lyall, one could argue most days even more, but she is paid a fraction of what you earn," Robbie quipped. From across the table Tom shot his sister a look, but surprised Meg when he did not take the opportunity to tease her.

"The argument could be made it is because I will have a family to support," Lyall said evenly, but he had turned bright red.

"But you don't right now," his mother said gently.

"I think Mrs. Roosevelt made the additional point that there are many women who *are* supporting families," Isobel observed. "Should supporting a family be part of the criteria of how pay is determined, regardless of being male or female?"

"What if the females in the office are actually doing better work than their male counterparts?" Ellen Prescott smiled at Julie and Vivian, who were sitting near her.

"In that case my payroll would have to be increased significantly," Captain McClaren said seriously.

"Perhaps you could take some of the men's wages and reallocate them," Cynthia suggested. As Cynthia met Tom's eye and he nodded appreciatively at her comment, Meg realized Cynthia had been studying more than baseball scores. She was definitely trying to impress Tom.

"This is a fundamental challenge to the market," Dr. Prescott interjected. "How do we measure how much people are or are not working? It is much easier when tasks are clearly delineated. When an individual has a specific job on an assembly line, I can easily measure his—"

"Or her," Vivian interrupted, and then looked down at the table in embarrassment.

"Or her," Dr. Prescott agreed, "productivity. It's much harder to measure when you have several people who are contributing to a task as a committee or a team."

"Which happens when you are working on an intellectual project," Robbie noted. "You need new algorithms and models."

"Well, get to work, son. I understand you have a lot of free time on your hands."

The entire table laughed.

"I think," Robbie turned to his father, "making wages more equitable is something your alphabet soup of commissions and projects should be addressing. Are they?"

"It's hard to know where to start demanding needed reform. Especially since, as a resident of Washington, DC, I do not have a senator who represents me," Isobel said.

"As everyone at this table would agree, we're not doing everything we need to be doing. I know that longtime residents, the so-called Cave Dwellers—with notable exceptions," Dr. Prescott smiled at Isobel, "miss the mainly middle-class town and middle-class government with modest ambitions."

"In just a matter of a few years, war has transformed a slow-paced town into a crowded city. Even though the District has become the capital of the free world, it hasn't had any time to prepare for its role," Ellen Prescott remarked.

"But should Roosevelt be allowed to exercise so much more power than any President in history has? He's moved power and money from private ownership to public institutions," Robbie said, pushing his father.

"Didn't your liberal Columbia professors teach you that is the solution?" his father replied.

"Pop, I don't know where you get that idea. I majored in

mathematics. Numbers have no ideology. Econ is another story. But, unlike you, I'm not an economist."

For a moment it was as if they had all been transported from Isobel's elegant dining room to a large university lecture hall. Father and son appeared to be completely at ease debating each other this way. Meg had barely acclimated to dinner at Isobel's; she could not imagine dinner at the Prescotts'. She saw Tom watching the two men debate with interest. None of her brothers would have spoken in this manner to their father, but she also had never seen her father question her brothers' opinions in quite this way.

Meg expected Dr. Prescott to get up from his chair to start pacing as if in the classroom and to use arm gestures for effect, but he remained seated as he said, "There's no question FDR built a new government rather than try to modify the old one. The old one was broken. We've been called pompous and ill-bred, but the economic challenges of the thirties and now the war demonstrate a more sophisticated approach is needed, even if the town misses the gracious living and social engagements once associated with being in government. This isn't about organizing a country club; FDR needed the wherewithal to force businesses in wartime to manufacture what the government wanted and not what they wanted."

"There endeth the lesson," Robbie quipped. "Finished with your sermon, Pop?" Meg looked at Tom as the rest of the table laughed. Either he knew what Robbie meant or he was readier to fake that he did than she.

"What was your secret to studying for exams, Meg?"

Meg realized Robbie's father had changed topics and was asking her a question from across the table. He continued, "I always struggled before mathematics exams. I could cram before a history exam and read until the last possible moment, but math was more difficult."

"I would go the Brooklyn Museum and walk through the exhibits. And try to get a good night's sleep. Sometimes I swam before an exam, especially in the spring. It was more difficult when the pool was closed in the winter." The table laughed.

"See? You gave me a hard time when I said I was out rowing, but I was just clearing my head!" Robbie said.

"No, you were out rowing," his father teased him.

Cynthia asked, "Meg, why do you think your family all became swimmers?" Meg watched as Cynthia smiled at Tom when she said *swimmers*. Inwardly, Meg rolled her eyes before answering,

"For me it was because I got a chance to be with my older brothers. William and Tom taught me, mainly at the beach during the summer after I had a few lessons at the city pool. Tom, how did you get started swimming? I'm honestly not sure."

"The church took a group of us to the beach on a summer trip. I remember someone showing me how to paddle. One of the chaperones must have told Ma, who thought it was a good outlet for my energy. I was able to take lessons at the city pool. Later, I took lifeguarding classes when I was old enough." Tom smiled at Cynthia as he said this and continued, "I think it's our Armada blood. We are descended from one of the sailors who was able to swim to the Irish coast where some lovely Irish lass saved his life." The table laughed.

"All of this talk of swimming is making me think of the outdoors. Can I entice you all to relocate to the garden, where we can have dessert?" Isobel proposed.

Robbie and Tom were the last to come to the garden; Meg wondered what her brother and Robbie had been talking about before joining the group. She hoped it was not a list of things to tease her about. As Robbie entered the garden, he grabbed his mother's arm and guided her to Meg's table, where she was enjoying a slice of carrot cake and a cup of tea.

"I didn't realize you drank tea, Meg," Robbie said.

"I prefer tea, but I usually drink coffee."

"Why not tea?" Mrs. Prescott asked.

"I can't get used to drinking tea without milk and sugar." Meg surprised herself when she smiled at Robbie, even though she still felt he had used her. "As Robbie knows, I can drink coffee black."

He laughed. "Not really. That's why I bring you milk."

Meg chuckled. "True. I thought I was okay with strong coffee until I took this assignment." She turned to Robbie's mother and said, "You must understand the coffee at work is practically tar, but it does keep us awake."

"I'm sure Robbie told you I grew up on my family's farm in Maryland and we were tea drinkers." Meg tried to look as if Robbie had already told her this. Maryland. Robbie's mother might have grown up Catholic. An interesting fact, but not one her son had previously mentioned.

"Someone in Mother's family probably started the Great Fire in London and they had to escape, so they moved from England to Maryland in the late seventeenth century," Robbie joked.

"That isn't funny, dear. Someday someone will take you seriously."

"I am serious." He grinned at Meg.

Ellen smiled fondly at her son before turning to Meg. "My grandmother used to make wonderful, hearty, crusty bread for afternoon tea—not a formal, dress-up type tea, but a meal to fill the children up until a much later supper. She would brew tea in the pot, and the children would sit with her and tell her about the day. Children were not allowed to talk at the evening meal, only adults could talk, but we could talk during tea. I loved tea. She told wonderful stories and encouraged us to talk about anything we wanted to. I always associate tea with good conversation."

"Is the earthenware tea set in the kitchen the one your grandmother used?" Robbie asked his mother.

"Yes. I've kept it because it reminds me of some very happy times," Ellen said. "It should be used again."

Tom started to walk up to Meg but changed his course, joining Lyall and his parents instead. She could hear Captain McClaren talking to Tom about swimming. Meg couldn't help but notice that Robbie and Tom appeared to avoid each other after the meal. Meg guessed Tom had said something to Robbie about Cynthia and Robbie probably wasn't pleased.

After the other guests had thanked Isobel for a wonderful party, nothing more was said about FDR or the economy. Rather, at Isobel's direction, Tom built a small fire in the library and Julie asked him to read to them. Meg could not shake off the fact as she left for work that night that Cynthia's shoulder was touching Tom's as she sat next to him reading from *Little Dorrit*.

## 46

For the next two days, Meg slept until early afternoon and then took Tom sightseeing. As Meg showed him the new Jefferson Memorial, dedicated earlier that month, she regaled her brother with the story of the memorial's controversial start.

"In 1938, FDR announced plans for a memorial for Jefferson, but a group of local women led by Eleanor Cissy Patterson—"

"Publisher of the *Washington Times-Herald*," he interrupted.

"Yes, publisher—"

"And Cave Dweller."

"Yes. Cave Dweller." She smiled at him. "Are you going to let me continue my story?"

"Only if it promises to make things better for society."

"It doesn't. But it is a clever story."

"Do you like clever?"

"Not sure."

"There's a fine line between clever and arrogant, especially in naval officers," Tom observed.

"Noted. Mrs. Patterson opposed the memorial because fifty

of Washington's famous Japanese cherry trees would be felled to clear the designated spot. She gathered a group of her friends—"

"More Cave Dwellers . . ."

"There's a fine line between charming and obnoxious, my dear brother." He put his finger on his lips to indicate he would be silent, at least for the rest of this story.

"A group of Washington's most well-known women tried to stop the construction by chaining themselves to the trees to block the bulldozers. The Assistant Secretary of the Interior offered the women lunch and served them cup after cup of coffee. The women finally had to unchain themselves to use the restroom. As soon as they left, the bulldozers moved in."

Tom laughed. "New government outwits old."

Tom declared his favorite spot was the Library of Congress, until, on his last day, Isobel arranged a special tour of the Smithsonian aerospace collection early in the morning while Meg slept. Tom was scheduled to take a mid-afternoon train that Wednesday, but Meg convinced him to take the early evening train instead, allowing Cynthia to get there from work. As soon as she saw Cynthia arrive at the station, Meg hugged her brother quickly and departed to let the two of them say goodbye.

Meg had convinced Aunt Isobel to let her take the bus. The compromise was that she caught the bus around nine o'clock, which meant Meg arrived at the Annex early and had time to swim before work. Cynthia was a night owl and under Aunt Isobel's orders, waited with Meg at the bus stop. To pass the time, Cynthia discussed the books she was reading. There was no mention of Tom, Robbie, or Lyall. Meg liked this Cynthia much better.

Inspired by walking around the city during Tom's visit, she left the Annex shortly after seven in the morning to take advantage of a gorgeous late spring day. The thunderstorm during the night had wrung the humidity from the air the way she would twist water out of her washcloth, making it a good day to walk around. Her route to the Mall took her past several embassies. Meg took a few moments to watch the party preparations, surprised by the number of delivery trucks unloading wine, food, and linens on the circular driveways. The tablecloths were a dazzling white in the bright sun and the bottles sparkled. It had never occurred to her that embassy parties took place on weeknights as well as on weekends.

Meg decided to explore the Lincoln Memorial. With any luck, she told herself, there might be an ice-cream stand open later that morning. She was making up for the lost time of having given up ice cream during Lent. She had seen the memorial from a distance and its etching on the five-dollar bill but had not realized how massive the structure was. She read that it was one hundred feet tall, and that each of the thirty-six columns represented a state that was part of the Union when Lincoln died. From force of habit looking for patterns, Meg counted the twenty-nine steps from the Reflecting Pool to the plaza surrounding the monument and the fifty-eight steps from the plaza to the chamber housing Lincoln's statue. She marveled at the stonework, in which were carved both Lincoln's second inaugural address and his Gettysburg Address, as well as symbolic decorations such as eagles, laurels, and oak leaves.

Lost in thought, Meg found herself walking back along the Mall, near the Washington Monument, where she was surprised to see men playing a baseball game. From a distance, she could see one of the teams had uniforms. As she got closer, she saw the front of their shirts had the names of different repair garages around town. The opponents looked more like out-of-uniform servicemen. The ground was still damp from the previous night's rain and smelled fresh. The smell made her stop and stand with a small group of fans to watch for a few minutes. Meg realized as she watched that going to a Senators game at Griffith Stadium should be her next adventure if it was not improper for her to go by herself. She could ask Aunt

Isobel's advice, but realized Isobel probably knew the team owner and her simple outing to a game could turn into a big deal. As she looked around, Meg thought she saw Mr. "X," the man she had seen on the bus and at Easter. She shook her head and told herself it was time to go home and get some sleep. She was seeing things.

Although Meg wished for some female company on the night watch, she was surprised by how much she liked directing the seamen. As a schoolteacher she was used to directing people, but she had never led an all-male group. Meg reminded herself many of the seamen were new recruits and could have been in her math class the year before, which made it a little less daunting. For her second week on the night shift, she baked soda bread with Davis, bringing several loaves to share. Meg gathered the group together to eat bread.

"Great bread, ma'am," one man complimented her.

"Sure is," said another.

One of the lead radiomen suggested, "She wants something from us. She's bribing us with the bread. Are you about to announce we have to move all the furniture?"

"Nothing like that," Meg reassured them. "No heavy lifting involved," she said with a smile as she noted Warren watching her from the edge of the group. "What I would like you to do is to tell me if we could make the sorting process we do overnight any more efficient."

"We've got a good process for sorting the messages," one man replied.

"We're already pretty fast," confirmed another.

"I don't think we are doing enough with the style of the messages, ma'am," suggested a man sitting near Meg.

"Can you explain what you mean by that?" she asked.

"You may not know this, ma'am," the senior enlisted radioman said, "but Morse code transmission is sort of like handwriting. I can tell when there are different operators."

"We all can," added another man.

"Really?" Meg asked. "Is that true?"

There was a chorus of "yes" and "you bet" in response.

The radioman continued, "I think we all can. When we're transcribing the radio transmissions, we know when the operators have changed. I think it might be helpful if we track the operators and what sort of messages they send."

"That's an excellent idea," Meg confirmed. "Will you help me brief the commander when he comes in this morning? He usually comes in early, so we should be able to finish before the watch is over."

"You should brief him, ma'am."

"I can't describe the nuance of the operator style, but you can. He'll need to hear you to understand that part," Meg reassured him.

Out of the corner of her eye Meg could see Warren scurry back to his desk, and she noted Robbie entering the coding area.

"Throwing parties without us?" Robbie teased.

"Bribing the radiomen to tell me about choke points," Meg retorted.

"You've only been on nights two weeks, and you're reengineering the process."

"Not at all," Meg said. "But I did uncover some potentially important information, and I need you to catch Lewis as soon as he comes in so we can brief the two of you."

"Your wish is my command. Lewis just arrived. 'We'?"

"One of the radiomen."

Commander Lewis frowned when he saw Robbie and Meg approach him. Meg thought Lewis looked as though he had not slept more than a few hours and did not envy the next watch putting up with his bad mood.

"Commander Lewis, could Radioman Thorton and I meet with you for a few minutes?" Meg asked. "The men have noticed some important technical patterns with the communications, and we'd like to brief you, sir."

"Can I get a cup of coffee first?" Lewis asked groggily.

"There may even be some bread left to go with your coffee," Meg suggested.

"You make the bread?" Lewis asked, and Meg nodded. Lewis gave her an attempt at a smile. "Give me a minute and I'll meet you at my office."

Meg caught Thorton's eye, and he walked over to join her outside the office. He shuffled his feet nervously as they waited.

"Just tell him exactly what you told me. Be brief. There's nothing to it," Meg reassured him.

Meg could smell the fresh coffee in Lewis's mug as he approached the pair waiting outside his office.

"Where's Prescott gone?" Lewis grumbled.

"I'll fill him in if needed. We want Radioman Thorton to finish his shift on time," Meg said in a professional tone.

Lewis raised his eyebrows at her, opened his door, and gestured to Meg and Thorton to come in.

"Take a seat," he urged.

"Got the last piece of bread," Robbie said as he rushed in and stood in his usual place in the corner behind Lewis's desk.

Lewis began the conversation. "So, Seaman, what's going on? What should I know about?"

"We know there is a pattern to the style which radio operators use to transmit certain messages, sirs." He looked at Meg and quickly added, "And ma'am."

"How could the style help us?" Prescott asked.

"Among the group of us, we have begun to wonder if only certain operators get certain messages. The better ones might get the more important messages," Thorton continued.

"How would that help?" Lewis asked.

"Given the volume of messages we are processing, it would help guide us to working with the more important ones first," Thorton replied.

"Can you give me any specifics?" Prescott asked.

"We know the style of one of the operators who has been

sending potential battle coordinates. My understanding, sir, is that his information has always been useful. I know the weather is important," he paused to glance at Meg, "but knowing where ships plan on maneuvering before they do is critical information."

"I agree," Lewis confirmed. He tilted back in his chair and sighed. "Prescott, put Osgoode on this task. He has a good track record for deciphering patterns." Meg frowned when she heard Osgoode's name. She was still furious that he had reported her as a security threat, even if she had not gotten in trouble. One of the best things about being on the night watch was not having to see him. Lewis continued, "He should be able to figure out some frequency patterns among operators in a few days." He turned back to Thorton. "During your watch, mark the transmissions from the different operators so we can work on analyzing patterns during the day."

"Yes sir," Thorton replied.

Both Meg and Robbie looked at Lewis expectantly. Initially he gave them both a confused look until he understood their silent communication.

"Great observations, Radioman. Make sure you tell your team I said so," Lewis finally said.

"Yes sir!"

"Dismissed."

"Sirs, ma'am," Thorton said with relief as he left the office.

"I'm going to go find Osgoode and get him going on his assignment," Robbie announced as he followed Thorton out of the office.

"May I be excused, sir?" Meg asked as Lewis sat silently.

"Lieutenant Burke, I don't think you were here when I told the team how useful the decoded message describing Admiral Yamamoto's upcoming visit to the Solomon Islands was."

"I'm glad to hear it," Meg responded.

"More importantly," Lewis continued, "the Army Air Corps was able to use it to target Yamamoto's plane along with flying several patrols as decoys, so it looked to them like we got Yamamoto with pure luck rather than their thinking we were breaking their code."

"Very good to know, sir," Meg said.

"What we do continues to evolve," he continued. "At first it was a success to break their code. Now we need to be sophisticated in how we act on the information so we don't give our knowledge away. Strategy is important. That's what you have just shown."

"Sir?"

"I'm not sure recognizing operator style is going to win the war, but allowing the men to share their ideas and be innovative is important. We need minds like yours to help with that type of strategy." He leaned back in his chair again. "Asking the radiomen shows ingenuity on your part."

"On the men's part, sir," she countered. "I merely passed on what they told me."

"It shows good leadership, Lieutenant," Lewis confirmed. "Go home and get some sleep. You get to do this all over again later today."

"Thank you, sir."

As Meg exited Lewis's office, she realized the day shift was well underway and Lyall was walking straight toward her.

Lyall greeted her with a huge smile. "Howdy, stranger."

"Hi, Lyall. How are you?"

"I'd be great if you would go down to the Mess with me to get a cup of coffee," he suggested. "Tell me what you have been up to."

"Sure," she said brightly, and was surprised to see Lyall frown. Before she could ask why the frown, she heard Robbie from behind her order, "McClaren, go find Osgoode. I don't know where he has disappeared to, but I have a project for him."

"And then coffee," Lyall said to Meg.

"No coffee. Lieutenant Burke needs to get home and get to

sleep," Robbie reproached him. "Go home, Lieutenant Burke. Dismissed."

Lyall rolled his eyes at Meg and she smiled back. Robbie might have prevented her from grabbing a cup of coffee with Lyall, but he was not going to stop her from seeing Julie. She walked over to the library and had just given Julie a hug when Robbie and Osgoode entered the room. Meg clenched her fists when she saw Osgoode.

"Ensign Bowen, we need your help locating maps of the Pacific," Robbie requested.

"Prescott's got me on preschool duty," Osgoode grumbled.

"Let me see how I can help," Julie said pleasantly, with a forced smile.

Cynthia walked over to Meg and greeted her by asking curtly, "What do you need?"

"Just saying 'hi' since I hardly ever see you and Julie anymore," Meg said. "Lieutenant Prescott has already told me to go home, so I probably shouldn't stick around."

"Speaking of following orders, could you please get the night watch to stop making a mess in here? If it doesn't stop, Julie's going to have to report it and you're going to get in trouble," Cynthia advised.

"I didn't know. I'm glad you told me," Meg said earnestly. "It's hard to focus on codes and managing people at the same time. I'll try paying greater attention to who is accessing this area at night." She noticed Osgoode was watching her from where he was standing across the room and she dropped her voice to a whisper. "Maybe we should prohibit access to the library when you and Julie aren't here."

Cynthia lowered her voice as well when she replied, "Julie even came in early last week to tell Warren he was going to get *you* in trouble if he kept making a mess. Warren denied knowing anything about it." Cynthia sighed. "Of course."

"I don't think this project is going to give us anything useful, Prescott, especially for the time it's going to take," Osgoode exclaimed as he and Prescott walked across the room to Meg and Cynthia and smirked, saying, "All you WAVES do is gossip and drink coffee."

"Which is more than you do most days," Cynthia retorted.

"Oh, I assure you, I do much, much more," Osgoode answered.

"Osgoode, get to work. Collingsworth, you've got transmissions to file. Burke. GO. HOME," Prescott commanded.

"On my way, sir." Meg stood as if she were leaving. Once Robbie had left the room, she quickly sat back down and hissed, "Why do you think it's Warren?"

"The things left out always have to do with the weather. Only you and Warren care about the weather and you are too much of a rules follower to leave things out. That leaves Warren."

"True," Meg acknowledged.

Cynthia continued, "Warren says he never comes in here and wouldn't know how to find anything, but who else cares about the weather around here?" Cynthia tossed her head to indicate she didn't believe him and dropped her voice to an almost undetectable whisper before saying, "One of the copies of the Yamamoto transmission is missing, which is why Julie is really worried."

"Maybe misfiled?" Meg suggested.

Cynthia looked at Meg for a moment. "Maybe if you were not so caught up in your social life, you could play detective and figure out what is going on." Cynthia's remark surprised Meg.

"You used to be very concerned about my *lack* of social life," Meg replied. For the first time since she had met her, Cynthia gave her what Meg believed was Cynthia's true smile.

"You have been very gracious about leaving mine alone and I appreciate it. I've tried to do the same." Cynthia paused before asking, "Has Tom said anything to you?"

"Not a word." Meg smiled. "About anything. But there's something I have always wanted to ask you."

"Yes?"

"What did he say to you the morning he took us to the train station? You were miserable but whatever he said made you smile."

"Ah." Cynthia looked Meg in the eye and replied, "Be nice to her. Someday she might be your sister-in-law."

"I see. On that note, I'm going to go home to bed."

## 47

As soon as the fans came out, Meg experienced her first battle in this particular form of office warfare. There was a very narrow margin between being close enough to the fan to experience the relief of the air movement and having her papers blown away. Not surprisingly, Warren was often the prime target, as others moved the fan direction away from their area and toward another. But he was also a veteran of this trench warfare. Every time he left to go to the head or to get something from the cafeteria, he secured all his work with something heavy to withstand the brunt of the air stream, and Meg quickly learned to follow his example.

The humidity also increased the number of cockroaches. One night, several of the seamen lay down a track using cardboard so they could race cockroaches. Assigning names like Waltzing Walter or Shinny Sam, one of the seamen called the progress of the contest as if they were at the horse races. As watch officer, Meg knew she probably should have told them to stop, but it gave them a moment to relax and to step away from the frustration they were all experiencing and the war news they were hearing about and reading in the paper. She even thought it was practical for them to take a break. They were sweating so much that the paper they were working on would get damp and stick to the desk. If they were not careful when they moved their hands as they wrote, they were in danger of tearing transmissions. It was only a few days into the real heat and Meg found the conditions draining. It was going to be a long summer.

So far, her surveillance of Warren had been straightforward, especially without distractions from Cynthia or Julie. In fact, Meg needed no excuse to spend so much time with Warren since they were the only two people on the night watch working on decoding transmissions. Warren, Meg noted, appeared to spend most of the time moving pieces of paper and dozing rather than doing any actual decryption. Meg spent a few uncomfortable nights skipping going to the bathroom and not eating so she could pretend to leave the workspace and then hide in a darkened corner to see if Warren went into the library in her absence. He never did. When she returned to her desk following her clandestine attempts, she found him in his seat, often barely awake. If he had been moving files and possibly taking transmissions from the library as Cynthia and Julie had suggested, he appeared to have stopped. But someone was still moving things in the library. Julie had grabbed Meg on the previous day during the watch change to tell her that files were still being misplaced; Julie had given a formal report to Robbie to alert him to the issue and to brief Commander Lewis. Meg knew Warren couldn't be the culprit but had no idea who was responsible or why it was taking place.

Since she had not been able to solve the library file mystery, Meg decided to use the cover of the warmer weather bringing crowds outdoors to track Warren outside of work. One challenge of following Warren was to devise a way to deceive the brilliant Isobel about what she was up to. One evening, Meg fabricated a church event and slipped out of the house wearing tired civilian clothes she'd found in a charity shop, with her hair wound into a scarf. She hoped she looked like any other tired young woman at the end of a day of cleaning. No one appeared to question that she was a domestic or cleaning woman at one of the many federal buildings. Once she was sure her outfit was not getting a second look and confident her disguise was effective, Meg took a bus to Warren's neighborhood and read a newspaper while sipping coffee at a corner soda shop near his home. When she saw him leave home around seven, she began following him, while carefully staying several yards behind him. She felt her elaborate ruse might be wasted, as Warren was not looking around. Even if he had been, he would probably not have recognized her. Meg had forgotten what it was like to be out of uniform and able to walk in a crowd without attracting attention. When he waited at the bus stop, she stood half a block away, partially hidden by a tree until she saw the bus approach.

Once on the crowded bus, Warren appeared to be lost in reading the newspaper and not paying attention to anything around him, not even the attractive woman sitting across from him who appeared to be trying to catch his eye. Meg slouched to make herself less obvious and tried not to make eye contact with anyone. When they got to a stop near work, Meg let Warren get off and start to walk down the street before jumping off the bus just as the driver started to put it back into gear, ignoring the driver's well-deserved hiss at her.

Meg was surprised when Warren turned toward work and approached the barracks on Nebraska Avenue, near the Annex. She giggled to herself that Warren was just like most single men living in Washington, DC, who knew this was one of the best places in town to see and to hopefully meet women. Men could not go inside the barracks, but in good weather, men and women would sit outside and enjoy listening to the dance music on radios placed in windows or plugged inside using extension cords, while others retreated to the shadows of the still partly wooded neighborhood.

Meg watched Warren take out a picnic supper of chicken brought from home and noted that he, much like herself, looked content to find a seat on the periphery where he could safely watch and listen. He remained one of many faces in the crowd rather than standing out within the group. Meg was disappointed, but not surprised, that Warren did not speak to anybody and, as far as she could tell, did not approach anyone, or make any type of nonverbal contact.

For a week, she found excuses to leave Isobel's early and follow Warren as he left home to go to work. It was monotonous, exhausting work, as she was constantly stopping and making sure she was far enough away from Warren that he did not notice her while also checking to see if anyone was following her. A few times she worried that he would recognize her, but remembered it took Robbie several encounters with her to connect Lieutenant Burke with the Taylors' maid and she had not been actively trying to look different. Context and clothes made a huge difference in perception. Although Meg was sure Warren had not seen her, frustratingly, he was on time to work every night she followed him. She had not figured out what he was doing before that made him late.

As the days grew longer, the additional sunlight not only made it easier for her to observe Warren, but also for him to see her. To improve her cover, Meg increased her following distance and was left flat-footed when one evening Warren crossed an intersection just as the light turned red. He continued in the general direction of the Communications Annex rather than pausing at his normal bus stop. Forced to wait through a traffic cycle at the busy intersection, Meg fell behind by several blocks and was having trouble spotting his figure in the growing twilight. She increased her pace and realized Warren was making good time; usually he idled, challenging her ability to stay discretely hidden. As Warren passed a small arcade of offices, a previously concealed figure emerged from one of the arches and approached him. Meg thought, excitedly, she was about to have proof of an encounter between Warren and Avila to report to McClaren and Lewis.

Taking advantage of the shadows cast over the sidewalk, she walked cautiously next to the buildings, keeping her face down, and readjusting her scarf to cover more of her hair. Adopting a shuffle step to disguise her characteristically long strides, she crept closer to hear the conversation. She stopped abruptly and pushed herself against the façade of the nearest building when she realized, rather than Avila, it was the same man she had seen on the bus and who followed her from the bookstore. How was Mr. "X" linked to Warren? Although she could hear their voices and the tone sounded angry, she could not make out what either was saying as Mr. "X" repeatedly pressed the pointer finger of his right hand up against Warren's chest. The scene reminded Meg of a bully taunting a smaller child on the playground. After several jabs, Warren started to slouch and resumed walking in his original direction. Warren had only taken a few steps when Mr. "X" grabbed his arm, pulled Warren roughly towards him, clasped Warren's shoulders, and shook him violently. Meg desperately wanted to rush over to the couple and break up the confrontation but knew she could not help Warren and it would only expose her.

After several seconds of shaking, Mr. "X" pushed Warren away from him, briskly crossed the street with his back toward Meg, and faded into the twilight. As much as Meg wanted to approach Warren, she was not sure who else might be watching and waiting. Mr. "X" might only have pretended to leave. She backtracked to the nearest corner and went in the opposite direction from Mr. "X" until she found a bus stop where people waited. For once she was grateful to see the bus was crowded and took comfort in being surrounded by others. At the Annex, she ducked into the women's barracks to change into her uniform and realized she needed to report the incident to Lewis or McClaren even though they had gone home.

As Meg walked into the research area, she was surprised to see Robbie sitting at her desk. She looked at him questioningly.

"Couldn't sleep," he responded to her expression. "What have you been up to? You're flushed and jumpy. I know you weren't swimming."

Meg quickly reviewed the chain of command. Even though she questioned Robbie's motives for flirting with her, technically he was the correct person to report what she had seen of Warren's encounter with Mr. "X". Before she started to explain, he interrupted her thoughts saying, "What do you need to make tea?"

"Boiling water, milk, sugar, and a teapot," Meg replied, unsure of where the conversation was going.

"Then come with me."

They went over to Robbie's desk, where he opened the large bottom drawer and extracted a brown, earthenware teapot, creamer, and sugar bowl. Meg was surprised to see he would have something so functional.

"Where did you get this?" she asked.

"After talking about it at Easter, Mother insisted I bring it in. It took me several days of bringing it in, piece by piece, so security did not ask any questions."

"Is this *the* tea set she used with her grandmother?" Meg was surprised.

"I assume so." Robbie grinned when he saw Meg was a little flustered. "Mother sent tea and sugar. We just need milk and boiling water."

"Where are we going to get boiling water?" Meg asked.

"Let me show you." Robbie led the way down the corridor, to the staircase, and down a half landing to a door that said "No Entry." He pulled out a key and opened the door into a small galley kitchen with two electric burners, on which sat a kettle.

"How many people know about this?" Meg asked.

"Open to officers," he replied.

"*Some* officers," she said tartly. "I'll boil the water if you bring down the tea set and get some milk."

"Only if you promise not to fling the boiling water at me."

By the time Robbie returned, the water was boiling. Meg carefully poured some water into the teapot, swished it around to warm up the pot, and dumped it out. She carefully spooned three tablespoons of tea leaves into the pot before adding the remainder of the boiling water.

"One for you, one for me, and one for the pot. We need to wait three minutes for the tea to steep. Just enough time for me to tell you what I witnessed tonight."

"What did you see?" he asked.

"More who I saw," she said slowly.

"Meg! What is the matter?"

"Do you remember how I told you about a man I thought was following me? I know I saw him on the bus and once walking after work. There have been a few other times when I thought I've seen him. Tonight, rather than following me, he was pushing Warren around." She made a face. "He was pretty rough with Warren."

Robbie did not respond immediately and as Meg waited for him to speak, she grabbed two mugs sitting on the counter and poured the tea, which was the perfect color, a shade darker than light syrup.

"It's important that the tea steep but not stew," she explained to fill the silence.

When she took the lid off the sugar bowl and saw sugar cubes, she raised her eyebrows before catching herself.

"A treat from my mother," Robbie clarified.

"For all of your tea parties?" Meg asked while looking at him pointedly, but he barely noticed her. She put a cube in her mug and stirred as he shrugged his shoulders and inclined his head to one side. He finally took a sip from his mug and said,

"This is wonderful tea. Much, much better than sludge coffee," Robbie complimented Meg. He took another long sip, put the mug on the counter, raked his hands through his hair, and started to pace in a small circle. Abruptly he stopped and said, "Is there any chance either one of them saw you?"

Meg shook her head. "I was against a wall. Given the angle, Warren might, might have been able to see me but he was being attacked. I don't think Mr. "X" could. He had his back to me most of the time"

"Think or know?"

"Think."

Robbie moved in front of her and put a hand on each of her shoulders as he looked intently at her. "Going forward, if you are outside Isobel's house or the command area, you need to be with at least one other person. Take the bus. Let George drive you the next few nights. You've got to be careful Meg."

"His issue was with Warren, not with me."

"Meg, this has become an issue far bigger than us. I will brief Lewis tonight. Until I do, not a word about this to anyone. Got me? You never saw Elliot tonight."

Meg did not respond but carefully extracted herself from Robbie's grasp and silently started to wash the tea set. Robbie moved next to her and dried each item. When she lifted the tray holding the now clean set, Robbie took it from her.

"You saw the drawer where I was keeping the tea set. We'll do this again when we are a little more relaxed." His mouth smiled at her, but his eyes conveyed his anxiety as she held the door so he could carry the tray.

## 48

When Meg left at the end of her shift, Prescott and Lewis had been talking for more than an hour in Lewis' office. At one point, Lewis had called her in and asked her to describe the incident. When she finished, he asked her no questions and dismissed her without comment. Warren did not come to the night watch and never returned. Two days later, as watch officer, she was directed to make a brief announcement indicating Mr. Elliot had returned to the Department of Agriculture. Meg felt she was the only person who noticed he was gone. The day watch had forgotten about him weeks earlier and no one on the night watch, other than herself, interacted regularly with him.

Not realizing how much of her time had been spent trailing Warren, anticipating him being late to work, and filling out paperwork to document his tardiness, were it not for wondering about Mr. "X", she would have felt almost light-hearted to focus only on her assigned work. While riding on the bus, as directed, she speculated about what had happened, but Lewis said nothing and Robbie had not come to work during the night watch for several days.

A week later, as she concentrated on Bay of Japan weather reports, Meg looked up to see Robbie pulling a small, waxed paper package out of his pocket.

"Have a cookie," he suggested.

"I can't eat cookies at one o'clock in the morning."

"It's closer to two, so it's okay."

She grinned at him, sniffed the bag, and moaned slightly. "Oh! They are homemade. Where did you get these?"

"I went home last night for dinner. Mother still has butter for cookie baking and my father is in denial about her flouting the ration restrictions. By the way, while I was there, she asked how the tea set was doing. I told her you were taking excellent care of it and were teaching me how to steep and not stew tea."

Meg felt her stomach lurch slightly. She was not sure how she felt about Robbie discussing her with his mother, so she quickly changed the subject and asked, "When do you sleep?"

"I can't sleep when it's this hot," he answered. "I figured I'd come in and see if you were making any remarkable break-throughs."

"I may have made one of sorts. Come with me to the library."

"The library?" As he asked, he put the bag of cookies back in his pocket and hurried to fall into step with her strides across the room.

"Yes. And be sure not to make a mess," she warned over her shoulder.

"Julie gave me the report," he whispered as he caught up to Meg. "In addition to "X", Lewis and I are worried about the Yamamoto transmission going missing. That's more than someone being lazy. That's a security problem. What do you think is going on?"

"I have no idea, but we know it can't be Warren since it's continued even though he's gone." She looked at him searchingly. "You'd probably know better than I if it involves counter-intelligence," she added coyly.

Robbie turned bright red. "You've got to admit it wasn't a bad idea for you to join the choir or to follow Elliot," he said gruffly.

"If you trusted me enough to be part of your project, you should have trusted me enough to brief me." She stared at him for a moment. "I don't like being used."

"Message received and noted."

"It better be. Can you tell me where he is?"

Robbie stopped as they walked down the hall that would take them to the galley kitchen. "Maybe over a cup of tea," he grinned mischievously.

"After . . . Did you hear that sound? It sounded like someone dropped some books."

"The noise is definitely coming from the library!" Robbie bounded ahead of Meg, opened the door, and flipped on the lights. There were several folders on one of the tables and an atlas on the floor lying facedown with its spine splayed, but no one was there.

"I don't think it is anyone on the night watch," Robbie said. "We would have seen them coming from the transmission room. Someone is sneaking in using the stairs in the back corridor, which are not guarded at night." He sighed loudly. "Meg, would you mind making some tea? I have a report to write. Lewis and McClaren need to be briefed as soon as they arrive. Remind me, what were we looking for in the library?"

"There's something different about the recent weather reports and I can't put my finger on it. I was going to compare them to old ones to figure it out," Meg responded.

Robbie cleared his throat before saying, "Make a mental note to revisit that project. But not tonight. It's more important to document someone sneaking in."

Making tea without Robbie was faster but less enjoyable. When Meg returned to the office with two mugs of tea, Robbie was sitting at his desk, tapping his left foot in agitation and racking his fingers through his hair. There were several crumpled balls of paper in the wastebasket, as well as a few on the floor where Robbie's throw had missed.

"Why is the report so hard to write?" she asked.

"I don't want you, or me, for that matter, to be blamed or to get a black mark on our record. I'm wording the narrative to suggest the night watch needs the double set of guards at the back stairs that we have during the day and swing shift by explaining you're required to be in too many places at once to also watch the door."

"Ah." Meg hadn't thought about how the mysterious visitor or visitors could specifically get her in trouble.

"Want to read it over?"

"Sure." Meg scanned the report quickly, finding it not only factual but almost lyrical. Not surprisingly, in addition to being mathematically gifted, Robbie could write. "Looks good to me."

"Great. You should probably sign it too."

As she applied her signature, Robbie said, "I checked the schedule. You're off on Thursday night. You can sleep that night and go to the Senators game with me on Friday afternoon before work."

Meg was surprised by the dramatic change in subject. She said evenly, "You seem confident I'll go," even though her heart was pounding.

"I know how much you like baseball. You'd go with Osgoode to a baseball game if he asked. I'm just lucky McClaren isn't smart enough to figure out that's the way to your heart."

Meg noted Robbie was not smiling as he said that.

"I'd like to go." She took a breath and paused. "With you."

"Good. I'll get tickets. Leave the mugs to me."

With the heat of late spring, the atmosphere in the Research section was becoming thicker with the smell of cigarette smoke, burnt coffee, and increasingly, body odor. Even so, she could not entirely blame the closeness of the workspace for being a little light-headed. Meg could feel herself blushing furiously as she thought about the invitation to the Senators game as she walked out of the department.

Although she had swum before her watch since she had not been following Warren, Meg decided to go to the pool again. It would help her to sleep if she cooled down and washed away her tension from work. For the first several laps she thought about the upcoming baseball game. She was glad to be in the pool by herself, where she could reflect on her earlier conversation with Robbie. Then she turned her mind to the work problem that was bothering her, which was the weather reports she was tracking. There was something very different with this current weather transmission, and it had to do not with what was being sent but when it was being sent. Meg knew she would forget her ideas about transmission patterns if she did not go back to work.

She got a few strange looks when she returned to her desk, in part because she had come back and in part because once she took off her hat, her hair was still damp. Several of the "professors" put ice packs on their heads when they had headaches, and another walked around in slippers while he paced and went over patterns in his mind. She hoped she could have some latitude on the wet hair. It would dry soon enough. She called Aunt Isobel's house and left a message with Davis to say she would be home later. Then she went to the library.

"Cynthia, do you mind helping me pull some of these weather reports?"

"Yes. I do mind. Can I ask why you need weather reports when you should be going home and getting some sleep?" Cynthia said in a loud voice. "Your lack of sleep is making you delusional."

"Help me pull them and I'll help you put them back. I need them to look for a pattern."

"Hmph," Cynthia muttered.

"Thank you for your confidence," Meg said with a smile.

"Would you like me to do your ironing as well?" Cynthia retorted.

"That would be great," Meg responded.

Although there was more room in the library for Meg to spread the transmissions in sequence, she went back to the main area away from Cynthia's sighs. Meg started to lay the transmissions in chronological order on her desk when the fan blew them in several directions. She yelled in frustration, "Could someone please turn the fans off for just a minute?"

Her uncharacteristic outburst not only brought Robbie bounding over to her desk, but Lewis also rushed out of his office and stood with his arms across his chest, wordlessly shifting his weight slightly from one foot to the other while he watched her work. Meg thought, in retrospect, it might have been more relaxing to stay with Cynthia in the library as she circled the transmission times on most of the communications while marking others with a rectangle. After she finished and confirmed they were in order, she whistled under her breath.

"This had better be more than an exuberant geometry lesson," Lewis demanded. "I've got a few pressing issues this morning, as you well know."

Meg looked briefly at Robbie, whose expression indicated the report of the files left in the library was at least as stressful as expected. Meg took a deep breath.

"I had an idea while I was swimming," she said by way of explanation. "I have something I want to show you." Meg pointed to the first two months of reports.

"What am I looking at?" Lewis asked.

"Transmission time. The transmissions are within a few minutes of six a.m. local time, twenty out of twenty-one days. Every three weeks, the weather reports come at seven a.m. local time. Why?"

"How long has this been going on?"

"I can track it back at least six months. Probably more. I

pulled six months to show a pattern. Every three weeks it is delayed by an hour. Why?"

"I wonder if something else is being transmitted?" Robbie pondered. "What are they using this network for and what are we missing? Or is something happening on the primary system?"

"Solid work, Lieutenant Burke. Go home and get some sleep," Lewis said. "I want you working on this when you return this evening. Prescott, give it to McClaren to work on today," he directed. "He has a knack for this sort of puzzle and will move it along before Lieutenant Burke comes back tonight."

"McClaren?" Robbie asked in an incredulous tone.

"Sure. Why not? Do you think he's misplaced here?" Lewis asked.

"Maybe not misplaced, but specially placed?" Robbie said tartly.

"Recommended based on his math scores before his father took command, not that it is really any business of yours," Lewis clarified. Robbie looked dubious. "It's an act, Prescott. He hides how smart he is." Lewis turned to Meg. "Why are you still here? Go home."

Meg barely noticed the heat and humidity as she walked home. She was busy thinking about who or what was using the communication network every three weeks, when she wasn't thinking about the baseball game.

## 49

M eg would have been content to walk or even take a bus to the baseball game and join Robbie there, but Robbie insisted that he would meet her at Aunt Isobel's so they could travel together to Griffith Stadium. She was prepared to meet him on the porch and whisk him away before he could have any contact with the household, but Isobel outsmarted her. Isobel cornered Meg in the library a few minutes before Robbie arrived so that she was unable to get the door when he arrived.

After Davis showed him in, Isobel announced, "I am sure you have time for some tea in the garden." Davis brought tea as well as soda bread for a late morning snack. Meg was on edge, but Robbie seemed completely at ease.

"Neither of you is really a Senators fan, so I'm not sure how much you know about Griffith Stadium. I think I should prepare you," Aunt Isobel said, "especially as it is not like Ebbets Field or Fenway."

Meg never ceased to be amazed by the breadth of things Aunt Isobel knew. Even though Meg loved baseball, she didn't know a thing about Fenway but made a mental note that if the conversation lagged during the game, she would ask Robbie about Boston's ballpark.

"The Senators are usually in last place in the American League," Robbie commented. "Their stadium is ancient, has no parking, and is regarded widely as a firetrap."

"Even so, it is where Washington's leaders gather," Isobel explained. "I wasn't there, but on the Sunday of the Pearl Harbor attack a football game was underway when the press box received the news over the wires. Some of the spectators overheard the press talking about the air strike and the news spread through the stadium. Initially, no one had made an announcement over the PA system. Apparently, the stadium manager thought it would be a crowd control hazard if it were announced. Instead, the fans realized it was true when they started making a series of announcements asking for one general or admiral after another to report to duty immediately. One story I heard was when a newspaper reporter's wife learned the news from her home radio, she dispatched a telegram to her husband sitting in the grandstand to inform him."

Robbie laughed. "Sorry, Isobel. I shouldn't laugh about something so tragic, but your story so quintessentially captures life in Washington, DC, and how it's so different from New York or Boston." He had finished his soda bread and grabbed Meg's barely touched slice to eat.

Isobel smiled fondly at him before asking, "How are your parents?"

"They're going to Maine for ten days in June. I won't be able to join them, *again*, this year. Another summer of not finishing the book I'm supposed to be writing." He looked at his watch and said, "Speaking of being late, Meg wants to be there for batting practice, so we'd better be off." Out of the shade of the garden, on this late May day, the sun was blinding. "Are you sure you don't want to take the bus?" Robbie asked. "Or even a cab?"

"I can walk. It's under two miles and I need to be in the sun. We're spending so much time inside that we're going to look like escaped prisoners or part of a science experiment when people do see us."

He laughed heartily. "They wouldn't be entirely wrong, would they?" Then, changing the subject he said, "That didn't taste like your soda bread."

"My soda bread?"

"The best part of being on the night watch if you talk to the men. Why didn't you make it when you were on days?"

"Davis made today's bread. But to answer the other part of your question, it's easier to do things for the night watch, like bake bread, than for those on days. It's more relaxed," Meg explained.

"And Cynthia isn't there to tease you."

"Exactly!"

"Has it crossed your mind you may need to get used to that teasing?"

"No." Although of course she had thought about it, after her conversation with Cynthia about Tom, but she did not want to discuss that with Robbie.

"I refuse to believe she and I will have anything to do with each other after the war beyond memories of having been housemates and colleagues."

"Right," Robbie said.

Meg continued, "I'm sure her pretending to be interested in my brother is all about winding me up somehow, and maybe even worse."

"It sounds as though she already has. Wound you up, at least." Robbie looked amused. "One way or another, you're going to be stuck with Cynthia. Isobel isn't going to let you go after the war. You're the daughter she should have had. Besides, I predict you'll be at Thanksgiving with Cynthia for the next fifty years." Smiling wickedly, he added, "You'll be godmother to their first child."

When Meg lightly punched him in response to that statement, Robbie grabbed her arm and tucked it into his. The street
around them was busy with other people going to the game.
The stadium was in a run-down section of the city and Meg was
comforted being close to Robbie. Moreover, Isobel had not
exaggerated when she referred to Griffith Stadium as a firetrap.
With faded green-painted steel and worn wooden grandstands
and bleachers, it looked as if it belonged in the Minor Leagues
rather than hosting spectators such as military brass and
ambassadors. Meg had not asked Robbie about their seats but
assumed he had gotten bleacher seats, which is what she would
have purchased for a game with a friend. Once the usher took
their ticket stubs at the gate, Robbie steered her toward the
tunnel for the section behind home plate. She said nothing but
looked at him in surprise when she realized they were in some
of the best seats at the game.

"I knew it was going to be hot. I figured we might like some
shade," he said in answer to her expression. "Am I wrong? Your
uniform hat may be 'darling,' but it doesn't do much against the
sun. It is what I would call highly decorative."

"Are you suggesting the WAVES are highly decorative?"

"Only some of them. Not you."

Once they sat, Meg was not sure what she was supposed to
do. She had not really thought through what she was going to
do or say to Robbie at the game. She put off any planning
because if she did not think about it, she did not have to
admit to herself that their going to the game was a date.
Working nights, she infrequently had the opportunity to talk
with Julie as they fell asleep. Only Aunt Isobel and Davis
knew Meg was going to the game with Lieutenant Prescott.
Meg could not talk to him about work and desperately tried
to think of something to say. She wasn't sure how to work the
Red Sox into the conversation and ask about Fenway, so she
remained silent.

"Why are you so quiet? Are you hungry? You didn't eat any

bread. May I buy you some peanuts or a hot dog?" Robbie asked.

"Um, no."

"What, then?" He smiled but seemed annoyed. She was sure she was not acting like any of the women with whom he normally spent time. She might as well tell him what she really wanted.

"How would you feel if I kept score?" Meg asked.

"Kept score? You mean you'd get the tickets next time?"

She blushed. "No. But I can." Would he really want to go to another game with her? "I meant kept score during the game. I like to do that. Sometimes I keep score when I listen to a game on the radio. You know. When Red Barber describes the Dodgers 'tearing up the pea patch'."

Robbie laughed loudly enough he startled the people sitting a few seats away, but they smiled when they saw the couple. When he watched Meg nervously nibbling her lip, he smiled gently.

"Of course you can keep score." He looked for a vendor and gestured to get his attention. "Can we have a program and a scorecard?" He turned to Meg. "Do you need a pencil?"

"Um, no. I have a pencil in my purse."

"Of course you do. Mechanical, right?" She nodded.

"Do you want to do the Browns and I'll do the Senators, or vice versa?" she asked.

"Nope. I'm going to have to watch you. There aren't score-cards in rowing and I have no idea how you do this."

"You didn't go to Red Sox games growing up?"

"Of course I did. Still do when I can, but I don't keep score."

"As a Sox fan, you don't go to Yankee games, do you?"

"Only when the Sox are in town. You are still going to hate me, maybe even more than if I were a Yankee fan. When in New York, I follow the Giants. I don't get to many games. Either I'm busy with school or I'm away during the summer. During the summer before the war, I was holed up in our Maine summer house because I was supposed to be turning my dissertation into a book. I still have a book contract and a deadline. Believe it or not, I'm still trying to snatch a few minutes here and there trying to finish it. More and more, it looks as though I am going to miss the deadline, though."

"Were you working on it the night after the concert at the National Gallery?"

He looked at her silently for a few moments. "Yes, I was, as a matter of fact. How could you possibly know that?"

"You looked as though you had been up all night the next day, but I knew everyone came home fairly early."

"You should be a detective." *Or a spy*, was left unsaid as they stared at each other until he broke eye contact and Meg focused on her scorecard. Her heart thumped against her chest as he leaned over her shoulder to watch her making her scribbles, marking strikes and balls, with a special flourish for the backward "K" when the batter was caught looking at a third strike, bat on his shoulder.

Finally, he said, "Will you go back to teaching after the war?" She was glad she was scorekeeping and could avoid making eye contact when she answered.

"A few months ago, I would have said I was absolutely going to go back to teaching high school math, but now I'm less sure. I didn't have much time with the instructors during Indoctrination, but I think I'd like to become a professor if that were possible."

"Of course it's possible."

"I would need to get a graduate degree."

"Meg, when has school ever been a challenge for you? In fact, it might be good for you if it were to be a challenge. It's easy to get in trouble when you are bored."

"Well, maybe." She was silent again for a few minutes.

Robbie said quietly, "With your recent experience, people will fall over themselves to give you a graduate fellowship."

She was so focused on capturing a short fly ball to right

field and a throw to pick off the runner who had left second for third that she did not notice he had put his arm around her until she leaned back in her seat. Should she say something? What was she supposed to say? Was she supposed to do something? Meg decided to ever so slightly lean into his embrace. He responded by lightly squeezing her shoulder. When they got up to sing at the seventh-inning stretch, she let him take her hand. Then she noticed huge thunderheads forming as they looked toward the outfield.

"Do you think it's going to rain before the end of the game?" Meg asked.

"We should get the game in. But with no umbrella, we'll get soaked walking home. Do you want to leave now?"

"Leave church before communion?" she replied.

He laughed. "In that case, maybe you'll let us take a cab after the game?"

"Maybe." She smiled.

Too soon, the game was over. The Senators won four to two and Robbie had taken her arm to help lead her out of the ballpark. They walked a few blocks away from the stadium before he was able to hail a cab. As Robbie pulled the door closed behind them, it began to pour. "Just in time," he declared. "Italian food alright with you? I know a good place in Georgetown."

"Sounds lovely."

Meg was grateful for the sound of the rain pinging against the roof of the cab to cover the awkward silence caused by her anxiety about making small talk. It was a few minutes, and several blocks, before she was able to say, "We probably saw one of the Senators' few wins this season. We should consider ourselves lucky."

Robbie pulled his arm through Meg's crooked elbow so that their shoulders overlapped and whispered in her ear, "We were definitely lucky." A bolt of lightning hit a tree about a block ahead of them and the accompanying thunder shook the cab.

Meg bumped Robbie's jaw with her shoulder as she jumped at the noise.

"I am so sorry!" she exclaimed.

"Nothing a few drinks won't help." Robbie laughed when he saw her shocked expression. "Maybe you'll have a glass of Chianti with me? For medicinal reasons? Since we were almost hit by lightning?"

"Okay. Just one." Robbie pulled her back close to him and seemed content to sit in companionable silence as the rain poured down and the windshield wipers kept an even tempo. The gentle rhythm allowed Meg to relax enough that she was surprised when the driver said, "Here we are, sir."

Robbie quickly paid the driver, then bounded out the door to Meg's side to help her across the rushing water in the gutter and onto the sidewalk. The restaurant was several steps down from street level and even after the rain-darkened early evening light, it took a few moments for Meg's eyes to adjust to the restaurant's dim interior. As she looked around, she saw most of the tables were filled, although it was barely evening. She and Robbie were among the few customers in uniform; most of the diners were wearing suits and dresses. A presidential administration hangout, she concluded.

"Dr. Prescott. Nice to see you again." The maître d' shook hands with Robbie. Meg noted the use of *doctor* rather than *lieutenant*, suggesting Robbie came here with his parents. Robbie grabbed her elbow, gently guiding her as they followed the man to a booth in the back. She wondered if they were going to join Dr. and Mrs. Prescott, or at least run into them that evening. After Meg slid onto the upholstered bench, Robbie followed and sat next to her. Meg looked searchingly at him.

"It's easier to people-watch and whisper our observations to each other if we sit on the same side," Robbie explained as he grinned at her.

"I'll send Eduardo right over," the maître d' promised, and Meg thought she saw him wink at Robbie.

Eduardo must have been hovering, Meg realized, as he appeared almost instantaneously with a basket of bread. "What would you like to drink?" he asked.

"A bottle of Chianti," Robbie responded. "How does the fried zucchini to start followed by the veal sound Meg?"

"Perfect," she replied.

"I'm working tonight, Robbie. I shouldn't be drinking," Meg objected after the waiter left.

"Don't worry. We probably won't drink the whole bottle, but they're short staffed and it's much easier to make one trip with a bottle rather than several trips to bring glasses."

"We're ordering a bottle of wine for the war effort?" Meg asked.

"Exactly. It's your patriotic duty," he responded, and gently squeezed her arm. "Don't worry. I'm not going to let you go in to work drunk. Although you wouldn't be the first."

"First WAVE to do so."

"Hardly." He grabbed the bread basket. "Here. Have a roll. It'll help soak up the alcohol." Meg was grateful to have something to do with her hands and broke a roll into small pieces as Robbie asked, "If you had more time to play tourist, what would you go see?"

"That's a long list. I thought I'd have made more progress by now."

"What have you seen?" Robbie inquired.

"The Smithsonian and the Art Museum, briefly. The first day we got here, when you had nowhere to put us." They both laughed as they thought back to that day. "I've had several hours at the Lincoln Memorial, and I took Tom to see the Jefferson Memorial as well as to look through the fence at the White House rose garden. That's been about it. Oh. And I have seen one of the informal baseball games on the Mall."

"And the Senators win, which puts you in a small sample of people."

Their wine arrived, and Robbie poured a third of a glass for Meg and a full glass for himself. "You can always have more," he explained.

"What are your favorite parts of Washington, DC?" Meg asked.

"The parts not in DC."

"What do you mean?"

"I love being around Chesapeake Bay," Robbie explained. "I enjoy fishing and being out on the water. My father loves to sail, and I wish I were as good a sailor as he. It took me a while to become seaworthy when I was growing up. I was always on the wrong side of the boat deck or not ducking the boom quickly enough, which could make the boat capsize."

"But you row?"

"I do. I know it doesn't make sense that I can balance a scull, which can tip over if you look at it the wrong way, but I was a late bloomer when it comes to sailing. My sister, Elizabeth, is a much better sailor. You still haven't met her, have you?"

Meg did not remember the salad arriving but was glad it had, so she could move a few lettuce pieces around before answering, "No, I haven't. Isn't she at school?"

"She was at the McClarens' at New Year's."

"I barely remember New Year's," Meg replied. "We'd just arrived."

"That's right. You spent most of the party hiding in the corner when you weren't dancing with Osgoode." Meg started to blush as she remembered her panic that Robbie had discovered she had worked as a servant. As if reading her thoughts, Robbie squeezed her knee gently under the table. "Hope you think you've found a better dance partner." Meg felt herself glowing and smiled at him in response.

Robbie stopped speaking and started to pour more wine into Meg's glass.

"No more! It's just going to go to waste," she protested.

"You need something to drink with your veal."

"Okay. But just a little," she conceded.

"And right on cue, Eduardo has our main course."

Meg hadn't wanted to tell Robbie she had never had veal and was not entirely sure what to expect. She fussed with her knife and fork to cover her uncertainty, watching Robbie as he quickly sliced a piece of veal and murmured his pleasure at the taste. She realized she had never seen him without a healthy appetite.

"Now that I've had a bite of mine and haven't passed out, do you think it is safe to eat?" he teased.

Meg felt her face flush, which seemed to be an almost constant condition when she was with Robbie.

"You know me better than I know myself sometimes," she said so quietly she didn't think he could have heard her, but even if he did not hear, he sensed her self-consciousness. Robbie gently pressed his leg against hers and whispered, "You're doing fine." In a louder voice, he asked, "What's something you want to do before the summer is over?"

She had just taken her first bite of the veal when he asked. She had never had such a tender piece of meat; it felt almost velvety in her mouth. She had expected a heartier essence, more like steak, and was delighted with its more delicate flavor. Robbie watched her expectantly as she finished her mouthful.

"Don't worry. I'll be glad to finish yours since you don't like it."

"Not a chance," she said as she moved her arm protectively around her plate and turned to look him in the eye. "I want to rent a canoe and listen to the Washington Opera one night."

"Great idea," he confirmed. "I think they perform *La Bohème* in a few weeks. I'll make sure we get to a performance." Robbie paused before asking, "With the group or just us?"

"Just us," Meg said. He smiled delightedly at her. From that moment on, the conversation came easily. Although she did not eat as quickly as Robbie, Meg made short work of her meal as they discussed baseball and debated who currently was the best player at each position.

"One thing we haven't had time for is bridge," Robbie remarked. "I was really surprised during your Smith interview when you said you didn't play. Do you really not play or didn't you want to talk about it with me?"

"I don't play."

"We've got to work on that. Especially if you are going to be spending any time with my parents. They're bridge devotees."

Meg was grateful for the Chianti's protective effect against the nerve-wracking thought of playing bridge with Robbie's parents.

"Would the lady and gentleman like dessert or coffee?" Eduardo had reappeared at the table and as Meg looked up, she saw that not only was every seat taken, but several people were waiting in the vestibule.

"Should we skip dessert so they can have our table?" Meg asked.

Robbie shook his head. "Nope," he reassured her and turned to Eduardo. "Two coffees and two spumonis."

"Very good, sir," Eduardo replied before disappearing again.

"I assume you're still catching up on your ice cream consumption after giving it up for Lent. Their spumoni is amazing. Huge pieces of candied cherries. And before you protest, it looks like the rain has stopped, so we'll walk to work so you can have your ice cream without too much guilt."

Meg started to open her mouth to protest, closed it, and grinned at him instead.

## 50

As they left the restaurant, Meg noticed the air was much cooler and drier after the thunderstorm. In fact, it was an unusually pleasant evening in Washington, DC, although Meg acknowledged to herself as she walked toward the Annex holding hands with Robbie, it could have been blisteringly hot or below freezing and she wouldn't have cared. As the pair approached the security gate, Meg reluctantly said, "I don't think you're on the schedule tonight, so I'll say goodbye and thank you for dinner."

"I put myself on the schedule," Robbie replied with a deep chuckle, which made Meg tingle. "I need to make up the hours during which I played hooky this afternoon."

"Oh, I see." Meg quickly dropped his hand and looked around as they approached the guard to see if any of their coworkers had spotted their display of affection. In the shadows near the barracks, she spotted a familiar figure and casually put her arm around Robbie. He looked bemused until she whispered in his ear, "Mr. "X" is across the street."

Quickly, Robbie grabbed her arm, they flashed their badges, and he practically dragged her into the Annex. Once inside, Meg realized they might as well have continued to hold hands, since Robbie walked so protectively with her down the corridor. As they arrived in the work area, for once Meg welcomed the industrial fans and stood close to one in an attempt to cool her flushed face.

"Lieutenant Burke, you've noticed a pattern with the weather reports. Could you walk me through what you are doing? I think we'll need to look at a couple of months of trans-missions in the library." Robbie announced as people settled into their work for the night. Meg appreciated his ingenuity in providing a reason for them to go to the library and discuss Mr. "X" without an audience.

"To the library?" Robbie asked.

"To the library," Meg confirmed. As the pair walked down the corridor, Meg said softly, "Now I *am* worried."

"Me too," Robbie agreed.

As they approached the library, the door was closed, but there was a dim light coming from the gap between the door and floor. Meg looked at Robbie and whispered, "There shouldn't be anyone in there."

"Someone is about to be surprised," Robbie responded quietly. He quickly opened the door, and Meg gasped as she entered the library and saw several folders of decoded ciphers strewn across one of the tables—as well as Lieutenant Osgoode!

"Lieutenant Osgoode, what are you doing in here?" Meg asked.

"I was just looking something up. Isn't that what we are supposed to use the library for?" Osgoode was looking at the doorway rather than Meg.

"During the day," Meg replied. "Why have you made such a mess?"

Osgoode didn't answer. Instead, he stared at Meg, starting at her feet and moving slowly up her body, lingering at her waist and at her chest. Meg clenched her toes and fists to keep from trembling with rage and revulsion.

"Osgoode, what are you doing?" Prescott demanded.

Osgoode leered at Meg. "You think you caught me? You're already completely entangled in your own web."

In seconds, Osgoode was not only near enough for her to smell whiskey on his breath but also close enough to grab and pin her against the table. From this angle, she could see a camera resting on the corner of the table.

"Robbie, he's got a camera." Meg's voice broke as Osgoode twisted her arm. She could hear Robbie moving behind her. As Prescott leaped to tackle Osgoode, he took his hand off her arm and unexpectedly put all his weight into Prescott's moving body. The momentum pushed Prescott backward and he bumped his head on the corner of a nearby desk before landing on the floor. When Prescott did not cry out or move, Meg was shocked still. Osgoode grabbed the camera, pushed Meg out of the way, and rushed out the door.

Ignoring the fleeing Osgoode, Meg crouched next to Robbie to check he was still breathing. In a moment, Robbie's eyes opened and he looked at Meg in confusion.

"What happened?" he asked.

"You fell against the desk and I think you were briefly unconscious," Meg replied.

"Everyone okay? I heard voices. What's wrong?" asked a guard from the door. He looked puzzled when he saw the two dazed officers.

"Sentry, Osgoode can't escape. Radio the gate for back-up!" Prescott commanded. "C'mon Meg. We can't let him get away."

"But you just hit your head," Meg responded.

"I've rowed after worse. Let's go!" The sentry followed as Meg and Robbie dashed out of the library and toward the gate.

Meg rapidly tried to process what was happening. It made sense that Osgoode was breaking into the library. He left out weather reports, she worked on, to get her in trouble. It also made sense to accuse her of suspicious activity to deflect attention from himself.

At the gate, Prescott called out, "Did a short, heavy officer come through?"

"He did sir."

"Which way did he go?"

"He went north on Massachusetts Avenue toward Fort Reno Park."

Prescott turned to let Meg catch up. "Stay close to me. I think "X" is probably out here as well. I know we can catch Osgoode. We're in better shape and he's on foot." He grinned at her, and Meg felt a surge of adrenaline as he said, "We can do this."

## 51

Only a few rain clouds lingered from the earlier thunderstorm, occasionally blocking the moonlight Meg and Robbie needed to see in the darkened city. As they jogged, they fell into a comfortable pace moving in unison along the quiet street. After a few blocks, Meg confided, "Osgoode has a big advantage. He's not wearing heels. I'd ditch my shoes, but I'm afraid I'll cut my feet."

"You're doing great. All that marching has finally come in handy."

"It's the swimming," she retorted.

"We've got to find him before we lose him in the park."

"Robbie!" Meg exclaimed and pointed to her right. Four or five blocks ahead was a man who looked like Osgoode.

The ground was still slick from the rain and, despite the extensive practice at Smith, Meg was afraid she'd slip. The two had started to gain on the figure when they saw him make an abrupt turn into the park. The moon came out from behind a cloud and Meg could make out a grove of trees, several maintenance sheds, and a reservoir reflecting the lunar glow.

At that moment Osgoode turned to look around and saw

them. He bolted toward the reservoir, climbed onto its berm, and started to run. Meg knew she would skid on the slick barrier and slowed while Robbie sprinted to overtake Osgoode. Meg watched as Osgoode darted surprisingly quickly along the diameter until there was a loud *splash*. She ran up to the reservoir edge and saw him thrashing in the water.

"Meg, I don't think he knows how to swim," Robbie shouted.

Meg found her lifeguard training taking over. Instinctually, she kicked off her shoes, threw her hat to the ground, and, not knowing the basin depth, slipped into the water. Keeping her head out of the water as she swam, she saw Osgoode had stopped splashing and was now bobbing in the water. With each breath, he submerged further under the surface of the water. Meg approached him and shouted, "I'm going to help you! I'm going to put my arm around you and swim you in!"

Osgoode bobbed once more and swallowed water as Meg approached him from behind. She was forcefully jamming her arm between his chest and right arm when Osgoode grabbed her legs with his other arm and pulled her under the surface. She jabbed him hard in his back with her elbow and felt him react in surprise. Startled, he inhaled water. His arm was still around her leg and they continued to sink. Meg felt Osgoode splutter as he tried to force water out of his chest. Instead of exhaling, he was bringing more liquid into his lungs. Having started to drown, he would be unconscious soon. *Luckily*, she thought, *I can hold my breath while I wait.*

Osgoode's body went limp and Meg's feet hit the basin floor. Using all her strength, she propelled both of them to the surface. Osgoode's body fat provided the buoyancy she needed to turn him on his side, put her right arm across his chest, and swim him toward the berm. In the distance, she could hear sirens as Robbie waded into the water to take Osgoode from her, carry him out of the reservoir, and place him on a patch of flat ground.

Robbie rolled Osgoode on his side and whacked his back until water began to gurgle out of Osgoode's mouth and he began to make spluttering noises. Meg was not sure who had put a blanket around her shoulders while she watched Robbie applying resuscitation. Once surrounded by men carrying flashlights, Robbie quickly moved from Osgoode to hold her as she desperately tried to stop shaking.

"Meg, I can't believe you just did that. Now breathe. And again. That's it. Nice, even, deep breaths. Just a few more. Just like that." She knew it was Robbie speaking to her, but he sounded like he was talking to her through a tunnel.

"Ma'am. Sir. I need you to get into the car. I've got to take you back to the Annex," a man in a naval guard uniform told them.

"Meg. You with us?" Robbie asked gently.

Meg focused on nodding her head but was unable to speak as Robbie guided her into the back seat of the waiting car. As she settled, he put his arm protectively around her and kept it there until they reached the gate and the driver rolled the window down. She felt for her badge and discovered it had disappeared.

"I must have lost my badge back there," she explained to the guard with chattering teeth.

"It's all right ma'am," the sentry replied and waved them through.

Meg tried to smile as the car came to a stop and Robbie reached across to open the door, but her facial muscles did not want to move. She slowly formed the words in her mind before she moved her mouth to say, "I don't have my shoes or my hat."

Robbie squeezed her shoulder. "We'll get you new ones," he reassured her. "We need to go in and brief Lewis and McClaren. Lean on me until we get to the room and then you can sit. I promise we'll get you some coffee. Some brandy if you want it."

Meg knew she was wet and her uniform dirty, but the shocked looks of the sleepy guards as the pair walked into the command told her just how disheveled she looked. In the light, she looked down at her feet and saw they were bleeding.

"Can you find an extra pair of shoes or boots?" Robbie called to the seamen on duty behind the information counter. "Even socks and a dry tracksuit will do."

Robbie led Meg over to a chair and helped her to sit. She could hear cupboards being opened and closed. Quickly a man came out with dry clothes and a pair of thick socks, which he handed wordlessly to Robbie. Robbie bent down and tenderly put the socks on her scraped feet, giving each foot a gentle squeeze as he did so.

"Can I use the washroom and clean up?" she asked Robbie as he handed her the clothes.

"Do promise you are not going to keel over on me if I leave you alone?"

"Promise. Although you'd better stand at the door and listen for a thud."

"Your sense of humor is coming back. Thank God."

"I'll be just a few minutes," she reassured Robbie at the door of the lavatory. When she entered the washroom and saw herself, she jumped. Her wet hair was plastered to her head and when she removed her blanket-cape there were brown spots on her no-longer white uniform. After putting on the dry t-shirt and sweat pants, she spent a few moments splashing cool water on her face and finger-combing her hair. When she was convinced no more preening would help, she opened the door. Robbie was leaning against the wall as she entered the hallway holding her wet uniform in a ball.

"Ready?" he asked as he quickly righted himself and grabbed her arm to guide her down the hallway. They entered the small windowless room near security, the same room where she had been brought weeks ago when previously accused of being a spy. A seaman was placing a pitcher of coffee, mugs, a smaller pitcher of milk, and four diagonals of toast with strawberry jam on the grungy table.

"Captain McClaren told me to tell you to eat all the toast. You wouldn't have to order *me* to eat toast with jam, ma'am," he noted. "Also, he asked me to bring you two aspirin." He put down a napkin in which he had twisted the two pills. "Can you take it with the coffee, or do you need water?"

"I can take it with coffee," Meg replied hoarsely. There was a frog stuck in her throat. She collapsed into a chair and Robbie lowered himself into the one next to her. From the moment she had started her special training at Smith, Meg had known that she was working on a top-secret project, but she had never anticipated the assignment could involve her jumping into the water to save the life of a likely spy. As the seaman exited the room, Meg wove her fingers around the warm mug, taking comfort from this small ritual. Once her fingers were no longer numb, she reached across the table, grabbed a slice of toast, and took several bites before she realized she was being rude.

"Sorry. I should have offered you some toast," she apologized to Robbie.

"No need. It's all yours. You need it after the shock," he replied with a grin as Captain McClaren entered with Commander Lewis. As the four exchanged salutes, Meg thought how much older Lewis looked than when she had met him six months ago. Each day of his assignment was aging him.

McClaren and Lewis exchanged a look before McClaren said, "Lieutenant Burke, I think you'll feel better after we review tonight's operational success."

"Sir?" she questioned.

McClaren continued, "Immediately after the war started, one of the ensigns in OP-20-G was approached by a Japanese man working in the Library of Congress. This librarian was willing to pay dearly to find out how many of the Japanese additives we had been able to crack. The ensign, correctly, went directly to Naval Intelligence to report what had happened. Intelligence decided to send the ensign back to meet with the librarian, behaving as if he were willing to play ball with the

Japanese. But the poor guy was way too green for such a challenging and delicate situation. Intelligence saw the ensign was the wrong operative but did not want to waste the opportunity. Intelligence substituted the person you know as Warren Elliot to work with the librarian."

"He's not a civilian?" Meg said in surprise.

"Actually, he's an experienced intelligence officer," McClaren confirmed.

"But you had me shadowing him? Why do that if we were on the same side?" she exclaimed.

"It's a complicated story," Lewis began. "With the influx of Navy officers, both career and reserve, into the command, nobody was sure who had been here before the war. It was a good cover story for Elliot to pretend to be a civil servant."

"Lieutenant Prescott, I can't believe you didn't see through the story," Meg replied skeptically.

"I wasn't here yet. And when I first got to the command, I spent all my time breaking codes, not really paying attention to anything else," Prescott replied.

"Prescott had only been attached to the command for a few weeks, however, when he recognized we needed to make sure the Japanese did not know how much success we were having uncovering their encryption techniques," McClaren said as he gave Prescott a smile. "He designed a plan for spreading disinformation, which he presented to Commander Lewis and me. Given Elliot's remit, we got Elliot and Prescott together to see if they could kill two birds with one stone. We also gave Prescott the cover of helping Lewis so he wasn't chained to a desk and was not expected to work on codes as much."

Lewis chuckled ruefully. "None of us anticipated that Prescott would spend much of the time redirecting you so you didn't notice Elliot wasn't ever breaking any codes," Lewis explained. "Elliot told stories and walked you through the mechanics, but every day Prescott, Elliot, and I waited for you to notice Elliot never cracked anything. We thought the weather reports were a safe dead end for him and then you managed to find information in them. It was a godsend to get Elliot onto nights to make his limitations less obvious."

Meg shook her head before admitting, "I was so caught up in not wanting to be the weak link, I never noticed Elliot's shortcomings." She folded her hands together and unfolded them as she thought about this information. "But why was I following Elliot if he wasn't doing anything wrong?"

"I can answer that," Prescott replied. "As Elliot distributed disinformation, we knew he was being watched. Knowing about Avila, who was so low on the food chain, was not enough. We wanted to identify Avila's boss. If we were very lucky, we might even uncover his boss's boss. I suggested that since Avila already thought you were spying on him, having you tail Elliot might change the dynamics of who was watching whom and flush out others who were involved in the espionage."

"Hmmm," Meg replied softly before saying more firmly, "So I became part of your disinformation campaign."

"I know you thought I wasn't taking you seriously when you told me about the rearranged church pamphlets," Prescott chuckled as he remembered. "But I was. Avila realized you had noticed the signal and insisted Elliot move their drops from the church to the embassy, which allowed us to spot and follow an expanded cast of characters, leading to a better understanding of Avila's network."

"Also, you were there to alert us to Elliot being roughed up. Because of you, we were able to get him to a safe place," Lewis explained.

"He's not back at the Department of Agriculture, is he?" Meg asked and Lewis shook his head slightly in response.

"Mr. "X" was upset because Elliot's doctored information did not match other intelligence the Axis operatives were receiving. He was questioning whether Elliot was providing good intel. Tonight, we confirmed "X" and Avila were comparing our doctored information to transmissions Osgoode was photographing in the library," Lewis clarified. "Since both of you were working with Elliot, you are in danger."

"But why was Mr. "X" following me? Why was he following both Lieutenant Prescott and me tonight as we walked to work?" Meg inquired.

"We have some of our best people grilling Osgoode as we speak to help figure that out," McClaren said. "Based on Elliot's description and the surveillance pictures we have, we also have a team searching for "X." Once we capture him, we'll know more."

"I've disliked Osgoode from the day I met him. I've never understood why Lieutenant Boller and Lieutenant McClaren were helping him tail the other WAVES and me when we first arrived in Washington, DC," Meg admitted.

McClaren's eyebrows shot up when Meg mentioned Lyall and he looked to Lewis.

"It was supposed to be Prescott with Boller and McClaren to run the security test, but I couldn't spare him that day. Boller grabbed Osgoode and a classmate of theirs to help at the last minute. The three reported Osgoode for being completely out of line and I never sent him on a similar mission," Lewis clarified.

"But it continued after that. Osgoode didn't hide his disdain for WAVES in general and me, in particular."

"He was completely out of line numerous times with Lieutenant Burke," Prescott confirmed. "Some of the things he said to her made *me* blush."

"But he was never so horrible that you completely ignored him. He could stay close enough to be aware of Lieutenant Burke's activities and point suspicion at her, but dislikable enough that none of you spent time watching what he was up to," McClaren explained. He turned to Prescott and briefly glared. "One thing I don't understand is why, when you knew better than to go to the dance at the Portuguese Embassy, you brought Osgoode with you."

"Yes. Why did you invite Osgoode?" Lewis inquired.

Meg and Robbie exchanged a look before he shrugged his shoulders slightly saying, "The outing was organized at lunch. Osgoode was sitting next to me and was winding me up. I got angry when Osgoode asked me if I was really a math professor or if it was a cover. In the moment it was better for him to be part of the gang rather than deconstruct what he'd said. Especially since Osgoode's taunt indicated he had his suspicions about me. I didn't know Elliot was going to be there playing the drums that night."

"Unfortunately, I noticed Elliot," Meg added. "And since I was supposed to be tailing him, I had to report it."

"In turn, I had to submit a report to Lewis. It would look like I was covering up something if I didn't." Prescott sighed. He shifted in his seat and turned to Meg. "How are you doing Meg?" he asked as he discretely put his arm behind her chair and put his hand against the small of her back.

She tried to smile but feared it was more of a frown. "I think I'm observant but I feel like I've missed almost everything going on around me."

---

## 52

"Osgoode may have been smarter than we thought," Lewis commented.

"Agreed," Prescott said. "I think Lieutenant Burke moving to nights alerted Osgoode to the fact that we were aware information was escaping"

"Why do you say that?" McClaren asked.

"If you're interested in decoding Japanese transmissions, it was ridiculous and ineffective to move Lieutenant Burke to nights, away from working with the 'professors' and the A-team analysts. The only reason to put her on nights was because she was doing something other than code-breaking." Prescott explained.

McClaren nodded his head at Prescott's statement.

"But why was Osgoode trading secrets in the first place?" Meg was still confused. Osgoode had never struck her as particularly committed to anything other than whiskey. She was surprised when Lewis took up the narrative.

"Osgoode first caught my attention because of his drinking problem, which is unfortunately not unique in the Navy. Since he was sober on duty, there was not much I could do. He was a rake to the WAVES, but collectively you generally ignored him, which was much better than my making a big deal of it."

"It wasn't easy," Meg said with feeling.

"Then I found out Osgoode had developed serious money problems," Prescott continued.

"How did you find that out?" Meg asked.

"Osgoode thought I would be good for a pretty substantial loan," Prescott explained while avoiding every eye in the room.

"We are still filling in the gaps, but it looks like he has been betting on horses, ball games, and even dog races. It probably goes back to his days at Annapolis," Lewis said. "Osgoode should never have passed the background check to be doing this type of top-secret work."

"Gambling!" Meg exclaimed. "Gambling!" She shook her head in disbelief. "I should have let him drown." She stood up. "I'm sorry sirs, but I really need to go home and change," she declared.

"About that," Lewis began.

"You can go home and quickly pack your things. We're going to have a car take you there and then bring you to a troop train at Union Station," McClaren stated.

"What? Why?" Meg asked.

"We need to get you and Prescott out of Washington," McClaren explained.

"Where am I going? What do I tell Julie? Isobel? The others?" Meg stammered.

"San Diego. And you don't need to say anything. It will all be explained for you," McClaren replied.

"Lieutenant Burke don't even think about going upstairs to see people. I'm ordering you to slip out to the car and not speak to anyone on base," Lewis commanded.

"I'll wait for the car with you. You shouldn't be alone," Prescott said.

Lewis's words gradually sank in. Meg could not say goodbye to Julie, Vivian, or Cynthia, the three women with whom she had shared the experience of growing from a provincial teacher to a more worldly military officer. She would never be able to share her introductory foray into intelligence work.

"Hell of a night," Prescott commented as they waited in an alcove near the security gate. The sky in the east was turning purple. He grinned at Meg "It was great fun until McClaren said we both need to be reassigned."

"Is Mr. "X" really that dangerous?" Meg whispered to Robbie, who shrugged his shoulders.

"He knows you're working for our side and are aware information is being passed, so yes. You may be in real danger," Robbie whispered back. "But I'm also being sent away for a different reason."

"What did you do?"

"I got tired of slightly modifying Japanese communications for distribution to Avila. I've gone off-script a few times. Each time a little more fanciful than the previous one. I've been on borrowed time," Robbie explained.

"You write surprisingly well for a man who plays with numbers for a living," she admitted.

"Thank you," Prescott said. He grabbed her arm and pulled her toward him. He said quietly, "Letting the group go to the embassy party was the nail in the coffin."

"It was so much fun to dance that night," Meg confessed.

As a black car with government plates approached the pair, Robbie pulled Meg closer and kissed her softly. "I'd get in trouble again to have a chance to dance with you," he said. "This is only goodbye for now."

Meg did not trust herself to reply. Instead, she looked into his eyes and bit her lip to keep from sobbing. As Robbie opened the door, she reached up to give him a brief embrace. Quickly, she got in the back seat and after Robbie closed the door put her hand against the window to match where he had placed his in a final gesture.

Meg closed her eyes to hold back the tears, opening them

only when the driver announced she was home. Home. When Meg thought of how happy she had been living there, she felt a stabbing pain. She did not want to leave Julie, Vivian, Isobel, Davis, and even Cynthia.

Meg was surprised when Isobel rather than Davis answered the door. Before Meg could say a word, Isobel greeted her. "Hello, my dear. I'm going to come upstairs with you as I know you are packing quickly; I want to make sure you are not overlooking anything." When Meg opened the door to her room, she saw her suitcase was waiting on her bed. She was sure everything she had brought to Washington, and probably more if she knew Isobel and Davis, was in that case.

Isobel sat down on Julie's bed as Meg changed into a fresh uniform. "You know, Meg, I enjoy reading spy stories. It's not unusual for those on assignment to know nothing about the assignments of the other people with whom they are working. Some people are used as decoys. Others are passing information constructed to be just true enough. It is a tremendous challenge to be able to play any of these roles with the right precision. It's also exhausting and very dangerous work. You can only do that for so long before you need a break." She paused. "Or at least that is the way it works in books."

Meg thought of the oath she had signed to keep secrets for life. She would never be able to confirm what Isobel suspected or even knew.

"Writers have to get their ideas somewhere, don't they?" Meg tried to give Isobel a smile but instead began to cry. "I've been so happy here. I really appreciate everything you've done. Even the things I don't know about," Meg said, and Isobel smiled. "What am I going to do without Julie, Vivian, and Cynthia?"

"Meg. This is temporary. You'll see them again soon. You will all be in each other's weddings and godmothers to each other's children." She smiled at Meg. "I expect the first of those weddings will take place soon and we'll both be invited, although perhaps from different sides of the family." Meg chuckled in spite of herself. They both stood, and Meg hugged Aunt Isobel for several moments.

"You'll write and let us know how you are doing as soon as you can?" Isobel inquired.

"Of course," Meg replied.

Isobel smiled at her. "One chapter is over, but another one is beginning."

# POSTSCRIPT

A few weeks later, Meg found a package on her new desk in San Diego. The parcel stamped "Military Mail" was addressed with block handwriting she did not recognize, but it clearly contained a book. She waited until she returned to her quarters that night and cautiously opened the paper wrapping expecting to see a card or a note, but found only a book entitled *The Moving Finger* by Agatha Christie. This particular copy had been published in London and still had a price tag of seven shillings and sixpence affixed to the back. Carefully opening the cover, she looked for an inscription on the flyleaf. Nothing. Gently shaking the book, nothing fell out.

After brushing her teeth and changing for bed, Meg propped the pillows against the headboard. She settled herself into bed and started the first chapter. The story set in a Devon village was a welcomed change, specifically from her hurried relocation to San Diego and more generally, from the past several months of her life. After a few chapters, she noticed some of the words had a shadow. Probably the publisher was contending with wartime printing issues. The paper was rough and cheap.

Looking more closely, she noted there was a pattern to the blotching. The last letter of the last word of seemingly random pages was faintly traced. Grabbing paper and pencil, she went back to the start of the book.

*"Doing interesting work. Would like to get you assigned to the project. Miss your soda bread. Hope you are swimming as much as you can. Love Robbie"*

# ACKNOWLEDGMENTS

The idea for this book first emerged when I undertook an oral history assignment for a Princeton seminar on the American Way of War. I had always been curious about my great aunt's experience in the WAVES in World War II, especially as she had always been less than forthcoming in response to my inquisitive questions about her military experience. I played upon Irish-Catholic guilt, knowing my aunt, a retired school-teacher, would be unable to refuse my request to interview her for an academic assignment. The result was an unforgettable afternoon of drinking tea as she reminisced about her experiences.

I learned despite having a bachelor's degree in math, she initially was directed into the enlisted WAVES program. It was only after her first duty assignment as a weather mate when an officer noted the quality of her work, that she was selected to attend officer training at Smith. She was commissioned as a lieutenant and received orders to "work on something that helped to track ships" in Texas along the Gulf Coast. While she refused to be specific about what she did, my aunt did share that her experience at Smith was among the happiest of her life.

As I transcribed the interview, I realized her eventual selection for commission and success in the WAVES was a story that needed to be told. In 2020, when the world shut down for the COVID pandemic, I realized I had finally been given the time to do so. Building on materials gathered at the Princeton

University library, I relied on the support of the University of San Diego interlibrary lending program, which helped to identify digitally available resources, when I needed materials to support my main character as a cryptologist. I also received the personal assistance of librarians in the San Diego Public Library system who helped me to locate physical copies of wartime periodicals to provide extra "color" for Meg and her fellow officers.

I am indebted to Joe Avery, Mary Claire Allvine, Erika Carrington, Kathy Chiang, Sabrina Comizzoli, Erika Dale, Marty Dicker, Mei-ling Marshall, David Melchior, Jill Melchior, Lucy McMurrer, Sara Turner, Vijay Vemulakonda, and Sean Zielenbach who read and offered suggestions to improve earlier versions of the manuscript. Special thanks go to Colleen Huschke, who not only read multiple versions of the novel but also prepared dinner several times while urging me to keep writing and revising.

Through a few coincidences, the type which seemed to abound during the pandemic, I met my editor Cornelia Feye— virtually. I would never have predicted the medium of Zoom could be so constructive or permit such creativity. Our weekly meetings became a much-anticipated appointment and a reminder to me that there was a world outside of our house.

A debt of gratitude goes to my family who learned to tip-toe around me when they saw I was sitting at my desk and "working on my book." My sons, Mike and Trip, provided invaluable suggestions, especially for improvements to the dialogue, allowing characters to leap off the page rather than remain two-dimensional.

Lastly, and most importantly, to my husband Steven who married an epidemiologist rather than a writer and found himself rapidly adapting to several new, unanticipated roles including sounding board, subject matter expert, reader, cheerleader, chef, project manager, and editor. It is because of him that my dream became a reality.

# ABOUT THE AUTHOR

R. Ann Bush is a southern California native who studied history at Princeton University as an undergraduate and received her Masters in Women's History at the University of London. One of her scholarly assignments was an oral history project featuring her great aunt's experiences in the Women Accepted for Volunteer Emergency Service (WAVES) during World War II. She received her Ph.D. in Public Health at the University of California San Diego, and currently is a professor in Health Sciences at the University of San Diego. An experienced scientific researcher and academic author, Ann used the pandemic lockdown to weave together family narratives and first-hand naval experiences to tell the story. Ann lives with her patient husband and two inquisitive sons.

Made in the USA
Las Vegas, NV
24 May 2023

72506438R00266